The Unending Light

Quest of Fire

BRETT ARMSTRONG

Expanse Books

This book is dedicated to the glory of God without Whom there would be no hope of the King's Day nor the unending light beyond the dark.

It is also for my family, earthly and spiritual, who walk this journey alongside me and make it immeasurably better by being there through all I face.

Pre
(24 F

ICE
SHELF

Gulf of Fenres

ECTHELOWALL COMMONWEALTH

Caldoness

VOGTEREMARK

Ecthalon

Brockenburgh

Grimndale

Falconclett

Port Jarreth

Stormridge

Falkirke

REHALCYON

Carvenna

Lecfortes

Lyrscony

Cennomar

SURCALIDO

GARCENILLES-ECTHELOWALL PROTECTORATE

PUERTOLICA

Majadesar

Riconue

Dos Avos

Mykum

Photas

THERATOS

Nescador

Durellean

KNORLAND

Opwk

Krak O'ysailles

Urkhastvania

REHALCYON

Montégris

Lesjou

AUSTORA-CUENT KINGDOM
OF REHALCYON EMPIRE

Chomigby

I'jen

ZILNEN

N'jofu

Ruins of Gerisk

Fort Varas

ZILNEN

Eshtal

Rushmid

Pezund

Vadanaya

Ivberria

Memsar

Reccaknor

Dôra

KNORLAND

Lesnoygora

LOV

LOWER
HIGHLANDS

LO

Prastiha

Qirthen

Iptihfur

Phosphan

YUSBILSI

Hündlürgala

Ikes

Sigmazraj Yeri

Ho

Suseleh

C
H

War
odem Era)

Giaknervo

Kepkevina

Leknuk   Novoknorstok

Far Pointe

Ujón Fjord   Wroghcart

FYOWSIK

Ixylo   Ildholm

Eoitling

ARNUK   Psilmos

ARNUK

Muzby

Hifonest

POSEK

Sophak   Cyzrol

Minathsui

Sorland

Avangaluk

Nimues   Cleviu Flats

Baleyo

Nhiponi

Bham

JHI

Voodgin

Fizhourd

Froc Red

Omsawwe

Virrasba

Jhi City

Luongua

Togaman   TIKBOK

Dor Waihei

Wuhu Tong

Pingwebi

Longshe

ZHGULONG

NDARVU   Ciyarem City

Feptoya

Mbisai Moun

Songarch

Grutoj

LOWER
HIGHLANDS

MBISAI   Apisidisi

Beeg Daan

Green Walls

Oloyoisa

Shenzhou

Pekadesh

Hean   Peyohili Koro

Fusinla

Weitonkai

OKYN
ECHELOWALL
PROTECTORATE

Seabring

Vuhoso

Baňhua

Jhipore

Exenrah

Isokachvak

Geghelsík

Nicarro

Quilona

Montse Rego

Cunahus

FARA

Occibayar

VOV HILON

Wasstoa

Corsairington

Avonchauk

Uxilitepec

Dor Lessa   Safira

Aseriell

Favbas

Wonarchea

Sol Uldim

KERAXLACO

Poguessa

Xolni

LENUMO ISLANDS

ULDIQUIM   Zunri

Srasilla

ECHELOWALL PROTECTORATE
Albortswren

Endochora

Rerocita

Mmoni   Qaimethra

Qishni   Sailiton

Doggeron

Por Vástad

Costa Yikarté

Nueve Deep

Pegdono

Inguim

Tzekar

SEYCHLONESIA   PASHTARI   Cuarconah

Nizkarta

Gedim

Siparia

Lowlands War
(24 Daraleath 358 Modern Era)

☐: Confede
☐: Alliance
☐: Neutral

ICE SHELF

GULF OF FENRES

Pezund
Vodanaya
Memsar
Ivberria
Dor
Recoaknor

KNORLAND

KNORLAND

Opusk
Lesnaygora
LOW

ECTHELOWALL COMMONWEALTH

Esthglas
Brackenburgh
VOLGTERGMARK
Grimmdale

Falconcleff

Port Jarneth

Stormridge

Falkirke

REHALCYON

Carvenna

Lacfortes

Lyrsceny

Krak O'ysailkes
Urkharivania

REHALCYON

LOWER
HIGHLANDS

Momègris

Lesjou

Chomigby

Prastcha

Cennomar

I'jon

GARKENVILLES-ECTHELOWALL PROTECTORATE

JURCALIDOOR

REHALCYON EMPIRE

Qirthen
Isltfur

YUSBILSI
Hündürqala

Phosphan

Ike

Igmacaa
Yeri

N'jofu
Ruins of Geriek

Fort Varas

PUERTOLICA

Suseleh

Majadesar

Riconue

Dos Avos

Mykum
Phatas

Eshtal

THERATOS
Nescador

Durellean

Rushmid

by Confederacy

☐ : Alliance of Realms

▨ : Confederacy territory occupied by Alliance

Lowla:
(15 Glad

Bay of Crozma

ZAR

Caldoness

Gulf of Fenres

Avon-caroon

ALBARON •Ordumair

•Ivarsbad

KNORLAND

Grand Knorstok

KNORLAND

VOUTS VI PARK

Estonbury (Estona)

Ermvia

•Bechast

Tislatnean Sea

•Fair Winds (Bonus Mare)

Versik

LIBERTAS

•Stormridge

Einwis •Black River

•Kirke

Port Jarreth

Pete's March

REHALGY

TYREENES

Lacfortes

•Carvenna

SHIELD ISLANDS

Lyrscony •

•Parthes

ANSTARA

YUSBILSI

LYSCEA

Hundurqala

•Cennamar

Straits of Calboa

SURCALIDO

ZILJAFU DESERT

ZILNEN

RED DUNES

Bouquemeral

N'jafu

PUERTOLICA

Notiosanemos Sea

Riconue

Photos

THERATOS

dle Era
(dle Era)

Quaqu
Sea

Glacial Sea

FYOWSIK

Ild

Trang Sea

ARNUKHAN

Palimos

F ARNUK

POSEK

Cyzral

D

JHI

Jhi City

Longhe

ZHOULONG

EAU

Gulf of Pilroc

MBISAI

Apisidiu

Okyniko

ORUN

Uyderpei Strait

SHANFARA

Ermonh

Quilon
Bay

VOV HILAN

Dor Leasb

Maisorient
Sea

Uldim

KERAXLACO

ULDIQUIM

Axala

Cuorconoh

PASHTARI

SEYCHLONESIA

Nizkarta

LINK TO FULL-COLOR MAPS

https://brettarmstrong.net/quest-of-fire-maps/

DRAMATIS PERSONAE

MIDDLE ERA (Anargen's Era)

- **Anargen**: Twenty-year-old Knight of Light from small town of Black River and part of the Quest to defend the mysterious Tower of Light.
- **Seren:** Anargen's fiancée and Knight of Light originally from Stormridge and swept into the Quest during an attack on Black River.
- **Glewdyn:** Anargen's father and elder Knight of Light. He and Sir Cinaed of Black River helped rescue Anargen and the others in Stormridge.
- **Sir Cinaed of Black River**: Anargen's mentor, Meredith MacCowell, Defender of the Northern Realm. He sacrificed himself in Stormridge to save everyone.
- **Caeserus**: Anargen's best friend who had the initial vision of the Tower of Light that pulled them

all into the Quest of Fire, but abandoned the Quest after the events in Stormridge.

- **Bertinand**: Anargen and Seren's friend and another Knight of Light on the Quest who kept up the group's spirits with his humor. He, like Caeserus, abandoned the Quest after the losses at Stormridge.
- **Terrillian**: Anargen's friend and Knight of Light who opted to aid Ecthelowall in the early days of the War of Restoration during the events in Stormridge.
- **Count Eidolon**: The ruler of Stormridge and wielder of dark powers from Tislatna. He was defeated and destroyed with Stormridge after attempting to create a dragon.
- **Maldes Ilyron**: Usurping Monarch of Ecthelowall and son of Ecthelion. Leader of the Monarchists and wielder of dark powers like his mentor Count Eidolon.
- **Viceroy Ecthelion Halifax**: Deposed rightful ruler of Ecthelowall and leader of the Loyalists in the War of Restoration. Adoptive father to Thomas.
- **Ords**: Race of northern dwarfs who were delivered from destruction in large part thanks to Sir Cinaed, Anargen, Caeserus, Bertinand, and Terrillian's efforts.
- **Dag Votere**: Citizens of the Vogteremark, a northern nation that sent Knights to aid Anargen and the others in liberating the Ords.
- **Viscount Geralian**: Ruler of Libertias, Anargen's home nation.

- **Thomas (Fenwrest) Halifax**: Ecthel teen who joined the Knights of Light while rescuing Mia and Gregor from the collapse of Loyalist defenses in Ecthelowall. Later adopted by Viceroy Ecthelion and succeeded him as Baron of Halifax.
- **Mia Sornfold**: Daughter of the murdered Baron Sornfold, and heir to his lands. Sister to Delia Sornfold the bride of Monarch Ilyron. Thomas's fiancée and new Knight of Light.
- **Gregor Fenwrest**: Thomas's cousin and the last remaining legitimate rival claimant to the Monarch's throne. A new member of the Knight Order though crippled during Delia Sornfold's attacks on Albaron.
- **Captain Strathmore**: Loyal soldier of the Restoration who assisted Thomas in the battle at Dirkforge and in rescuing Mia from Wyvares.
- **Monarchists**: Those belonging to the Ecthelowall faction that supports Maldes Ilyron's claim to the historic Ecthelish Monarch throne.
- **Restoration**: The allied groups from Ecthelowall, Ordumair, Albaron, and Libertias who oppose the Monarchists and actively fight to restore Viceroy Ecthelion Halifax back to rule over Ecthelowall and its Commonwealth.

MODERN ERA (Jason's Era)

- **Jason (Wernstrum) Landsby**: Twenty-year-old who stumbled upon the Quest of Fire while trying to rescue his brother from their sordid

family. Knight of Light and student of Cinaed
Black.

- **Dorian Wernstrum**: Jason's younger brother
  who embraced the dark powers offered him and
  tried to imprison and execute Jason. Secret leader
  of the Rehalcyon Empire and thereby the
  Confederacy of Nations.
- **Aria Black**: Jason's fiancée and a wise and skilled
  Knight of Light who has lived in hiding with her
  grandfather since childhood.
- **Cinaed "The Storyteller" Black**: Aria's
  grandfather and current Defender of the Northern
  Realm. His stories about Anargen's adventures
  drew Jason into the Quest of Fire initially. Plans to
  unite all the Defenders of the Realms to stop the
  coming darkness.
- **Melania Tsyket**: Jason's childhood sweetheart
  and heir to a rival gang. Believed to have died years
  ago, but resurfaced in service to Dorian and
  possessing powers from witchcraft.
- **Dr. Gregorio Antoni**: A Knight of Light from
  the Lyscea province of the Rehalcyon Empire who
  secretly supported Cinaed Black's efforts and saved
  Jason by sacrificing himself.
- **Yúzé Guo**: Jhi'ish Knight of Light and Defender
  of the Northeastern Realm. The last Defender
  needed to hold the Council who had to be assisted
  in escaping his homeland.
- **Tirzah Kharoum**: Sadiq's middle daughter and
  Knight of Light. Shares a sisterly bond with Aria.
- **Kaveed Amine**: Tirzah's husband and former
  heir to the throne of Zilnen. Current Defender of
  the Southwestern Realm.

- **Sadiq Kharoum**: Former Defender of the Southwestern Realm and father to Tirzah. Executed during Mesnara's betrayal.
- **Mesnara**: Ex-wife of Sadiq and noblewoman of Zilnen who bargained for rule of Zilnen as a client kingdom of Rehalcyon.
- **Kazim Cuzibaum**: Current Defender of the West Central Realm.
- **Yohanan ben Davidiah**: Knight of Light from Centros and Defender of the Central and Lower Highlands Realm. Young, uneasy in his prominent role amongst the Defenders at the historic Council.
- **Boris Tooadama**: Knorish Knight of Light and Defender of the North-Central Realm. Almost deposed and executed by Dorian's forces, after which he became a staunch ally of Defender Cinaed Black.
- **Rindo del Miguelso**: Vov Hilanese Knight of Light and Defender of the Southeastern Realm. A level-headed Knight and key supporter of Defender Black.
- **General Cywjzi Gorsk**: commander of all Poseki armed forces. A gruff, stubborn and ruthlessly efficient leader. Fascinated and intimidated by the fiery implements Knights of Light wield.
- **Professor Theodore Goulder**: Eccentric Ecthel academic, old friend of Defender Black, and Aria's godfather. A key resource in arranging and coordinating all the parties needed for the Council of Defenders.
- **Dr. Hua Jing**: Jhi'ish physician and secret Knight

of Light who has become mutually taken with and involved in assisting Professor Goulder's efforts.
- **Alliance of Realms**: Collection of countries fighting to thwart the Confederacy of Nations and their brutal conquest of the Lowlands. Initial members include the Commonwealth of Ecthelowall, Surcalido, Theratos, Arnuk, Posek, Mbisai, Keraxlaco, Vov Hilan, and Fyowsik. Later joined by the breakaway Sykonos Republic.
- **Confederacy of Nations**: Group of countries seeking to conquer the rest of the Lowlands and impose a new order. Led by Dorian Wernstrum and deeply influenced by darker forces. Initial members include the Rehalcyon Empire, Knorland, Jhi, Tikabok, Uldiquim, and Pashtari. Also controls a puppet state in Yusbilsi.

CREATURES/BEINGS OF BOTH ERAS

- **Werebeast**: Massive monster that transforms from a human to werewolf/bear-like creature in dark and at night.
- **Sombra**: League of assassins who use dark Tislatnean sorcery to merge in and out of shadows. They can also form tools and weapons of shadows at will. Their enchanted hoods allow for their sorcery.
- **Carrion**: Ordinary individuals controlled by Tislatnean sorcery such that they cannot feel pain and single-mindedly follow the bidding of whomever cast the spell.

- **Doppelgangers**: Creatures capable of changing their appearance to that of another person's in order to replace that person. They serve Dorian and others wielding the dark powers. When lacking a suitable replacement choice their faces revert to a blank void.
- **Direnoir**: Hideous parasitic monsters that feed off their victim's fears until they've destroyed their host. They serve Dorian and those like him.
- **Boggart/Troll**: A massive beastly creature of decidedly evil nature. At least fifteen feet tall and covered in stoney plates. Boggarts are cruel and arrogant but not as bright as they imagine, and in spite of their slovenliness are very strong and dangerous.
- **Wyvern**: Enormous flying reptilian beast with an incredibly tough hide and breathes fire. They have largely gone extinct from the Lowlands and are regarded as a myth in the Modern Era.
- **Dragon**: A wyvern that has been bonded with a goblin through a forbidden Tislatnean ritual to create an even more deadly creature that has heightened powers of a wyvern and the calculating and malevolent mind of the goblin.
- **Goblin**: Also called dark elves, they are elves that rebelled against the High King with the Dark Prince before the foundation of the Lowlands.
- **Elves**: The first servants of the High King and beings of flame and light and have remained loyal to the High King. Aid the Knights of Light as directed by the High King.
- **Vif**: A high elf who aided both Thomas and Jason

during some of their most trying moments in the Quest.

THE STORY THUS FAR

(Covers critical events from *The Gathering Dark*, *Shadows at Nightfall*, *Desperation*, *Resurgence of Dawn*, and *Devastation* in brief)

Jason returns to Brackenburgh after living on the run. He stops at an inn to escape the rain and there is captivated by the innkeeper's daughter, Aria, and the innkeeper's story of another teen from centuries past, Anargen.

Anargen lives in Black River, a small village of Libertias, and has just joined the ancient order Palatini Lucis Aeternae, or Knights of Light, who serve the divine High King of All Realms. Few in the Lowlands outside the Order still obey the High King's laws or submit to his rule. Soon after joining the Order, Anargen's friend, Caeserus, tells him he had a vision of four Knights defending a Tower of Light from an attack that would topple the tower and leave everything in darkness and ruin. He believes he and Anargen are part of the four and enlisted their mentor Sir Cinaed's help in determining how to fulfill their part in the quest. This is heart-breaking for Anargen who has just started a courtship with the girl he loves, Seren. Following his oaths; Anargen, Caeserus, Sir Cinaed, and two other teens from the village—Bertinand and Terrillian— all leave for a location Sir Cinaed vaguely hints at being of importance.

As they travel, the group is assaulted by a centuries old monster, the Grey Scourge, and Sir Cinaed reveals they are traveling far north to Ordumair, the homeland of the Ords, a group of dwarfs who are signing a peace treaty with the men of the powerful Commonwealth of Ecthelowall. Cinaed has been summoned to witness the historic moment and believes it to be key to the tower quest.

However, on arriving, Anargen and the others find the Ords hate Knights almost as much as the Ecthels and when the peace talks falter, they are caught between the two sides as a battle breaks out. Very quickly it becomes clear that the Grey Scourge was orchestrating the false accord and uses his dark powers to transform parts of the Ecthel army into werebeasts like himself. With the combination of evil sorcery and the latest siege weapons the Ords are overwhelmed and all seems lost.

Rallying the battered Ords, Cinaed reveals he is actually Meredoch MacCowell, Defender of the Northern Realm and has rescued the true leader of Ecthelowall, Viceroy Ecthelion, whom the Grey Scourge tried to execute. The Scourge wants something in Ordumair, a lost treasure that had at one time been shared jointly by the Ecthels and Ords.

As the defenses start crumbling the Grey Scourge breaks in and is confronted by the Knights who defeat the Scourge and discover an oracle from a past ruler of Ordumair that is remarkably similar to Caeserus's vision.

Outside the fortress walls the battle for Ordumair takes a turn as the dark powers of the Scourge have been broken and aid arrives in the form of Knights from Albaron and the Vogteremark, sent for at Sir Cinaed's request.

Back in Jason's time, the Storyteller is interrupted by a city councilman who places him under arrest along with Jason who is charged for conspiring with the old man. Outside the inn, however, the councilman reveals himself to be a doppelganger, a changeling, who posed as the councilman to get the Storyteller alone and murder him. The Storyteller, also named Cinaed, reveals himself to be a Knight of Light and defeats the councilman. He then invites Jason to come with him as he goes back to the inn to get Aria and promises to explain more once there.

Upon arriving back in the inn, the pair splits up to find Aria. Jason succeeds but is forced to run with Aria from the inn as her grandfather defends them against an attack by werebeasts serving the same mysterious master as the doppelganger.

Aria, also a Knight of Light, is soon after forced to defend them both from a Sombra, mystic assassins who can merge in and out of shadows at will. The Sombra, once defeated, reveals he was actually after Jason.

The pair flees Brackenburgh and hides out at an inn in the nearby town, Windward, to wait for Cinaed the Storyteller to rejoin them. While there, Aria begins to reveal more of Anargen's story.

With Ordumair delivered, it is decided that Anargen, his friends, Viceroy Ecthelion, and a group of Ords will travel to the ruins of the Ord city Glastonae to search the archive there for more about the Tower of Light. There they find an oracle from the Ord ruler that is almost identical to Caeserus's vision. The group however must defer completing the quest as it becomes clear Ecthelion's son orchestrated the Grey Scourge's coup and has taken control of Ecthelowall.

The group pledges to help retake Ecthelowall but must sneak back into the country to rally restoration forces for the Viceroy. To do so Cinaed recalls the kindness he and Anargen's father showed to a secretive man who arrived in Black River some time ago, Arnauld Nerebold, who is actually a famed Ecthel privateer fallen on hard times. Trusting Captain Nerebold can guide them secretly back into Ecthelowall the group heads for Black River and stops at Falconcleft where the Count of Stormridge, Eidolon, takes interest in them. Shortly after that meeting, they are attacked by a group of Sombra, intent on assassinating the Viceroy.

Barely escaping, to better mask their plans the group splits with Anargen, Caeserus, and Bertinand heading to Black River to send Anargen's father, Glewdyn, with Captain Nerebold, to meet the Viceroy, Sir Cinaed, and Terrillian at West Haven.

Anargen reunites with Seren, who reveals she pledged loyalty to the High King and became a Knight of Light as well. Their blissful reunion is interrupted when mercenaries raid Black River. Anargen and his friends lay down their arms rather than risk harm coming to the villagers.

Taken captive to a secret location to labor on an enormous construction project, Anargen and Caeserus have a chance to escape, but when Anargen realizes he would have to leave Seren behind, and the potential danger she would be in, he again surrenders.

Months pass with Anargen and his friends released to live in Stormridge under watch to ensure they don't speak of what has happened. Anargen forgets his oaths to the High King during the time and lives a normal life until one night he sees something that stirs his memories—the Grey Scourge has been watching him and that very night, Anargen discovers a package that contains his spiritsword. Holding the divinely blessed blade reignites his zeal for the High King.

Soon after he is brought to a Knight Hall in Stormridge where Glewdyn and Sir Cinaed have already rescued Caeserus. They travel to get Seren back while Caeserus and Anargen go to retrieve Bertinand. They find him beset by a direnoir. A monstrous parasitic creature that feeds on the fears of its host. After defeating it, the Grey Scourge attacks, intending to keep them from returning to the Quest of Fire. They defeat the Scourge and bring him prisoner back to the Knight Hall. He reveals that he has been working for Count Eidolon and that the Count's plans for conquering the Western Lowlands are almost complete. Confronting Eidolon, the evil ruler does not hide his dabbling in dark sorceries from the cursed land of Tislatna—long ago destroyed by the High King for its wickedness.

Escaping the encounter with their lives, the Knights try to rally the few members of their Order in Stormridge they can trust, only to find they're too late. Eidolon has used the sorceries of Tislatna and an enchanted fruit that grows in the region to take control of the entire city's population. Mindless servants of his will, called carrion, they overwhelm the Knights with only a handful escaping. Sir Cinaed, Glewdyn, Anargen, Seren, Caeserus, and Bertinand along with a Sir Kyreneas, Lady Lyncia, and five other Knights make it atop the enormous reservoir that holds a secret escape tunnel from the city. There they find Eidolon waiting for them. He intends to sacrifice them in a ritual that will allow him to summon a wyvern long dormant in the mountains of the region and fuse it with a goblin to create a dragon, the first of an army of such creatures he wants to use to conquer the Lowlands and the very forbidden sorcery for which Tislatna was destroyed.

A battle ensues as a storm threatens to overflow the reservoir. The Knights attempt to escape, but Sir Cinaed, Glewdyn, and Anargen are still on the artificial lake's retaining wall finishing off Eidolon when the wyvern he summoned arrives. The creature rejects the weakened Eidolon, destroying him, and then sets out to do the same to the Knights and the everything in its path. Sir Cinaed sacrifices himself, leaping onto the wyvern and slaying it as the reservoir gives and the water and stones plummet with the Defender Knight and the wyvern to the valley below. Anargen and the others escape, heartbroken.

In the Modern Era, Jason and Aria receive a message that her grandfather has had to slip out of Rehalycon to the Ecthel island Geisle and wants Aria to meet him there. Before Aria and Jason part ways, however, Jason is attacked by a group of mobster thugs who work for his family. The Wernstrums are the preeminent crime family of the Lowlands. They almost beat Jason to death when Aria steps in and rescues him. Jason confesses to Aria he had been running from being a part of his loathsome family till he received a letter giving him an ultimatum to either rejoin the family or his younger brother, Dorian, would be forced to take his place in the gang. Aria convinces him to come with her and they will figure out what to do next.

They arrive on Geisle and meet up with Cinaed the Storyteller. He leads them to the mansion of Professor Goulder, an old friend and fellow Knight of Light. Along the way, Jason and Aria acknowledge the romance between them and decide to formally begin dating, such as they can.

Once at the eccentric professor's home, he shares his secret communications and seconds a plan Cinaed proposed to have all the Lowlands' Defenders of the Realms assemble to address the disturbing signs and growing darkness they've observed and endured. While discussing their next steps, the mansion is attacked by werebeasts and again Jason and Aria flee while Cinaed defends them.

The couple almost escapes when Sombra ambush and overwhelm them, taking Jason captive. Jason is brought to the Gerisk Ruins in the Southwestern desert nation Zilnen. There the Sombra hold him in wait of word from their client on whether to bring him in or finish him off.

Jason escapes with some aid from the High King and after encountering the horrifying powers of Tislatna buried in the ruins, makes his way to a small desert ksar where he's caught by the Sombra but liberated by Cinaed and Aria. The Sombra vow revenge.

From there, the group travels north to I'jon where Sadiq Kharoum, Defender of the Southwestern Realm resides. Zilnen is hostile to Knights of Light, so they meet in a secret library. There Jason is introduced to Aria's close friend, Tirzah, and encounters some books that cast doubt on whether what he had experienced was truly marvelous or rather the whole Quest of Fire was a sham. While gripped in doubt and uncertainty, Sadiq flies into a rage, having learned Jason is a Wernstrum. The Wernstrums had been helping the Rehalcyon Empire with a secret project on southern shores of the Notioanemos Sea and Sadiq as a loyal Zilnian noble accuses Jason of treachery and espionage.

Cinaed, Jason, and Aria leave in a rush and on the train ride, Cinaed confirms he is not the Sir Cinaed from the stories

Jason has been told. Torn by not having helped his brother and convinced he'd been conned into believing a fairy tale, Jason jumps off the train and abandons Aria and Cinaed. He heads home to Brackenburgh and turns himself over to his family.

It was a ruse and a trap all along. Dorian isn't in danger at all, he is now the head of the family and behind the attacks on Jason. He reveals that he has embraced the dark powers used by Count Eidolon and others and chains Jason up to endure a slow and painful death.

While chained, Jason cries out to the High King, broken and penitent, realizing once and for all the Quest of Fire is real. In a blaze of glorious fire and light, the High King frees Jason from his bonds.

Meanwhile, Aria and Cinaed visit Dr. Gregorio Antoni to further their work in uniting the Defenders of the Realms. Aria is wistful and misses Jason. But they can't lament long as Sombra attack, forcing them to move on. Cinaed instructs Dr. Antoni to help Jason find them, because he is certain they haven't seen the last of the teen.

During the events in Stormridge of the Middle Era, Thomas Fenwrest is a squire serving his uncle Baron Fenwrest under the captain of his guard, Sir Hurstwell. Thomas and Hurstwell are tasked with delivering the Baron's young son, Gregor, to Yerst Castle along with his betrothed, Lady Delia Sornfold and her sister Mia. The war to restore the Viceroy has been underway for months and things seem hopeful when the group stumbles upon the ravaged field of a battle that dealt a decisive blow to the Restoration Army. Having lost his own family, Thomas comforts Mia who believes her father, Baron Sornfold, died in the battle. The group also finds a survivor, the foreign Knight and friend of Anargen, Terrillian.

Sir Hurstwell advises that they all retreat to Port Valence, a fortified position on the coast. They arrive along with a steady stream of refugees from the collapsing Restoration front lines just as the Monarchists launch a surprise attack on Port Valence. Fleeing inside the city, they only just catch their breath before it becomes clear Valence too will fall and they make a narrow escape from its docks onboard a ship bound for the island of New Ecthelowall, known to its residents as Emeral.

On Emeral, Mia discovers her father is alive and as Baron of Emeral welcomes the group, and Viceroy Ecthelion who also arrives at the same time, promising everyone safety. Things are quiet long enough for Thomas to think on the lessons Terrillian has been giving him about Knights of Light and for Thomas to begin to see he and Mia have feelings for one another. A celebratory ball is thrown by Baron Sornfold and Thomas is invited to attend as Lady Mia's guest. However, Gregor has fallen ill since their escape from Valence and must be tended to.

Shortly before the ball begins, Thomas has a vision of the Tower of Light under siege. He doesn't know it at the time, but it is eerily similar to Caeserus's vision almost a year earlier. He pledges himself to the High King and is at once aware that there is something unnatural about Gregor's illness. A dark force seems to be binding him.

Thomas delivers Gregor from the enchanted illness and is warned by Gregor that he had been poisoned by Lady Delia. The pair dash to the site of the celebration and reach it just in time to see Delia murder her father and proclaim her loyalty to Monarch Ilyron. Thomas, Terrillian, Sir Hurstwell, Mia, Gregor, Viceroy Ecthelion, and the Viceroy's guards fight their way out and make a desperate escape into the Emeral countryside. Their plan is to reach the other side of the island before word that they weren't captured reaches there and then sail to Libertias to plead for aid from the Viscount of Libertias.

The attempt fails and they are forced to turn back where they are intercepted by Captain Nerebold. The captain takes the Viceroy and Terrillian to Libertias to petition the Viscount as planned, but Gregor and Mia are deemed too valuable to risk keeping with the Viceroy, as they each now represent the most powerful noble houses in Ecthelowall's Restoration forces. They travel with Thomas and Sir Hurstwell to the Isle of Geists (later called Geisle) to hide until a safer passage north can be arranged. While hiding deep in the foreboding interior of the island, they discover a darkling creature that reveals an evil far greater than Monarch Ilyron is orchestrating the events unfolding.

The monster mortally wounds Sir Hurstwell, before he and Thomas are able to defeat it. In a frantic bid to save Sir Hurstwell and get needed supplies for Mia and Gregor, Thomas seeks help from the residents of the island only to find they've been slain by Monarchist forces after they failed to find Gregor and Mia. The trio remains on the island until Captain Nerebold returns. They sail with him, determined now to seize the hope that their most desperate hour was past and to warn the Viceroy about what they've learned.

Meanwhile, Anargen and the other survivors of Stormridge's destruction escape to a small town to grieve those they've lost, including Anargen's mentor and Defender of the Northern Realm, Sir Cinaed. There they are betrayed into the hands of Sombra intent on revenge for the embarrassing defeat the shadow assassins had suffered months earlier. Anargen and the others escape captivity and defeat the Sombra, but not before being taunted with the revelation that the Sombra would soon be eliminating an important target in Libertias's capital of Kirke on behalf of the evil Ecthel ruler, Monarch Ilyron.

Anargen and his father, Glewdyn, are eager to act on this information. However, Caeserus, Bertinand, and the others survivors of Stormridge are no longer convinced the Quest is real, matters, or is for them to pursue. All of them depart leaving Anargen devastated by the loss of his dearest friends and with little aid now to stop the Sombra from carrying out Monarch Ilyron's plot.

With just his fiancée, Seren, and his father to aid him, they seek allies in Estonbury. The Knights there refuse to aid them as the War for Restoration is causing political pressure and they aren't convinced the Sombra threat is real.

Dejected they travel to Kirke only to find it under a secret blockade by werebeasts. In a forest just outside the great city they meet up with Thomas, Gregor, and Mia who likewise need to reach Viceroy Ecthelion in the city with a warning and can't.

Together they break through the blockade and sneak into Kirke's palace only to find out a Sombra is already there preparing for his assassination attempt. They rush to find Ecthelion expecting the assassin is after him only to discover that he was really sent to murder the leader of Libertias, Viscount Geralian. His goal is to pin the blame for the assassination on Ecthelion and the Restoration. With the Sombra felled, Geralian pledges Libertias will support Ecthelion and the Restoration. The first rays of hope to break through the gloom since the tragedy at Stormridge.

In the Modern Era, Jason is freed from the chains of his brother, Dorian, by the High King, to whom he pledges himself as a Knight of Light. Escaping the Ministry of Justice's dungeon, he encounters Vif the elf. One of the High King's original and most powerful servants, he guides Jason to armor and spiritsword and instructs him to go to Windward seeking Jerome to learn where Aria and Cinaed Black are as he must rejoin them to help gather the Council of Defenders. The ancient council being the best hope for rallying enough Knights to counter the dark forces Dorian is leading.

In Windward, Jason receives Anargen's journal and reads of his struggles, encouraging and guiding him as he travels to the capital of the Rehalcyon Empire and former capital of the long ended Libertias, Falkirke. Falkirke marks the first step in reaching Aria and Cinaed.

While in Falkirke, Jason is approached by Melania, an old girlfriend from a gangster family that rivaled his own family. She has fallen in with Dorian and tries to capture Jason, but he escapes, horrified by the dark powers she now wields.

He travels south to Lyrscony where he meets with the cowardly Dr. Antoni who was planning to aid Cinaed in gathering the Council of Defenders, so long as he could do so in secret. He agrees to get Jason to I'jon in Zilnen where Cinaed and Aria are working with Sadiq Kharoum again.

During a train stop in Yuldistan, Jason and Dr. Antoni are attacked by Sombra. Jason's courage and zeal for the High King inspires Dr. Antoni and he sacrifices himself to make sure Jason is on the train south to continue the Quest.

In I'jon, Jason meets up with Kaveed Amine, a Knight of Light who secretly married Aria's best friend and daughter of Defender Kharoum, Tirzah.

Aria is icy towards Jason for having abandoned her and the Quest, refusing to believe the High King's rescue of him from

Dorian changed him. While Aria, Jason, and Cinaed are preparing to leave to begin gathering support for the Council of Defenders, Defender Kharoum returns and is furious having discovered Tirzah's secret marriage to Kaveed. He puts Kaveed in Lago Amurgo on the frontlines of the simmering conflict between Rehalcyon and Zilnen.

Tirzah begs Cinaed and Aria to rescue Kaveed. They agree and Jason, in a bid to prove he has changed, volunteers to be captured to relay Tirzah's plea to her father for Kaveed's release from the army. Jason also seeks to convince Defender Kharoum that the Council of Defenders is the only hope for victory.

Defender Kharoum rejects both premises and has Jason beaten, towing him to the frontlines to witness what he expects to be Zilnen's military victory. Except Defender Kharoum's ex-wife Mesnara has betrayed him and his army and pledged her loyalty to Rehalcyon in exchange for the governorship over Zilnen. Jason manages to escape while Kharoum is executed.

Hurrying to Port Amurgo, he warns Kaveed and his men to retreat to avoid being captured by Mesnara's traitorous forces. As they flee, they're bombed by Rehalcyon's airplanes and carrion created by Dorian signaling that, as in the past, the newest weapons of war were being mixed with ancient, evil sorceries.

Fleeing along a dangerous desert path known as The Lion's Back, Jason and Kaveed face dehydration and are nearly the only survivors left. Jason thinks he sees others following them but worries they're a mirage. Passing by the Ash Dunes they're attacked by a sand scourge and narrowly defeat the beast with some last-minute assistance by those who had followed them—Cinaed, Aria, and Tirzah. After catching everyone up on what has happened to Zilnen, the group flees to Yusbilsi, a neutral nation.

Yusbilsi's neutrality was tenuous, however, as thugs break

in and kidnap Cinaed, Kaveed, and Tirzah. Faced with being the only ones left to proceed with the Quest or rescue the others, Jason and Aria finally reconcile. Together they set out on a rescue mission but are intercepted on their way southeast. They're taken to the secret stronghold of Siğmacaq Yeri where Defender Kazim Cuzibaum informs them that Uldiquim slavers regularly kidnap Knights in Yusbilsi and sell them at auction in Varliliman.

Defender Cuzibaum helps them launch a rescue attempt. However, once again a betrayal overturns their efforts. Only Aria, Jason, and a former slaver named Efram escape. Efram offers to lead them to the location he believes everyone is really being held.

The location is Uthtar, an enormous mansion that once served as a manor house overlooking the lands. It is filled with terrible, vicious secrets. Not the least of which being that Jason remembers having been to this place before as a child. After freeing Tirzah, Kaveed, and Defender Cuzibaum; Jason and Aria head into the mansion to find her grandfather. They are attacked by werebeasts and get separated. After Jason bests his beastly foes, he finds his way down into the basement where he finds Aria battling Melania. Cinaed is there, weak from torture. Jason fights through some of Melania's direnoir minions, requiring him to conquer his most potent fears to do so, though one remains: that he cannot save his brother from what he has become.

Melania, defeated, escapes using dark sorcery akin to a Sombra's but not before teasing that Monarch Ilyron would soon be returning.

Escaping with Cinaed and the other Knights, they set their sights and hearts to the task of finishing gathering the Council of Defenders.

Back in the Middle Era, more than a year after rescuing Viscount Geralian, the War of Restoration is deadlocked. Though the addition of Libertias gave the advantage to the Restoration and helped bolster their efforts, a terrible disease known as the Devastation, or Ilyron's Hammer, has beset the Restoration armies and is threatening to shift the balance back to the Monarchists.

Sir Thomas Fenwrest is now Mia and Gregor's personal body guard as each have assumed their titles, Baronness and Heir-Apparent respectively. To keep them safe he has taken them to fortified area of Albaron, Kilkern's Redoubt, where Devastation patients receive what treatment and care as can be given. They stay under the protection of an Albaron noble, William Kilkern.

While there, they are surprised by an attack from Mia's sister, Delia, who has wed Monarch Ilyron and declared herself Queen of Emeral. Kilkern betrays them into her hands in exchange for sparing his lands. Delia takes Thomas, Mia, Gregor, and Mia's handmaid, Ilsa, prisoner. Marching them northeast for an unknown purpose.

Delia makes camp and summons Thomas and Ilsa offering one of them a favor if they reveal the location of Viceroy Ecthelion to her. Aided by her witchcraft, she tempts Thomas with the offer of a title, which he needs if he ever hopes to have a public, official relationship with Mia. Delia needs Ecthelion's location, because she wants to unleash upon him the arcane power of Wyvares. Thomas resists, relying on the High King's aid and refuses Delia's request.

Delia is forced to attend to a surprise attack on her camp and while away, Thomas frees everyone, though they can't escape, because Gregor was brutally injured in his leg and can barely walk. They are again captured, this time by Albaron soldiers led by Kilkern. He informs them he duped Delia into trusting him and would deliver them safely to Albaron's capital, Caldoness.

The group cautiously reveals that Delia, now Kilkern's captive, had wanted Wyvares's power. This terrifies Kilkern who reveals that Wyvares is a region of Albaron long associated with legends of wyvern and witches. Having seen Melania's dark powers, he believes that she intended to try to find and bend a wyvern to her will.

After reporting in Caldoness, the group is sent south to Dirkforge, the primary source of arms and armaments for Albaron. Viceroy Ecthelion has been keeping hidden there, directing the war effort for Ecthelowall's Restoration forces. While there, it becomes apparent that Queen Delia's army of Emeralans is on the move and preparing to attack Dirkforge. Thomas must join the defense but Ilsa comes to speak to him on the parapets.

At first, she tries to convince him they should both accept their common lot, she even hints that perhaps he is better off with her than Mia. When he rebuffs her, she informs him he has been summoned to see Mia before the battle starts. He had been avoiding Mia, accepting he could never be with her, because of her noble status and himself being a commoner.

Before he can go to her though, a messenger for the Viceroy summons him to make an offer. Ecthelion knows he needs an heir. His usurping son Ilyron once defeated won't be able to receive their family's title and he doesn't want the fragile Commonwealth that will emerge from the war torn up over a fight about his lands' succession rights. So, he offers to adopt Thomas.

Thomas accepts and rushes to tell Mia, intent on proposing to her immediately. He finds her in her room, cool and combative. She thinks he is having an affair with Ilsa because of things Ilsa had said since their captivity.

Thomas reassures her he has been faithful and presents the paperwork signed by the Viceroy that could allow them to be married. She refuses to give Thomas a direct answer, not wanting him distracted one way or another in the battle ahead.

A short battle ensues soon after he arrives to take his place. The Queen's forces are routed and flee. Thomas is concerned something is amiss but the other commanders of Dirkforge's defense disregard his worries and ride out after the fleeing Monarchists. As they do, Thomas spots werebeasts and another mysterious rider heading for the city.

Thomas follows the werebeasts and defeats two of them. The third he finds in a plaza as it battles Ecthelion and nobles of Albaron. He thinks he spots Kilkern tending to those injured. Ecthelion is seriously wounded in the fight before Thomas defeats the werebeast. One of the Albaron nobles cries out in pain, pulling Thomas from tending to Ecthelion. Kilkern had been replaced by a doppelganger and instead of tending to the injured he was finishing them off.

A new battle begins and Thomas defeats the doppelganger. Before it ceases to be, the shape-stealing monster taunts him that Queen Delia's capture was planned. She wanted to be in striking distance of Ecthelion, Gregor, Mia, and Albaron's bravest nobles. Thomas rushes to Mia's quarters and finds the mysterious rider with Delia, cornering Mia.

The mysterious rider is revealed to be Ilsa who had been planted by Delia in her sister's service. Ilsa is schooled in the dark arts like Delia and as Delia flees, with Mia as her prisoner, Ilsa battles Thomas.

For all her dark powers and prowess, Thomas is still able to best Ilsa and has the regrettable burden of informing all remaining that Mia was taken. Matters darken further as he discovers that Gregor has contracted the Devastation through his leg wound and though he's endured an amputation to halt its spread, he hasn't much time left to live.

Even as he struggles to comfort a fading Gregor, Viceroy Ecthelion is brought in, his prognosis just as dire.

A soldier arrives and informs Thomas the battle for Dirkforge has ended. It looked as though he had been correct about the retreat being a ploy, but what would've been a devastating loss as an army of carrion swarmed Albaron's forces, turned into a victory as they all suddenly collapsed inexplicably. Though since all of them were ill with the Devastation plague it was harder to figure out how the carrion hadn't fallen sooner.

Thomas realizes that the Devastation plague is being used in conjunction with dark sorcery and uses the flat of his spiritsword on Gregor's leg. It works, burning away the arcane infection. Gregor has the vision of the High King and pledges himself to the High King as a Knight of Light. He also informs Thomas that the High King has revealed to him that Queen Delia is on her way to Wyvares to summon a dragon.

Assembling a small party of soldiers, Thomas sneaks to Wyvares with the group and prepares to face Delia and her army. Within the snowy valley surrounded by jagged mountains, Delia only has a handful of soldiers with her.

Entering an enormous ice monument, Thomas watches as Delia prepares to sacrifice her sister to transform a wyvern freed from the ice into a dreaded dragon. The ritual is disrupted by a sudden blinding light and Thomas finds himself next to the high elf, Vif, who has brought Mia to him. He warns they must fight the wyvern but he was permitted to prevent the summoning of the dragon for the moment.

Thomas and Mia rush outside into the snowy valley around Wyvares. Mia, armed with a spiritsword provided by Thomas, faces off against her sister while Thomas must stand against the wyvern. The soldiers Thomas brought help ensure none of Delia's troops interfere nor escape.

The battles rage and Thomas is able to triumph over the wyvern. He hears a woman's shriek and rushes over to find Mia, standing over her slain sister. Thomas comforts her as they return to Caldoness to report what had transpired.

There they hold a funeral for Viceroy Ecthelion and Thomas assumes his new baronic title and name, a name he will share with Mia as she had said yes to his marriage proposal all along. Bittersweetness deepens in sharpness as a letter from Monarch Ilyron arrives. He is annoyed at their felling his Queen, but undeterred. So much so he informs them of his imminent plans to march to Ordumair and claim from it the wyvern he knows to be hidden there. A revelation which forces Thomas, Mia, and Gregor to move swiftly to aid Ordumair or await the same grisly end they thought they had just averted.

THE LOWLANDS WAR

24 Daraleath 358 Modern Era

Black smoke rolling off the ruined landscape seared the sky. A hundred yards ahead, a shell whistled from the darkness and crashed into what had once been a verdant plain of long swaying grasses on gently rolling hills.

"Whatever happens next—no fear," Jason vowed.

Tremors raced through the ground, reaching all the way to him. Or perhaps he was only imagining that, much the way he imagined that the explosion's despicable sound was the land crying out in anger and agony.

Jason lifted the face plate of his helmet and wiped the sweat from his brow. About the best that could be said for the cold sweat and the increasing tempo of chilly raindrops pelting the landscape was that they cut the layer of grime on his face. Steam curled from his mouth. His nose wrinkled at the stench of fires started by the bombs and artillery shells.

He gagged and spat, wiping at his mouth, which only smeared his face with the mixture of mud and ash. Just beyond the earthen rampart concealing Jason, bullets whizzed and charred dirt erupted in all directions.

The sea and the crumbling ruins of once-vibrant Novoknorstok stretched behind him. His arrival yesterday had discovered only the village's smoking corpse, littered with the bodies of those trapped by the merciless bombardment. The attack leveled the city before aid could arrive, forcing a

I

stalemate between the Alliance of Realms, led by the Commonwealth of Ecthelowall, and the Confederacy of Nations, controlled by the Rehalcyon Empire. Never mind that here in the northeasternmost stretches of Arnuk, the armies of both sides were thousands of miles from Ecthelowall and Rehalcyon's heartlands. The sad truth was that this was only a tiny blip in the war that had engulfed the entirety of the Lowlands. But the terror and despair were tragic enough.

Enough to convince Jason that, whatever the cost, Rehalcyon must be stopped.

A fresh whistling quickly became a scream. Jason threw himself down, instinctively covering his head. The shell impacted a few feet away, pelting him with a cascade of dirt and stone shards. His ears rang from the sound, and he felt the reverberations in his arms. Most of his precious concealment had been obliterated.

Keep it together. The motorcycle isn't too far from here.

Jason closed his eyes and drew in a breath. Silently, he thanked the High King that the guns hadn't aimed slightly farther back. Eyes open again, he raised from his prone position as much as he dared and dashed along the trench. It had been carved out days ago for an advance by the Alliance forces from the bordering nation of Posek. He was the only one still this far forward.

He gripped his satchel strap tightly. These risks weren't for nothing. He had received vital correspondence from the contact he met amidst the rubble of Novoknorstok—a message from Psilmas, the capital of neighboring Arnuk, which was currently under a Confederacy siege. But one did not simply walk into the middle of No Man's Land.

Staggering over the remnants of a soldier's pack, Jason stiffened. Dirt exploded into dust just above his head. The sniper's bullet didn't have his name on it.

No, he could not think that way.

Everything happens as the High King permits, not by fate or circumstance.

He clambered over the sodden debris until, in the dark, his hands found the thing he desperately needed. For just a moment, he felt the gentle touch of relief. His motorcycle.

More shells joined in a symphony of bombastic fury. Jason lifted the bike off the permafrost exposed by the trench diggers. He threw his leg over the seat, securing the precious satchel he carried to his chest, the straps pulled so snug they would leave bruises.

One more deep breath as he revved the motorbike's engine. Its little combustion motor growled like an ocelot staring down an elephant. Until recently, Jason had only seen either in a zoo. One of the great tragedies of the war was that he'd visited much of the Lowlands in those two years. So much beauty and wonder to discover, marred by so much death and malevolence.

A final shell's explosion rang through the broad clearing. Minutes later, all was silent, except for Jason's own heartbeat. He double-checked his watch. The Alliance had paused its firing as promised. In the dark, the Confederacy couldn't know where to shell without the flares of light from the cannons firing on the Alliance side. Jason had less than fifteen minutes to make it across No Man's Land to his destination before the Alliance resumed its bombardment, and the Confederacy followed suit.

This is it, my King. Either I make it across, or I join you in the City of Light.

Popping the clutch, Jason squeezed the accelerator, and the motorcycle shot forward. It bumped along the uneven soil, careening through the trench. Several yards ahead, dirt sprayed from bullet impacts, and he could faintly hear the crack of sniper rifles firing. He took it as a good sign. They knew someone was in this trench, but they didn't know where, or they would've completely obliterated the area he was in. His younger brother, Dorian, had ensured he was a primary target for all Confederacy forces—those of a conventional sort and those servants of darker powers.

The trench ended in a slope upward, and Jason popped up into No Man's Land, completely exposed. He kept the bike's light off to prevent tipping off the Confederacy gunners. Dark and long, the trench coat he wore kept the gleaming armor of the Knights of Light from alerting the darker foes he was there.

Cutting back toward the stable Posek front line, Jason poured on speed, not caring that the motorcycle's engine growled twice as loud. He was past the point where complete stealth would aid him. Now he needed to move fast. A bullet whizzed past him as if to confirm that fact.

Dodging a bomb crater, Jason swung the bike left and right, trying to find a level path to return him to headquarters in one piece. He came up on a crater too fast and soared over it, briefly in the air. As he landed with a jarring thud, he glimpsed ochre eyes gleaming with malice in the night.

Werebeast.

Sleek and black as midnight, the creature—wolf-like but with an arched back akin to a bison and a build closer to a bear —must have spotted him. Its eyes, filled with the cunning of a man, were trained on him. At once, it loped swiftly in his direction.

There was no outrunning the thing, especially not through this pockmarked ruin of a plain. The best Jason could hope for was to get as close to his destination as he could before the monster overtook him.

CONVICTIONS

J ason revved the engine on his motorcycle, fighting to coax
more speed out of the spindly bike. To his left, the
creature was gaining on him, its muscled limbs bounding
with all the grace of a wolf, yet so much faster than any natural
beast could. The Posek town he sought, Kezmarepos, was two
miles away. Jason realized he'd have to face the beast, and the
important message the informant needed delivered was on the
line.

A familiar growl came from behind. He had seconds before
it caught him. Peering ahead in the gloom, he spotted a ridge—
his best shot.

Jerking the bike onto its slightly adjusted course, Jason's
muscles tensed. Inches away, the beast's jaws snapped shut.
Sparing precious seconds of attention, Jason watched the beast
skitter through the muddy soil. Its attempt to leap and snag him
off the motorcycle had just missed.

Thank you, my King!

The werebeast recovered and continued its pursuit with an
unfair speed advantage. Its claws barely slipped amid the mire.
The ridge Jason sought loomed about two hundred yards
ahead.

Beside him, the beast surged past, blocking him. He veered
off his intended path, and a shudder ran through his arms that
nearly ripped his hands off the bars.

Cutting back onto the line he needed to hold, he ducked as

the beast swiped at him. He felt a tug along his back and, over the bike's whining engine, heard the shredding of his coat.

The howl loosed into the storm told him the hidden armor had held. He had expected the beast to be frustrated. The claws couldn't overcome his righteous cuirass—*Thorax Dikaiosyne* in the ancient tongue—but it couldn't deliver him from the fearsome jaws.

When they were about fifty yards from the ridge, Jason swallowed back his anxiety. He must be crazed, or else supremely confident in the High King's favor resting on him.

"Help me, Great King. The Alliance is depending on me!" he mumbled.

Forty.

Thirty.

The beast was closing in.

Twenty.

Good.

He shifted his position as much as he dared. The bike shuddered.

Ten.

A feral growl sounded just behind him.

Too late.

He reached the ridge, and the bike soared off as intended. Liquid as quicksilver, Jason spun around in the seat and kicked off it, reaching for the hilt of his spiritsword. The werebeast was there, jaws open wide and terrible claws reaching for him.

Drawing his spiritsword in an arc of fire, he felt the blade connect with the monster's furry side. The impact twisted him around and away from his attacker. And he found his sight filled with the ground as he plummeted toward it.

Jason landed with a roll and tumbled several feet away as his momentum bled off, skidding in the mud, aching in every part of his body. Taking a shaky breath, he forced himself to his feet. He couldn't lose time.

The werebeast lurked ahead on the road, about thirty feet away, where his bike had crashed. Its massive frame heaved as the beast drew itself up to its full height on its back legs.

Gripping his spiritsword tightly, Jason advanced. The beast stood there, baleful eyes tracking his approach.

Jason closed the distance and took up a guard stance. His foe snarled, its lupine lips pulling back over wicked fangs. It took one step toward him and then stumbled.

A lump formed in his throat. This was the moment. The one in which Defender Black had taught him to reach out to the beasts, to warn them they could be free of their curse. But he couldn't do it. He couldn't say it. Not after everything he'd seen in this war. Not with the carnage he knew these creatures inflicted everywhere they went. His skin prickled with a flush of heat as he resisted the urge, the need to call out to his foe with hope of deliverance. Had the familiar whisper of guidance from the High King come to him? It couldn't have, not this time.

With a heavy, wet *thwump*, the beast collapsed. A whimper issued from it, and a twitch seized its body before going still.

Moving closer, Jason could see the still-sizzling wound he'd inflicted, a glowing slash across its chest.

He released his tension with a shuddering breath. It had been enough. His crazy plan had worked. Thankfully, because he wasn't sure he could have faced down the thing.

A couple of years ago, standing against such a monster would've terrified him. How many had he overcome since?

Too many. He felt a stirring in his chest. He could almost hear Defender Black reminding him that every one of them had been a person once, consumed by the dark sorceries wielded by those overseeing Rehalcyon's campaign. People who had become monsters.

"Dorian," he murmured, the familiar white-hot pain that thoughts of his little brother always induced seared his chest. His dear Dorian, who was chief among those practicing such vile arts, would be much satisfied by Jason's demise at the claws of his craven creatures.

A sound reached Jason's ears—shrill, cutting through the bluster of resumed artillery and munitions firing. Another of the beasts.

It had perhaps caught his scent or witnessed his kill, or it might simply be on the hunt. Whatever the case, Jason wasn't in the clear yet.

Gritting his teeth, he dashed to his motorcycle and verified that the bike was damaged beyond use. Too bad. Securing his leather satchel, Jason pushed back his body's protests and set off at a jog toward the town of Kezmarepos, just across the Arnukan border with Posek.

I

BESIEGED

*"The Monarch's forces are as determined as they are dangerous.
Port Jarreth's defense is essential to defending Libertias's interior
lands, and may not be enough. No. I promised to always be
honest, especially in what I write.
It IS NOT enough."*

—Anargen's King's Day Journal
15 Gladiol 1610 Middle Era

Whena hand was offered to help him up, Anargen gladly accepted the aid. His heart and hand—all of him—felt heavy, weighed by the burden of what lay ahead. "Thank you."

Terrillian grinned. "You're one of the few Knights of Light who still kneel to make your pleas to the High King. It draws some stares."

"Really?" Anargen regarded his fellow Knight with brows raised. Terrillian's all-too-rare smile broke on his face, which had a long scar along the jawline from a battle nearer the war's beginning. His taut, almost hollowed cheeks and shaved head made for quite the contrast to Anargen's long, wild dark hair and gentler expressions. Both were about twenty now, a fact that still seemed impossible, and yet completely real. They had endured much in their short lives—all the more since pledging oaths of loyalty to the High King of All Realms.

"Indeed, quite a few eyes on you, especially among the others about our age ... and younger."

Earlier in his time as a Knight, Anargen might have been self-conscious and looked to see who had watched him. "Good. Perhaps it will help clear the path for them to have the vision as well. There are so few of us now, and the need is so great."

Clapping him on the back and giving Anargen's shoulder a shake, Terrillian chuckled. "You haven't changed a bit since I last saw you. I'm glad for that. This war has been costly enough without losing ourselves to it."

Anargen followed as his long-time friend led the way out of the forebuilding and into the quadrangle. A long double column of soldiers marched ahead, most on foot. They were moving through the inner and outer wards toward Port Jarreth's castle's gatehouse to take up positions along the sea walls. He felt favored by the High King to have his friend at his side once more, to march into this fight with him. Terrillian from Black River hadn't been lost to the horrors and hardships they'd each endured. That in itself was more than Anargen dared hope for.

"You're awfully cheerful, given the blockade around the port is being reinforced and an attack is almost certain," Anargen commented, wishing he could project the ease that Terrillian was right now.

Some of the brightness of Terrillian's expression slipped. He shrugged. "Well, we both knew this day was coming. If the Monarch wants to get to Kirke, this is the most direct staging point for that campaign."

"Exactly." Anargen glanced over his shoulder, hoping to catch sight of Seren or his father, Glewdyn, on one of the towers or ramparts. It always gave him extra drive having a visual reminder of what and to whom he was returning after a battle. As expected, this time was different. He tried not to begrudge them for it. "We know what is at stake and have both been fighting this war long enough to know the depths of darkness our foes belong to and wield without hesitation. After what happened at Castle Letolk, it will be hard to stand against—"

Terrillian gripped the hilt at his belt, glancing both ways as they passed outside the castle's gatehouse. In one swift flourish, he drew his weapon. Before he brought it around fully, the lettering on the blade glowed, and fire traced its way up the spiritsword's length, its rush of heat and sudden brilliance sent tingling through Anargen's length.

"Point made," Anargen allowed. Even being Palatini Lucis Aeternae, Knights of Light, with divinely empowered armor and implements of the High King of All Realms, there was no getting around the hard reality. The odds were not in their favor in the long term. Outnumbered many to one. The Libertian weapons here in Port Jarreth were damaged from the last attack, as were the walls. Worst, the Monarch resorted to darker sorceries that filled battlefields with werebeasts and mindless, unyielding carrion soldiers, who continued marching onward, even as their bodies were destroyed, not stopping until they had torn their targets apart.

"It's too bad we don't have Sir Thomas here with us," Anargen added. The young Ecthelish Knight had been instrumental in thwarting Monarch Ilyron's assassination attempt on Libertias's Viscount. His aid now would have been appreciated, but he was busy serving Ecthelowall's Restoration armies in Albaron by guarding those essential to the war's success. On Thomas's mission hung the hopes to restore Viceroy Ecthelion, the leader of the Commonwealth, to Ecthelowall, before the power-hungry Monarch consumed it, Libertias, and all of the western Lowlands.

Terrillian's brows knit for an instant. "I thought you were going to say Caeserus and Bertinand."

Anargen's gait faltered. He still hadn't had the heart to tell Terrillian what had happened after their mentor, Sir Cinaed, sacrificed himself in Stormridge. It was hard enough to tell Terrillian of that, but the fact that the other two teens from their original group of four had abandoned the Quest hurt too deeply to share. How had he ever thought life in Black River was difficult at all compared to this?

The other Knight huffed. "But we'll make do ... or Libertias will fall."

"Oh, well, given those options." Anargen rolled his eyes.

Terrillian jabbed Anargen's shoulder pauldron. His armor of an easy smile was once more in place.

An instant later, they both walked out onto the sea walls around the port. The echoing report of distant cannon fire reached them, obliterating the coast's peace. An enormous fleet stretched ahead, flying the black and green flags of the Monarch and utterly outgunning the defensive squadron of ships assigned to Port Jarreth. Whoever thought that Bonus Mare was the more likely point of attack for the Monarch after his last costly defeat here had made a gross miscalculation. When the last of the defensive ships sank, their failure was made complete.

Soon, terribly soon, the towering frigates and carracks of the Monarch would be in firing range on the port. There was no repelling this amount of firepower. Even the best defensive points for the port would be smashed to dust by a fleet this large. The banter between Anargen and Terrillian earlier about the danger to them from the Monarch's forces suddenly felt crude and profane. Everything tragic they had discussed was much more real, more likely to come to pass now.

"Sometimes I wonder if we're meant to win this war," Terrillian mumbled, his earlier humor stripped away.

Anargen glanced at him out of the corner of his eye, weighing whether or not to say anything. No, this wasn't the time to bring up arguments he'd had with his father. "We can't think that way," Anargen replied, clearing his throat. "Not if we're going to stand a chance in this battle."

A rush of heat enveloped Anargen on the breeze, startling him. Riding on the wind was a whisper, which pulled his attention away from the imminent attack by sea and far into the distance. At first, all he saw was the castle and city of Port Jarreth. But he felt strangely pulled away.

Neither sensation nor focus was foreign. The timbre of the summons—its gravity and magnificence—was very familiar to him. Treasured by him. Rather, it was the strength of the pull from this place, this moment, that took him aback. As if he shouldn't be here, shouldn't be fighting this battle.

And yet, that couldn't be true, because where else could or should he be but on the front lines? Stopping the evil armies of the Monarch from snuffing out the wick of the one remaining western Lowland nation still fully sovereign over its domain and still committed to liberty, justice, and truth—all of which he knew the High King prized. Still, he could not escape it. The draw to be elsewhere. Far from here by so many leagues.

What are you telling me, my King?

"Anargen?" Terrillian gave his shoulder a sharp shake. "Are you well?"

Blinking, Anargen was pulled in two different directions. "I, uh, I think so."

Terrillian chuckled, but with an edge of concern to the sound. "Yeah, well, you'd better *know* fast. The Field Marshal is about to address us all."

That grabbed his attention. Count Forsmythe of Jarreth County had been given command over the Libertian armies of the coast. Anargen had never met him, but a host of superlatives were attached to his name, including valorous and ingenious. If anyone stood a chance to claim the title Viscount from Geralian in the next council of counties when this conflict ended, it would be Forsmythe.

Anargen felt an almost boyish eagerness to hear the Field Marshal speak. To be one of the few who could look back and say he'd heard his address and was there at this pivotal moment in the Lowlands' history. A part of him understood how foolish he was being, given that he had been granted the vision of the High King of All Realms, heard His voice, and experienced the edges of his fiery presence.

Now Anargen felt abashed. All the same, he drifted after Terrillian, heading toward the seawall—against the pull he felt from the Highlands and its Lord. His Lord.

Forsmythe was already standing atop a hastily erected platform. A crowd of Libertian soldiers—dark blue tunics with their gleaming silver armor looking like sun-crested waves—surrounded the vaunted leader. The anticipation rolling over the gathered was palpable. This man and what he stood for could sway the battle. His words could rally them now to overcome what looked to be a sure defeat. He had done so at the Siege of Tenchford, where he earned his legend and cemented his title and command.

"Men of Libertias! Dawn greets us on shores that soon will be hallowed by the courageous defense we must mount. Our enemy's ships are moored just off our nation's coast. An enemy so despicable, its own people are determined to thwart it at the cost of their lives.

"It is no small irony that the enemy is the resurgent Monarchy of Ecthelowall. The very viper your forefathers struck down to craft the country we have been nurtured and protected by. Libertias, the bright and shining beacon of justice and freedom, a tower looking out onto the Lowlands—"

A twinge of hot anxiety seared Anargen's chest. His eyes instinctively flicked toward the Highlands. A "beacon." A "tower." The very things he, Terrillian, and the others had been summoned from Black River to defend. The same Tower of Light spoken of in oracles by Thane Ornand of Ordumair in the far north, centuries before. Naturally, the proposition that Forsmythe's words sat before him had to be considered. The "shining beacon" and the "tower," was it truly Libertias? Was Libertias the Tower of Light they must defend?

"... which might light and guide the Lowlands for a thousand generations. Or it may fall in this Era. In this war. On this day." Forsmythe paused his speech, letting the words seep into the sinews of his hearers. Anargen felt his natural impulse to deny it, to reject it, well up within. Even as another voice pointed out that every nation of the Lowlands ends. Only the High King's would never end.

Forsmythe began again, his voice dropping an octave into a cold and gruff register. "No. It will not."

A wild cheer rang out from the assembled. Forsmythe drew his ceremonial rapier, lifting it high to glint in the sunlight. "No. It will not fall. Not Port Jarreth. This County. Libertias. Not ever! Our forefathers spilled their blood to forge this nation, and now we will safeguard it till the last drops of our own. So when our children's children look back, they will feel the same swell of pride and comfort that on this day, in this place, the beacon of freedom and justice was not extinguished. It burned on and set ablaze those who would dare defy its righteous justice and the inalienable freedoms for which it was founded."

The raucous cheer built in volume and verve to a feral roar

of defiance aimed at the Monarch's ships floating in the choppy waters of the Muiruaine Sea. Dark lines of seaweed drifted in bands on the waters, agitated by a recent storm. These appeared to rise and fall with the pumps of Libertian soldier's arms. The very stones of the wall on which they stood seemed to vibrate with the resonance of their zeal. It was infectious and exhilarating, and Anargen ... grew more and more torn. Every whoop and shout of victory and valor only scored deeper a wound he perceived himself receiving.

A whisper powerful in its subtlety gripped Anargen's attention. The whisper demanded he fall back, that he leave. Now.

Why, my King? Why can't I celebrate this? Don't you allow nations to rise, and Libertias above all the others? You favored it so! It was born from Ecthelowall. The secession of Libertias is what paved the way for the Commonwealth of Ecthelowall to replace its cruel Monarchy. We've been estranged, but amicable with the Commonwealth since, and with this war, we now link arms as brothers. Is this not the Tower of Light that you've been drawing us to safeguard?

Silence was his answer. And a wave of unease—of something being amiss both within and without—so potent he thought he might collapse. Holding his head and drawing in shaking breaths, he barely caught Count Forsmythe announce over the chants for victory, for Libertias, and for the Count, "Now, men of Libertias, stand at the ready. Your company commanders have my orders. Form up on them and receive the pathway to triumph."

Anargen's discomfort doubled with the bombastic, almost frantic outpouring that followed. He felt like he'd been cast overboard, and every shout was another wave slapping him in the face, stealing away the air from his lungs. Spots danced in his vision, and he knew he was going to collapse.

He tried to take a step as those around him dispersed, and he staggered. A strong arm shot out and steadied him. Terrillian's. "Are you well? I know you're not a sailor, but you really don't need sea legs to stand by the shoreline."

"I, uh, I ..." A new shout went up all around, but Anargen could scarcely make it out. His vision went dark, and he fell.

2

FALTERING LINES

"Why did I resist? Is this my punishment for defying the High King, or was it an attack by the darkness to keep me from being of aid? After so many trials endured, I'm still struggling to find the correct way forward."

—Anargen's King's Day Journal
16 Gladiol 1610 Middle Era

"The Tower of Light ... must defend ... it's ... it's ..." Anargen struggled against the dark. "No! It cannot fall!"

He bolted upright, the cold sweat of a fever dream running down his temples. Anargen looked around, his heart pounding. Under him was a simple bedroll, and someone stood at the doorway to the small stone room he was in.

"Anargen!" Seren called out and was at his side a moment later, holding his hand with the ferocity of love nearly doomed to be fate-spoken.

Words eluded him for a moment, and he put an arm around his fiancée, drawing her close. She felt so warm, even through his soaked tunic. With her was also the familiar fragrance of honeysuckle that he treasured so much. It was the scent of memory and Black River, their hometown.

The soothing balm of her closeness, however, was not the bulwark against his distress that he needed. Cold air assaulted his flesh, sending shudders through him. The dream, the vision.

Whichever he had just experienced was so vivid, so immediate, he couldn't yet be sure he was beyond the borderland between domains of the body and the mind.

He felt Seren's other hand gently brushing back the damp, black strands of his hair. She placed a quick, gentle kiss on his forehead. "Speak to me, my love. Are you hale?"

No, he wasn't well. Seeing the panic in her warm brown eyes almost convinced him to lie, to deflect her concern. But he could not. The will to deceive was so far removed from him, having been pinioned to the truth for what felt like days without end. "I saw it being attacked. From a distance. I felt like I had to help, but I couldn't ... I ... it's going to fall. It's going to fall, Seren."

"Shh," she said soothingly, moving to wrap her arms around him in a comforting embrace. She seemed to absently remember something she had been planning to do a moment earlier and let go of him just long enough to retrieve a cool, damp cloth. She applied it to his forehead and resumed her comforting lilt, "I know. They've taken the seawall and are sending their troops into the city below. If Count Forsmythe's replacement does not sound the retreat soon, then we'll all be taken when the castle falls."

Anargen blinked, his eyes fixed on the distance, suddenly regaining awareness of his surroundings once more. "What? What do you mean?"

Seren's brows furrowed, and she gnawed at her lower lip as if struggling to decide whether he could bear what she had to say. "Port Jarreth is going to fall."

The words, so brief, were weightier than the stones of the castle around them. "It's going to fall?" he asked, feeling it difficult to breathe again.

She swallowed hard. "You were out on the seawall with the others when the Monarch's forces surprised us all. They'd drifted some explosives along on the beds of seaweed and kelp washing ashore. They detonated them and damaged the seawall, along with injuring many troops. You among them."

"What?" That wasn't at all what he remembered. "How did I get here?"

"Sir Terrillian brought you. You fell when the attack took place, and he thinks a chunk of stone must have hit you. Your *Perikephalia Sosterios* saved you."

Reflexively, Anargen reached up to touch the helmet that had rescued him. Instead, his fingers found his bare head, and he compulsively tried to find and feel an injury he wasn't sure he'd incurred. His head did ache, but that wasn't what felled him. He was on the verge of defying the High King again. He knew it in that moment, right before things grew dark.

Sitting in silence for a moment, he understood the silence to be his bride-to-be wisely allotting him time to come to terms with the Lowlands he had awoken to—one far darker than the one he'd last seen. "You said, 'Count Forsmythe's replacement.' What do you mean?"

Seren's soft, round cheeks showed one of the deepest frowns he'd seen in months. "He was one of the first casualties of the surprise attack. The Monarchists may have even detonated their bombs earlier than planned because they saw him on the wall giving his rallying speech." Her voice took on a haunted quality, "At least, that's how it seemed to me when I walked out onto the parapets just before it happened. I saw it all unfolding. Every terrible moment, including when Terrillian drug you off ..."

Tears welled in her eyes, and Anargen rallied himself to hold her closer, transitioning from comforted to comforting. "That's awful. I'm so sorry you endured that ..." He hesitated for a moment before adding, "It will be all right."

She pulled back, sniffling and wiping away tears. "How can

you say that? I haven't even told you about your father and Terrillian being out there now, fighting to hold back the Monarchists."

That news sent a ripple of concern through him, but he knew he had to hold himself together for Seren. Who knew how long she'd tended him. From the slight droop to her eyelids, he could tell she was exhausted. Emotionally and physically. He had to be strong for her now. "There isn't a Monarchist in their whole army who can contend with either of them," he said, not having to feign his conviction on that point at least.

With a deft shake of her head, she dispelled it. "They're carrion. Every one of them. There wasn't a single normal soldier unloaded from those ships."

It was impossible to mask his initial revulsion at what she revealed. Even a handful of those held under the sway of the carrion curse could be trouble. Ordinary men, women, even children, transformed into mindless machines, bent upon ravaging whatever or whomever they were commanded to destroy. If they comprised the whole army, there would be thousands. How had the Monarch managed to conjure enough dark power to control so many at once? Count Eidolon had tried something of similar scale and only hastened his own demise. Perhaps the Monarch was the master and Eidolon the apprentice in the dark arts, or the student simply surpassed the master.

Whatever the case, things were far more dire now. As dire as the dream he'd just had. Leaning back from Seren, he looked at her intently. "I need my armor. I have to get down there to help the defense."

Her eyes widened. "No, you're not ready. You just woke up. You've been unconscious for a day. Who knows how severe your injuries are!"

"Seren," he countered, his voice even and as gentle as a feather on the wind.

"No. I will not lose you now!" Her eyes filled with tears.

"You won't." He lifted her gaze to his. "Remember, we've talked about this. Finding a nice place, building a home, starting our family when the war ends. Growing old together in quiet and peace. Do you think I'm going to let the Monarchists steal that from us?"

There was a thoughtfulness in her eyes, and at last, she answered, "If you go to fight, I'm going with you. We've fought together when things were at their worst, and if Libertias's army allowed women to fight, I would've been by your side through everything this past year."

His brow briefly furrowed. Having her safely away from the battlelines had been something he'd greatly appreciated since they'd rescued Count Geralian in Kirke. But she was right. Knights of Light, men and women, stood for the High King at his calling. Seren was going to be his wife, which meant they would share each other's lives, including those moments when the Quest meant facing danger.

"There's no one else in the Lowlands I'd rather have by my side," he replied, squeezing her hand.

She returned the pressure and then was up in a flurry of motion, gathering their armor. No further words passed between them until each was fully suited. Which was for the best, because Anargen wasn't yet steady as he worked to apply his own armor. Fortunately, they gave each other privacy to dress, so Seren hadn't seen him struggle.

Gripping the hilt of his spiritsword, Anargen felt the rush of warmth and with it the strength beyond himself he desperately needed. Deep inside, he knew that his blacking out and the intense visions he'd endured would need many hours of contemplation to properly understand. Presuming they survived the castle's defense.

Anargen tightened the *Alethia*, the belt that held his armor together in surety and verity. Lifting his helmet's faceplate, he looked over at Seren. Her pronounced feminine curves, midnight hair, and quiet smiling lips were hidden beneath her armor that, like Anargen's, burned with the High King's fire, defining her a warrior for his honor. In spite of it, she was beautiful. Or perhaps it was because of what the armor obscured and declared that she was all the more beautiful to him. If he wanted his future wife just to be an attractive woman, there were plenty in the Lowlands. A woman who was devoted to the High King as through and through as himself, wise beyond her years, with such a tender heart and quietly fierce spirit? He knew all these only existed in her.

She caught him staring and her cheeks reddened. "You're looking at me like I'm in my bridal gown instead of armor for battle."

Try as he might, he couldn't help wincing at that. They would have already been married by now if not for the war. Every day it continued, every battle entered, and every new danger faced made it feel less and less likely they would both live to see the war's end. Along with the outer war, he thus fought an inner protracted one to banish such melancholy.

Removing a gauntlet, he tenderly brushed her cheek with his hand. "You are the most beautiful of all the High King's works. Whatever you wear, wherever you are, you embody every groom's dream for his bride in beauty, wisdom, and compassion. The day I truly see you in your wedding gown will rob me of all words, of my very breath."

Tears began to well in her eyes, and she held his hand to her cheek for a moment. The soft warmth of it was more precious to him than all the gold in the canyons of Aridgulch.

Her voice was tight when she pulled his hand away. "We must go. Whatever happens next ... I love you, always."

"Always," he agreed.

Sliding his faceplate down, he let her lead them down to the castle's quadrangle. The few servants and others they found were bustling with anxious and aimless energy, unsure of what to do. Where to go. One maid clutched two young children close to her and winced at every sound of cannon fire.

Out in the courtyard, Anargen gaped. He could see well where the defensive line had been pushed to. It was within the inner wall. Townspeople streamed past as the keep's gate opened to admit them. Interspersed were soldiers in the blue of Libertias who mostly tried to form back up into regiments in the courtyard, but were in such a disarray that some fell back with the people they needed to defend.

A cannon boomed in the distance and with it came a tremendous cracking sound. Anargen's attention whisked to a billowing cloud of dust from where the shot had crushed stone inside the inner wall. Several more volleys sounded, and a five-foot section of wall crumbled inward.

Over the damaged wall they clamored—the carrion. Barely noticing the impact from the drop or worrying over the feat of scaling to the damaged point in the wall. They only cared about one thing: the death of everyone in the castle.

"I see Glewdyn," Seren had to yell over the intensifying din around them. "It looks like he's limping."

Immediately, Anargen's attention jerked from the breach to his father. The older man did seem to be struggling, and he half-carried Terrillian. The other Knight's left arm hung limp at his side, and he seemed to be doing little of the work to escape the pressing danger.

"Dead. Their eyes, their faces, their insatiable hunger for murder
—everything about the carrion screams death. But they bleed,
and you cannot escape the truth that they are really living
prisoners of death."

—Anargen's King's Day Journal
16 Gladiol 1610 Middle Era

"Ｎo, it's Terrillian," he said, regretting his tone carrying a sort of mixed relief. "I have to help him. They'll never keep ahead of the Monarchists at their pace."

He started to dash toward them when he felt a tug on his arm. The look in Seren's eyes through her faceplate was fierce. "I'm not letting us be parted."

Gnawing at his lip, Anargen glanced once more at his father, who had had to drop Terrillian's weight and whirl to face a carrion leaping to attack them. "Then come with me, and you can go ahead of us and guide us to the keep."

This earned a curt nod. Both of them sprinted down to where Glewdyn was already dispatching a second carrion. Pushing through and around fleeing people as if fighting against a strong current, Anargen reached his father in time to shoulder charge a fifth carrion that had almost gotten the drop on Glewdyn.

The older Knight whirled around; his breathing ragged.

His hazel eyes widened. "Son! I wish I could say it is good to see you up and hale so soon."

"What's wrong with Terrillian?" Anargen asked, dropping down to a crouch and then raising with his shield to batter back another carrion, which in turn crashed into two others and sent them spiraling in a wild tangle of flailing limbs.

"Ah, his shoulder is dislocated," Terrillian replied with a groan. "Don't ask how right now."

Looking his friend over, Anargen knew he was hurt worse than just the shoulder, but that would have to wait. Hooking himself under Terrillian's right arm, he called to Glewdyn, "You give the rearguard and I'll help him up to the keep?"

Glewdyn brought his spiritsword around, bashing a halberd aside and thrusting forward, finishing the weapon-wielding carrion. "Go."

Anargen trusted that was approval for the plan and took three steps to tow Terrillian forward before he was clubbed over the head from beyond his peripheral vision. Staggering, he nearly lost his footing and took himself and Terrillian down to the stones of the street.

There was a mad snarl, and he felt another heavy smack onto his arched back. That put him on one knee. He managed to keep his hold on Terrillian, knowing that if either of them went fully down, they wouldn't be getting up again.

His eyes finally glimpsed his attacker. It was a carrion, wielding the smoldering, shattered remnants of some kind of wooden beam. Scavenged from the carnage near the docks below, no doubt.

He managed to raise his sword and deflect another swipe, but he was off balance, Terrillian's weight and apparent wooziness making it impossible to set his feet or hold a solid guard.

He stared into the deadly still eyes of the carrion as it

brought its wooden chunk up again for another strike. It didn't even seem to flinch as the wood shifted and ground into its palm, adding to the mangled and bloodied ruination of its hands.

Anargen gritted his teeth, intending to bear the blow and maybe sneak in a quick lunge, but not hoping much for either. From behind the carrion came a screaming war cry, and suddenly the carrion was launched past them at an angle that sent it crashing into some barrels down a street to the right.

Seren stood in front of him, her chest heaving. Less from the exertion of the run or the effort of her surprise attack, he imagined, and more from the shock of how very near they all were to death.

"This way," she gasped.

Though he could ill afford it, he spared a glance back at Glewdyn as he hauled a half-conscious Terrillian after her. His father was keeping close, though far too busy for them to be making good progress. Nearly all the other defenders had moved beyond them. They weren't going to be able to make it to the keep's gate before they locked it.

Despair was beginning to sap some of his strength when a horn cut through the air, stilling all but the carrion, whose senses were sorcery-dulled, and Anargen's little group, whose flight was too frantic to falter.

"It's a rout," Terrillian commented groggily. "That's the signal to abandon the defense and retreat back to Einwis."

Not losing a single footfall's rhythm, Anargen challenged, "But what about Jarreth? The castle hasn't fallen yet, the defense—"

"Is finished," Glewdyn announced, coming alongside and lifting Terrillian from the other side, which elicited a screech of pain from him. "Sorry, lad, but we need to move quicker."

Ahead, Seren called over her shoulder, "I think I can get us out of the city faster. There's a side entrance to the inner wall that should lead out into the lowlands by the port. It's where they have the clay pits for the city."

Bitterly she added, "One of the wives of a local potter told me about it while we were stuck watching things from the keep. Before her husband was lost in the defense."

"Then lead on," Anargen and Glewdyn said in near-unison.

They moved much faster with Glewdyn helping to carry Terrillian, even after the other young Knight passed out from the pain. Anargen dared not look back to see how they were faring relative to the Monarchist advance. Snarls and occasional grazing swipes impacted his back and arms in turn. Still, they pressed on. Stopping was death. Hesitating was death. All around them was death.

Sounds of chaos echoed from the keep, but all he could focus on was moving as fast as he could. Even as the crowds thinned and the sounds of the carrion curiously faded. Soon, only a handful of other townspeople and soldiers appeared to be with them in using this particular path out of the city.

Most of the population of Port Jarreth was already in the keep. There was a secret tunnel leading out of the keep for a retreat of this sort, but it would be nightmarish within the tight stone corridors as people scrambled to make use of it.

The loss of it all stung. All the more knowing that he was of no help to those poor people clamoring to get out. Even as he breathed in the evening air beyond the city's outer wall, he did not feel free. He felt weighed down by failure. And the anxious tension of understanding that this escape was only a brief reprieve from the danger now firmly moored to his homeland.

ANOTHER INN

I t was almost ironic. Here he was standing outside an inn, drenched by a downpour. Just like he had been when he first came to the Black River Inn in Brackenburgh.

Checking either direction to ensure he wasn't being watched, Jason drew in a deep breath. He wrapped his knuckles against the worn spruce door.

A slat slid open a moment later. Stern eyes peered out at him. "Who sent you?" the one answering the door asked in a gruff voice, laced through with wariness.

"He who broke my chains," Jason answered. His throat tightened. It always did when he recited his passphrase. That moment when his life was at its miserable end and he at last understood who the High King was and accepted he had been a fool. Ready to die for his rebellion. Then he had seen it. Jason had seen him. The vision of the High King was forever seared into his mind's eye and the literal chains he had been bound with were burned away even as the figurative ones binding him shattered as well. A thousand lifetimes could pass and he would never forget it.

The man within opened the door and hurriedly motioned for Jason to step inside. An instant after Jason complied, the door shut behind him. He didn't recognize the Poseki man admitting him. The doorkeeper was burly with bushy bronze mutton chops wrapping around his round face. Probably twice Jason's age, with clothes dirtied and wet from being out in the

29

storm as well. If he hadn't so quickly recognized Jason's passphrase, he would have been suspicious of the stranger.

Even so, his stomach clenched as he followed his gruff guide through the poorly lit passage to another door. The Poseki man assessed Jason up and down once more and then swung open the door without ceremony. The tightness in Jason's stomach intensified as smells from beyond the door drifted in: honey mead, smoked sausages, and fried potato cakes.

Jason swallowed hard. At the other end of the room, he saw her.

Aria.

It took every ounce of his will not to race across the room and throw his arms around her. To rain kisses on his fiancée like the torrents falling outside. Especially when her green eyes found him and he saw the relief and joy in them, dawning with the beauty of the morning sun.

A cocksure grin drifted onto his lips. The one that never failed to make her roll her eyes, but also to smile back.

Except it didn't work this time. She did roll her eyes, but the smile was tight. Something was worrying her, despite his safe return.

He wanted to stride over and ask her right away, but two Poseki soldiers flanking their leader, General Cywjzi Gorsk, were on Jason before he could move. Gorsk gripped Jason by both arms as was Poseki custom for serious talks. His bushy brown and silver mutton chops seemed to bristle with excitement as he spoke, "You have word from double speaker, yes?"

Jason offered a weak smile. General Gorsk had not yet mastered Ecthelish, not that Jason had even attempted to grasp more than a few key words of Posekyn. "Ah, you mean the informant? Yes, I was able to meet with him." He nodded to the satchel strapped over his shoulder. "He sent a scouting report for you from Psilmas."

"Scow-ooting?" Gorsk repeated, his heavy brows furrowed.

"Um, his words on what is ahead?" Jason tried.

"Ah," the Poseki nodded enthusiastically. "Very good, scow-ooting was thorough?"

Jason chafed under the other man's tight grip. He would have loved to shrug and avoid this tenuous game of probing for words they both understood. It was probably for the best he couldn't. If he remembered rightly, either the Poseki or the Arnukans viewed that as a highly insulting gesture. Emulating the chill of dread or fear, or something to that effect.

"I don't know," he admitted bluntly. "Our contact said the letter addressed to you is for your eyes only. He was adamant about it."

"Ada-da-mant?"

Fighting a sigh, Jason amended, "Very insist—ah, he was very firmly planted on it."

Not his best translating work, but the general seemed to get the idea. He released Jason. "Give to me. Now."

Reaching into the satchel, Jason produced the parchment with its crude leather cord and handed it over to the Poseki.

The general's dark brown eyes scoured the document, widening as he read, and his brows began to knit over his eyes like clouds of a gathering storm.

"Bah!" Gorsk grumbled and ripped the parchment up. He threw the tatters into the air and began muttering words in Posekyn that Jason guessed were curses. With dramatic waves of his hands, he summoned the other Poseki leaders to him. The impromptu confab was tightly grouped, so Jason took it as an unspoken dismissal and drifted over to Aria's side. "Missed you," he whispered and snuck a quick kiss on her cheek.

"Missed you too," she replied and gave a meaningful look to her left.

He moved to stand beside her, arms crossed over his chest. The Poseki didn't approve of men conversing with women in public. Not even one's fiancée.

Careful to keep his words clipped so it wouldn't be so obvious he was talking to her, Jason commented, "Wonder what's going on."

"Me too," Aria admitted. "My Posekyn is ... limited."

"Where's your grandfather? He's the expert."

Aria was silent for several seconds before sighing lightly. "Later."

The impromptu war council of Posek's military leadership concluded as suddenly as it had started. General Gorsk cast a long, meaningful look at Jason.

"Guess he wants to talk to me," he mouthed to Aria. Jason took a step toward Gorsk. A sharp pain radiated from his wrist, and he looked down to see that Aria had gripped it so tightly her nails were digging into his skin, though her face was an impassive mask. "Hey," he muttered under his breath, "What is wrong?"

"Whatever he says to you," she whispered out of the corner of her mouth, "Don't agree to anything. Please?"

"Uh, sure," he replied, somewhat puzzled. Her long dark hair was done back in a traditional Poseki ponytail, and she was wearing the cream and light green billowy dresses Poseki women wore. Aria had made a lot of concessions and overtures to get along with General Gorsk and the other hardliners in Posek, so whatever they were about to ask must be beyond the pale.

General Gorsk pointed at Jason. "You have brought us terrible news. This will not be accepted." The stocky man sliced his hand through the air as if sweeping away the ill-received correspondence.

"I apologize, sir," Jason replied with care. He shot Aria an anxious glance. "The contact didn't indicate the nature of his intelligence, only to whom it—"

"Silence," Gorsk cut him off. "Those traitors have played us for fools. Calling us to their aid while secretly surrendering to the Knors. Bah! We will table the turns on them!"

Under his breath, Jason murmured, "Turn the tables on them." He didn't dare interrupt the tirade by offering the correction loud enough to be heard. From what he had just said, General Gorsk believed the Arnukans had somehow brokered an armistice with the Knors and, thereby, the Confederacy. How they managed that with the near entirety of their territory under Knor control was a mystery. Even now, their capital Psilmos was an island amid Knor conquests. Not to mention the Arnukans were known to be a resolute people, stubborn to the point of their own harm. Jason never imagined they would give in, unless ...

"You say the Arnukans have surrendered, could it be—"

"They were always belong to the Knors," General Gorsk spat. "Superstitious mountain swine ... believe the 'Mother Moon' is guiding them right fight for the Confederacy—" he lost his tenuous hold on Ecthelish and finished the curse-colored remainder of his rant in Posekyn. Mentally, Jason plotted out the rest for himself.

The Knors must have struck a deal with the Arnukans. Perhaps this was all an elaborate means for the Knors to sort out the Poseki military's capabilities before committing wholly to an assault.

The general made it back into Ecthelish. "You. You will command the fire to consume them."

Eyes widening as he recognized their meaning, Jason shook

his head. "I'm sorry, but there is a grave error. I do not command the High King. He commands me."

Gorsk rolled his eyes. "However you choose to say, you will join our grand counterattack and use your fire to burn them to deep ash heaps."

It was almost impossible to guess if he had meant to say the exact words Jason heard. He shot another quick look Aria's way.

The tension in her posture was undeniable. Was this what she urged him to refuse?

She couldn't have forgotten the Posek were full of bluster and unafraid to act to whatever degree of cruelty and harshness it took to reach their aims. That said, they were all staring down the second year in what some had already termed the Lowlands Total War. Defender Black had consistently spurned opportunities for them to take a more active role in fighting to stop the Rehalycon-led Confederacy. That insistence on skirting the edge of battle with what he knew to be genuinely evil was so perplexing. Frustrating. Unconscionable.

Jason cleared his throat. He needed to choose his words carefully. Either he would have an angry Poseki general or an angry fiancée. Which of the two would be more dangerous was up for debate.

"Your Honor," he began.

"Your High Honor," one of Gorsk's aids corrected.

Jason nodded. "My apologies. Your High Honor, to fight alongside you would be a great ... honor. But I am constrained by the decrees of my Order. We—"

General Gorsk held up his hand. "What mean you, 'decrees of your Order'? I thought Defender Black and the Knights of Light are on the side of the Alliance. Do you now ... make ..." the general struggled for the right words in Ecthelish.

"Make this false?" the aide from before supplied.

"Yes. False. False!" Gorsk proclaimed, his expression growing severe. "Speak, Knight."

"I ... uh ... I ..." What was he supposed to say? Poseki regarded their leaders as eminently wise. Disrespecting his conclusions out of hand was an insult. But equivocating on their truthfulness of supporting the Alliance and thereby the Poseki would definitely go badly. Especially given his misgivings that their allegiance to the Alliance deserved to be questioned.

Jason's brow furrowed in frustration. There was no winning here, but there was a way that he felt made sense. Hopefully, Aria would forgive him. He took a step back and bowed. "You are right, Your High Honor. It would be false not to support the Alliance. Despite the orders otherwise, I will fight for—"

Jason wasn't able to finish. A familiar buzzing sound overhead stole his attention. It took only an instant to recognize the subsequent whistling sounds accompanying it. He had to move! Jason leaped at Aria and dragged her to the floor as the bomb from the planes flying over the town struck the building they were in.

4

ABANDONMENT

*"Some say that it is a tragic malady of the heart to see great evil
and to watch it unfold without action. I cannot say for certain
after what happened in Port Jarreth that I wholly agree, but it
seems a still greater wrong is about to be perpetrated on the
people of Einwis."*

—*Anargen's King's Day Journal
24 Gladiol 1610 Middle Era*

B elow Einwis lay in hushed tension, taut as the strings of a
well-tuned lyra. Over it hung a waning crescent moon,
the pale light of which was withering perilously to the void of
another new moon. Perilous, because Anargen remembered all
too well the old rhyme about werebeasts:

*"Doors locked tight,
Fear's full height,
Glimmering white,
Dread fangs in the night,
New Moon's bane,
Full Moon's gain."*

Under the cover of the dark, the creatures loved to strike.
Anargen had faced such, felt their sweltering breath on his face,
had his skin crawl with the piercing sound of their howls, and
stared into their gleaming ochre eyes. And the fangs, slick with

saliva, wicked sharp and hungry for destruction... Anargen wasn't sure if he could take it if what he'd seen elsewhere befell Einwis before his very eyes. Even if the werebeasts did not come, the Monarchists armies scorched the earth behind them and were not interested in the significance or beauty of anything they encountered. They rendered everything to ash. Which was tragic, because Einwis had become prominent in Libertias as a city dedicated to stirring people's souls. Whether through poetic verse or lyric songs performed on plazas across the city, it was impossible to spend more than a day here and not be moved.

Anargen had spent four so far and already seen two of its museums and taken in multiple performances. Weaving the vibrant melodies that ranged from melancholy to hopeful optimism before great stone edifices bearing the remnants of the past, from ancient to recent, had a potent effect on him. This place insisted on the power of memory. It's ability to shape a person, or a nation, as each event's impact reverberated across the years. Like a string plucked, its sound propagates further and further so that even long after the first strum the savor of that sound is still tasted. If this place fell, who would record its fall in verse? Who would impress its memory onto the Lowlands to instill the lessons that could keep this from happening again?

What lesson would that be? Moreover, did it matter after the nightmare he'd suffered? That the Lowlands suffered now?

"I thought I'd find you up here," Glewdyn commented. The elder Knight walked up to the balcony on which Anargen stood and leaned against the polished marble balustrade. He too seemed to be regarding the state of the moon, though the lines of his aged face weren't deepened with anxiety the way Anargen would expect.

"Yeah, I can see why the people here put balconies on all of their buildings. It helps to take in everything ... especially one last time, before the battle comes here. You know. Before it's destroyed like Port Jarreth."

Glewdyn glanced sidelong at his son and sighed. "I had hoped you had been spared hearing the worst of it."

"They slaughtered more than half of the population as they fled. We failed them. They trusted us to keep the city safe." Anargen slammed his fist down on the balustrade in frustration. "If we'd held them off for even a week, that would've been enough to evacuate the population and draw additional troops to the fight."

To this, his father had no reply. The muscles in his jaw worked, visible under a stubbly grey and black beard. This war was aging all of them, sapping the life out of them as effectively as Count Eidolon had the victims of his vampirism.

In the absence of anything else said, Anargen's thoughts were overloud. The ones he'd tried to suppress for so long about his guilt in the midst of all of this tragedy. "I let them down. Port Jarreth needed every soldier there in its defense, and I was ... I still don't even know what I was doing in the tower. What even happened to me. How many people could have lived if I hadn't been hiding up there?"

Glewdyn stirred. "You were injured. Terrillian told me you went down in the first volley of strikes. It isn't your fault that Count Forsmythe's pride left us all vulnerable to a cruel enemy. There are no rules of engagement with the Monarchists, and Forsmythe should have remembered that instead of trying to build his 'legend' and smooth the path to his Viscountship.

"Besides, you're not a soldier, son. You're a Knight of Light."

"I know I'm a Knight of Light," Anargen replied, as much for himself as in agreement. "But aren't we all soldiers for Libertias? It's our duty to defend it. To stop atrocities like Port

Jarreth from happening, even if it costs us personally everything. That should be all the truer of Knights like us."

Heavy brows furrowed, Glewdyn huffed. "I've been giving that some thought. What happened at Port Jarreth was terrible ..." He began scratching at his beard the way he did when trying to find the right words as they eluded him. "You know I fought for Libertias's armies years ago, but things were different. Our enemies were different. Not flagrant or blatant in their evils or service to the Dark Prince ..."

Anargen nodded. "You've told me stories about it. Parts of it anyway." He wasn't sure how he could help his father right now. The older man looked as torn as he'd ever seen him. Maybe Seren, with her gentle wisdom, could coax out what he wanted to say, but she was already asleep for the night. She'd told him how fitful her sleep had been since Port Jarreth, filled with recurring nightmares related to the death of the Jarreth potter and his wife, whom they discovered later hadn't been able to use the very route of escape that had helped rescue them. "It's because of how evil the enemy is that it's all the more important we don't fail, that we don't back down, right?"

"You didn't fail. You were injured, you had to recover," Glewdyn insisted.

"No, Terrillian said that's what happened, but the truth is I just collapsed," Anargen blurted out in a rush, before his sense of personal pride could bar the shameful admission. "I blacked out and slept through the destruction of Port Jarreth. If I hadn't had the nightmare about the Tower of Light, you all might've died having to come to carry me out of the keep's infirmary."

Tears welled in Anargen's eyes and his cheeks burned, betraying him, just as his weakness had almost betrayed those he cared most deeply about.

Glewdyn frowned and regarded his son for a few seconds before slowly putting his arms around him in a comforting embrace. It felt to Anargen like he was nine years old again and had just ruined his father's potato crop by playing in their family garden. The worst that had come of that was a slightly harder winter in terms of meals.

When Glewdyn pulled back, however, his expression wasn't filled with the same sort of consolation and compassion he'd had for the younger Anargen and his rambunctious games. His gaze was intensely thought-filled.

"You said you had a nightmare about the Tower of Light?"

Anargen shrugged. "Yeah. It was awful. Almost as much as living out the fall of Port Jarreth."

"What happened?"

"You were there. You saw more of the terribleness while I was asleep."

"No, no. The nightmare. What happened to the Tower of Light?"

"Oh. Well, it's kind of—" he almost said 'hazy,' but then realized the dream wasn't as fuzzy as he'd expected after so much had passed. Vividly, it replayed for him as if he were experiencing it afresh. "It's cold and the sky is dark. There are mountains all around, and the Tower is standing in the middle of them. It's being struck over and over by attacks from all different angles. There are all sorts of beasts and wicked men attacking it, and suddenly a great dark shape takes to the sky and crashes into the Tower of Light, toppling it over."

The memory of it sent a chill racing along his back and arms. Details stood out that he hadn't noticed before, like the nature of the dark shape. Though he'd only heard about them in legends and seen them drawn in books, he was fairly sure it had been a dragon that had toppled the Tower of Light and that he and other Knights, maybe three others, were at the base, watching helplessly.

Glewdyn scratched his chin again. "Son, I don't think that was just a dream. I think we need to—"

Behind them, the doors leading out onto the balcony swung open. Terrillian, his arm still in a sling, rushed out to them. "Good, you're both here."

"What's the matter, lad?" Glewdyn asked, sounding a bit exasperated that he was cut off in mid-sentence.

"Ill news, I'm afraid, sir. I was just passed orders from Acting Field Marshal Moreslyson. We're to ride for Peter's March right away."

Anargen scowled, a flood of abashment striking him like breaking waves. "What? But why? Is this a punishment?"

"No," Terrillian replied, his gaze falling to the balcony floor.

"He didn't just mean us, son," Glewdyn surmised. "The whole city is being evacuated."

That wasn't a light decision. Abandoning Einwis meant losing countless documents and artifacts from across the Lowlands and its history. Buildings that were among the earliest in Libertias's history would burn.

But at least the people of Einwis will be safe. And they are—

"No. Not everyone. Only the defensive forces. Marshal Moreslyson believes that if we pull back, then the Monarchists will ignore Einwis or occupy it instead of destroying it." Terrillian banged his fist against his leg as he delivered the news, not raising his gaze.

"You don't really believe that, do you?" Anargen countered. "We know these aren't just invading armies. Monarch Ilyron is consorting with goblins. Thomas told us as much when we were in Kirke. They will destroy everything in their path!"

"We have our orders."

"Terrillian!"

"We have our orders," Terrillian reiterated. "I don't like

them, but from Peter's March, we can make a real defense and have enough troops to launch a counterattack. If we try to defend Einwis, we're going to lose, and there won't be enough of us to push the Monarchists back."

"But the people of Einwis—"

"If we don't chance this, Anargen, then they're going to march straight to Kirke, and that will be the end of it. Libertias will have to surrender and then the war will be over. There's no way the Restoration Armies and Albarons can fight off the Monarchists on their own.

"We have to think about what is best for the Libertias and the Lowlands as a whole, not just Einwis."

Backing away, Terrillian splayed his hands. "I'm sorry. Those are the orders." Just before he turned to leave, he hesitated, seeming to remember something.

"I already woke Seren and told her to ready both of your things for travel."

Almost too afraid to ask, Anargen muttered, "Did she?"

"No. She's waiting on you. You'll need to hurry, though. We leave for Peter's March before the midnight hour."

As the echoes of Terrillian's retreating steps faded, Anargen looked at his father, crestfallen. It was as though the entire Lowlands were off kilter and everything was sliding into an abyss to match his nightmare. "How could we possibly leave these people to this fate?"

Glewdyn was leaning on the balustrade. After a minute, he straightened. "Gather your things and Seren's as fast as you're able. We'll ride through the town and pass on the warning to the city constable. That's the best we can do ... for now."

DEBRIS

T he force of the explosion almost threw him off of Aria, and he cried out in pain as shattered bits of a beam holding up the roof raked over him. He didn't have time to think about that pain, though, as the smoke and dust billowing from the impact cleared enough to see that a fire had caught in the mostly wooden structure.

"Come on," he yelled to Aria, ringing building in his ears so that he wasn't sure if he was whispering or shouting. "We have to get out of here."

"We have to get out," Aria yelled back, which didn't bode well for her hearing. Jason was relieved to see she got to her feet without any problems, but there was a twinge in her expression as she looked him over that made him think he might be in worse shape than he felt. He knew the armor the High King bestowed on them held, but he had his helmet off.

Liquid dribbled down his cheek, sweat or blood, and he brushed it away without verifying which. As he turned around, he gaped. The entire front of the building was smoldering wreckage. Where he had been standing a moment before was now buried beneath a heap of broken and burning bits of what had been the secret meeting house.

"Where is the General?" he asked.

She shot him a quizzical look. It quickly morphed into concern. Aria cupped a hand around her ear. "What did you say?"

"Where is the General?" he repeated, louder and with careful enunciation.

His fiancée's brows knit. Much like him, she began to peer at the wreckage of wood and stone kindled around them. A hand flew to her mouth, and she pointed to the portion of the building closest to the bomb's detonation.

Jason looked over and instantly regretted it. The sight waiting for him was one that would haunt him in his worst nightmares as long as he lived. All of the other Poseki were in like states, beyond the arts of any physician in the Lowlands. The brutality of this war was as great as any mauling by werebeast, but it was accomplished without the dark powers behind such a creature.

Oddly, in the midst of the flames, something shimmered. A quirk of light or flame that seemed distinct from the fire.

What?

Under him, the boards of the floor began to groan. A warning that they too would soon break and burn.

Taking Aria by the shoulders, he gave a gentle but insistent nudge away from the horrific scene. Choking smoke was already burning his eyes. Another minute in this place and they wouldn't be leaving. Ever.

Thankfully, the gesture was enough, and she raced out of the burning shambles of the structure and into the street. She led the way for a couple of blocks before coming to an abrupt halt and dropping to her knees on the stone pavement, coughing and retching as her body fought to expel the toxic smoke inhaled while they had struggled to piece things together.

Jason was beside her a moment later, unable to keep from spilling the contents of his stomach. After a couple of minutes, he was empty. His eyes were shut tight from the tears rolling down his flame-seared cheeks that felt far better than his now ravaged, aching throat. That was when he heard it again. A plane was buzzing overhead.

"Get down!" Jason yelped and tackled Aria to the ground, using his body as a shield for hers.

Braced for the searing heat and concussive blast from the bomb, the sound of a muted thump was almost as unnerving as what had been expected. Daring to lift off Aria, he peered in the direction of the impact. There was a grey parachute unassumingly collapsing behind a wooden crate to which it was tethered. Jason glanced down at Aria, seeing if she understood better what he was seeing.

Her brow furrowed in thought. She huffed and gave a little shrug. "Let's take a look."

Still wary, Jason tried to keep between Aria and the crate. It worked for all of ten seconds before she slipped around him and crouched to examine another side.

Brave she most certainly was, which made it hard to be protective of her. Sighing, he dropped down and began looking over his side. For all his suspicions, it appeared to be a plain wooden box of rough beige wood, only about three feet cubed.

"Hopefully they keep dropping these instead of those infernal—"

"Jason," Aria called, her hesitance pulling him up short.

"Yeah?"

She rotated the crate so that the side that had faced away from them was in view. On it was stamped in bold black letters,

"TO: JASON WERNSTRUM
FROM: D.W."

Without hesitating, he tore off the top, forgetting about possible danger from a booby trap or other cunning con. Inside was a hat, seated on some straw. But not just any hat. As he pulled it from the box, his hands shook a little.

"Is that the newsboy cap you lost?" Aria asked, the pity in

her voice again betraying how she really felt. She knew it was just as surely as he did.

"My father's cap," he gently amended. He hadn't seen it since the sombra held him prisoner in the Gerisk Ruins.

As he turned it over in his hands, he found a little note folded inside. His heartbeat picked up, and he knew he did not want to read what was on the paper slip. Only pain could come with it, but he was equally certain he had to know.

"Dearest brother,

"Thought you might want this back, seeing as how you just lost Posek as your allies. Try not to keep misplacing important things. It would be a shame if you lost something else important to you.

"Warm regards,

"Dorian.

PS. Which name do you think she'll take, the fake 'Landsby' or despicable 'Wernstrum'? Guess time will tell ... or not."

Crumbling the note into as tight a wad as he could make it, Jason grumbled and tossed it down another street. He'd hurl it straight in his wicked younger brother's face if he could. But it was a childish impulse and as petty as the note and gesture of sending him back the cap after the bombing deaths of the Poseki leaders was, it was not a childish threat. The intention was clear. Back off, or Aria would be next.

"What did it say?" Aria asked, placing her hand gently on his back.

The ringing in his ears had faded enough that he could hear her relatively soft-spoken words clearly. He kept his tone even. "Nothing. Just my brother trying to torment me."

"By appearances, he succeeded. Don't let him," she insisted, gripping him tightly and wincing as she did. They were both still banged up, their faces and clothes dark with sooty ash. It only made the threat feel still less idle and impossible to ignore.

He turned and embraced her, holding on for a moment longer. They needed this. Needed each other for strength after what just happened. The sound of a ringing alarm bell and wagon wheels bumping along stones echoed from the direction of the destruction.

"We have to go," she whispered.

"Looks that way." He began to hobble along beside her. The complete silence from any further planes sent a message: this wasn't random. It was a targeted attack. An assassination. His brother had sent a couple of other messages too. Jason couldn't ignore who he was and what Dorian had become.

He waited until they were more than a mile out of Kezmarepos and he felt like he would burst if he didn't say it. "The informant was a trap. Dorian knew exactly where the meetup spot was and even had that plane waiting to drop off my 'gift.' I wonder who the spy is and how long we've been under his watch."

"Does it really matter now?"

He wrung the newsboy cap, a nervous tic he'd had before he lost it. Forcing himself to stop, he replied. "Nope."

"We were about to lose the Poseki as allies even before the attack," Aria commented, pulling her dress up some as they forded a small creek. Bouncing from stone to stone, she added, "What they wanted was impossible. They asked us to betray the Order to fight a battle that their army was struggling to manage."

"I wish your grandfather had been there. Defender Black would've been able to sort that mess out."

"He might also be able to explain why the Confederacy allowed us to live at all. Why not kill us outright with the Poseki leaders?"

"I don't know," he answered numbly. He didn't want to think about the bombing. Or about the package he'd been given, even if he still held onto the hat returned to him. All of it was just a special kind of awful, the sort of hurt only someone close to you can achieve.

Jason kicked at the last bit of water between him and the dry path ahead. He only succeeded in soaking his pants leg and socks.

Aria gave him one of her looks that said she had so much she wanted to say but couldn't begin to do so. Usually, he chalked it up to him being a mess. Too much of a knotted morass to untie. Rather than address the disaster that was this night, she opted to redirect the line of conversation. "Betrayals and political wrangling, it sounds eerily like what happened to Anargen and Seren at Ordumair." A little shudder ran through her.

"Anargen and Seren were at Ordumair together?"

Aria shot him an askance glance. "You mean you haven't read that far in his King's Day journal?"

Jason gnawed on his lower lip. Lying right now would definitely not be good, but admitting he hadn't read a bit of it since the war began might be the last thing he ever did ... "Not that far?"

Her look became a full and very knowing scowl.

"Okay, no. I haven't read anymore. Things have just been ... we're in the middle of a war. Maybe THE war!"

Bracing himself for an angry diatribe against his failing, Jason was more worried to see Aria not respond at all. She simply looked down at the path before them and fell silent.

Not good.

"Listen, I'm sorry. All right? I know you said we can't get married until I've finished it and seen what happened to Anargen and Seren, but—"

"No 'but,'" she interrupted coolly. "You have to read it to understand my concerns and until you do ... I can't pledge myself to you, not for life. Maybe not at all."

He wanted to yell, "You've gotta be kidding me!" The old Jason would have done it. Probably thrown in some other choice words about her love for that story and then stormed off. That wasn't him anymore, though. He was a Knight of Light and neither his oaths to the High King and all they implied, nor his surprising depth of love for the feisty and often opinionated woman he wanted to marry—which of itself felt a crazy change for him—would allow it.

Taking hold of her hands, quite the opposite came from his mouth. "Fine, then let's have it. Where is it, and I'll read it cover to cover right now!"

Aria looked very much like she wanted to sigh, deep and long as the canyon of Aridgulch. To her credit, she didn't. In a quiet, tight voice, she informed him, "Grandfather has it. He took it with him on his trip."

There was no further elaboration on the mysterious trip. And her entire countenance was as deeply sullen as he'd ever seen it.

She had been in this sort of melancholic funk ever since they became engaged, which was one of the greatest mysteries of all for Jason. The proposal itself had been all he could've hoped for. They had just delivered food and supplies to villages in Vov Hilan near the Jhi border, where attacks were intensifying as the war moved into the region. While traveling back by rail, the train had to make a stop in Keraxlaco's famed Varipuram Crystal Desert. An indigo night with a full array of stars awaited them. The crystalline desert seemed to reflect the pattern from above so that where land and sky met was indistinguishable. The gleaming beauty of the starry expanse felt like a picture of how their lives had already become one fabric. He had had the ring for some time and been searching for just such a moment. When he pulled it out, the joy in her eyes, radiating from her face, eclipsed all of the desert's beauty. She had gushed so about it all, about the life she wanted for them, that he felt full enough to pull the train to the next station with his bare hands.

But then something happened. Somewhere en route back to meeting her grandfather in the newly established Sykonos Republic, centered around Siğmacaq Yeri, she had grown pensive, introspective, as if something heavy lay on her shoulders. She'd been like that intermittently ever since, drifting further and further into gloom. Which, if he had minded closer, he'd have realized it was more than four months now.

The stipulation that he finish reading Anargen's last journal was almost an afterthought as a condition of marriage. He wasn't even sure she was serious until he teased her about it a month into their engagement. Her response had been so heated, so pointed, he thought she might break it off there and then. She hadn't, of course, and cooled. But he hadn't understood her insistence on it then any more than he did now.

Guess that's what I'll have to find out from reading.

"Okay, we'll just go meet up with him. We need to let him know what happened with the Poseki anyway. Posek is going to be reeling after this, and if Arnuk is lost, the Alliance doesn't need to be caught flatfooted in shoring up the Poseki."

Her brows knit. "No, he asked that we not come and to keep his trip a total secret."

"From whom?" Jason pressed, not able to mask all of his annoyance and surprise.

"Everyone," she fired back. Aria stopped in the middle of the road and put her hands on her hips. "No one needs to know where he went. Especially not you right now, Mr. Alliance."

"What is that supposed to mean?" he shouted, so that his voice echoed in the night.

Aria folded her arms over her chest. Her lips were pressed in a tight line, and though he expected to see anger shimmering in her green eyes, there was only a glassiness. She was tearing up.

All of his being longed to wrap her in his arms and soothe away the hurt. But he was apparently the source of that hurt, and he wasn't even sure what he was doing to cause it.

He folded both of his hands behind his head. When they had stood there without words for more than a minute, he slapped his thigh with the hat held clenched in his fist. "Listen, I'm sorry. Okay. I know I ... don't understand everything your grandfather does. Or have a need to. I just ... I do need to know what is eating at you."

"It's nothing," she mouthed tartly.

"Ugh, see, now that's the one thing I know it's not. Because if it really were nothing, I'd have to be holding you at arm's length with all my might to keep you from smothering me in kisses."

His attempt at humor earned a roll of her eyes. But it seemed to crack the tension between them a little. Or at least he hoped that it had.

"Aria, please. Talk to me. I'm clearly too dense to sort this out on my own and among the things I want in the Lowlands, your happiness is at the top of the stack."

"That's the problem," she mumbled. And when he shot her a quizzical look in response, she threw up her hands. "If you had read the journal, you would understand!"

Jason had to fight not to scream. "I know you really like that story, but it's a story!"

"It's more than that! It's history. It's my ..." she paused and caught herself. "It's my favorite story. And because it's true in

51

the deepest sense, it's instructive. If you kept up your practice with your spiritsword, you might have found the inscription that says, 'For whatever was written in former days was written for our instruction.' The words of the Great King and the lives of Knights who have lived since are meant to produce endurance and encouragement in us, to keep fresh our hope for the King's Day."

Her voice had almost cracked at the end, and her small hand was under her nose as if its presence there could keep any tears at bay. Little tremors ran through her frame.

Working moisture to his suddenly dry mouth, he replied, "You're right. I was confronted with my lack of diligence earlier tonight."

That seemed to brighten her gaze, so he pressed on. "And hearing Anargen's story is what helped guide me to becoming a Knight of Light as well."

Carefully, he took her hand in both of his and held it with all the care due it if it were Jhi'ish porcelain. "I want to understand. I do. Since we can't get the book from your grandfather, maybe you can fill me in some on what I'm missing till I can get a hold of it?"

Emerald-tinted starlight gleamed in the teary sheen of her eyes. "Only if you promise to read the account for yourself. His words, his realizations, are important. They'll help keep perspective."

"I will. I promise."

She cocked her head as if to say, "You did that once before already."

"I will," he insisted.

Closing her eyes, she rubbed away tears and took several steadying breaths. Once she'd composed herself, she looked up at him and asked, "Do you trust me to lead the way without any questions?"

"Of course," he answered rather quickly, which earned an arch of her brow. He gave an emphatic nod to add earnest to his words.

"Then come on. I'll tell you what you're missing and ..." she shot him a warning look. "You may be right about needing to warn Grandfather of what's happened here."

"Not again. Please, don't let this be happening again! How are
we supposed to complete the Quest when everyone and
everything seems against it, even those we lean on so heavily for
the strength to complete it? To where are we supposed to turn
now?"

—*Anargen's King's Day Journal*
30 Gladiol 1610 Middle Era

"You called for me, Father?" Anargen looked around them, noting that the room he'd been beckoned to in the barracks of Peter's March was empty save for Seren. She hadn't been mentioned in the summons. Despite having cleared the room already, Anargen did a quick second check to verify they were truly alone.

"Seren? What are you doing here? If anyone finds you in the barracks, they'll put you in the stocks! I know you should be fighting alongside us as much as anyone, but they're being sharper about rules for those they approved to fight in the army and those allowed in support roles."

He left off the painful and obvious points that it was all born of the panic pervading Libertias since the retreat from Port Jarreth. After abandoning Einwis, superstition and paranoia were at a fever pitch.

"Neither of us is here to stir trouble," Seren replied gently. Her hands were clenched in front of her, and her gaze was on the floor. Oddly demure, given how heatedly she argued against both her and Glewdyn being kept out of the fray on other occasions.

"That isn't necessarily true," Glewdyn countered. He crossed his arms over his chest and cleared his throat. "We called you here because we both think it's time for us to withdraw."

"Withdraw? You're both going to stay in Kirke?" There was a note of relief in his voice that Anargen could not fully mask.

"No, son. All of us, the Knights of Light from Black River, need to withdraw. You and Terrillian included."

Anargen eyed his father and fiancée in turn. Not certain what to say, other than, "Why?"

"You know why," Glewdyn countered.

"I don't—" In that instant, his compulsion to leave at Port Jarreth returned to him. As did his dream of the Tower of Light falling. He hadn't grappled with the significance of all of it together, especially after forsaking the people and city of Einwis. All of it, as he stood back, became a mosaic. One with a clear picture. "We aren't following the Quest by fighting this war, are we? At least not fighting it this way?"

"I don't believe so," Glewdyn replied solemnly.

"We don't," Seren amended. "It's been harder for you to see fighting on the front lines of the battles, but from a distance ..."

"Libertias is becoming calloused and focused on winning a political victory, not on stopping the darkness within the Monarchists faction from spreading," Glewdyn said. "Worse, I fear Libertias has lost sight that many of those fighting in the Monarch's armies, the carrion, are not doing so by choice but by compulsion. I have sought the High King's guidance on this many times, and on every occasion, He has confirmed that we need to step back from this conflict and focus on the heart of the Quest."

Anargen ran his hand through the long, wild black strands of his hair. He might be able to argue with Seren or Glewdyn individually, but together they made a more salient point. Tension was building in his chest, an insistent ache to depart.

"Where will we go?" he asked, his voice hollow.

Rubbing his chin, Glewdyn took a beat to find an answer. "We'll travel north. Return to Estonbury. You said there was an oracle from centuries past about the Quest kept in Glastonae; perhaps there's more. We can see if there's anything to find to add to all that we know so far."

Recalling the desiccated corpse of a city that was Glastonae, Anargen doubted much was left to be salvaged from its ruins. More pointedly, though, an admittedly selfish part of him thrilled at this turn of events. They would pass through Black River and Maple Point. And he could finally show Seren many of the sights from his first journey and— Anargen reined himself in. "Then it's to Bonus Mare to begin with?"

Glewdyn shook his head. "First, you must do your best to convince Terrillian to come. The dreams of the Tower have always involved four individuals defending against the darkness. There are others we may yet convince to join us, but it must start with Terrillian."

Anxiety filled Anargen from his hair to his feet. This wouldn't be an easy or pleasant task. "Understood," he replied. Glancing at Seren, he shot her a weak smile and then stalked off to complete his task.

It took less time than he was prepared for to find Terrillian. The other young Knight was tending to a sorrel-colored horse in the stables. As Anargen struggled to find the words he needed, his steps slowed, so that he ended up stopping a couple of yards away.

He gnawed on his lower lip, dithering over whether to turn

back. How could he argue they needed to leave when he barely accepted it himself?

"Anargen?" Terrillian called to him, having looked up from feeding the nearest horse a carrot. He was still wearing a sling. In the perpetual dusk of the stable, the scar on his face stood out more angrily as well.

"Terrillian! Hale evening."

"Hale evening," he replied and rubbed his hand against his leg once the last of the carrot was gone. He patted the horse on its muzzle and walked over to Anargen. "Is everything as it should be? You look pale."

At length, he let what he'd been holding in out in a rush, "I'm afraid not. My father doesn't believe the war is part of the Quest anymore. He thinks there's something else, something more we should be doing."

Terrillian scowled. "He wants to abandon us in the middle of defending Peter's March?"

"No, no," Anargen waved his hands as if to dispel any notions of betrayal and cowardice, neither of which applied to his father. "He's taking up positions in the castle with the other older defenders and Seren. When the defensive line breaks, they'll be ready to help reinforce us."

"*If* the defensive lines falter," Terrillian corrected.

"Terrillian ..." Anargen tried to begin. His friend had to see that, whether the line held this time or not, something darker was at work. Something that had to be stopped, and not by the strength of common arms and armor.

"Don't 'Terrillian' me. Aren't you the one who argued at Port Jarreth that we can't afford to give in to such thinking?"

Sighing, Anargen nodded. "I did, and you saw what good our resolve did us there. We survived, but you were right too. We might not be meant to win this war in terms of battlefields and which flags fly over which parts of maps. We—"

"I can't believe what I'm hearing!" Terrillian's tone had grown as heated as Anargen had ever heard it. His friend was nearly shouting. The Knight rubbed his face roughly. His eyes were hard on Anargen, as though he were checking a measure that should be coming out to more than he was finding. He gestured off to an indistinct point in the distance. "Does Sir Cinaed's sacrifice mean nothing to you?"

It felt like Anargen had been sucker punched in his abdomen. Had Terrillian seriously just said that to him?

"And if his isn't enough, what about the thousands of our people and those in Ecthelowall and Albaron who are dying to make sure their families and our families aren't terrorized and enslaved by that madman Ilyron? This isn't just about some abstract dream Caeserus may or may not have had anymore. This is the Quest. This is about preserving something worth preserving."

Am I the only one who still believes the Tower of Light is real? And that dream was real? How in the Lowlands did that happen?

"We both want Libertias and the Restoration to succeed, but Terrillian, they aren't the one to whom we've ultimately pledged our fealty. The High King works through the nations of the Lowlands, but he also has a task we as Knights have been entrusted beyond all of that. I fought seeing that for so long now, but I think this is where we have to tread carefully and not let our desires pull us from the true Quest."

Terrillian's face reddened, and his fist clenched. As Anargen watched, it shook with barely contained rage. "You told me how you failed in Stormridge, and you're going to lecture me about how desires can distract us from the true Quest? How do you take up your spiritsword and such hypocrisy at the same time!"

Anargen closed his eyes and gritted his teeth against the

shame and anger that rose instantly to meet and batter back the attack levied against him. He still had his eyes shut when he replied, "It is because of my failure that I'm extra sensitive to that error. And if you think for one moment that I haven't hated myself and struggled with that every day since I turned from my error and back to the High King's service, then you clearly think I'm the most irredeemable fool in the Lowlands."

His friend's gaze was so hard that Anargen was sure it could grind granite to powder. It softened only fractionally when he spoke. "I don't think you're a fool for returning and failing. I think you're a fool for fleeing like a coward now and claiming it to be for the High King's honor. It's what Caeserus and Bertinand did, right? That's why they aren't with us? They forsook the Quest?"

As much as he tried not to gape, Anargen knew from the way Terrillian's expression seemed to cement in its resolve that his own face had betrayed everything. "They didn't flee in fear," Anargen replied weakly.

"Are we really going to get into a battle of semantics on their behalf?" Terrillian challenged.

Swallowing against the tension between them that felt very palpable as if it was crushing him from all sides, Anargen countered, "I can't speak for what drove them away. All I can say is that they departed. And every day, I hope the High King summons them back to the Quest. What I can tell you is that I can't escape the pressure on my heart that the Quest and the War of Restoration overlap in places, but they aren't one and the same."

Terrillian spun on his heels and walked away, his free hand on his neck. He let out something between a groan and a growl. Then he whirled back around and splayed his arm wide. "Then I don't know what to tell you, Anargen, other than go. Just go. Right now."

"What? The defense—"

"We don't need you for the defense. Not when your heart isn't in it. You'd just be a liability. If you're so convinced that you know better than all the rest of the Lowlands what is right and true and good ... then go. I'll inform the marshal ... I don't know what I'll inform him. But ..."

From the quavering in Terrillian's voice at the end, he was trying to wrestle with an emotion that threatened to rob him of his voice. After a moment, he tried again, "But ... you need to go. And may the High King be with you."

Anargen gaped, unable to move or to speak. It was happening again, a fracturing among those who should be completing the Quest. In retrospect, he could see how the Stormridge Knights or even Caeserus might have had issues with how the Quest was being pursued and with him, respectively. Their departures were understandable. Bertinand's was harder to grapple with, but this ... Level-headed, affable, and intensely devoted Terrillian was dismissing him, permanently.

Seconds dragged past without either of them moving, speaking, or Terrillian's expression softening in the least. Ultimately, practicality won out. If they were leaving today, which they would have to do to escape court martial, they'd need to go now so they could make it to the next town over before nightfall. He made his halting way to the door, calling back over his shoulder as he left, "May the High King be with you."

THE COLD TRAIL

There had been no sweeping chill nor oppressive weight of darkness and fear that fell upon Jason when he crossed from Posek into Jhi. Thereby leaving the lands of the Alliance and entering those of the Confederacy. And not just the Confederacy, but one of its three pillars. Uldiquim, Tikbok, and Pashtari may have been willing partners in the Confederacy, but they were merely opportunistic, playing the side they anticipated would win. Not that any one of them was overly noble otherwise, especially not the despicable slaver state of Uldiquim. Knorland and Jhi, however, were fully ensconced in Rehalcyon's aims to conquer the entire Lowlands. From hints and whispers gleaned since the Lowlands Total War began, they were quickly adopting the darker practices and devotions of the Rehalcy. The sort that Jason's brother, Dorian, was behind.

So, as they mountaineered along the treacherous faces of the jagged Jiānshān Mountains to sneak across the border into Jhi under the cover of twilight, he expected a stronger sensation of its evil to strike him. As though he had crossed an intrinsic line in morality or was in danger of doing so just by being here. While it was rather cold in a physical sense, they had found Shānkou to be a quiet village, where the inhabitants mined ore from the peaks they carved their homes into. These squat, round, stone homes with their simple hearths and dirt paths hardly evoked the industrialized brutality displayed in propaganda posters of Bengesparr and Jhipore much farther south. The villagers were welcoming, even taking in two strangers who were clearly foreigners. They shared thick woven blankets made from their other key mercantile superlative, a thick wool from mountain sheep. Not wholly different from Hoarcrest in Ecthelowall's Albaron region, which Jason had visited briefly and found to be quite lovely. Likewise, Shānkou's hospitality and generosity were unshakeable.

Following the village's traders down the slopes to the base of the mountains where the Bham River flowed off the same Jiānshān Mountains somewhere to the east, they then encountered Xiaoxīn. It was more like the stories of old Jhi he had heard about with pointed terracotta rooftops, brightly colored buildings, and billowy clothes. The people there spoke faster and had more fluid movement in their city, which was filled with a diverse array of everything from rice and apricot farmers to textiles and smithing merchants who took the Shānkou wool and made much "finer" things than the practical but plain garments, blankets, and tools they'd seen in Shānkou. There was an abundance of rugs with intricate interwoven geometric patterns that somehow still captured nature's scenic beauty. Elegant candelabras and hammered work sculptures to decorate homes abounded.

The bustle reminded Jason a bit of Varliliman. While he didn't care for Varliliman, it was disconcerting to relate familiar localities with the Jhi'ish, a tendril of the evil kraken that was the Confederacy of Nations. He didn't want to appreciate them or their aggressive charity and respectfulness. Even less because he caught glimpses of Aria smirking when he interacted with them. Particularly when he taught a local noodle house proprietor who had discounted their meal heavily how to shake hands and pronounce "Ecthel" properly. How was he not supposed to grin when the wrinkled old man beamed and almost jerked Jason's arm off, shaking it so excitedly.

Jason was now the one playing the sullen and dour card. Which he suspected Aria had fully expected after she had abruptly redirected their cautious southerly progress from Sephak in Posek to the headlong rail ride, slipping into Jhi without formally explaining her plans to him. In fact, she had basically told him nothing the entire trip. Oh, she was definitely talking now, especially as she recounted here and there bits of Anargen's journal to him or spoke of Anargen's contemporary, Thomas. Her silence, though, on where she was leading them and why was deafening. If he hadn't given his word to trust her and made such an affair of it, then he would've put an end to this trip more than a thousand miles ago. They had burned two weeks and by necessity kept such a low profile he wasn't sure the Alliance would believe they were still alive once they got back in contact with them. It almost made them seem suspicious of treachery, all the more now that they were mingling among the Jhi'ish, riding a steamboat down the Bham River to its namesake city.

"We're almost there now," she informed him, the lift in her brows implying a smile he couldn't see beneath the green and white-patterned scarf covering the lower half of her face. An outbreak of disease in the city necessitated facial coverings, and Jason was happy to blend in. His pale countenance and very Western facial features would've been solid giveaways that they didn't belong. Though he might've passed for Rehalcy and by his somewhat brawny build—earned through all the trench work and efforts on behalf of the Alliance—maybe Lyrsconian. Either of the latter would work as cover until his halting Rehalcy was asked of him.

Thanks to a tailor in Xiaoxīn, Aria was wearing a *liangmao*, a hat that was a sort of bamboo disc with a hole atop the crown, with fabric draping like small curtains. Between that and the scarf, gauging her expressions was an exercise in trust. If he kept a journal like Anargen, he would probably have summarized this time with: "Trust is hard."

Not that it was all bad. He had sketched a few things. One evening while out on deck, Aria had let down her mask and hair as she looked out over the water while the sunset's rich palette edged the river and her in ways that were almost heartbreakingly beautiful. He kept the sketch, but he treated it almost as if it were a traitor. Sullen and dour, those were the things he was to be right now. Not some lovesick puppy running around her feet yipping for her attention. Maybe his log for this would need two sentences, "Trust is hard. Love can be harder."

That last bit ironic, because it was easy to love Aria, even in the midst of being utterly furious with her over the risks she was taking upon herself. Upon them both, if he was honest, but he seldom took danger to himself as worth accounting. Jason was more than prepared to lay down his life at any moment for the Alliance and for Aria.

For the High King too.

The thought was jarring. Of course, for the High King, above all. The other two were synonymous with that. Or, well, not synonymous but corollary. Or coincidental. Or ... they were all part of the same fabric. Weren't they?

"Something has confused you enough to break through that brooding façade you erected," Aria observed, giving him a nudge with her shoulder.

He scooted a step away and shot a look around them. Jhi'ish were far more accepting of men and women interacting in public than the Poseki, but playful banter and fraternizing like this wasn't the norm from what he'd observed. "Low profile," he reminded her.

"No one is watching us," she reassured him. "I checked. You forget, Grandfather and I have lived hiding in plain sight my whole life. I know how to blend into spaces I shouldn't be able to, and"—she gave another playful nudge—"just how far to push things."

That earned a grunt from him. For some dumb reason, he wanted to kiss her. Probably because Aria, his Aria, was decidedly restored from the tragic statute of her he'd been accompanied by for so long. But her lackadaisical handling of these tenuous moments was in no one's interest. "Careful not to get cocky."

"I'm fairly certain a particular hustler I know from Brackenburgh would have said in similar circumstances, 'It's not being cocky if you're that good.'"

Ugh, he probably had said that at one point. He hoped he'd fastidiously put to death that side of himself. But, in all likelihood, that facet of his personality hadn't yet been polished away to humility. He was about to make a comment to the effect that she was going backwards if she was imitating him when she looked up at him and bounced her brows as if in challenge. And to seal it, she nudged him for a third time.

Oh, all right, that's it.

Time to one-up her. Quick as a whip crack, he jerked down his facial cover and hers and laid a heavy kiss on her. Except, a second into it, his bold shock-and-awe campaign of gamesmanship crumbled, because this was the first full kiss he'd had from her in months. And he was ashamed of how much he'd missed it. At least he thought he should be ashamed of it. The longer the kiss lingered the harder it was to focus.

He should be upset with her, or something... He'd sort it out later.

Their kiss lasted only a few seconds longer, making it both too short and too long. When he pulled back, there was a mischievous glint in her eyes. She adjusted her face covering with delicate care. Likewise, she reaffixed his. "There, it's good that we took care of that. Because it will be too dangerous for any significant displays of affection or uncovering of our faces for the next couple of days."

And as if unable to resist one more verbal nudge, she added, "Especially since we're only engaged right now."

Wow ... the student is now the master.

Then again, Aria had always been feisty. Alluringly so.

He sighed and did a quick check around just to make sure she hadn't been overconfident. Nobody else was in sight and they were still a few hundred yards off from an enormous red and gold painted stone arch that indicated they had officially passed into Bham.

"We play dangerous games sometimes," he said wistfully, the tingle from their kiss still occupying his thoughts.

"No. No games," she replied, more serious. "There is a time for laughter and playfulness as much as for mourning and austerity. The latter two may be in greater supply all too soon and, well, I do love you. I perhaps made that less than clear in recent days."

"Not as recently as I," he admitted, taking her hand.

She didn't pull free but did drop their linked hands behind the side of the boat as they passed under Bham's archway. Jason watched it shrink away before turning his attention to the array of taller prismatic towers of fuchsia glass and grey concrete intermingled with the more vibrant and smaller structures similar to Xiaoxīn they'd left days ago. In the distance, dark plumes of smoke rose from what must be factories.

"Aria, I trust you," he said, shaking his head as they steamed full on toward one of the jetties in the broad river that would allow them to disembark. "But at some point, you will need to tell me why we're here. We work best as a team."

66

"We do, when we are focused on the Quest," she amended lightly. Pressing his hand, she continued before he could interject anything. "We're here to find Grandfather. While some of our sentiments are in conflict, you were right, he does need to know what happened at Kezmarepos."

Jason worked hard to suppress any annoyed sounds from escaping his lips. The best he managed was to reply, "Okay," on a rush of pent-up air. "Laying aside that you could have told me that at any point in the trip ..." She started to speak, and he gave her hand a squeeze much as she had his and barreled on, "What brought him here? This is deep in Confederacy territory. It's a risk for us, but for him it's doubly so. Neither of us is the Defender of any realms."

The boat began to slow and turn as it sought to dock at the jetty. Aria took note of that before she added in a whisper, "True. Which is why we couldn't discuss it till the last possible moment. I know you're protective of me, and I treasure the feeling of safety you give me. Truly. However, we had to come, and we still need to keep quiet about the reason for doing so. There will be spies watching us, and as long as they don't catch on to what we're doing till it's too late, then everything will be fine."

There was just enough tension around her eyes that he could tell, even with the optimistic lilt to her voice, that any smile she wore now was tight. This was no sure thing they were about to attempt. There was a thud as the boat reached its docking, a little roughly. A crewmate was already lowering a ramp to disembark. It was too late to find out why Defender Black was in Bham.

"Sure thing," he said, suppressing an ironic tone.

"How often had I heard it said, "You cannot go home," and never considered any of its truth or substance to be worth a single moment's considering. If only I ever had, I would've been spared such a grievous injury ..."

—*Anargen's King's Day Journal*
5 Aurigids 1610 Middle Era

"We should already be there," Anargen protested, urging his horse to a quicker gait. "We reached the Black River's mouth half an hour ago."

Glewdyn sighed heavily. "Lad, it's been less than half as long. I told you already, this area flooded. The rain has swollen the Black River over its banks, and it's flowing farther south than usual, even for this time of year."

In spite of hearing his father, Anargen urged his horse ahead still faster. The older Knight didn't seem to have the same force, stronger than gravity, pulling him back to Black River. It was more than just visiting his childhood home and gathering supplies. Black River meant so much to him. After the tragedies of Port Jarreth, Einwis, and losing Terrillian's support at Peter's March, they needed a reset. A return to where the Quest had started, for them to find its new direction. More personally, Anargen desperately needed not to have his clearest memories of it be those tainted by the attack that had put him and all those carried off into Count Eidolon's wicked hands.

"It's a shame we're not passing through a month later. Maple Point and the whole region would be fully ablaze with the colors of fall," Anargen gestured to the abundance of maples and oaks they rode among. "Though I suppose the greater shame is we weren't here a month earlier when the blackberries are at their ripest and haven't yet all been picked over."

He beamed at Seren, whose soft, pallid skin contrasted with her midnight hair in a manner akin to blackberries and crème. Fittingly, he'd found her picking the berries during his last visit to Black River. It was the one memory of the event not wholly tainted by the sorrow of the atrocity that took place soon after. He'd expected to see a knowing smile on her face, but long strands of hair obscured her expression from his angle. She whispered something to Glewdyn, who nodded.

A moment later, her horse was matching pace with his while Glewdyn hung back. She reached out her hand for him to take, requiring him to rein in his horse and slow to a canter.

"What's wrong?" he asked, rubbing his thumb gently against the soft skin of her palm. Memories of the first times he'd done so, not more than a mile from here, were sweet morsels he savored.

She cleared her throat, as though choked. "Your father thought it would be best for me to be with you. We're almost to your family's cottage."

Brows furrowed for an instant in consideration, Anargen's brooding lifted with a shrug of his shoulders. "It would be good to have a few moments alone with you. Amidst all we've endured, we've talked precious little of what comes after." He rubbed his thumb along her hand still more gently, a light caress. "Returning to Black River, it made me wonder if we might not come back here, after. Build our home. Start our family."

There was no missing the sudden flush in her cheeks and the smile that parted her lips. The very sort of smile that, even aside from her wit and wisdom, beauty and strength, could bind all his affections firmly to her. It was, however, equally impossible to overlook how something caught her eyes, and the joy in her expression faded like the bright sun masked by rolling storm clouds. She gnawed at her lip before giving a little nod. "We're here."

Anargen grinned. He'd been so fixated on her, he hadn't noticed that they'd cleared the bounds of the forest and entered the clearing where he'd grown up. He brushed the back of her hand with a kiss and looked at his family's land. The breath within him wasn't stolen but locked within, unwilling to escape where the warmth of his happiness a moment earlier was so much more pleasant.

A steady pressure on his hand from Seren helped coax him back into breathing. Even so, it was choked by a sob. "It's ruined."

The modest cottage lacked most of its roof, and the door his father had made himself was missing from the shattered entryway to the darkened structure. Thistles, briers, and small sumacs grew up over where his father's sprawling garden plot— his pride and pleasure—once stretched.

He scarcely halted his horse before he slid out of the saddle and jogged over to it. Tall grass grew up over the path to the house and swayed wildly as a cool breeze cut across the clearing. It shook the shattered remains of the roof, and part of it collapsed inside with a thump. The danger of further collapse didn't deter Anargen, but he could not bring himself to pass beyond the doorway. He slumped against it and immediately had to back away as he felt it nearly give.

Once again, Seren's fingers laced through his and squeezed. It was almost a minute before he found his voice. "I don't know what I was expecting. I knew Mother wasn't here, and Father has been away since nearly a month after Eidolon ..."

"Took us all," Seren finished for him, her voice soothing, calm. "Your father got word about its condition some time ago. Bandits have been roaming through the area. The war has taken away most of those who used to secure the region, so they're freer to pillage homes left behind by those fighting or displaced. He ... we ... struggled with how to break the news to you."

It took a great deal of intention on his part not to ball both hands into fists of rage. Count Eidolon and Monarch Ilyron had taken yet another thing from him.

"My parents' house was too far from Black River's town center to be damaged by the raid that happened ... well, you know."

"I do."

Seren's words were so wistful, so unburdened by any tones of happiness or hope he desperately wanted for her. It made it all the harder to ask, "How bad is Black River proper if ..."

"Your father is riding ahead to see. He thought you might need some time here and, depending on what he finds, may advise we take a different path. One that skirts around the town."

He shook his head. "No. I have to see it."

She just nodded and laid her head against his shoulder.

Closing his eyes, he tilted his head to rest on hers. Unlike other times, like Sir Cinaed's death or the other horrors he'd witnessed, this didn't numb him. All of his senses were agitated, raw, roiling with a turmoil of emotions. Among them, guilt. Hadn't he already said goodbye to Black River years ago, when he and the others followed Sir Cinaed out of the town and first joined the Quest? He'd known then the High King might not ever will for him to return to this place and accepted it. Somewhere along the way, with his reunion with Seren and their engagement, he'd allowed himself to slip into wishful thinking. Imagining a simple life like the one he'd left. Growing a garden as his father had and working a practical job, perhaps even the smithing trade he'd once been so eager to escape. Visions of growing old with Seren as their children and children's children brought a depth of beauty and significance to his days that he'd always been told made the passage of time and life a blessing instead of a burden.

A sudden, sharp pain within forced him to suck in an equally pointed breath. It did not appear to be the High King's path for them. Even if he and Seren were together and got to wed as they hoped, how could the Lowlands ever return to something so simple as that quiet life? More pointedly, how could he go back to such a thing when the High King had called him to the Quest and his part seemed so much more fraught and demanded so much more valiance than most?

Absently, he'd begun towing Seren and himself back to their horses that each munched on the overgrown grass. He helped her up into her saddle and managed to shakily seat himself on his own mount. He let Seren set their pace the rest of the way to Black River proper, and once more it was well that she held fast to him. A lone tear streaked down his face as they came up the deteriorating road to find Glewdyn looking on the only remaining stones and timbers of his smithy still standing. One great work-worn hand pressed against the scorched remnants of the forge where he'd earned every callous.

All of it, the quaint town Anargen had known all his life, was gone. Most of what remained was a black slurry of ash and mossy stones poking out from the forest's encroachment. Barely any indication of the shapes of what had once stood in their places remained. The mayor's house, the shop where Hilya had sold honey and candles, the corner where Ernest and his musical family had performed during festivals—all rendered nothing. Less than that, where once they gave goods and purpose to this land, their corpses blighted it. Not unlike the werebeast massacre at little Bracken or the centuries-old battle that had destroyed Glastonae in the north. Most tragic of all though was the slightly more protruding, jagged remnants of the Knight Hall.

Since the Hall had been of stone set with wooden beams, it had best survived the fires the raiders had set. But at some point, someone or something had felt inspired to inflict greater damage and torn down whatever was left of it. Once the pride of the town with its colored glass windows and tall tower that shone out a light on the darkest nights, it was laid lowest.

Amid the ruins were remnants of the spots with the greatest significance to him. The library from which Anargen had devoured all the tomes available, learning of far-off lands and long-past days. An expansive commons where Anargen pledged himself to the High King of All Realms after receiving the vision that summoned him into his majesty's service. The room where his fingers had first brushed the hilt of a spiritsword and set his hair on end as the flames coursed along the tang and burned within him as much as on the blade.

Another cool breeze cut across the land, whistling as it passed through the devastation that was Black River. The ache from earlier returned intensified. These buildings lost were just that, buildings. He mourned the people. Scores of young and old who should be bustling through their mid-afternoon chores and causes. This was the weekend near the month's end, and the markets should be swarmed with miners bringing home the meager wages they earned with back-breaking labor. Despite it, he'd seen such joy in the dust-darkened faces of those miners reunited with their families.

Sir Darius and the other Knight elders would have been tending to those in need around the town. Sir Cinaed, laughing boisterously and encouraging dour Arnauld in his muddled attempts at improving his squat home. Those images, above all the others, tormented him and made the haunting stillness of this place all the more tragic.

Anargen closed his eyes and dropped to the ground.

He felt Seren wrap her arms around his neck as she crouched beside him. Leaning into her embrace, they stayed that way for so long, long enough for Glewdyn to come over and join them. Long enough for the sun to start to pass behind the tree tops in the distance. Long enough for Anargen to finally and firmly say goodbye to Black River. Both the town and its citizens were tragically lost. Long enough to release his hold on the dreams and ambitions and desires he'd been building up within him, an idol to which he was devoting allegiance dangerously comparable to that which he'd pledged and owed to the High King.

Very well. I understand, my King. Your wisdom is greater. Your will better. May it be done.

No one had to say that they could not stay there for the night. Without a word, they all mounted their horses and rode until the sun set away from Black River. Though Anargen did not say it aloud, he was certain that this time, whatever happened with the war, with the Quest, he would never come back to this place again.

FITTING IN

As the shudders from the boat settling into place faded, Jason gave Aria a tight smile. They had to drop hands, but he gestured for her to precede him, especially seeing the way a crewmate eyed her with more interest than Jason cared for. Hoisting their bags and following her down the ramp, he was sure to give the man a wink and nod as he passed by, just to let him know where he stood in no uncertain terms.

Being the first pair off the boat, they were able to weave quickly through those waiting on the dock to embark and got up to the streets. Thoroughfares here were made of two differently colored granites, the street grey and the edging ruddier-hued. It was a commonly held ancient maxim that "Jhi becomes more fixed with time." Apparently, that carried over into their choice of construction materials. Their cities would literally become harder with the passing years.

A disconcerting notion, given the Alliance very much needed not only to bend but break Jhi to win the war in the Eastern Lowlands. Perhaps it was of some comfort that even the proud Jhi'ish had resorted to Western construction methods for their modern city spires and factories. Still, the colorful banners they hung off the concrete portions and the fuchsia-tinted glass made them distinctively Jhi'ish, and he grudgingly admitted they were more attractive than the drab western cities like Brackenburgh.

"Jason," Aria called, coming to stand in front of him. If he had been looking up slightly higher, he would've missed her.

Even though she was about a foot shorter, the withering look she gave him made it feel like she was eye-to-eye with him. "Don't get distracted."

"Just doing some locational reconnaissance," he offered with ease.

She rolled her eyes. "Right, well, you can take a rest from topographic mapping for now. Just follow me. I have an address to try."

"Okay," he answered. But she didn't move. "What's up?"

From the window into her expressions formed by her *liangmao*—the wide circular brimmed hat with a hole at the top from which her braided hair draped—and the facial covering, he knew she was irked. "You'll have to walk slightly in front of me. It's a Jhi'ish custom for husbands and suitors to do that in new places."

"You're kidding. This is going to be the most awkward trip we've made yet. Can you just give me the address?"

She cocked her head to the side and gave him a knowing look. Blending in meant there was no point in arguing that they flout the custom.

"Fine, fine." He shook his head. "Sort of lead the way then."

It was perhaps the most ridiculous way of getting around they had yet tried. He had to keep shooting discreet glances back at Aria to make sure she was still headed the same direction as him. There was no conversation between them. It was too tricky to manage with him in front and the restrictions on what they could ostensibly talk about. At more than one intersection, he had crossed the street before finding that Aria had intended to take a left or a right and go down a different street.

Along the way, Jason also came to realize that their decision to wear more traditional Jhi'ish garments, based on Xiaoxīn's tailor's suggestions, was a mistake. The *shenyi* they wore were black with light trims, and Aria's was slightly more ornate in its folds and draping than Jason's. Both robe-like garments had seemed ideal with how loose they were, because concealing their Knight armor underneath was so reasonable. But here in the more modern city of Bham, it was quickly becoming apparent that newer styles of clothes were in use. More functional vested garments and trousers were employed, though at least the sort of skull cap Jason had been given to wear wasn't too out of place. The women he spotted typically wore some variant of *shenyi*, but more fitted than Aria's by a good degree. They garnered more than a few stares.

Yup. Keeping a non-existent profile here. No way any spies are tailing us.

Mentally, he began practicing his Rehalcy in case someone stopped them. He really hoped that no one would try to stop them.

Aria cleared her throat.

Jason glanced back. He had walked several feet past where Aria had stopped in front of a building that was clearly a newer, more Westernized addition to the city. It was roughly the same height as either of the two traditional architecture buildings beside it. None of them looked particularly well-maintained or desirable. When had they wandered into the less reputable parts of the city?

Aria tilted her head, the fabric of her *liangmao* gently shaking. He bustled over, his *shenyi* making the jaunt less fluid than he'd like. "This is it?" he inquired.

"Mhm," she replied and gestured discreetly for him to go in first.

He did so and was ushered into a plain foyer with what looked like some locked postal boxes embedded in the wall on one side and a set of stairs leading upward on the other. They appeared to be alone.

"It's an apartment complex."

Aria seized the moment alone to grab him by the arm and tow him up the stairs. He almost tripped on his *shenyi* three times on the way up, but by the time they reached the seventh floor and peeled off to the third door, he had sorted himself out.

From inside the elaborate folds of her own *shenyi*, Aria produced a key. "Let's hope the locks weren't changed from when I was five," she informed him.

"Whoa, it's been that long since you've been here? Why would—"

A click of the lock disengaging cut him off, and Aria jerked him inside, shutting the door and removing her *liangmao* and scarf. Jason set their luggage to the side and likewise removed his cap and scarf. If Aria hadn't looked so haunted at that moment, he would've seized the opportunity to sneak another kiss. The room was curtained off at the windows, so it was dim inside and presumably safe from prying eyes.

"What's wrong?" he asked.

"It's too neat, too kempt," she informed him. "Grandfather hasn't been here for some time." Walking slowly into the room, she fussed with a few bits of paper on a desk to the left.

There wasn't much to the space. A telephone sat on the desk along with a stack of papers and other stationery essentials. To the right was a narrow bed, made up with very spare covers. There was one old wooden chair for sitting and a coal stove in the left corner of the modest-sized space. The absence of any smoke or even its scent signaled it hadn't been lit for some days. A rug was about the homiest thing in the room, and it was plain, not at all matching the typical Jhi'ish flourishes he'd seen so far.

"This is a very Western room," he noted. As if confirming it, he spotted a small painting on the wall beside the bed that he believed to be an artistic rendering of the dwarf fortress-city Ordumair.

Aria sighed, opening and slamming desk drawers. "This was effectively his embassy as Defender of the Northern Realm. At least from before the Jhi'ish leaders became so isolationist and xenophobic."

She went back to rifling through the contents of the desk.

"Ah, from a time when fitting in wasn't as important."

Without pausing, she replied, "We never fit in anywhere. Not really. We're in the Lowlands, but not of them ..."

"Strangers until the King's Day comes and we're called home," he completed her trailing thoughts. It was a fact of being a Knight of Light rather than them in particular, but the perspective shift didn't alter their present situation.

Lacking further instructions, Jason drifted around the room, checking for any signs of recent occupancy. There were none. He even inspected the cupboard beside the stove pipe and found not a crumb in it.

Walking over to the chair, he dropped into it and sighed. "Well, I guess this will be my bed this evening unless you're feeling masochistic tonight and want the chair."

Shaking her head vigorously, Aria replied, "We're not staying here. As soon as I find some trace of where he's gone, we're leaving."

Jason leaned forward with steepled fingers, about to point out that they had precious little to go on and, if this was where Defender Black typically stayed, it made as much sense as anywhere in town to be here. But the frantic energy with which she searched brought him up short. She was scared. Scared for her grandfather.

He tilted back in the chair, which immediately wobbled under him. Flailing, he fought to stabilize himself, and the front legs slammed to the floor. The board under him made a muted thud.

Aria stopped working and looked at him, a chastisement dying on her lips as Jason's own expression became knowing. They were each on their knees and prying at the board right away. Scooting the chair aside, they lifted away the loose board and were rewarded with the sight of a secret compartment. Tucked inside was a thick, bound tome that was at once identifiable. "Anargen's journal," Jason announced as he produced it.

"There's something else," Aria replied, reaching in with hungry hands. A scrap of paper with the text. "Ears that aren't yours may hear, fears shed may call on tears."

She dropped back from her knees onto her bottom and moaned. "Not a riddle, Grandfather."

Jason reached out and rubbed her hand with his thumb, holding onto it with a gentle firmness. "Hey, this is good. We know he was here, right? And now we know, he knew you'd come looking for him and this is how he's going to help us find him."

Moisture was already welling in her eyes and dribbling down her cheeks, threatening to mar the pale facial makeup she had insisted she must wear to match Jhi'ish women. Already, some of the dark kohl around her eyes and vibrant mascara seemed to have suffered. A snuffle, and then through a choked throat she concluded. "That's true. He—"

At their backs, there was a rattling of keys, and the doorknob rotated. Someone else was coming in, and as the door creaked open, the shadow that spilled in immediately betrayed it wasn't Aria's grandfather.

OLD ACQUAINTANCE

There was no time to prepare to face whoever was entering. The room wasn't large enough to accommodate more than a couple of people, so if they were about to be raided, he and Aria would only have to face a few foes at a time. Of course, the limited space meant wielding their spiritswords would be a challenge. Even brandishing them would be a feat, given that their spiritswords were both in the luggage and nearer to the front door than they were.

Aria was quicker-thinking at that moment and jerked the journal from him to stow it back in the hold. She'd covered it with the board by the time he was on his feet and dropped into a boxing stance. He couldn't fight an army of armed guards, but he'd sure make sure the first one through the door smarted for his efforts.

Whoever was entering must have heard the scuffling from within, because there was some hesitation, and the door pulled closed for just a moment. Footsteps clomped in the hall, followed by a punctuated quiet.

The door flung open and in leaped an average-sized man wielding—an umbrella?

Jason caught the first sortie with it, deflecting its swipe, and drew back to deck his attacker square in the face. He pulled up short when he realized not only was the intruder not Jhi'ish, but Jason knew him.

"Professor Goulder?" he asked, not sure if he believed what he was seeing.

Engaged in trying to extricate the umbrella from Jason's iron grip on it, the quirky academic perked up and looked at Jason with scrutiny made comical by his over-thick little glasses. Realization blossomed on the old man's face, and he chuckled in his hearty Ecthel country way and beamed a great toothy grin that sent his bushy mustache whiskers twitching. "Jason Landsby, by the High King's favor, it is good to see you!"

Offering his hand to shake, Jason was instead pulled into a surprisingly tight hug. "Good to see you too, Professor," he squeaked out.

The professor eyed him up and down like an uncle assessing a dear nephew after a long time apart. At least Jason imagined that was what a caring uncle might have done. He'd personally only ever gotten a good smack across his chops from his "dearest" blood relatives. Seeming to fixate on his attire, the professor fussed with the *shenyi*. "Why in the Lowlands are you wearing a *shenyi* while about in Bham?" he asked. "You must stick out like a sore thumb here."

"Well, I—"

"It's my doing, Professor," Aria spoke up, stepping into view. "I wanted us to blend in, but the tailor in Xiaoxīn seems to have misled us."

"Oh, Aria, my dear girl!" exclaimed the professor, who edged over to Aria. With a bow, he took her hand and kissed it. "It does my old heart good to see you well."

He squinted at her hand and suddenly his eyes behind the thick glass enlarged comically. "I say, and engaged, perhaps to this strapping young lad, by chance?"

Aria's cheeks flushed, "Yes, Professor. I'm sorry, I meant to write to tell you of it. With the war, it's been hard to keep in touch."

"The war's made a great deal hard, I'm afraid. Though I must confess, I was playing the part of a thespian just now.

Your grandfather actually informed me via letter a month ago. Along with his summons for me to, uh, come render my assistance."

"Our assistance, Professor?" a feminine voice called from the entryway.

For the first time since Jason had known the professor, he saw his cheeks redden for a moment. "Oh, quite right. I'm frightfully bad at this, but I must introduce my astute colleague. This is Dr. Hua Jing, and certainly the flower of my aged eyes."

The thin woman who entered was wearing a simple grey dress, like many Jason had noted before. Not so form-fitted as others, but certainly not as loose as the *shenyi* with which he and Aria had been outfitted. Dr. Jing's eyes were lively, and like Goulder, she noticeably relied on a small pair of spectacles for seeing. Her hair was dark with streaks of grey. Tiny wrinkles around the corners of her eyes and mouth betrayed she was as given to smiles as the professor. And they were treated to their first from her. A shy, coy one.

The effect of it on the professor's demeanor wasn't beyond noticing, and Jason shot Aria a knowing smirk and cleared his throat pointedly.

"Oh, my, my etiquette is in shambles." Gesturing to each of them in turn, he introduced Aria and Jason, emphasizing with each the designation of "Lady" and "Sir." Dr. Jing noted this with an appreciative nod. With a gentle grace, she closed the door behind her and locked it.

"Now, my children," the professor began afresh. "Pardon my barging in here, but Hua—er, Dr. Jing—and I were coming to call upon your grandfather. I see now he has, by appearances, not been here in some time."

Jason managed to keep from looking shocked, but had to give it to the professor. He might feign disorderliness, but he was certainly observant.

Aria's face fell. "Oh, Professor, I'm afraid you're right as usual. We were coming to see him about events from Posek. Ill news, I'm afraid."

"Intensely so if you would risk crossing this deeply into Jhi territory to deliver it," he noted.

She nodded. "Indeed. It appears we've missed him, and he hasn't left an obvious note behind explaining his absence."

Goulder twitched his moustache. "Ah, no, Defender Black is far too sensible for something of that sort."

"Speaking of sensible," Jason piped in. "How did you and Dr. Jing make it into Bham? I know our attire isn't exactly the latest on these streets, but you couldn't look more Ecthelish, professor."

"What?" Goulder exclaimed as though he had been caught completely off guard. He turned to Hua as if needing support.

She wore the sort of quiet smile that Jason could see complementing Professor Goulder's boisterous ones nicely. "He is right, my dear. You are very distinguished, but also quite noticeable on the streets."

"Dash it all," Goulder said. "And here I've been strutting like some sort of peacock before my lovely guide to this country and all her kith and kin!"

"At least you speak Rehalcy fluently," Aria noted, shooting a pointed look at Jason.

"Indeed, I speak eight languages fluently," Goulder commented, gripping the suspenders he wore with no small measure of pride.

From across the room, Dr. Jing called out something in a language Jason had never heard before.

The professor bowed to her graciously and replied in like-sounding words. Turning back to Jason and Aria, he informed them, "Once more, I'm rescued by the good doctor. My ninth language is Dar, the tongue of Ndarvu's river valleys."

Eyeing the younger pair of Knights with more focus, he waved his hand. "But none of us are here for trifles such as my polyglottery. No doubt, one as wise as Sir Cinaed would not have summoned me here so urgently and not imagined that his loving granddaughter and her gallant paramour would deign to lollygag about during these precipitous times. Mark my words, the crafty old confrère no doubt has left something for us. We need only find it."

That said, the professor began to look around with Dr. Jing. The pair began quietly evaluating the contents of the desk, much as Aria had done.

Aria retrieved the journal once more and handed it to Jason. "Here you go. Keep it safe."

"With my life," he replied. As soon as he stood from stowing it in their luggage, Aria called out to Professor Goulder and Dr. Jing, "I need to mention, we did find something."

Both Goulder and Jing adjusted their spectacles at roughly the same instant, which would have been adorable under other circumstances. "Yes," Goulder said, "Let's have a look at it then."

Producing the paper, she handed it to them and read aloud again: "Ears that aren't yours may hear, fears shed may call on tears."

Giving a shake of her head, Aria shrugged. "He's never said anything like this to me before. No stories, no proverbs. Nothing to explain this."

Brows furrowed, Goulder nodded. "Indeed. It is unlike him to leave a clue without the key already embedded in one of our persons. I haven't the faintest notion of ever having conversed with him about a matter that would elucidate this riddle."

Perking, of sudden, Goulder looked over at Jason. "But Aria and I wouldn't have been expected to come alone. What do you make of this, Mr. Landsby?"

"Well, it's a lovely rhyme?"

Goulder tittered. "Indeed. What else, though? Anything Defender Black said or did?"

"Nothing," Jason shook his head. "At least nothing I can recall."

"Of course," the professor said, glancing at the paper and twitching his bushy whiskers once more. "What about things you said to him?"

"Oh, um, I don't ..." Jason hesitated. It was so improbable he was certain he'd just look like a buffoon. But Aria and Professor Goulder were well aware of his shortcomings. What harm was there in showing Dr. Jing? "Perhaps the word 'call.'"

"Call?" Aria repeated, dubious. "Like summon?"

He shook his head and walked over to the desk. There sat the telephone he had spotted earlier. "We talked after I decided to propose to Aria. I wanted his blessing, and he asked what skills I had that could provide for us after the war was over.

"Besides street hustling and some parkour? Not much, but I did help a guy with some work before. He was stringing lines along some poles on the side of the road. Since he was an older man, I offered to help him with it—honestly, I needed some money too. The pay wasn't much, but he taught me all about telephony and telegraphy."

"The telephone!" Aria exclaimed. Her enthusiasm quickly receded. "But I looked all around it earlier."

Jason nodded, gnawing on his lip in thought. "Just a second." Picking it up, he turned the phone around and around in his hands and then smiled. As he twisted the bottom, a note dropped out.

Quicker than he could've blinked, Aria had the note in hand, reading it. An instant later, she shredded it into fine bits. "I know where he is," she announced.

"Excellent!" Goulder crowed. "Where is the old boy?"

"Don't say another word," Jason yelled.

All eyes turned to him, each face a different shade of surprise. He put down the phone. "Look in here, Professor, what do you see?"

After a quick adjustment of his spectacles, he announced, "There's a second wire. This phone has been tapped!"

"What does that mean?" Aria asked, looking over the disassembled device.

"It means someone has been able to listen in and record every word spoken over this telephone," Goulder explained. Looking sharply at Jason, he added, "But look here, there's no cause for shouting about it, young man. The line only picks up sound when the receiver is off the hook."

"That's true," Jason admitted. "Except this telephone had the portion that sets the cradle internally removed. It's been able to pick up every errant word spoken in this room since we arrived."

"Oh, dear," Goulder mumbled.

"Is there any way to know who was listening in?" Dr. Jing asked, wringing her bony hands.

"I think it would be a safe bet to say it was Confederacy spies," Jason replied.

Aria was already by the window, looking out the curtain. "A wager the Jhi'ish authorities would pay. They're surrounding the building!"

<blockquote>
"Has all the Lowlands gone mad, or has it always been so and I was until recently a happy participant in it? Is it too much to try to have even a moment of untempered romance and fond memories with Seren? Perhaps I'm still being too selfish and naïve for my good, or the Lowlands', for that matter."
</blockquote>

—*Anargen's King's Day Journal*
21 Aurigids 1610 Middle Era

Anargen kept the cloak spread as wide as he was able, but pockets of collecting water hampered his efforts. "Hurry!" he called and began to jog faster, his hair plastered over his eyes and obscuring his vision. Normally, he would have stopped to brush the strands away, but both his hands gripped the corners of the cloak as he tried to keep Seren dry in the torrential downpour.

"You need to take more cover for yourself," Seren chided, trying to pull the cloak more in his direction.

There was no point in doing so, in Anargen's estimation. He was already soaked through, every stitch of fabric on him saturated to its capacity and dripping with still more. A roll of thunder blocked his counter, and he just accepted Seren's offer. They were only a dozen yards from the inn they had chosen for lodging earlier in the day. He focused on keeping every footfall steady on the rain-slicked stones of Bonus Mare's streets. Colorful bits of shell embedded in sandstone pathways streaked past until they were under the welcome shelter of the cypress timber and sandstone that was the Breakers Inn.

"Such an odd and ironic name for an inn," Seren commented as they dumped off the downpour's contributions and Anargen wrung the garment out.

Once finished with that, he noticed Seren was taking her long raven hair, even darker for the soaking, and winding it into a ponytail. Anargen held open the door for Seren to enter. "I'm sorry," he offered.

She took his hand. "You had good intentions. I think it was romantic to want to take a moonlit walk with me. I'm sure Bonus Mare's coastline is lovely under different circumstances."

Despite his best efforts, her light grey dress was sodden, her hair was dripping, and slight shudders ran through her from being cold. By all accounts, their outing was a miserable one. He returned a tight smile and squeezed her hand. Seren was exceedingly understanding, which only made the situation feel tragic. She deserved so much more, so much better. "Once again, I was being naïve. Thinking things would be as marvelous as they were the first time I visited Bonus Mare."

Seren shrugged. "I don't know. Last time, neither of us knew if we'd ever see the other again. And you hadn't even read my letter yet to know how I felt about you. This time ..."

She looked up into his eyes, her expression gentle, earnest, alluring—all in one. "We are together, and you know I'm irrevocably in love with you."

Despite the chill from being soaked, warmth flooded Anargen. He lifted her hand to his lips and brushed it with a tender kiss. "I suppose you must be to put up with such a soaking ... And for such patience and wisdom, I will always love you."

"It does an old heart good to witness your young love,"

Glewdyn commented as he strode up. In spite of what he said, his tone was somber. "I do not mean to intrude, but now that you've returned, there's something I must show you."

Anargen glanced at Seren but found she was equally mystified by his father's vagueness. "Lead the way to our rooms then," Anargen gestured deferentially to his father.

It may have only been in Anargen's imagining, but it looked as if Glewdyn did quick sweeping checks of all the passages around them before he headed to the stairs up to his and Anargen's second-floor room. There was something very off, which became even clearer when he overloudly asked, "I take it they barred you from reaching the shores?"

Hesitant, for pain and perplexment, Anargen answered, "Yes. They also made us sit through a brief interrogation as to our intentions for coming down to the shoreline. The entire waterfront is closed off from public access since the attack on Bonus Mare years ago, and it's only become stricter with the war going on. They're paranoid about spies and saboteurs slipping in."

"They were at least gentle with us," Seren added. "Something has them spooked, but fortunately, it is not us."

Pushing open the cypress door to their room, Glewdyn waved them through hurriedly, his eyes fixed beyond them, scanning the way they came. "Well, can't be too careful these days." Assessing them each, he added louder still, "It's a shame about the storm blowing in on you too."

Trying not to look at his father as though the elder Knight was edging into insanity, Anargen nodded. "It was rather sudden."

Apparently, he failed at masking his confusion, because Glewdyn's brows knit in consternation. Seren spoke up, "Rather sudden and very thorough in soaking us. With your leave, sir, I would like to go back to my room and change into drier clothes."

Glewdyn eyed Seren thoughtfully, then crossed the room in a few quick strides, jerked open the door, and gestured for her to go. "Of course. But do hurry back so we can discuss your evening in greater detail ..."

He let the last bit trail off because his abrupt opening of the door had sent a gangly middle-aged man sprawling to the floor. From his cerulean tunic, he was easily identified as one of the innkeeper's servants. In his hand was a cup.

He was spying on us!

"My humblest apologies, sir," the servant began. "I was coming to ... uh ... help ... you with your ... wet garments?"

"Were you?" Glewdyn replied, the challenge clear in his voice.

"Oh, um, certainly. And to stoke your hearth's fire."

"Very thoughtful of you, though it appears you've forgotten the coal. Bustle off and get some, and we'll be sure to repay your trouble."

The servant must have imagined a double meaning there, because he paled. "Of course. Thank you, sir."

Glewdyn didn't shut the door again until he'd watched the other reach the bottom floor. Whirling back on Anargen and Seren, he stalked back to the room's desk and produced from it a rolled parchment bearing a green wax seal. He handed it to Anargen. "Came by a very cautious courier while you were both out," Glewdyn whispered. "The courier mentioned this letter has been due for some time, but the chaos after Port Jarreth disrupted getting it to us."

Anargen glanced down at the seal and immediately up at Glewdyn, his eyes wide. "It has Viceroy Ecthelion's personal seal on it."

"Indeed."

No wonder his father had been acting as he had. Rightly so, given the spy who had just been attempting to listen in on them.

"Sorry," he mumbled.

"Be quick, open it," Glewdyn instructed, his face as lined with tension as Anargen had ever seen.

Heeding his father, he broke through the seal and unrolled the parchment, glancing up to see if he should read it aloud. Glewdyn shook his head. Apparently, it was better not to speak aloud unless necessary.

Swallowing as he braced himself for what he might find, Anargen had to fight not to cry out. He covered his mouth and looked at Seren and then Glewdyn and then re-read the horrible section of the elegantly scrawled letter. Finishing it, he passed it first to Seren and then to his father.

Both looked visibly shaken by its contents:

"By the hand of the high court accountant Quentin Devos on behalf of the honorable Baron Thomas Halifax, to Sir Glewdyn, Sir Terrillian, Sir Anargen, and Lady Seren of Black River,

"Greetings,

"Would that I could say I write to you with words of joy and hope. But I have precious little in my stores, and time quickly erodes what I do possess. Much has happened since we last saw one another, and it is with the deepest sorrow I must report that Viceroy Ecthelion Halifax was killed in battle more than a week ago.

"As you have no doubt noted, I now bear his surname and the title accompanying it. That is his last gift to me and all I have left of him.

"Yet my own loss is nothing compared to what I must relay with all urgency and haste. Thus, I shall speak my part, and you must burn this letter as soon as you have taken in its dire news.

"Darkness lies heavy on the North, crushing it in suffering and struggles exceeding the expanse of both time and space to tell. In that pain, however, the High King has seen and favored us. We scored a deep blow to Monarch Ilyron in the defeat of Queen Delia and her army. Bitterness and hubris have blinded the Monarch, and he has revealed his aim to conquer Ordumair. His obsession with enacting the Tislatnean rites to create dragons is insatiable, and he believes Ordumair will aid in this endeavor. I do not know how for certain; only that the whole thing is made more plausible by the fact that this war began when he usurped Viceroy Ecthelion and tried to overthrow Ordumair before. Since you, Sir Terrillian, and you, Sir Anargen, are veterans of that defense, I thought it prudent to reach out to you.

"Now, I want to share my full hand. We are in desperate need of allies. The north lands are poised to fall. Albaron and Ecthelowall's Restoration armies are spread to their limits and can scarcely spare more than a token contingent to shore up Ordumair unless something drastic changes in the war elsewhere. We need you and whoever you can gather to fly to our aid with all haste. I have written to you directly because our need is dire, and the nobles of both the Restoration and Albaron have agreed not to alert Libertias of our weakness. I do not mean to impugn your land's honor, but we are certain your leaders will sue for peace and leave the war once they learn of the Viceroy's passing. Keep wary, there are spies everywhere.

"Please, my friends, my brothers and sister of the Order, help us deliver Ordumair and the Lowlands from this desolate hour. You are all so much wiser and more experienced than I— If you come, I cannot say for sure any of us shall survive, but without aid we will die, and these shall be the last words shared between us till the King's Day.

"Lady Mia and Sir Gregor send their regards, and I bid you a hale evening, ever before the dawn of Ecthelowall's Commonwealth and all the more that the High King may be with you and favor you in all things.

"Sir Thomas Halifax, Baron of Halifax"

Anargen watched for the others to finish reading, but his attention drifted. A familiar numbness was spreading, the poison of dread. How could things have deteriorated so far so quickly? The Viceroy was gone. Thomas was right to instruct them to burn this letter. If the leaders of Libertias knew he was dead, then they would certainly sue for peace to avoid total defeat by the Monarch. Perhaps even change sides.

The thought was so odious, so despicable, Anargen physically shuddered. Worse, Thomas was in mortal danger. Young Thomas, who was truly a brother of the Order. Anargen didn't have any siblings, so he had no frame of reference for this hollow feeling.

No, this feeling was indeed one he knew, because he had lost a brother of the Order before, one who was closest to a blood brother of anyone he'd known. His childhood friend, Caeserus. When he walked away from the Quest and the Order, it had nearly destroyed Anargen. Once word finally came of Thomas's demise, would it hurt worse or less than the tragedy of that supreme betrayal?

Not that anything they've done is as bad as my period adrift from the Quest.

Glewdyn cleared his throat. Anargen started to speak up, to shout, to wail over it all, but a stern gesture from his father cut him off. The older man took the edge of the parchment and made a little slice in his forefinger. Drops of red immediately beaded up on his skin, and Anargen watched aghast as

Glewdyn dabbed his finger over the paper in seemingly random dots.

Anargen's gaze flicked to Seren, and she was tilting her head, as if trying to see something more clearly.

Anargen focused on the parchment, on the scarlet dots already made. His eyes widened. There was a pattern. The letters touched meant nothing alone, but formed a message together.

Wemustg ... We must go to ...

"We must go tomorrow?" he blurted out.

An immediate scowl formed on his father's face. He gestured with a nod of his greying head to the next letter. An "n."

This time in control of himself, Anargen waited until his father had finished his dabbing. The moment he met the older man's hazel gaze, he mouthed, "To where?"

The bleeding had stopped, and his father looked like he was caught in an internal debate. At length, he huffed, twitching his bristly mustache that would hide some of his own mouthed words. He tapped on the letter again, this time without leaving a rouge trail.

E-S-T-O-N-B-U-R-Y.

Seren shook her head, sending her damp tresses in the makeshift ponytail swinging like a pendulum. "Why? They didn't help us before; they certainly won't now."

Tapping on his ear, Glewdyn suddenly drew his spiritsword and touched it to the paper so that it lit ablaze.

"What?" Seren mouthed. "I don't understand."

Anargen did, and took Seren's hand. "The High King commanded him to."

From the twitch of her lips, that wasn't a wholly satisfying answer. Why would they react differently? But Anargen knew well enough that the High King could do anything he chose.

Glewdyn either didn't notice or didn't care about the concerns simmering in Seren. He had taken the slow-burning letter and tossed it onto the room's hearth, watching it burn with intensely thoughtful eyes.

In the silence ensuing, Anargen worried a rift might form between his father and fiancée over this matter. He wasn't sure he could survive such a thing. Nettled, he wondered how many more people he had lost to disagreements and dissent instead of death? Horribly, he found himself pondering which was worse. In the latter case, Sir Cinaed and Viceroy Ecthelion had died in battle, nobly serving the High King of All Realms. There was purpose and significance to those losses. Their sting, while not erased, was at least eased. Knowing that others like his closest childhood friends: Caeserus, Bertinand, and Terrillian, had all left him and regarded him little better than a brigand ... that was a wound that didn't have any end or relief to which he could lay claim.

A rush of heat swirled through the room. Not from the hearth, but seemingly from everywhere and nowhere at once. When the whispers reached his ear, he did not have to guess their source.

"The others, they aren't rejecting us or abandoning us. They're turning their backs on the Quest," Anargen gathered.

Seren tilted her head. "Who do you mean?"

Anargen blinked. He hadn't meant to speak aloud what he was being guided to. "Oh, um ... Terrillian. Caeserus. Bertinand. Kyreneas—"

"I get your meaning," Seren cut him off. She folded her arms at her waist. "There is an enormous difference between Caeserus's cowardice and Terrillian's commitment to his nation."

There was, and yet there wasn't. In the end, both had departed from the Quest, and the thoughts and intentions of the heart were the High King's to divide. Anargen hesitated to argue that point with Seren, given his own thoughts weren't settled.

"Even Bertinand ... I could understand," she continued, her voice sounding strained.

Anargen had no interest in delving into that particular parting. His friend had been jealous of Anargen's courtship with Seren. In their particularly dark hour after the ambush at Cattingsford, he had left. As much as it might have been to try to retrieve Caeserus, Anargen guessed from Bertinand's absence that he couldn't bear to see Seren choose someone over him. What made it worse was that Anargen could understand it. Wouldn't he be torn to bits if he had to watch Seren love and build a life with another right in front of him? Hating Bertinand's choice, judging it, meant hating and judging a fault he feared was deeply within himself.

Leave judgment of Bertinand and his motives to the High King. His oaths are to the Great King, not me. To him, he must answer. We must answer ...

"Bertinand would've made a terrible joke right about now," Anargen mused.

"The worst," Seren agreed.

"I remember, during harvest one year, he kept telling everyone that Black River had seen its 'hay day,' and it was all downhill from there."

Seren snickered. "Did he ever tell you about seeing his first clock in Stormridge? He said it was 'about time.'"

Anargen burst out laughing. "Even if he'd kept that clock, the timing of his jokes was the worst too."

"Ooh, don't you start doing it too," Seren giggled, holding her sides.

They bantered back and forth for several more minutes, welcoming the levity, before Glewdyn came over and rested his hand on his son's shoulder. The gravity of it pulled Anargen sharply back to their present. "We should leave now. The storm is picking up. It will help to frustrate any followers."

Anargen swallowed with some difficulty. "I'll prepare the horses."

"Bring them around the back," Glewdyn confirmed.

The storm had intensified, and Anargen had to fight through the boisterous winds and driving rain to reach the stables. They left within half an hour, wrapped in cloaks and striving against the tumult, departing into the dark plains that led to Estonbury and ultimately once more the dwarf fortress city of Ordumair.

FOUR CORNERS

"I s there another way out of this building than the front?" Jason asked, already hoisting up their luggage and strapping it over his shoulder.

"Well—" Goulder began.

"Wait!" Jason called and rushed over to the phone. Gripping its cords and receiver in each hand, he jerked them apart. "There, now tell us."

"Jolly good show, lad," Goulder said, giving him a pat on the back. "Now, Sir Cinaed did once tell me about a service entrance that was left unfinished in the building. It was part of why he chose it. If you can reach it, you won't be able to leave that way, but you can wait out the authorities and sneak away under the cover of dark."

"How will we do that? Won't they be looking for us?" Aria asked. "Surely they had a tail on us and know what we look like."

"Particularly given your unfortunate garb. It is impossible you went without notice," Dr. Jing lamented.

Smack! Professor Goulder slammed his fist down on the desk. "That's the answer. Whereas it is unlikely Hua and I have been tracked, you both have. Your painfully obvious outfits are the key! If you swap clothes with us, I can guarantee we'll be able to distract the authorities long enough to give you both a chance to escape."

"Oh, Professor, that's the noblest of offers, but we can't let you do that!" Aria protested, her voice catching.

"She's right," Jason concurred, rubbing her shoulders comfortingly. "If you do, there's a chance they might kill you on sight, and even if they don't, they're not above arresting and torturing you."

"We Jhi'ish are not so brutal as you imagine us," Dr. Jing said sharply.

"It's not your people I worry about. If the Jhi'ish were alone, I fully believe they would respect captives. But as long as my brother is secretly pulling the strings of Rehalcyon, they will not show you any mercy."

Clapping his hands, Goulder commanded, "There is no time for this folly. If they will kill us for helping you escape, they will kill us for speaking with you now. Cruelty needs have no bounds or distinctions, but you each are young and carry with you the seeds of tomorrow. And as your godfather, Aria, I cannot allow you to be taken. That would truly end me."

There was no exaggeration in his voice, only earnestness. Glancing out the window, Jason guessed they had only minutes until the building was stormed and all of this became moot. From the way Aria's shoulders tensed and then fell slack, she could not deny Goulder any longer.

"Very well," she conceded.

Goulder shot Dr. Jing a look of apology, and she merely smiled and nodded. "Everyone to the corners. We shall pass our clothes about with care for each other's dignity, yes?"

"Yes, Doctor," Jason affirmed.

"May the High King be with all of us," Professor Goulder solemnly intoned.

A few minutes later, the swap was complete, though Jason knew right away he was in trouble. Goulder was shorter and slighter than him, so he could not button the vested shirt nor tuck it into his belt as the professor had. The trousers were also more like breeches than pants on him. All the same, it had to suffice.

One quick glance at Aria almost stole his breath away. She was more curvaceous than the doctor, so where the dress had been somewhat loose on Dr. Jing, it was tightly fitted to Aria's body. With the makeup from the town and a quickly supplied hairpin from Dr. Jing, Aria looked like a statue one would find carved from marble by one of the great artists of Lyrscony and placed in a museum. He whispered to her, "Wow," as he shouldered their bags once more. "You look like the definition of beauty."

Her cheeks reddened. "I never felt plump before, but I'm definitely not breathing too deeply in this."

"Hey, at least you aren't like me, I'm basically a person sausage."

That earned a snicker from Aria. Final moments of levity before the severity of what lay ahead descended on them. The worst part of the too-small clothes was that their armor had to be stowed in the suitcases, leaving Jason feeling more exposed than if he were naked.

Sounds reached them from below. The authorities were coming. They were out of time.

"Go quickly, children. The chute you seek should have an access at the far end of the hall when you turn left. It will seem like a fire escape. Enter it as usual and feel along the wall for a release. It will open a dumbwaiter to carry you down the shaft. Do not move a muscle from it until you have counted enough seconds for it to be after nightfall. Which should be"—he squinted at his watch—"approximately 16,500 seconds. Understood? Dash it all, don't answer me. Just get moving if you do."

Rushing to the doorway, Aria hugged Goulder and kissed him on the cheek. Jason shook his hand smartly and said, "This is the second time you're buying me an escape. I fully expect to see you again after this one as well."

The smile Goulder wore was tight. "Nothing is more certain, lad. We will all meet in the Highland if nowhere else."

With a nod, Jason was off. He careened down the hall to where Aria waited, the service door held open. He had to finesse the luggage in, but less than a minute later, the door was shut, and they were by the dumbwaiter. Looking it over, he nodded to her. "Ladies first."

She scowled. "Not a chance. If you lower me, they could be all over you by the time I'm at the bottom. I say we raise the dumbwaiter and we climb down together."

Rubbing the bridge of his nose, he nodded. "Okay, I don't like you risking the fall, but I'm with you till the end."

Aria was already raising the dumbwaiter to the next floor for them. "Just say, 'Yes, dear,' and get over here. They'll be up to this floor any minute!"

"Yes, dear," he muttered and, against his better sensibilities, let all of their things drop to the bottom of the shaft. Hearing the thumps below, he hoped the leather bags had handled the drop. The spiritswords and armor he was certain would survive, and the clothes should be fine. Anargen's journal ... he hoped it had been cushioned by the clothes. There was no telling from this height. It was too dark to make anything out.

Well, that's good, right? We want it that dark—

"Jason?" Aria prompted as she clung to the top of the shaft's cable.

"Right, get going, I'm coming along right after." Part of him worried over the strength of the rope used for the service elevator, holding them both on it at the same time. Crouching in wait at the top of the shaft, he heard echoes of footsteps and shouts in Jhi'ish from the corridor beyond.

He grabbed hold of the cord. More yelling, the footsteps

were approaching the door into the room. Heartbeat picking up, Jason risked it and ducked inside the shaft, letting himself slide down several feet, before tightening his grip in an attempt to slow his descent. Friction bit into his hands. Heavy footfalls of the Jhi'ish soldiers entering the room echoed down to him. Already halfway down, he had to stop entirely, which only made the ache in his hands intensify.

Clenching his teeth against the pain he looked up the shaft and leaned as much against the shaft wall as he could, allowing the shadows to garb him.

His heart felt like it was leaping into his throat when a face appeared at the top of the shaft. A Jhi'ish soldier looked left, right, up, and, of course, down.

Jason held his breath, counting the precious seconds ticking away as he waited for the soldier to sound an alarm.

One. Two. Three. Four.

What was he doing, lingering there? Could he see Jason? It felt like he was staring directly into Jason's eyes.

That's when he spotted it. That same peculiar shimmer from the bomb fire in the Poseki village Kezmarepos. This time, it almost looked like it was moving toward them. If it shone down in the shaft, it could reveal them!

Five. Six. Seven.

The soldier had to see him. And certainly, the orb-shaped light hovering next to him.

Jason hadn't moved an inch, and his hands and muscles ached in concert, threatening to turn him into a twitching, sliding mess.

Eight. Nine. Ten. Eleven.

How long was this guy just going to stare blankly? Something, anything, would be better than this interminable peering into the dark.

Twelve. Thirteen. Fourteen. Fifteen.

Still no movement from the soldier or the peculiar light. Was he watching Jason by the light so he couldn't move, couldn't possibly get away? Riveted to this spot for as long as the soldier had his eyes on him?

Sixteen. Seventeen. Eighteen. Nineteen. Twenty. Twenty-one.

There was no getting around it; his grip was going to fail any second. Jason's heart beat frantically in his chest, railing against what was happening.

Twenty-two. Twenty-three. Twenty-four.

All at once, the soldier backed out of view and called out in Jhi'ish to someone unseen. If only Jason spoke Jhi'ish.

Twenty-five. Twenty-six. Twenty-seven.

The soldier didn't reappear, nor did the weird light that had been with him, but Jason knew he didn't dare move when the other man could return at any moment.

Twenty-eight. Twenty-nine. Thirty. Thirty-one. Thirty-Two.

Sounds of the door to the room opening and then slowly, slowly, slowly swinging shut meandered down the shaft to Jason.

Thirty-three. Thirty-four. Thirty-five. Thirty-six. Thirty-seven.

It was no use. He had to resume his descent or drop the last three and a half stories or more, which would not serve him or Aria well at all. Was that playing right into that soldier's hands, though?

Thirty-eight. Thirty-nine.

His grip slipped, and he barely caught it again after dropping another half floor. The whole length of cord jerked and twanged from the sudden shifting of weight tugging at it.

Well, forget counting now. If he's there, there's no way he missed that.

All the same, Jason gritted his teeth and waited. And waited.

Nothing.

Renewing his descent as slowly as his raw hands and intensely annoyed muscles would allow, he moved down, down, and then his feet were on the uneven stones of the shaft floor and sliding off a suitcase. For good measure, he banged the back of his head on the shaft wall as he wobbled to a balance.

Aria's hands shot out and steadied him. Holding him by the suspenders and pulling him close to her. They barely had enough room for the two of them down here. Inches separated their bodies.

"I think we're alone," she whispered so faintly he almost missed it.

"Yeah? I couldn't tell if all of them had left the room above." He left off the part about the recurrence of the strange light. He had failed to mention it before, and he wasn't sure if he'd really seen it this time or not.

In the dark, he couldn't really make out her expression, but he knew the moment she lay her head against his chest. "Professor Goulder," she whimpered, little tremors signaling her battle against crying for him.

"I know," he said, enfolding her in his arms. "He and Dr. Jing are going to be okay. They might even let them go."

"Knowing how things have gone in the past for us," she replied. "Dr. Jing probably is double-crossing us right now."

As if to confirm it, the wan light from above flickered as a new Jhi'ish face appeared over the shaft opening.

HAPPY ENDING

J ason bit down on his lip, partly wishing he and Aria could
separate and hug the walls, but the movement would only
make them more noticeable. Besides, if he was going to be
betrayed and hauled up for who knew what tortures to come,
he wanted to be holding Aria every second he was able.

This time, Jason had counted out more than a minute
before the onlooker muttered something in Jhi'ish, stalked
noisily to the door, and departed. This time, neither of them
dared to utter a word until Jason had counted out more than
five minutes in seconds.

"I don't want to talk crazy," he began. "But I think this
might be working."

"Shh, don't say that. Just let it play out."

"Right."

How long did they need to wait until they climbed out?
Sixteen thousand and some seconds, if he recalled Professor
Goulder's estimate correctly. How many minutes and hours
was that exactly?

Seconds later, his mental math was completed. They would
need to be down in the dark, barely moving, barely speaking,
for about four and a half hours.

Oof. Well, I did want to hold Aria like this as long as I could
…

Only his steadied heartbeat was audible, making the shaft
unnervingly quiet. His imagination threatened to panic him.
Absent sight and not trusting sound fully, Jason focused on

smell, such as the distinct fragrance of Aria's hair. Her particular, familiar scent, with distinct notes of cinnamon. A nice break in the otherwise overwhelming mustiness of the unfinished shaft.

Even if smell weren't wholly reliable either, touch was, because his arms were fully aware they held the woman he loved tight to his chest. Registering each subtle movement as she breathed in and out regularly. He rested his chin atop her head and began making small circles on her back with his raw, rope-burned hands. The last bit aside, touch was proving to be his favorite sense right now.

Minutes blurred into hours, and he realized just how hard it was to actually stand still and awake in one spot for so long. Even doing nothing, the experience was leaving him exhausted.

A gentle pressure on his cheek surprised him. Aria's hand had found its way to his face. Her soft fingertips brushed along the stubble of his chin until they found the back of his neck and pulled downward. It wasn't a perfectly smooth union on the first try, but moments later, the pressure of her lips on his flooded his senses, all of them in one with plenty to consider, to savor, to treasure. He was more than willing to return his fiancée's kiss. Not even caring, however long it had been, that they had made noticeable noises.

"There," Aria said breathily. "Now you won't go to sleep on me again."

"Asleep? What are you talking about?"

Had he gone to sleep? It was difficult to distinguish between sleep and wakefulness in their current location.

"What's your second count?"

"Around ten thousand," she replied.

"Ah," he replied. His was at more like nine thousand, so maybe he had drifted off. "Well, for the record, any time you want to wake me like that again, please do."

She giggled. "Duly noted."

Silence rushed back in to fill the space, and the next sound he heard was Aria sighing.

"You okay?"

"I'm thinking about Professor Goulder and Dr. Jing. I don't think she betrayed any of us."

"Yeah, it doesn't look like she did. She was courageous to sacrifice herself like that for a couple of strangers."

Aria shrugged. "She was, though the Jhi'ish as a rule do not execute their own people. Professor Goulder is in danger, but the worst they may do to Dr. Jing is place her in a work camp. Which, of course, is awful in its own way. If the war is won, she'll be free to live the rest of her days in peace."

Jason was triumphant. "Ha! So, you admit that we need to fight. We need to win this war."

"Shh!" Aria shushed. If there were anywhere to go, she would've pushed him away and taken off. The best she could do was stop laying her head on his chest and lean back. Much quieter than his outburst she countered, "No. That is not what I'm saying. At least, not as you understand it to mean."

Shaking his head, Jason saw no point in gamesmanship. "I have no idea what you mean by that."

With a measured tone as if working to keep the keel of their conversation even, Aria began again. "I want the Alliance to win the war. But the war itself isn't our Quest. If only you had finished Anargen's story, I think you'd understand."

"Then just skip to the end for me. What's the moral of it all? War is bad?"

He felt some of the tension in her relax, and she stopped pushing back away from him. "No. And I can't just tell you the end. The purpose of a story is to lead you to the end, so that when you arrive there, you'll understand it fully. If you skip ahead, you won't have all that makes the ending significant woven into you."

Jason whistled softly. "You have an awfully high opinion of storytelling."

She chuckled. "Have you met my grandfather?"

"Ha, fair enough."

Silence resumed briefly before she added, "It's too bad it's so dark and cramped down here. You could get some reading on the journal done."

"Yeah, right," he replied and leaned his head back against the chilly stone of the shaft.

"Do I detect some reluctance?" she asked. Sounding genuinely vulnerable, she pressed, "You aren't rethinking it, are you?"

"No, no," he was quick to reply. "I just ... with all respect to 'the journey is the destination' type talk ... I already know how the story is going to end. What I haven't sorted out yet is what you want me to glean from it."

"First, the journey isn't the destination. I said it's what makes you ready to properly appreciate the destination fully. Second, you think you already know the ending, hmm? Do tell."

"And they all lived happily ever after," he stated with storyteller flourish. "The end."

He couldn't see it, but from the subtle shifts in positioning, he could tell she was looking up at him. Was he the only one who couldn't see down here, and all the while she was boring into him with one of her thoughtful gazes?

Another sigh. "You know it isn't a fairytale, right? These things really happened."

"Yeah, yeah, of course. I do know it all really happened. But I mean, that's just how stories like that end. Why tell it if it's not going to end happily ever after?"

"And what exactly does 'happily ever after' mean to you?"

Uh-oh. That felt like a thorny question to sort out. She hadn't said it with the tone that usually forewarned he was being baited into a skewering over something. But he had resolved not to trust his hearing down here.

"You know. Everyone makes it to the end all happy and stuff. The bad guys lose. The good guys win. Happy. Ever after."

Aria's tone grew somber, quiet. "Not everyone makes it to the end. And it certainly isn't happy for everyone. Besides, what would make the ending a happy one? Everyone surviving and Ordumair being saved—those didn't happen. We know that from history alone."

"Well, yeah," Jason protested, though in fairness, he hadn't actually known all of that strictly from history. "I guess, you know, none of the main characters die."

Clucking her tongue, Aria asked, "For how long? Till after the siege ends? Till they're married? Till they have a dozen kids, grow old together? Either way, death would end each of those otherwise happy points in life."

"Well, yeah, I guess when you put it that way ..."

"So, they should never die? But if they still grew old, that would be tragic in its own way, with the pain of old age. And what if they're poor or sickly or suffering in some way? Do they need unlimited riches and bodies immune to harm and illness? Not to mention what about those they care for?"

"Fine, fine," he muttered, frustrated. "I haven't given it a lot of thought about what a 'happy ending' means."

Sounding more tired than anything, she asked, "Then how could you know the story will end happily?"

Jason just thudded his head against the wall. She hadn't even been smug over her total victory here. What exactly did he expect? What did he want for Anargen, Seren, and the others? For that matter, what did he think a "happily ever after" would look like for himself and Aria? It all did seem to be futile, a chasing after the wind.

Once more, he felt Aria's hand gently caress his cheek.

"I'm still awake," he informed her rather tersely.

"I know," her voice was as gentle and comforting as her touch. "I'm sorry. Grandfather grilled me in the same way once too. I didn't fare any better than you."

"Oh, well, that's comforting."

Ignoring his sarcastic retort, she continued. "Would you care to hear what he told me?"

"Shoot."

Taking on a deeper tone to mimic her grandfather, she began, "'You know you are a Knight of Light now, and there is one true happy ending. One that solves all the ills I put forth. The one for which everyone has been longing since the Original Rebellion ... The King's Day.

"Reunion with the High King in justice, peace, and joy, with the renewal of the Lowlands as truly part of His kingdom.

"It is what every Knight yearns for, and when it comes, it will be the happy ending that is not an end, but a beginning, as all good endings to stories must be.'"

Jason looked down at Aria. Even though he couldn't see her, he could guess she knew how he felt in that moment. Chastised, humbled, hopeful. It was a potent concoction of emotions swirling together. Though he didn't feel he fully grasped it all, he felt full from it. Satisfied.

After several seconds of silence between them, he said, "That was a great impression of your grandfather."

Aria gave a light laugh and lay her head against his chest again. "Thanks. I may have needed that particular lesson more than once."

"Somehow I find that hard to believe."

"It's true. To be fair, he's been telling me those sorts of things since I was old enough to speak ..." She trailed off, became wistful. "He's always been there for me, trying to teach me the fullest truth I can handle at any age. I hope he's all right."

That was his cue, and he tightened his hold on her, planting a kiss atop her head. His first impulse was to tell her that everything was going to be all right. To not worry about her grandfather. Though after everything she'd said, he didn't think that was the right thing to say, not the truest thing to say.

Clearing his throat, because he felt a sudden swell of anxiety at the answer that did seem best, he said in his cracked but soothing voice. "I don't know what has happened in this land. But if any of us will see the King's Day and have THE happy ending, I think it would be him."

"Jason," she said quietly.

"Yeah?"

"I love you."

"I love you too ... cinnamon cake."

She sighed and shook her head, but he didn't have to see her to know she was smiling.

That was all they said until they both reached a count of seventeen thousand. In perhaps the most awkward dance of their life, they loaded the luggage onto Jason. It felt mostly intact, including the journal.

The climb up hurt almost as much as the descent had. He wouldn't complain. Not when they had to get to Defender Black as soon as possible. He didn't know what was going on, but the moment he stepped into the Jhi'ish night and felt a rush of cold air, he guessed the dark things of the Lowlands wanted very much to ensure there was no happy ending of any kind for anyone.

*"It feels so odd, retracing so many steps of the fateful trek to
Ordumair. Our first steps in the Quest ... well, mine. It feels
equally strange that of the five of us who first embarked to the
Ord city state, only one of us is still committed to keeping the
Tower of Light from falling. I cannot shake the sensation that I
owe the Lowlands an apology that I am the one."*

—*Anargen's King's Day Journal*
12 Aurigids 1610 Middle Era

Anargen dashed down the street and ducked around the
corner. Instantly, he flattened himself against a creamy
beige stucco wall with dark wood half-timbering and fought to
still his breathing. From the alleyway, he could hear heavy
footfalls. His pursuer was close.

Looking up at the argent sky, he peered in the direction of
the Highlands and pleaded, "My King, please, don't let them
find me."

His hand drifted to the hilt of his spiritsword, though he
wasn't fully resolved to use it. An ordinance against
brandishing it in public unless first attacked had been passed
since he had last been to Estonbury. Striking first would be a
major problem, landing him in the stocks at best, and at worst—
well, he wasn't sure. The skies over the city weren't the only
thing darker here than he remembered.

The footsteps halted near the last intersection through which he had dashed.

Anargen's grip tightened further on the hilt, and he clenched his teeth. His father had warned him to stay inside, but Seren loved the cinnamon cakes they sold in the bakery here, and he gave precious little to his future wife while feeling he took a great deal. She deserved a little comfort, a little overture of conventional love and care. Despite the foolishness of doing so, he eyed the bag hanging from his shoulder. It would be a feat for him not to have smashed the cakes into mush by now.

A sound echoed in the largely empty portion of the city. It was almost like a hound's nostrils tasting deep draughts of the hunt's air.

The creature's human form took several steps away from Anargen, each lessening the tension in his body. A sudden gust, a precursor of the impending storm, cut through the alleyways encircling and blowing past Anargen.

His antagonist stopped and spun on his heels. With four purposeful strides, he was within a dozen feet of Anargen.

Whatever the rules, Anargen was ready to draw the spiritsword, beginning to slide it out of its sheath. The other man stopped fixedly, however, and called out in a husky voice, "Phosphila, do not insult us both by thinking you can hide. I know your kind's wretched stench. Rare as truffles to come upon as it may be."

For an instant, Anargen debated about revealing himself. There was no probing lilt to the beast-man's speech. He wasn't hoping to lure Anargen out. He knew exactly where the young man stood. "Your own odor is rather pungent, werebeast—even if you can't take your full beast form yet."

There was a low growl that shifted out of human octaves. "You're fortunate I'm just here to deliver a message from the

Monarch ... 'You may believe you are something, racing to Ordumair's aid. The damage you and your pitiful squad of ruffians did to the last campaign against Ordumair was an inconvenience. This time, however, I forewarn you that I intend to grind the Ords' home to dust, and if you stand against me, you with it.'"

Anargen tugged at the hilt of his sword, ready to rush out and face the beast. To his surprise and frustration, the spiritsword wouldn't slide free of its scabbard. Wiggling it around, he tried with increasing concern and futility to extricate it.

No use. It wouldn't come out.

Anargen peered around the corner, his heart hammering in his chest. If the darkling being just down the street were to find him and attack, Anargen would be in serious trouble.

His worries doubled as he saw the creature, partially transformed into its beast self, balanced on the balls of its feet, and ready to charge.

Once more, Anargen tried his blade.

Again, only failure. No, something more, a heat that made the hilt difficult to hold.

Shaking out his overheated hand, it occurred to him that he might be obstructed from initiating battle by the High King. If that was the case, then whatever came next wasn't up to him.

"Fear has finally mastered you, phosphila?" the monster that looked deceptively man-like crooned. "Finally realized how weak and worthless your whole order is?"

The last was all but a shout. Every fiber of Anargen felt torn, anger surging in him that he knew wasn't wholly misplaced, but for some reason, he was denied the right to act upon it. Not that the High King needed Anargen to defend his honor.

"Fool! You're making a scene!"

Anargen stiffened. There was someone else with the creature.

A snarl tinged the beast's retort. "What if I am? I don't serve you."

"Perhaps," the new speaker allowed. "But the accord with your master doesn't allow room for such folly. I've worked my influence in Hildecrest to make sure the Vogteremark stays out of your master's war. You terrorizing Estonbury is undermining my efforts."

That voice ... it's the town's mayor!

Anargen had only met the mayor once, during their last trip to Estonbury. They had been seeking allies in the early days of the War of Restoration and in hopes of shoring up support for the Quest. That trip had been an utter failure, and the broad-shouldered former soldier who had claimed the mayorship not many months before then had laid low two centuries of Dag Votere tradition of support for the Knights of Light. In fact, during those two hundred years, the mayors had all been Knights themselves.

"You also promised you'd hand over all the Knights of Light to us. Yet, here I am, following one now."

The mayor snorted. "I never said I'd hand them over to you, only that I'd keep them from interfering. And I have. No Dag Votere Knights have dared to step out of line."

"You had best keep it so. The Monarch will not suffer those to live who cannot keep their word. Understood?"

There was a beat of silence before the mayor answered. "I'll consult with the Knights of the local halls. Apply pressure to get them to turn over these foreign Knights you seek. The Vogteremark is committed to peace with the rightful government of Ecthelowall."

It took all Anargen's restraint to wait until he heard both sets of steps clomping over the cobblestone of the street before moving. He didn't waste a moment more before sprinting from the alley and wending his way back to Estonbury's Knight Hall. He went straight for the quarters assigned to him and his father and burst in to find Glewdyn and Seren in discussions with the Knight Errant of the Hall, Matthias.

Taking in the surprised expressions, Anargen struggled to rein in his breathing, knowing he needed to explain himself. It wasn't easy. If what the mayor had said was true, then Sir Matthias was complicit in everything. Would it be wise to tip his hand that he knew about the arrangement? Or would it be better to confront him?

"Anargen, son?" Glewdyn prompted. "What is wrong?"

Swallowing and finally evening out his breaths, Anargen opted to be direct.

He told everything that had transpired—including, to the reddening of both his Seren's cheeks, acquiring the cakes for Seren.

At the end, Glewdyn's hazel eyes rested heavily on Sir Matthias, somewhere between anger and expectation. The former was a rare thing to see in his father. "When last we were here, you told us you could not give us any aid beyond well wishes because your people did not want to become entangled in the war. Tell me what my son overheard isn't true. Tell me you have not turned your back on your brothers in arms and on your oaths to the High King!"

Sir Matthias leaned back from the accusation. His old face seemed all the more weathered by time, the little gullies of worry deepened around his brows, and his spindly thumbs twiddled with anxious energy. "We are not so loathsome as we've been made to sound. But we are enough."

Deep-set blue eyes, steeped in regret, fell on Anargen. "Child, are you certain the mayor saw the agent of the

Monarch in his beastly form? Does the mayor truly know what sort of pact he has made?"

Anargen nodded. "He saw him partially transformed. Whether he understands the depth of the darkness with which he bargains, I can't say. He has a reputation for being a bold warrior, decisive and fierce, yes? Perhaps he thinks he can best the dark if it betrays him."

"Don't all Dag Votere have that reputation?" Seren chimed in. "Just because they were warriors in the past doesn't mean that heart still beats in them."

"Hmph," Sir Matthias grunted and started to speak, but let his long jaw stay slack as he appeared to reconsider his words. "My people have that reputation and perhaps have grown softer in the years of peace and abundance. Comfort has sapped our strength less than our virtue, I daresay. Our mayor likes the money we earn from trade with the Ecthel Monarchists. It keeps us atop the Knors, who are still as brutal and ambitious as our people began. It makes such a treaty—"

"Forgive me for any impertinence," Glewdyn interrupted. "We need not stand here and talk of Vogteremark politics, nor its history, nor even what has already passed between us. What matters is what you intend to do today. That will define you.

"We have witnessed Estonbury's mayor consorting with agents of the Dark Prince."

Matthias began to protest, but Glewdyn held up a finger, his own aged face hardened by severity. "There is no point in questioning whether Monarch Ilyron is serving the Dark Prince. We have witnessed the darkness and spoken with others who confirm it. Believe what you will, but the matter at hand is whether you will help us stop the destruction of Ordumair or not."

"No one has seen a dragon since Tislatna's fall!" Sir Matthias insisted without much resolve. What solidity his words had melted under the fiery fury of Glewdyn's gaze. "It's just so hard to ... you don't understand what dangers it will present for ..."

"We all face grave danger on the Quest, but we must trust the High King's plans and ways are above ours."

Flushing red and scowling, Sir Matthias shot back, "Don't jest. The mayor is well-connected to Hildecrest. Going against him would ruin life for the Order in the Vogteremark's lands. Do you genuinely expect us to risk this Hall and every other in the country for your rumors?"

Glewdyn sighed. "There is no need for us to speak further. We will gather our things and ride on at first light. You need do nothing more for us. Except leave us. Now."

"Yes, well, perhaps it is best you leave Estonbury swiftly," Sir Matthias concurred. Then, as if uncovering something disgusting, he added, "That's your problem—you Libertians have always had an inflated sense of your own righteousness, haven't you?"

Anargen gaped at the insult and turned to his father. The older man said nothing until Sir Matthias had shuffled over to the door out of the room. "And that's your problem—we aren't Libertians. We are Knights of Light. We were born in Libertias, but our hearts belong to the Highland and its King. Do yours really belong to the Vogteremark above all others?"

The elder of the Hall stiffened. He returned Glewdyn's hard stare for several seconds and then slammed the door shut behind him.

MORNING WAS JUST as bleak as the evening before. A storm was likely to roll in and buffet them most of the way to Ordumair. After he helped Seren up onto her horse, Anargen went to his father, who had just finished loading the last saddle bag. "We're ready to leave?"

Glewdyn glanced at his son, his expression almost apologetic. "Looks that way."

"Very well." Anargen rocked on his heels, wrestling with how he felt about their sudden departure. None of it felt right. But when did it feel right or good to be betrayed by friends? "It's customary to depart with a blessing or admonition in the High King's name," he blurted out.

"It is, for Knights of Light departing from brothers and sisters in arms. I don't know that we are."

Anargen could hear the hurt in Glewdyn's voice. It was Sir Cinaed's high regard for the Knights in Estonbury from the years he had lived there, Sir Matthias in particular. It felt almost a dismissal of Cinaed to not honor their hosts.

"I dropped a satchel of money on the steps to the Hall's entry portico," Glewdyn noted.

That pretty much sealed the slight. Knights for centuries operated with the expectation of hospitality from one another fully at the host's expense and with no mention of the cost. That Glewdyn paid them for their stay was a sharp if subtle rebuke.

"Then we should get going," Anargen mumbled and scurried over to his horse, mounting it before the clouds of inner turmoil could catch up and match those overhead.

He undid his mount's tethering and gently urged the sorrel horse out of the stall, coming alongside Seren and his father. Glewdyn raised his arm to give the command to ride.

"You there! Wait!"

Anargen half turned to look back. Sir Matthias bustled toward them, a small satchel in his hand. It took him almost a minute to reach them with his age-labored gait. Once he did, he tossed the bag up to Glewdyn. "May the High King's favor be yours on the road ahead."

Frowning for an instant, Glewdyn dithered before seeming to concede something. "And may his favor rest upon you as well."

Seemingly satisfied, Sir Matthias backed away and shuffled back into the Hall.

Once he was out of view, Glewdyn motioned for them to leave, and they got a few miles out from Estonbury before he opened the sack. Immediately, his brows knit. From the bag, he produced another smaller pouch and a rolled bit of parchment in addition to the coins.

Tossing the tiny pouch to Anargen, it took only a second of holding it for the young Knight's concern to turn to amusement.

"What is it?" Seren asked, looking befuddled by the range of reactions the others had.

Anargen sniffed in the sweet scent of the sack and handed it on to Seren. "This is meant for you."

Looking uneasy, she undid the cinch on the sack and then chuckled. From it, she produced a single cinnamon cake. This one undamaged. She didn't waste a second more in taking a bite of the treat and let out a little satisfied moan of contentment.

"It looks like we owe them for this," Glewdyn commented with an air of dismissal. He passed the note on to Anargen and then spurred his horse on.

The note was simple: "We serve the High King. I make no promises, but if we are able, look for us two nights hence."

Anargen felt a tension that had held him since Peter's March relax. They weren't in this alone, and not all of those they depended on had betrayed their trust.

73

FATE

"This is it," Aria whispered to him. "This is where Grandfather wanted us to meet him."

Jason whistled. Standing before an enormous gate with oxidized copper bars as thick as a man's arm, he had to say, Jhi City was certainly an interesting place. Unlike Bham or any of the other Jhi'ish cities they'd been to so far, it was neither stuck in the past nor barreling toward the future. It was both. For more than a mile in all directions, there were towers of the same fuchsia glass and grey concrete as in Bham, though taller. There were also more factories and every conceivable mark of a modern city of the Lowlands, including rail lines, cars, an air strip, and a bevy of dirigibles drifting like specters over the city, going to and fro.

The city's layout appeared to be a series of concentric rings. Most modern outermost, with the next reflecting slightly older influences from across the Lowlands that would only have trickled in since the Middle Era. This was followed by another still older-looking ring of development. And at last, the heart of Jhi City, which was an eerily well-preserved iteration of itself from almost a millennium past. Pointed terracotta-roofed architecture and an explosion of colored banners and lanterns strung about were present in this inmost circle. Old and new, existing side by side, seemingly organically, yet very much planned. As if the whole thing were a museum exhibit on Jhi City's past. Included in this was the Terracotta Palace that housed the Zhuhou of Jhi, its highest noble and ruler, who, if

Jason remembered correctly, hailed from a dynasty in its twentieth generation. Unbroken in all those years. Perhaps that was why Jhi City had such a long view of its history. The continuity from antiquity to present felt unbroken here.

Especially in what they called Dìbā Huán, "The Eighth Ring"—which he didn't know how they arrived at the count of eight, but it was Jhi'ish superstition that eight was the greatest and luckiest of numbers. Outside Jhi, it was known as the Jade Garden. More than a simple hedge maze, it had eight-foot terracotta walls capped with verdant bushy plants and a small forest with trees that had been grown into twisting patterns around one another and into all manner of shapes, from arches over paths to what resembled an enormous hand reaching into the sky. All along each of its eight concentric rings were also statues made entirely of jade, polished to glistening and expertly carved into poses and scenes that reflected every facet of Jhi'ish life and history.

Flowers of all sorts also grew in the garden, such that something bloomed every season of the year. A marvel of horticulture and architecture, nature and innovation synergized. It was perhaps Jhi's most famous monument and attraction. Which made it all the more curious a choice for Defender Black to insist they rendezvous here.

They had been walking through it for some time now, and it was almost midnight. Fortunately, the garden remained open continuously, lit at intervals by artistically crafted oxidized-copper lamps. In a few spots, it even incorporated electric lighting to enhance dramatic effects, though those were primarily in the two outermost rings.

"I'm going to go ahead and say it: I have a bad feeling about this."

Aria bounced one shoulder up. "I'm not thrilled either. Grandfather's note was eerily specific about the date and time we should be here. We're to meet him at the sculpted scene: 'The Aperture of Fate.'"

"Right. Not ominous at all ... did the Jhi'ish really name it that?"

Aria waited until they had slipped from ring six into ring five under what looked like thin cypress trees that had been coaxed into growing into a vaulted arch. "Well, it's my translation. I meant aperture as in an opening, not specifically the one for a camera. I suppose it just sounded more dramatic than 'The Opening in Fate.'"

"What, you, dramatic?" he chuckled.

She paused and turned to face him, her chin raised. "I don't know, am I?"

For an instant, he took the challenge at face value, then saw the sly smile turning up the corner of her mouth. "Oh, I don't know about that," he replied smoothly. "I would say, 'beautiful' and 'incredible' are only the first 'rings' in what describes you."

Her cheeks flushed red, and she grabbed one of his hands, towing him along. "Come on, you. I don't know where you got your smooth tongue, but if you're going to speak that way, I'd prefer it in safer and more private quarters."

"As you wish, my cinnamon cake," he crooned in his most velvet voice.

He thought he might have heard a little edge of contentment mixed into her huff in response to his new pet name for her. It was something of a tease for him now, but somehow, he thought she liked it. It echoed with the warmth, mystery, and tenderness of when they'd first met.

Clack.

Jason whirled around, looking behind them on the path they'd come from. There was nothing. Just the winding granite walkways, similar to the one in Bham, gleaming in the lamplight. Perhaps a bird had dropped a stone pilfered from one of the many jade fountains.

The disruption in the sounds of babbling waters and nighttime insects and birds didn't seem to trouble Aria. Continuing to tow him along, she reminded, "We don't have much time till we're supposed to meet Grandfather."

Along path after path, ring after ring, they made their way until they were at what looked to be the focal point of the whole garden. A giant ring cast in the same oxidized copper as elsewhere, bearing reliefs of all sorts of scenes chronicling Jhi'ish history around its curvatures in what was most certainly gold leaf if not solid gold. At the center was a mirror that made the whole thing seem like an eye.

Standing before it was a duster-clad old man. Sir Cinaed was waiting for them along with someone else.

Aria broke into a run, "Grandfather!" she called.

The elder Black turned, seeming unsurprised, and opened his arms to receive her. "Oh! My dear, you have come as I hoped. And with quite a squeeze for these old bones."

Jason came up and offered his hand, "Hale evening, sir! It does us good to see you well."

Giving Jason's hand a firm shake, Cinaed jerked him into a hug, slapping him on the back. "Ah, hale evening indeed. Well done, the both of you, for finding your way to me."

Glancing to his left, he placed his hand over his face and said, "My manners are withered to nothing. My children, this is Yúzé Guo, Defender of the Northeastern Realm.

"Sir Guo, this is my granddaughter, Lady Aria Black, and her fiancé, Sir Jason Landsby."

Roughly a head shorter than Jason, Sir Guo was still imposing. His armor was thick and segmented in such a way that Jason could tell he was powerfully built. A stern, angular face with few wrinkles meant he wasn't nearly so old as some of the Defenders of other Realms, though at least two decades Jason's senior. His ink-black hair was pulled back into a simple knot, and he sported a sleek mustache and goatee. His sharp eyes flitted quickly from person to person and then to their surroundings before returning to those before him.

The Defender bent his arm at ninety degrees to his body and gave a slight bow, a conventional Jhi'ish gesture of respect. "It is an honor, dear ones," he replied in very thickly accented Ecthelish, his voice both resonant and soothing. He exuded the aura of a natural leader.

"The honor is ours, sir," Jason said on his and Aria's behalf when she gave him a subtle nudge of her elbow to do the speaking. Jhi'ish must have some rule about that as well.

Stroking his thick grey beard, Sir Cinaed glanced at a watch on his wrist. "Should be any moment now, we'll be able to get out without notice."

"Forgive me, sir, but whose notice are we attempting to skirt?" Jason asked. "I know we aren't wanted here, but here we are all the same."

Valleys of wrinkles on Cinaed's weathered old face deepened, and his piercing gray eyes locked onto Jason, seeming to probe him for resilience for what he was about to say.

"Confederacy forces from the Rehalcyon Empire offered their services in rounding up and dealing with any foreigners and nationals accompanying them who are identified as dissidents against their cause."

"In short, all of us," Yúzé summarized.

"Yes, all of us," Cinaed agreed with such an emphasis that Jason guessed their meeting had been successfully concluded with Yúzé agreeing to participate in the Council of Defenders, which meant the last holdout was now on board.

"That's fantastic," Jason blurted out and then immediately

grimaced and had to backpedal when both men shot him a quizzical look. "Not that they're after us, but that we stand united."

"We are Knights of Light," Yúzé's tone indicated the matter was settled.

Placing his hand on Yúzé's shoulder, Cinaed grinned through his bushy beard. "Now that our dear brother in arms has agreed to come to the council, it is our duty to deliver him there safely."

Jason couldn't help sharing a look of sheer wonder with Aria at this tremendous news. The gathering of the full council would be the first in perhaps a millennium. It could marshal all of the Knights in the Lowlands against the dark forces Dorian was conjuring and planned to unleash.

Aria beat Jason to asking the next key question that inevitably resulted: "Grandfather, this is wonderful news, but why meet here? It is relatively exposed and open. Why didn't you and Defender Yúzé already leave Jhi City and meet us somewhere remote to make the rest of the journey?"

Their Jhi'ish compatriot spoke up, his tone solemn. "The High King spoke to me in a dream. The Tower of Light is once more at stake, and my joining the Quest successfully requires each of us to triumph."

His hard face softened some, even becoming a bit sly. "As for this place, you will see shortly why we chose here."

WHIZZ! CRACK! BOOM!

Jason leaped away from the source of the explosions, immediately moving to protect Aria. He found her crouched defensively but already breathing a sigh of relief. A green pall passed over her face and vanished.

Whirling around, Jason just caught the tail residual sparkles of the firework that had just been launched. He let out a breath that carried with it the tension in his chest as well.

BOOM. WHIZZ. BOOM. BOOM.

More fireworks joined the opening and soon filled the sky in a dazzling array of colors and shapes, some expertly placed to resemble flowers or a sunset. It was one of the most impressive displays Jason had ever seen. Rehalcyon had fireworks on key days of remembrance, but they were more about size and volume than artful presentation.

Brow furrowed, Jason tried to speak over the explosive sounds. "This is lovely, but how does it help us get you both safely out of the city, much less Jhi?"

"Hmm?" Sir Cinaed asked, his face scrunched as he leaned over to better hear.

"How does this help?" Jason reiterated.

The old man nodded and pointed at the mirror. "When the last rocket is spent, you'll see something special about this garden about which only a handful have ever known. It will help us to escape."

He patted Jason on the arm vigorously. "In the meantime, enjoy."

That was it then. Everything they had been hoping for over the past two years. A united army of Knights of Light riding out against the sinister forces to forever vanquish them. The Alliance would win the war and recognize the High King's sovereignty over the Lowlands once more because of it.

"The King's Day is upon us, isn't it?" Jason said like a child opening his presents on the week of Starshine. "We're living it!"

Cinaed cocked his head as if he hadn't heard again, and Jason just waved him off good-naturedly and turned to Aria, beaming.

She was watching the fireworks, her breaths halted as if she could scarcely take in all the richness of what was transpiring. Jason took her hands in his, which pulled her attention to him.

Her conflicted expression melted into a smile that parted her ruddy lips.

"Care for a dance?" he asked her.

Tilting her head, she laughed. "I suppose I would. Provided I have the right partner, you know, one who can actually dance."

He smirked and nodded as if saying, "Okay, okay," to her cheeky jab. Pursing his lips, he leaned forward and whispered into her ear, "We both have found the right partner, till death do us part."

Her eyes flicked up to his face, and he felt her pulse liven. With delicate care, he put one hand on her lower back and kissed her hand as he took it in the first step of the Brackenburgh Waltz. It was perhaps the most suave and romantic thing he had ever done. He hoped she wouldn't point out that it was the only slow dance he knew.

After a few seconds of gliding over the polished stones of the Jade Garden's heart, there was no denying that his words, this dance, and probably the news they'd received were intensely affecting her. Maybe it was his earnestness as much as his choice of words that had sent Aria off kilter. There was distance to her gaze, even as she rested against his chest and seemed to lose herself in the dance.

Almost dreamily, she murmured to him, "You know, this garden is considered good fortune for couples?"

At least that's what Jason thought he heard her say. As they spun toward the "Aperture," he rolled a shoulder. "I can believe that."

She nodded toward the enormous ring behind them. "Jhi'ish couples come here for a ceremony. Arriving separately and each walking up to the Aperture of Fate as individuals. They stand before the mirror together, embrace, and then leave together, confident their future together, their fate, is sealed with good fortune."

That made the mirror seem a little less random. The symbology of themselves reflected in this portal to a fate they desired all to see. "That sounds nice. Almost like a wedding ceremony."

"Oh, it usually is for them," she agreed, her voice choked.

She stopped dancing.

"Hey, are you okay?" he asked, giving her hand another kiss. It felt clammy, and her cheeks were flushed.

"We could do it. Here. Now. We should do it."

"Do it?" He watched her brows bend in a look of expectation and pleading that cut through his usual blockheadedness like a hot knife through butter. "Oh! You mean," he gestured to them and then to the Aperture.

Aria nodded, truly sheepish for maybe the first time since he'd known her. And why not? Throughout their relationship, she had, perhaps with some struggle, allowed him to lead. To make the first moves. This was her taking an enormous, spontaneous step.

"Okay," he said, knowing not to crack a joke or smirk or any of the other obtuse things he was given to do that would ruin the moment. And this most certainly was a moment. He could feel it, them on the edge of the fate they'd been moving toward ever since he walked into the Black River Inn. Together for life. Riding out in service of the High King as the Lowlands were made new. He had been wrong earlier. This was everything now. All his hopes wound up into a single night. In a foreign land, maybe. But a beautiful one, under the most spectacular fireworks and in probably the most romantic venue they would find—not that either of those were essential to the equation. The sum of him plus her balanced nicely with all the rest of the externalities subtracted away.

He realized when she tilted her head as if to say, "Okay?" that he'd failed to finish his answer.

Looking away to keep from bursting out into a goofy, raucous, joyous laugh at his own silliness, he beamed her the brightest, most effortless smile of his life. "Yeah. I'd love to. Like you said—let's do it."

Aria looked like a spring, coiled to its max compression and ready to launch straight into his arms and bowl him over. But she had always been more levelheaded and managed to rein in what was for his ego a very comfortingly deep well of excitement at the prospect of binding herself to him for life. "You have to tell Grandfather."

"Okay," he agreed, glancing over at the old man and seeing him standing to the side, silently staring off away from the fireworks rather than watching them with Yúzé. "And you're sure? Now? No more waiting till I finish the journal?"

"Now," she affirmed, shaking his hands, some of her exuberance leaking out and turning his arms into resonators. This was definitely a new side of her he was seeing. Weirdly— he really needed to stop thinking it was weird—he loved it. With every facet, every new angle of viewing Aria from, he only loved her more. Which was decidedly not something he had ever expected to find in all the Lowlands.

None of my life since meeting her has been what I expected.

"Right," he agreed, managing to regain control of his limbs from her. "I'll be right back." He couldn't resist now giving her a little wink as he walked over. He spun around to face Cinaed before she could roll her eyes or put her head in her hands and rethink the whole lifetime-with-him thing.

Jason sucked in a sharp breath. Prepping himself for this next conversation, which would feel very different from the raucous joy of the last. Yeah, he had asked the elderly Knight for his granddaughter's hand before he had ever proposed, but this was sudden. And final. And even if planned as an eventuality, this was the sort of profound change that, even if good, could strain people.

So, as Jason cleared his throat and tried to coax out the words that he should say, needed to say, he wasn't surprised at first by Cinaed's reticence and distractedness. "Sir, um, Defender Black. Hey, uh, hi, um ..." This wasn't going well. Or at all. When did the smooth-talking Jason Landsby turn befuddled?

His next bumbling appeal died on his lips as concern and gravity overtook Cinaed's wizened old face. Unease swept over Jason. "Sir?" he prompted.

Grabbing hold of Jason's arms as though he needed them for support, Cinaed looked up at him. There was a depth of dread there that Jason had never seen before in the storyteller. Cinaed's voice sounded choked, and Jason was afraid the elder man was having a heart attack. "Go ... go ... see if we have ... company coming."

That was an odd thing to say. But he obliged the elderly Knight and ran to the nearest hedge wall, climbing up onto the terracotta rim in one leap. Pulling himself up, he peered over the prickly green foliage. Jason's heart immediately sank, and though he could only speculate how Cinaed had known about it, he understood instantly both the apprehension on his weathered face and his comment about "company."

Arrayed before the entrance, and the only viable exit, to the garden was a small army. One hostile to them.

9

HAUNTED

"We left Ordumair when it was still in ruins, like a jouster who has only just marshalled himself enough to rise to his feet after being unseated. I had thought by now the jouster would be seated once more. Will my expectations about what I'll find along this journey ever align with reality?"

-- Anargen's King's Day Journal
15 Fylleth 1610 Middle Era

There were torches placed to light the way through the jagged stone remnants of Castle Valesgard. Eerie and still, the Ords did not bother to have more than a pair of lone sentries watching from the last teetering segment of curtain wall left standing. With all the pointed shards of broken stone and timbers still scattered about, it was as if they walked among the fossilized remains of an ancient beast instead of a vital defensive point and structure for securing the Valley of Ords beyond.

Whereas the first time Anargen came upon Valesgard, there had been hundreds of Ord soldiers stationed here and merely approaching prompted a cadre of soldiers to intercept them, these lone sentries waited until they were in the midst of winding their way through the wreckage before calling out, "You tharr! Halt where ya stand!"

Anargen had to suppress a smile. He had missed the thick

Ord burr. He almost failed to comply, but his father caught him by the chest and forced him to a stop. Good thing, too. A glimmer in the torchlight hinted that at least one of the two Ords had a bow with an arrow notched and ready to let fly.

"Good sirs," Glewdyn began. "We bring important news for your honorable Thane."

The Ord scoffed. "Are you wounded in your head? You cannot simply stroll into the Thane's private council on request!"

"Sir, we speak out of turn. It is not ours to decide who does and doesn't receive messages such as those we carry. Perhaps instead of your honorable Thane, there is another to whom we may deliver our report of impending danger? One for whom the message would be beneficial to hear and act upon swiftly?"

"What rot! You hunger— "

"Quiet, Guern," the bow-bearing Ord snapped. Lowering his bow, the sentry stepped forward so that his face was better illuminated. He seemed to be sizing up the group, as a fisherman might his catch.

"Very well," he concluded and shouldered his bow. Jumping down a series of stone fragments that served as makeshift stairs, the Ord strode up to them. He was of average height and build for an Ord and in his early middle age by the look of slight wrinkling and the braided, sandy blonde beard he sported. The bowman wore a deep blue tunic over silvery mail ringlets and had a helm dented and grooved from combat. On his tunic was emblazoned an insignia, but not the one for the Ords as a people. That crest looked familiar to Anargen.

Oh, ugh. Not him.

"Very well, hungerman. You will follow me.

"Guern, you run ahead and tell Elder Tengrath that we have ... messengers he may wish to interrogate."

The sharper-tongued and evidently younger Ord made the same trek down the rubble. He scowled. "Can't we send Brenor instead? I'd rather stay and guard the castle all night than walk a foot on behalf of this filth!"

"Do as you're told, boy," the archer Ord spat. "If you want to remain under Tengrath's banner, you'll take commands from your betters. Now be off!"

The welp took off at a clumsy run, eventually tripping over his own feet and tumbling through the grass. His captain sighed and grumbled something, eyeing Anargen and the others coolly, as if daring them to laugh.

No one did, especially now that they knew a third Ord who had never presented himself watched them even now.

Knowing Ords and their love of four, they probably have another sentry as well.

On impulse, Anargen blurted out, "Will the two sentries you've got left be an acceptable posting for Valesgard?"

The archer narrowed his eyes, but didn't correct Anargen, confirming his hunch about the second hidden guard. "This way, hungermen. The less you speak, the more likely you are to make it alive to see the Elder."

Glewdyn gave a nod of deference and spurred his horse slowly on. Anargen fell in line after him, gritting his teeth but trying not to let on his concern to Seren or his father. Given that they couldn't speak freely, it would be too difficult to convey the thorniness of their current situation. Elder Tengrath had attempted to depose Thane Duncoin during the battle to defend Ordumair from the Monarch's first attack. He was no friend of the Knights of Light, and though his coup failed, he had apparently managed to maintain his title and at least some loyal retainers. That meant he was connected and wielded influence. Passing this message through him would probably earn him favor with the Thane, which he could use later for who knew what ends.

Which in turn meant that the simple bowman guarding the castle wasn't so simple. That's why he deliberated about bringing them to Tengrath instead of just bellowing at them like a wild beast. He was shrewdly assessing the pieces on the political game board.

Despite his attempt to remain impassive, Anargen grimaced. On the frontlines of the war, he hadn't had to deal with intrigue and conniving. Enemies were obvious and direct about attacking, spears and swords out and swiping. Not daggers and poisons and whispered ruin dealt from shadows birthed by midnight deal-making.

They passed beyond the remnants of Valesgard and the valley opened up before them. In the pale moonlight, Anargen could make out the silhouette of Fior-sruthain, the massive mountain into which Thane Ordumair II had begun building an enormous fortress and city complex that had been the curse and pride of the Ords ever since. Seeing its shape again brought back torrents of memories, some good, many fraught. And many, many of Sir Cinaed. He sucked in a sharp breath as an ache spread through his chest.

He hadn't braced himself for this properly. Hadn't considered that seeing this place would make it impossible not to think about, to remember, his felled mentor. The pain deepened and spread. Cinaed had spent his childhood here, been victimized and cast off like a leper by those he'd embraced as his own, and returned ready to give his life for them. He would be here now, doing so again, if only ...

Anargen began humming the song that would forever haunt him. Though penned by someone else many years earlier, it was Sir Cinaed, singing it as they passed through Bracken's woods on their first journey to Ordumair, that had ingrained the words in Anargen's mind. Cinaed's mellifluous performance had sunk the melody into Anargen's bones. He skipped the first verse and jumped to the seasonally appropriate one. The first to darken with the understanding of its tragic quality.

> *"Clinking coins, through Autumn to spend,*
> *Your brow's sweat blesses where'er you wend,*
> *Empty place hearthside we would amend,*
> *Will you be home again?*
> *Will you be home, will our wait ever end?*
> *What friend may we seek, for our hearts' rends?"*

Though he kept his voice low enough to elude detection from their Ord envoy, Seren had caught the tune and watched him, her brown eyes filling with tears. She hadn't been here, hadn't known Cinaed as he did. But she knew what he had meant to Anargen, and so this song about a father who never returned from war, the saddest Anargen's mountain homeland of Walhonde had ever borne, had pierced her through as well. That keenness of insight, that tenderness of heart, and oneness of grief and joy shared between them were why he would love Seren fiercely to his dying breath.

A frigid breeze cut through the landscape, reminiscent of the next line that spoke of "Bitter winter winds ..." Anargen couldn't continue. If he did, he knew he would annoy their "host" at best and completely shatter at worst. This pain. This loss ... He needed to set it aside, box it away until a time when it could be handled with the care Cinaed's memory deserved. Only, he didn't know if any such time would ever come. Not until the High King's Day arrived and he made the Lowlands new. So, the lump in Anargen's throat that stolidly refused to be dispelled and the dull ache radiating from his core that would only deaden enough to tolerate but not abate—these he carried with him into Ordumair's half-repaired gates. It was fitting, in a way. Ordumair, like Anargen, had never fully recovered from its wounds and remained haunted by what it had endured.

10

ON A RAZOR'S EDGE

*"For decades, the politics of Ordumair have become increasingly
esoteric and dwelt with the specter of turmoil and scheming
lurking in the shadows. But the darkness has gathered, night has
fallen, and the shadows are all around us."*

*Anargen's King's Day Journal
15 Fylleth 1610 Middle Era*

At the gate was a small cluster of Ords. Some, Anargen could tell, had been assigned the duty of keeping guard of the primary entryway. A few more looked to be on patrol for the small clustering of homes and farms permitted outside the fortress and city. In the dark, it was difficult to determine how much of the late-season crop was planted and thriving.

Their guide walked them straight up to the largest group of Ords. The one centrally located, bearing the deepest blue tunic and cape with brilliant silvery plate mail encrusted with rare jewels and fine trim, was Tengrath. Still sporting ruddy locks, with little streaks of gray interspersed now, he, like the sentry Ord at Valesgard, had his beard braided, only his had gold beads dangling from his four braids. It was the hardness of his jaw's set and the calculating glint to his gaze that were the most memorable. This broad specimen of Ord was about as much a villain as any Anargen had ever met.

The galloping pace Guern had taken had given ample time for the Elder to make his grand appearance. Anargen could tell the moment that recognition of who he was registered with the dwarf. A little lift to his heavy brows, and then Tengrath's whole expression soured. With how much disdain the Ord held for Knights, it was a shock he had come down and not sent orders to imprison or kill them outright. To his right stood another Ord elder. Identifiable as such from his noble, if less ostentatious, garb. This elder was slighter and older than Tengrath. Oddly enough, he too looked familiar, though Anargen hadn't placed the face yet.

Once closer, the emblem this Ord wore was discernibly Elder Ironhold's. But this wasn't Ironhold, whom Anargen knew to be deceased.

Who can it be then? Wait, Feingohl!

He had been elevated to noble status after the disgrace and death of Ironhold. Anargen and Caeserus had convinced him to speak with Sir Cinaed during the siege of Ordumair, and through that simple act of tolerance and openness, Ordumair and the Ords had been spared much suffering. Though with sentries spouting insults and acting so dubiously, was there any chance he was still an ally of the Order? And why was he by Tengrath's side now?

"Anargen of Black River, you have returned to Ordumair's lands," Tengrath addressed him. "With an entourage of fellow ... Knights."

The last was so strained that Anargen knew he had only just held back from calling them by the old slur for Knights, "hungermen."

"Elder Tengrath and Elder Feingohl, it is an honor to be here and speak with you again. I am joined by my father, Sir Glewdyn, and fiancée, Lady Seren. I take it your servant has already informed you of our urgent need to speak with the Thane?"

Tengrath's eye twitched. "Yes, my subordinate delivered

the message during my meeting with Elder Feingohl," Tengrath replied, shooting a dark glance over his shoulder where the young Guern stood head down, quite piqued.

Looking over at Feingohl, Anargen found him to be strangely sanguine. Masking his true sentiments well.

"Wonderful," Tengrath grumbled. The fullest measure of cordiality he could muster, it seemed.

"I should escort Sir Anargen and his kin to see the Thane," Feingohl announced with a rather pointed look at Tengrath. "Much as I did during the Siege."

The faint pall of a scowl Tengrath wore deepened noticeably. Almost imperceptibly, Feingohl smirked in response.

Oh, no. Feingohl being here might've rescued us, but it wasn't because he's favorable to us. He's trying to use us to increase his favor with the Thane!

Suddenly, Tengrath's heavy brows lifted. "No, no, dear Feingohl. We should both stay here and conclude our business. I'll send my loyal bawrnig, Harold, here on with them. He brought them this far after all."

Tengrath didn't even look at anyone he had just mentioned. Rather, his full attention and the curling of his lip into a sneer were for Feingohl's benefit. Or torment.

Feingohl still managed to keep his features schooled, even if he did seem to bounce on his feet, seething. "Very well. I shall send my bawrnig, Wernsted, as well. Guests as important as these deserve a proper escort."

"Proper?" Tengrath bristled.

"Apologies, a fuller escort," Feingohl amended, his voice steady as stone, even though beneath it all, Anargen could detect the smugness radiating off him.

Within the gates, Ordumair was darker than Anargen expected. Lamps burned low, giving just enough light to navigate the thoroughfares and wind up the levels towards those at the top where the Thane and other nobles dwelt. Anargen remembered the rich glow and steady heat of many lamps and hearths burning, which made the imposing interior of Ordumair feel like more than just the place the Ords lived; it had felt like their home. Now, a heavy odor of mildew and mold permeated the lower levels, and green lines of moss traced the once-pristine stones of the streets and walls. From the chill in the air and little whistling gusts, Anargen could tell the upper levels hadn't yet been repaired sufficiently to seal all the gaps in the fortress created when the Great Bulwark was sundered by cannon fire from the rest of Ordumair. Most concerning was that there were so few Ords about. True enough, it was late, but within the mountain, Ordumair had been largely impervious to time's dictates on schedules and rules.

"So, few remain," he mumbled to himself.

Bawrnig Harold, whirled around in mid-stride. He was on Anargen in an instant, shoving him backward, so that Anargen had to wildly windmill his arms to keep from tumbling down the curving ramp that wound up the structure of Ordumair's civil areas.

"Careful with your temper, Harold," Wernsted chided, apparently as steeped in the power play between Feingohl and Tengrath as his patron.

Pointing a thick finger at the other officer, Harold seethed, "It's not enough that these hungermen keep coming one after another. They also dare to mock our suffering and losses that they caused!"

"How can we be responsible for what has transpired here?" Seren asked, her voice charged with emotion. Anargen tried to shake his head at her in warning. It was so rare for her to strike a strident note with others. Unfortunately, while her passion and point were valid, this wasn't the battle to pick.

"You'll do well to keep quiet, swamp hag," Harold spat.

Anargen was striding forward to deck the impudent dwarf when a stiff arm caught his chest and blocked him. His father had stepped between him and the Ord.

"Your opinions are your own, Ord," he said with as much calm as he seemed to be able to muster as well. "But they do nothing to relieve you of our company and indeed only forestall it. If you spent less time insulting virtuous women and taking offense at what is genuine empathy for your people's plight—"

"Our plight, you blighted cur, I'll run you through—"

"Quiet, Harold." This time, Wernsted was icier in his tone. "He's right in as much as we will be well rid of them sooner if you'd just walk without blustering. No one would dare lay a hand on this hungerman. He's favored by the Thane."

"'Favored,'" Harold repeated as if it tasted bitter on his tongue. To the Knights he addressed, "You three keep silent and maybe your being 'favored' will get you to the Twenty-third Round alive."

Seren shot a questioning look at Anargen, and he glanced upward meaningfully. There were twenty-four levels shaped into rounded floors. The higher one ascended in Ordumair's rounds, the wealthier and more prestigious its residents and purposes.

Abiding by their guides' ruthless contract, they followed up and up, with the transformation of the buildings failing to pair with a transformation in vitality to the city. If there were Ords of any class, they were either indoors or elsewhere. Given that almost every Ord for close to three centuries had spent their entire lives in Ordumair or its surrounding valley, where could they be?

Their unwilling guides ushered them into a large room

Anargen remembered as the convening hall for the elders of the Ords. Ever since Monarch Ilyron's forces destroyed the Thane's Hall and the Great Bulwark, Duncoin had been holding court here. However, as they entered the room, it was immediately apparent that this was not a day for ceremony and pomp. Duncoin wasn't seated in his high chair, but rather stood with a group of Ords around a table with a large parchment draped over it. A map of the region. They spoke in the hushed voices of those deliberating matters too weighty to dare burden any common Ord with and too precious for outsiders. So involved were the discussions that none of them noticed Anargen and the others for several minutes. As soon as they did, a hush fell on the group. Anargen recognized most of them, though there was a young fellow among the group he hadn't expected to be part of the Council of Elders. He was instantly delighted to identify his friend and mentee, Iaegon.

"Oh no," he mumbled as realization struck him.

"What is it?" his father whispered under his breath.

"An Ord I recognize from last time is here. A friend. But he can only be part of this group if his great-uncle Orwald can't. Which means he's either abroad or died, and at his age ..."

"Hush your yammering, hungermen," one of their Ord chaperones seethed.

Duncoin had strode out from the group and claimed a commanding spot on the dais where his elevated seat was. He didn't sit as he grumbled, "I see bawrnigs under the banners of Tengrath and Feingohl. What is the meaning of your intrusion into this council? And while we're at it, the absence of your patrons?"

The lighting was somewhat poor where Anargen and the others stood, but as the two sergeants squabbled over who should speak their humblest apologies on behalf of Tengrath and Feingohl, Anargen caught the moment Duncoin was able to recognize him. The stern Ord's gaze softened by a fraction, as much reaction as the schooled ruler allowed to show.

"Enough, both of you. If your patrons find the council's business so inconsequential, perhaps they would be better served by subordinating their banners to one of the other Elders present."

Feingohl's bawrnig stiffened noticeably, but there was an undeniable resilience, even haughtiness, to Tengrath's. Even if both replied, "Understood, our Thane. I shall deliver your summons."

"Do deliver them. Dismissed," he said, waving a gauntleted hand in open distaste.

After the sergeants departed, Duncoin stroked his beard. "Nobles of Ordumair, though our subordinates lack the good graces of court, I will take the honor of presenting one dear to our people's hearts. Sir Anargen of Black River."

"Hail, Sir Anargen of Black River, guest of the noble Thane!" the Elders called out as one.

Anargen stepped forward and nodded in deferral to the Thane. "Honorable Thane, it is my pleasure to come before you again. With me are my father, Sir Glewdyn of Black River, and my fiancée, Lady Seren of Black River."

"Ah, Sir Glewdyn, I do remember making your acquaintance briefly in your home country. Hail to you, sir. But Lady Seren, it is a true honor to meet the betrothed of our valiant Sir Anargen. A hearty and hale evening be yours."

In unison, the other Ord nobles called out the greeting likewise, except for Iaegon. His young brow looked furrowed in consternation.

There was no time to sort it out before the Thane boomed, "What brings you to the vaunted chambers of the Ords?"

Anargen glanced at his father, who merely shrugged. Clearing his throat, Anargen replied, "We received word that

Ordumair is in need of allies, dear Thane. Thus, we have come to render our aid to your cause."

Once more, there was only the faintest of physical indications of the Thane's emotive state—a faint tic in his jaw.

"Elder Strasmund, I'm going to escort our guests to quarters for their stay. You will guide discussions until I return."

"Aye, honorable Thane," a portly Ord with a silver-streaked black beard who wore polished steel plate mail from head to toe. His gaze was far less hostile for the Knights, but no one in the room seemed to feel particularly at ease and worlds away from the warm welcome Anargen had anticipated, particularly when he factored in the stony fixedness of Iaegon's stare.

Following the Thane out into the passages, no one spoke. They trailed without question, even as Duncoin led up a farther round to the highest level, which was essentially the Thane and his family's private palace carved inside the mountain. Once within the expansive entry area to the ruler's home, he turned to face them.

"Regrettably, I could not speak freely in front of the council. While they are privy to our need for aid, they are not all above suspicion. No doubt your encounter with Elder Tengrath and his minions left a foul taste in your mouths." He sauntered over and from a flask poured himself some kind of drink. It smelled strongly herbal, so Anargen guessed it was an Ord tea concoction.

"Your Honor," Glewdyn began.

Duncoin held up a hand. "Please, speak freely, Sir Glewdyn. Formality will only burn the wick on a candle we cannot afford to expend."

"What has happened?" Anargen asked, unable to mask how crestfallen he felt.

"Hrm," Duncoin rumbled. "After the Restoration was driven off Ecthelowall's main island, our armies supporting the

Viceroy began taking heavy casualties. We were forced to restore to full status some of the dishonored banners, like Tengrath's. Then the Devastation beset us. That plague has killed more of us than Ecthel steel. Including Uncle Orwald."

The Thane took a deep draught from his mug. While he usually seemed as solid as Mount Fior-sruthain, there were noticeable cracks in that façade now.

"I'm so sorry," Anargen said, feeling as though all of the air in him was being violently drawn out. "You know about Sir Cinaed?"

"Aye," he replied without looking up from swirling his remaining tea.

There was nothing else Anargen could say then. Once more, the grief, the regret, the guilt of Cinaed's death felt raw, the wound of his loss reopened. Cinaed had told Anargen stories about his childhood in Ordumair with some prompting. Duncoin and Cinaed had been the best of friends since childhood. Anargen's whole life easily fit within the expanse their friendship had endured, and he could only guess at how deeply the Ord missed him.

"Duncoin," Glewdyn spoke up, his voice gentle and halting. "I'm loath to speak into your pain, but as you said, time is precious to us. We received an urgent letter from Sir Thomas Fenwrest. Are matters as bleak as he portrayed them?"

"Hmm," was all he said before taking another sip of tea. "Thomas!" he bellowed, startling Anargen. The sound echoed through the corridors of the Thane's home.

After about a minute, a trio of familiar faces emerged from deeper in the quarters.

"Sir Anargen!" Thomas called out, his expression brightening for an instant before dimming.

Garbed in an Ecthel military uniform and with short shorn hair, he looked years older. Though it may have been the weight of his new title that aged him. At his side, his beloved Mia gripped his arm as if in support. Her copious copper ringlets bounced as she nodded in a more measured welcome. "Friends from Black River, it is good to see you again."

"Lady Seren," a much slimmer and therefore older-looking Gregor added.

"Your Honor, Gregor," Seren replied with a smirk. His crush hadn't evaporated in a year of absence.

Anargen had to swallow back a gasp. The young heir to Ecthelowall's throne used a crutch and hobbled. One of his legs had been amputated at the knee.

"I see you received my letter," Thomas commented, still doing only a passing job at masking some depth of discouragement. "I had not expected you all to travel all this way yourselves. I'm sure you will be much missed on the frontlines of Libertias's offensives."

"There are no offensives being waged by Libertias," Glewdyn replied.

"Ah, I see," Thomas looked down, as if this was only the confirmation of what he suspected. "And the aid we badly need?"

"We are the aid," Glewdyn confirmed. "We had hoped to bring with us Knights from Estonbury, but we have yet to see evidence of their coming to our aid."

Duncoin growled and threw his mug across the room, shattering it against a wall. He stood and stalked off, rubbing his face profusely.

After he was presumably out of earshot, Thomas cleared his throat. "You'll have to forgive our host. This wasn't the news we had hoped for."

"Clearly," Glewdyn commented dryly, eyeing the direction of the Thane's departure.

"You were hoping we'd be able to send an army from Libertias to bolster the defenses?" Anargen asked.

"We had hoped you would send an army to route the Monarch's forces entirely," Mia amended.

Anargen shot Seren and Glewdyn a look and sucked in a deep breath. "We could not send word ahead of ourselves, but Libertias is foundering. There has been a string of decisive defeats. The Counts are closing ranks to protect the interior of Libertias from further incursions, and if it gets any worse, they'll likely sue for peace."

The way the three Ecthel teens' faces fell, Anargen could tell this was the last thing they needed to hear right now. At his side, Seren offered, "Perhaps pressure from Albaron or the Restoration navy could help draw off the Monarch's advance?"

"That would be lovely," Gregor piped up. "Except the Albarons are struggling to hold their lands intact, and the navy is fortunate Admiral Nerebold is as gifted a commander as tales claim. They're far outgunned but managing to keep a full invasion from landing in the north."

"Little wonder the Monarchists had the forces to spare in the south," Glewdyn surmised. "You are all nobles of your homeland. Surely you did not come here alone."

Thomas glanced in the direction Duncoin had stalked off. "We have almost two thousand soldiers with us. But when we sent word to Duncoin of what we'd discovered about Ilyron's plans, he insisted our forces encamp in the mountains north and west of here. Only Mia, Gregor, I, and a small guard have been permitted to come into the valley."

"Hmph, those rockheaded elders don't even know we have an army at all," Gregor put in.

"What?" Anargen asked, looking at the three Ecthels in utter confusion.

Mia clasped her hands and took a steadying breath. "In his

wisdom, the Thane has not shared the news because he is convinced that revealing our army's presence would initiate a coup. Even his most loyal elders would apparently reject our presence as an occupation."

The room was quiet for a moment. Anargen's mind, however, was abuzz with protestations and frustration. How could the Ords still be so mistrusting? The war had not gone well for them, true. But it hadn't gone well for any on the Restoration's side. Did they have any clue that they were slitting their own throats to escape the danger of a knife to the back?

Clearing her throat, Seren spoke up. "From your letter, it sounds as if the Monarch is obsessed with creating a dragon. Given his fixation on Ordumair, does he believe a wyvern lives in these mountains?"

"He does," Thomas said gravely, and frustratingly added nothing else.

Seren nodded. "That is unfortunate. Perhaps if we find and destroy or bury it further, Ilyron will be deterred and refocus his efforts elsewhere?"

"Oh, we know where the wyvern is," Gregor grumbled and turned his sour expression away, perhaps to keep from looking so cross in front of Seren.

"Then that's something," Anargen said, his hopes rising. "For a moment, I feared researching its location would take scouring the library of Ordumair's entire collection."

"It very nearly did," Thomas admitted. "Unfortunately, knowing its location does us no good. We can't harm the wyvern or its location."

So solemn and defeated was Thomas's tone that Anargen feared to ask, but had to, "Why is that?"

"Because it would be the end of us all," Duncoin answered as he strode back into the room with a long, sleek knife in hand.

ESCAPE PLAN

A s the fireworks continued to explode in vibrant showers overhead, Jason dashed back to the others. "There's an entire division of the Jhi'ish army here. Artillery, trucks, foot soldiers, even tanks."

"Tanks?" Aria asked, aghast. "I thought only Rehalcyon and Ecthelowall had them?"

It was true Jason had only ever seen the hulking steel-plated trucks with cannons being deployed—to devastating effect—by the two primary nations on either side of the war. Having had one of their shells land next to a section of trench he had been in ensured he would never mistake the sight of them. "I guess Rehalcyon decided to share," he retorted more heatedly than he intended.

"No matter how they are here," Cinaed spoke up, arms crossed over his chest. "We cannot let Defender Guo be captured."

The Jhi'ish Defender hung his head. "I can appoint my successor. Nanxi should be waiting at the end of the secret passage. I will turn myself over to the authorities, and he will take my place as Defender of the Northeastern Realm."

Cinaed gripped Yúzé's shoulders. "You are noble-minded, but have to know as well as I do that if anyone but you appears before the Council, it could implode the whole thing."

Glancing up at the sky, Cinaed asked, "How much longer?"

The Jhi'ish stroked his tan chin. "Hard to say. It could be a minute. Or five. The big finale sometimes gets delayed."

"I'm sorry," Aria interjected. "But why are we fretting over fireworks right now?"

"There's a secret passage under the gardens that leads to a bridge across the river and away from Jhi City. We can use it to escape," Cinaed explained.

"I have some of the Order here waiting to meet us," Yúzé picked up. "To find the entrance to the tunnel, we need the final fireworks to go off. Under its light, a phosphorescent marking on the appropriate tile of this Plaza will glow. When it does, we may lift it away and flee."

Jason had already drifted away to climb up and check on the Jhi'ish army's approach. He climbed back down. "Whatever we're waiting on, we need to forget about. They're already halfway through the garden's maze."

"It's a secret exit marked in such a way that can only be seen in the light of the last fireworks of the show," Aria moaned.

Jason gaped, looking at each of the Defenders in turn. How had things tilted off their axis so quickly?

"Could we make a defense if we each take a side of the entry into this area?" he asked, already knowing the answer.

"They can drive a tank through that opening. And if Rehalcyon is involved in this at all, they wouldn't hesitate to burn this entire garden down and shell it into a crater to end us," Cinaed pointed out. His attention was on the fireworks.

It might have been his imagination, but Jason thought he heard voices and footsteps echoing from just beyond the maze's near walls.

Because of the way the maze encircled the Aperture of Fate Plaza, they were surrounded on all sides by soldiers now.

Jason shot Aria an apologetic look. He reached for her hand and found her buried in his arms an instant later.

Guess the wedding is off.

Thankfully, he had enough sense not to blurt that out loud.

The sky overhead suddenly burst into a sea of shimmering gold particles. They fizzled and simmered, seeming to move back and forth like the sea until another burst revealed a white blossom beneath it, seated like a water lily among the golden waters. It was beautiful, enough so that he would've commented on it if it weren't a paltry distraction from imminent capture and death.

Aria shook him. "Jason!"

He looked down at her and saw she was watching both of the Defenders dashing over to a stone slab at the edge of the garden. It looked as if it were dusted with some of the sea gold.

Holding on tight as she towed him after, Jason glanced over as they passed the Aperture of Fate and skidded to a halt and let go of her hand.

She took a few steps and whirled to face him, preparing to snap at him over his apparent lack of sanity. But she stopped short. They were both in the mirror with the giant flowery fireworks display still briefly brandishing the night sky.

He held out his hand, which she rushed to take, and then he bent down and gave her a hard, wild kiss.

"In case the worst happens," he said. "I wanted our fates to be one for even a little while."

Aria smiled, a tear rolling down her cheek. "I know."

"Children!" bellowed Cinaed as the slab was tossed aside.

At the other end of the plaza, the stamp of boots could be heard approaching. Shouts in Jhi'ish filled the air, and as he and Aria sprinted for the opening, a spray of gunfire replaced the now silent fireworks show, filling the night with the horrible bangs and booms that made its idyllic beauty of moments before seem completely illusory, a dream of a long-lost world that may never have existed except in the mind.

Jason put his body between Aria and the bullets and helped her drop into the hole. A shot zinged off his shoulder, deflected by the armor under his Jhi'ish clothes. It almost sent him headfirst into whatever waited below.

"In you go, lad," Cinaed insisted.

"You first, sir," he protested. "You—"

Cinaed jerked him by the arm so that Jason stumbled over the opening and dropped inside.

His feet had just splashed into an underground trough, which may have been for watering the garden's plants, when Aria towed him away. Cinaed splashed down next to him with a groan.

He helped the old man up from his hands and knees. He could tell the elder Black's descent had been more than messy and unpleasant. The Defender shook his head and waved off Jason's help. "Move, run for the rendezvous point!"

This whole family is absurdly stubborn.

Almost comically, he remembered that, according to Jhi'ish custom, this was now his family. Which meant he could and should be just as stubborn.

"Help me support him," he requested of Yúzé." The other Defender nodded, and between them, they managed to half-drag, half-carry Cinaed down the dark stone corridor running under the width of the garden.

Aria ran before them, her spiritsword drawn, its flashing flames guiding them through the inky blackness of the tunnel. They ran for what felt like an hour, exhausting Jason's lungs and muscles, until Aria reached a stone pushed up against a wall and turned to wait for them. Beyond must be outside the garden, somewhere in the city. Or perhaps they were even outside the city if they had truly run as long as he felt.

Leaning Cinaed up against a wall, he and Yúzé hurried over to the stone. Deeper in the tunnel echoed footsteps and Jhi'ish commands.

"They say, they may take us dead or alive," Yúzé translated, grunting with the effort of pushing against the stone. Incentive enough for them both to strain against the stone until at last it slid aside sufficiently to slip back out into the rich, cooler air of the night.

They were standing at the end of a long bridge across a chasm. Nearby were the sounds of the Jhire River's choppy waters. Though made of stone, the bridge was moss-covered and situated under a modern replacement formed from steel and concrete suspended, maybe two dozen yards above them. But it wasn't this that riveted their attention. Standing farther across the bridge was a group of people bearing torches.

Jason hoped they were the Knights they were to meet until he saw two bodies lying prone before them and another trio kneeling on the stones with hands behind their heads.

From across the gap called one of those stationed there, mocking them. The high, cruel notes of Melania's voice cut through the night air. "Really now, you weren't planning to leave Jhi City without seeing me first, were you?"

II

CONFLICTED

"Pardon?" Glewdyn requested as attention fixed on the returning Thane.

Trudging over to his seat, knife still bared, he dropped down and pulled a fruit out of a basket next to the seat and began peeling and quartering it. "We cannot do anything to harm or excavate or better obstruct access to the wyvern. It's politics." Duncoin said the last almost as a growl.

"We found an account from Thane Ornand the Orderer."

"He's the Ord ruler who had a vision of the Tower of Light," Anargen spoke up suddenly, excited to hear more in spite of the bleak proclamations. "Oh, sorry."

"It's quite all right," Thomas replied, cracking a smile for just an instant. "Having had a similar vision, I was excited to read more from Ornand's writings. As it turns out, Ornand had a curious scientific mind in addition to his ardent devotion to the High King and decided to investigate the nature of the Dual Springs by excavating around them.

"Which of course he did, but those discoveries were eclipsed. During the excavation, he stumbled upon a chamber. A vast one in which icy waters from above ran down into the molten core of the mountain. There he found, trapped in stone and dormant, a massive wyvern.

"Fascinated by it, he compiled several pages of notes about the beast and then ordered the cavern sealed off. Over it, he constructed the library and wells now in the Vault as you've seen."

"And there are Ords opposed to damaging the Vault?" Seren surmised.

"Hmph," Duncoin huffed from a chair he'd plopped down into.

"Not exactly," Mia picked up. "Since the Vault has the only surviving trees from Ecthelowall's Golden Forest and they've yet to grow anywhere else, we fear harming them. They're very dear to our people.

"Part of the treaty between Ecthelowall and Ordumair stipulates that the Golden Forest be restored. And with the passing of the Viceroy ..." Here, she paused and gently rubbed Thomas's back, then continued, "And how poorly the war is going, any divergence from the treaty could dissolve it and fracture the Restoration. Destroying it and guaranteeing all of us will be hunted down by the Monarchists as traitors."

"Never mind those silly trees," Duncoin grumbled. "If the wells and Vault are damaged, there will be no hiding how fragile my rule has become. My nobles already feel we've lost too much to gamble on a hunt for beasts of myth and lore. If we lose the treasures of the Vault, then I will be deposed, likely by Tengrath and his ilk. Then they will revoke the treaty with the Restoration, and Ordumair will be isolated. Easy picking for that vulture Ilyron."

Duncoin slammed down his fists on his chair, his gaze fierce and fixed on the distance as though he could see through the stones of the mountain to where Monarch Ilyron sat enthroned.

"That is rather bleak," Anargen sighed.

"Which is why we need help from beyond this valley," Thomas gestured to them. "If we don't, Ilyron's forces will descend upon Ordumair and claim their insidious prize."

"Either way, we lose," Gregor lamented. "Your reinforcements were our last hope."

Anargen scowled, his heart reeling. There was no escaping

this man-made trap that was forcing them into a devastating outcome.

"Do you know how many soldiers Ilyron is sending?"

"Thousands," Duncoin sneered. "Thousands upon thousands more than we have in Ordumair to defend with. It will be more devastating than the first siege."

"Surely not," Anargen protested unabashed in his desperation to find some hope. "These are just soldiers of Ecthelowall. The Grey Scourge is no more, no army of werebeasts follows."

Even as he had said it, Anargen knew that Ilyron's sorcery could create new werebeasts. And to Thomas's credit, he did not remind Anargen of that point. "He doesn't need them. There are thousands of carrion in his army. Enough alone to overwhelm an army twice the size of the Ords'. We believe the Monarch is personally marching out with them as well."

"That's an awful risk for him to take, deep in conflicted lands, far from supplies and support," Seren observed.

"He wants to perform the ritual right away," Anargen guessed. "Use it to create a dragon. If tales are true, he could be at Caldoness by the next day."

"Yes, and destroy the castle and force Albaron to surrender or withdraw," Gregor added.

Thomas shook his head. "He won't seek terms of surrender. He'll level Albaron and rebuild it in his image."

"After," Duncoin spoke up from in between furious bites of his fruit wedges. "Slaughtering every last one of my people. There's no escaping this for any of us."

Silence filled the room. It swelled until it became stifling, choking. Anargen dearly wanted to rush out and get some fresh, free air. But they were within a mountain; there was no such place. Only the deepening agony as he realized he had ridden with his father and fiancée into near-certain death.

A tremor began running its way through Anargen's body, born from a cry of anguish lodged in his throat by the oppressive force of the quiet. Strong hands gripped his shoulder, holding him still and together. His father spoke hoarsely. "There isn't much chance of victory by the look of things. But we are forgetting, the vision of the Tower of Light drew Sir Cinaed here initially—"

"And Cinaed is dead!" Duncoin roared, his fruit-paring knife clattering off the stone floor. "Just as we'll all be soon."

Glewdyn didn't even flinch at the bombastic prophecy of doom. "Cinaed isn't with us. But the High King drew him here for a reason, which we now understand. All along, the Monarch wanted the dark power of a dragon and sought it here. We cannot allow him to have it—"

"Were you not listening?" Duncoin snapped. "There is nothing left for us tah do." His burr thickened and escaped his control. "We arh doomed tah die ahn wahth my people tha rahst of yarr lands wahl burn!"

Pointing at the frothing mad Ord, Glewdyn spoke as forcefully as Anargen had ever heard him. "Sit down, Your Honor, and be silent. You are not speaking as a Palatini Lucis Aeternae ought. We are more than simple soldiers of a cause. Of any cause for any single people. We are Knights of the Unending Light.

"Many now in connection with your lands have had a vision confirming that the Tower of Light must not fall. We've all struggled for years to find the meaning and fulfillment of that vision. I feel it in every sinew and bone of my body that this hour, this danger is what that vision forewarned."

Gesturing broadly, Duncoin snarled, "Do ya see any towers hahr? My keep ahs ahn ruins. My people barely sahrvive."

Waving a dismissive hand like he was deflecting physical blows, Glewdyn pushed back. "We don't yet know in full what it means, but can any of us honestly dispute what I've said? Doesn't the High King's fire in your veins echo the very same to you?

"There is no giving up or turning back. We are in the very heart of the Quest of Fire. Perhaps the King's Day itself is upon us. Whatever may come, the High King would not have summoned us all and put it into our hearts to pursue this quest only to bring it to ruination. If we will just stand firm in our oaths to the High King, I'm certain we will see his deliverance."

"How can you say that the High King never allows us to fail?" Gregor protested. His gaze unmistakably dropped to his missing leg for an instant.

"Sometimes victory doesn't look like we expect," Anargen responded gently. "That was a lesson I learned the last time I was here defending Ordumair."

"Last time Ordumair's fortress wasn't already half destroyed or its people beyond decimated," Mia pointed out.

"We faced longer odds in Stormridge," Seren countered. "And victory did come with a bitter sting."

"Had it not, we wouldn't have been on the path that led to aiding you in Kirke," Anargen added.

"That does all presuppose the High King means for us to all be here," Gregor pointed out. "Didn't you tell us that the wyvern of Stormridge destroyed the Count who summoned it?"

Anargen nodded reluctantly. He tried not to remember that moment, because so soon after was the last memory he had of Sir Cinaed alive in the Lowlands.

"Perhaps if we evacuate the valley, this wyvern will destroy Ilyron," Gregor concluded.

"Even a common wyvern is a great threat to all around it. And if Ilyron succeeds, all of the older tales speak of terrible evil that comes with it," Thomas pointed out.

Throughout the discussion, Anargen noticed both Glewdyn and Duncoin were regarding each other. Almost as if they were combatants in a joust, evaluating their next opponent. The Thane's countenance darkened, and his nostrils flared.

KNOCK! KNOCK KNOCK!

"Uncle," a voice Anargen recognized called into the room from the hall. "Uncle, the council is ready to adjourn for dinner. You have been summoned to join them!"

"I will meet when and where I choose, not by their whims," Duncoin was like a volcanic mountain simmering, ready to explode. His eyes flashed, white hot on each of his guests until they settled on Anargen, and then suddenly the turmoil began to subside as though the sea had rushed in and cooled the magma before it could spread.

"Nephew, on considering the matter further. Please pass on my sincere apologies. I will be along shortly; I need only arrange for a special treat. Do make sure Elder Tengrath in particular is in attendance."

"As you wish, Uncle," Iaegon replied, still out of view, but his voice betraying all the misgiving and confusion that Anargen felt. Duncoin's mood had shifted so quickly that the wind off it was enough to send Anargen spiraling.

The Ord ruler smirked as he observed the clear puzzlement on Anargen's face. "Friends, perhaps we can prepare a better defense while reducing internal friction in one stroke. And offer you, the fate-spoken defenders of my people, a night richly deserved."

"Your Honor?" Anargen eyed the Ord in utter confusion.

Duncoin was already striding purposefully out of his quarters. In his wake, Gregor asked, "What does the Thane mean?"

Anargen shrugged. "I don't know, I've never seen him this way."

"He has been under incredible stress since our arrival," Thomas gestured to the stone around them. "All of the Ords have. It's as though everyone can sense what is coming, even if word has only been passed to those the Thane trusts most."

"Brace yourselves, young ones," Glewdyn said as he headed for the door. "The first blows of the battle for Ordumair are going to fall shortly, I fear. And the Thane will be using us to strike them."

SCHISM

"The machinations of the elite, the world of politics, are a fetid maelstrom that, unlike natural storms, are wielded in calculated attacks on the beautiful things of the Lowlands. And yet, whatever the malignant intentions and subterfuge that would seek to taint it, this one thing cannot be diminished. Can't be undone. Can't be put asunder. No matter what happens next."

Anargen's King's Day Journal
15 Fylleth 1610 Middle Era

As Anargen stepped up to the meeting hall, he tried to push aside the sensation of dread coiling around him like a serpent prepping to strike. Too much was happening too fast for him to sort it all out—the icy welcome and then the devastating news of Ordumair's inescapable fate. Duncoin's bizarre behavior might not seem so mad if he were to have as long as the ruler did to steep in the anguish and inescapability of it all.

He felt a light pressure on his hand. Seren's warm brown eyes were bright, but he could see past her well-placed mask of courteousness that she was worried, too, which meant that he needed to be braver for both of them. Giving her hand a reassuring squeeze, he linked his arm to hers and strode inside, behind his father, who was strangely passive about it all. The older Knight's words pushed back against the dark tide of doubt and fear oppressing him, but the chill of it was strong, and even the ardent warmth of the High King's whisper to heed that guidance was still battling mightily to dispel his misgivings.

The room quieted somewhat as they entered. Per instructions through a servant sent by Duncoin, they arrived somewhat late. The meeting hall from earlier had been adjusted to seat all of the Ord elders and their courtiers along a series of long tables. Already, the stocky elites of Ordumair were feasting on roasted game fowl and rooted vegetables. A basket with rolls as big as the dwarfs' fists was passed back and forth. A heady scent of honey mead and stronger ales mixed with the boisterous strains of conversation that had yet to be blunted by the Knights' arrival.

An elderly servant led them to stand at the room's center, before the greatest table, at which sat Duncoin and presumably those of highest position and favor with him. Anargen spotted Iaegon at the table, but once more the teen avoided his attempts to make eye contact. Among those at this high station, he wasn't surprised to find Tengrath, whom he supposed was there by necessity. But Feingohl's presence was an interesting development.

The servant bowed before Duncoin, and the Thane stood to grant a customary welcome to them as guests of the feast. All around the room at last quieted down to some hushed comments in anticipation of the formality.

"Venerable Duncoin, son of Denhard, great Thane of Ordumair, I present to you these guests," the servant began, but before he could reach the doubtless less-weighty introductions for Anargen, Seren, and Glewdyn, Duncoin waved off the gnarled Ord.

"My thanks for your service, Urald, but these three need no formal introductions. All here know already Sir Anargen. No less because most of you rough lot saw him earlier."

That drew a few laughs, which helped to dull the edges of

Anargen's nerves. Duncoin seemed to have slipped into a much lighter mood since leaving them to attend this meal. Had he drowned his worries with the heady ale?

"This son of Black River helped deliver our people from the greatest hour of danger we had ever known. We are honored to have him by our side now as we face a still graver test ahead. Many of you know the Monarchists of Ecthelowall are marching on our lands even as we speak."

The whispers spread and swelled like tinder catching fire. Clearly, some did not know, but no one spoke out yet to betray that ignorance. Anargen couldn't help noticing Tengrath's posture had tensed. Either he hadn't known, or he was irked that "hungermen" were being insinuated as coming to save the day.

"They bring numbers far greater than our own and weapons we are all too familiar with after the Siege and these years of war and toil. It would taste a lie to say I'm certain we shall emerge victorious. I am loath to give you a false sense of security and soundness, having no prognostication open to me beyond that which experience has given. Brutality and pain and bloodshed will once again be visited upon us ..."

Duncoin drew in a deep breath. His dark eyes glinted under his brows, and Anargen almost thought the Ord gave him a wink.

"Yet, this eve, I raise my tankard in celebration, because my fellow Knights and I know there is no reason to fear. All outcomes are in the High King's hands, including the fight ahead of us. He founded these Lowlands and he founded our nation. No evil shall overtake us while dwelling in the shadow of his banner. Thus, I know no fear—I know only the King's Day may well be upon us and that is the only future which matters."

Anargen sucked in a sharp breath. He could not help it.

While in substance he did not disagree with Duncoin's speech, it was so totally outside of what he expected, so completely unambiguous in its surrender to the High King's will, it scarcely felt it could come from the mouth of the brooding nobleman of earlier that day. Moreover, it was so utterly dangerous to speak brazenly about trusting the High King when seated within dagger's reach was an elder of his people who repudiated the Knight Order. Every individual who pledged themselves loyal to the High King was anathema to him.

Years ago, Anargen had asked Sir Cinaed why Duncoin hid that he was a Knight of Light, even after the Siege of Ordumair had been broken. The answer was simply for his own safety and that of his family. Though the Thane ruled with absolute authority, that authority was ultimately founded upon the loyalty of his retainers. Each elder's support truly mattered, even Tengrath's. Speaking so boldly was a bittersweet sound to Anargen's ears, especially seeing the way Elder Tengrath's face reddened, and he clenched his fists upon the table. Molten rock would seem as ice compared to the fury rolling off him.

Duncoin continued, "Now, raise your tankards and let us—"

"Enough!" Tengrath bellowed as he rose up from the table. "I canno' hear another word of this rot."

Addressing the red-faced Ord with a demeanor much as he might an upset child, Duncoin asked, "What has vexed you now, Elder Tengrath. You know well none are to interrupt a Thane's blessing."

"Would that Ordumair had a Thane I could so revere! Our people have been ravaged by the Devastation plague. Crushed by harsh winters. Slaughtered on far-off battlefields for our ancient Ecthel foes." Tengrath countered. "All because you have gone too far with your slathering over these hungerman and their deposed fairy king!" He slammed his fist on the table, sending shudders through its heavy oak frame.

"Bite your tongue, Tengrath!" an Ord opposite him at the table shouted as he stood as well. "The Council resolved that no one use that slur again. Never mind that you ought to be flogged for how you speak now to our Thane!"

Tengrath roared with a guttural laugh. "And who would do the flogging? You, Nedric? My newborn grandson hits harder."

At this, the room erupted into a barrage of insults and accusations levelled around the room. Petty grudges, old wounds, and deep divides found voice. All were caught in a raucous row of shouting except the Thane and Elder Feingohl. Anargen noted the latter was studying the room himself, stroking his beard as he did. His musing expression was well known to Anargen; he had seen it on the faces of other pragmatic opportunists in the past. Whatever Feingohl had in mind, any games being played at this point would only further seal everyone's doom.

Bringing his hands together with a resounding clap, Duncoin spoke over the din. "Silence. You're all bickering like children on the eve of our people's greatest test. How will Ordumair stand against its foes if he is busy bruising his own jaw?"

"This would not even be an issue if we had a true Thane over us!" Tengrath snarled. "Not some weak-armed, Ecthel-loving hungerman. If you weren't such a fool, we wouldn't even be in this position!"

"What would you do differently at this juncture, Elder Tengrath?" Feingohl asked, casually taking a draft from his tankard.

The ruddy-haired Ord glowered past Duncoin at Feingohl. "I certainly wouldn't be sitting back waiting for the enemy to come upon us and tear our dear ones to ribbons while I supplicate to these worthless hungermen and their imaginary master."

Splaying his hands, Feingohl said, "Well, what is stopping you? Haven't you been posting your men around the pass through Valesgard against the Thane's orders anyway?"

Tengrath leaned past Duncoin and across the table to glare down at Feingohl. "Aye, because at least one of us cares about Ordumair over carving a name for himself on its stone. Fancy doing that when all that it will be good for is a grave."

The calm in Feingohl's expression dissolved like snow in the sun. He stood and shoved Tengrath in one quick move.

Being as sturdy as he was surly, Tengrath didn't lose his balance and came back with a swing at Feingohl.

It never landed. Duncoin gripped Tengrath's fist and flung it aside. Turning to Feingohl, he jammed down on the other's shoulder, forcing him back into his seat. Casting a fierce glare over them both, he huffed, "Have neither of you any sense at all? What of shame? Our ancestors turn in their graves over this feckless prattling!"

Pushing off the table and backing away from Duncoin, Tengrath shook his head, the beads in his beard clacking as he did. "No. Our ancestors weep that weak-willed Ords like you allow us to hobble into oblivion. If you and your ilk cannot be made to see, then a true warrior of Ordumair needs to stand for us before it is too late."

To the whole room, he addressed, "True sons of Ordumair, all who would not see it fall, follow me! We will secure Valesgard and make sure not even one more Ecthel slime, Monarchist or otherwise, steps even a foot into the Valley of Ords."

Facing Duncoin, Tengrath spat on the floor in front of him and stalked out of the room. A dozen or more of those in service to him and those sympathetic to his vitriol followed after. Last, and most surprisingly, Feingohl stood once more, nodded to Duncoin, and exited with his underlings soon after.

In the stillness after the departures, Anargen still didn't dare move. He barely let himself breathe. At any moment, he felt they would need to run.

The room was on the knife's edge of chaos, and yet Thane Duncoin looked contented if not smug. He buried his pleased smirk under a more serious expression. "For those of you still loyal to Ordumair, who see beyond the mistakes and grievances of the past, you honor our ancestors. Though we will all be defending our people from terrible danger, those who have just departed do so for selfish aims. That is not our people's way. Tomorrow morning, we will convene our full war council and prepare ourselves, our fortress, our city, and our people for the greatest and perhaps final battle of Ord kind.

"Eat, gather your full strength. I take my leave for the remainder of the evening. Hale eve to you all."

Then, addressing the aged servant who had brought the Knights to the feast, "Urald, please see these guests back to their quarters and have Cerelah bring them their meals to dine there."

Urald waited until the Thane had exited to lead Anargen and the others back to and deeper inside the Thane's palace. This time, they were ushered into a series of small but impressive rooms joined by a broader, parlor-like area. The servant's voice quavered, either from what had just transpired or perhaps only his age. "Cerelah will bring your food shortly. Hale evening."

"Thank you," Glewdyn called after him.

The moment Anargen lost sight of Urald, from a trio of rooms emerged Thomas, Mia, and Gregor. "We didn't expect you back so soon," Gregor commented. "Did it go that poorly?"

"We're alive?" Glewdyn answered with a hint of humor. "So, as well as could be hoped."

"Elder Tengrath and two other nobles are rallying their supporters to go pitch their tents at the valley entrance and face down the Monarch's army there," Anargen elaborated. "They refuse to share the honor of defending their people with us and believe they can turn back the Monarch's forces by themselves."

"Can they?" Seren asked, sounding intensely dubious about it.

"Only with the High King's favor, which they reject. A castle once stood at the entrance to the valley, Valesgard. It was demolished during the last attack on Ordumair. Tengrath and his men are going to be obliterated."

"Aye," Duncoin agreed, coming up from behind again and startling them. "But they will die serving their fellow Ords and buy us precious time. Now, come, the lot of you. I promised this night would bear something you fully deserve for throwing in your lot with us dwarfs."

Pivoting and marching off, he called, "Come, come!" Apparently, to some degree, he understood how confusing his behavior had been.

After a few seconds, the whole group followed. Passing into the main reception area of the palace through a kitchen, larder, a smoke room, and a personal library, they at last entered the lavish interior quarters for the Thane himself. Draped with blue satin curtains bound by silver clasps, the floor was polished marble and had an expansive sapphire rug with patterned gold and silver symbols of the Golden Orchard and Dual Springs—the emblem of the Thane. Lit silver torches lined the walls and gold-embossed wood furniture filled much of the room, making it feel livable. Otherwise, it was devoid of personal touches and elements of a space truly kept as a home.

As if it were of no consequence to have them in his private chambers, Duncoin approached one silvery torch and yanked it. There was a click, and then several stones of the wall slid back to reveal a darkened passage. He motioned once more for them to follow.

"The secret passages," Anargen explained for the others' benefit. "There must be something of great importance he wants to show us."

Familiar musty odors presented and pressed themselves upon Anargen as he wound down along secret tunnels. A faint haze of smoke from the torches lighting the hidden passages hung like a curtain, adding mystery to the arcane tunnels used by Ord rulers for centuries. He made sure not to relinquish his hold on Seren's hand as he followed the surprisingly nimble dwarf down and around the maze-like network. Anargen hadn't ever expected to see these tunnels again. There was a tragic irony in that his part in the Quest began and would likely soon end here. Far from the only home he had ever known.

Though this time I have Seren and Father with me.

There was a stab of guilt. How could he take comfort that he wouldn't die apart from those he loved, when it was likely they too would meet painful ends?

But beyond it is the Kingdom of Light, and the King's Day is coming.

Yes, that was what he had to focus on. These troubles, which now felt so heavy and made the Lowlands feel utterly dark and hopeless, were made light and ephemeral as the smoke from the torches in comparison to the unending light in the High King's courts. He need only hold onto such wisdom when the fighting began, and the aches and weariness of battle beset him. And he may as well admit, when he would most need to steel himself if, perchance, he outlived, even briefly, those he loved.

Gripping Seren's hand all the more firmly, Anargen had to skid to a halt. In his introspection, he had almost missed seeing the Thane suddenly jerk out of the passages and through one of its many exits back into Ordumair's civil space.

He was unprepared for what he found as he emerged from the darker tunnels into a vaguely familiar room, decorated with hundreds of candles and deep maroon flower petals from a rose variant that grew along the valleys of these northern mountains. Waiting for them were a dozen or so other Ords in addition to Duncoin. The latter wore a sly grin.

"What is all this?" Anargen murmured, making room for all five of the other Knights to enter as well.

"A generosity that can scarce repay what you came to Ordumair prepared to give," Duncoin replied, somber. With a chuckle, he added, "I'd wager you don't recognize the dusty old Knight Hall you and your fellow Knights found last time you were here."

Of course. This is the forgotten Knight Hall!

Suddenly, its distinctive features stood out to him. As did the sharp twinge of pain at the memories attached to this place.

Terrillian, Bertinand, Caeserus ... Cinaed ... you should be here with us now.

Glewdyn stepped around Anargen and examined the spread. "This is lovely, Your Honor, but what is all this?"

Taking his place on the raised dais at the head of eight rows of seating, Duncoin gestured. "If you approve, then we should like to provide the young couples each with a ceremony of binding ties."

"You mean you want to throw Thomas and Mia and Anargen and Seren each a wedding?" Gregor summarized long before Anargen knew he would be able to speak. Gregor chuffed a bit petulantly, "Well, isn't that the biggest waste of time possible given our dire situation?"

"Gregor!" Mia scolded.

"I wouldn't call it a waste," Thomas said, taking hold of Mia's hand for an instant. "A surprise and a bit sudden perhaps."

Anargen finally found his voice, husky though it was: "I must say, I think I speak for Seren and I both when I say it is a tremendous honor, but we weren't expecting this either."

For once, the hard stone of Duncoin's face softened, even to the point of looking apologetic. "I know you weren't, young ones. But the ill news that we have no external allies to rely upon forced a difficult truth on me. We are all, likely as not, going to die."

Seren's grip on Anargen's hand tightened, underscoring for him the raw honesty of that admission. Before, the Thane had seemed depressed, pessimistic. Now, his words were resigned, as though he had already come to terms with their loss. In the face of its gravity, Anargen could only return Seren's pressure and keep himself composed, a stone amidst tumultuous breakers of the sea.

"Because of such noble sacrifice and because I understand the pain of lost love—" Duncoin's voice cracked, and Anargen knew he was referring to the death of his own wife, Caryn. Sir Cinaed had told him she was poisoned in a failed coup many years ago.

"Because I understand what it means to love someone with the vitality of a lifetime, even if only gifted by the High King a much shorter span, I want to offer you the chance to express your love for each other. To enjoy, however briefly, the reality of the commitment to which you've each already pledged yourselves."

At this, Anargen glanced over at Thomas. He and Mia were turned toward each other, him holding her in his arms, the younger man's expression an unreadable storm of emotions. He hadn't even realized Thomas and Mia were also engaged. The tragedy of their love, having endured as much and maybe more than he and Seren, drove the stinging barb of loss deeper. People called such love fate-spoken, destined from the beginning to meet a bitter end. It felt such a callous labelling to assign to Thomas and Mia, let alone him and Seren.

Duncoin finished, his hands held open towards each couple. "The choice is yours, of course, and I do not mean to presume. Inasmuch as I may give you my thanks, this is my best offer of it. I cannot give you a guarantee of a future, but if you choose, I—we here—will honor your present."

Anargen stared at Duncoin's outstretched hand, the silvery

rebrace on his forearm gleaming in the light of all the candles. He recognized now the scent of mountain flowers in the room. Lavender, hyacinth, and honeysuckle.

Honeysuckle. Some of his earliest memories of courting Seren were tinged with the fragrance of the delicate little blooms and summer evenings in the forests of Black River. So far from here and framed not in the certainty of war and death, but the uncertainty of a future unknown but ever so beautiful for the hope of being shared. Before he met Seren's eyes or even felt her shift into his arms, he knew deep inside what she would want, what she would say to this offer, because he felt precisely the same.

Brushing back a strand of her midnight hair behind her ear, he didn't take his eyes off her once they found themselves locked to hers. "Yes, Your Honor. This is not how nor where nor with whom we precisely envisioned this happening—" his voice faltered.

"But our life together has been full of losses that led to greater gains," Seren picked up, her voice rich if tremulous as she recited the same words that she'd started their relationship with years before. "We have lost our home but gained this one abroad. We have lost friends and family ..."

Now she could not continue, so he did in her stead. "Yet we have gained the family of all Knights of Light in the care of the High King of All Realms. And though we may lose tomorrow, by your kindness, and the High King's favor, we gratefully have today. For as long as life lasts, short or long, Seren has my love."

"For as long as life lasts, short or long, Anargen has mine."

Anargen touched his forehead against Seren's and held his beloved close, feeling deeply the weight and worth of each moment, knowing they were few in number. But were there an ocean's depth of days ahead, would they have been any less dear?

There was a quiet that fell over them then, though it took Anargen some time to perceive it. When he and Seren looked up, Duncoin heaved out a great sigh. "Well then, whatever blahssings I may have conjured to utter," he began, his burr slipping into his speech again. "I do not believe they would taste sweeter to any ear here than those. By your profession of love and commitment and my honor as regent of the Ords and servant of the High King of All Realms, I declare you man and wife."

Anargen's cheeks warmed as he realized they had been a bit dramatic in their declarations. It hadn't been their intent to usurp the traditional rites. Not that he was sure those given by an Ord would've matched those given in Libertias.

A firm hand gripped his shoulder and rested on Seren's as well. His father, hazel eyes shining with tears, smiled at them. "May the High King of All Realms grant your journey together be longer than the river courses, more fruitful than all the trees of the forests, and surer than the mountains before every storm. What began as twain ends as one. Hale, hale, hale tomorrows ever after for you," Glewdyn recited the traditional blessing spoken in their Walhonde homeland. It was devastating and dear to hear it over them now in this far-flung land.

"Father ..." Anargen began and then found he couldn't utter another word beyond "Thank you."

Glewdyn patted him on the back, a strangled chuckle rumbling in the older man's throat. "Don't thank me. Thank the High King. And thank this remarkable young woman, with the first kiss from her husband!"

That needed very little prompting, and though the heat in his cheeks was double stoked from embarrassment, the warmth that spread through him the moment his lips touched Seren's seared away all of it. Silly or not. Sorrowed over what lay ahead or not. Here, today, and always, he'd found his mate, and the mutual steadiness and reliance between them made it all fade into the background.

When he opened his eyes again, his first sight was his bride, and though her hair was slightly frizzed, her makeup not applied, and her humble travel dress not the finery typical of such an event, she was beauty itself to him. In that moment, he felt certain she always would be, whether age wearied her brows and wrinkled the soft skin of her cheeks or they parted the Lowlands fair and fresh as this day.

"Ehem," Gregor cleared his throat, jerking Anargen's and everyone else's attention to him. "That is lovely and all, but ..." He hesitated, starting to say one thing and then catching himself and resolving the unspoken matter with the shake of his head. "You cannot overlook my cousin and Baroness Sornfold."

The teen, as noble-born as Duncoin but also in less than lordly attire, gestured to the other couple. "I dare say it goes without saying what your decision is at this moment. You have each lost as much as any person can in these Lowlands. Yet you triumph over—"

"Gregor," Thomas interrupted with a smile and gentle shake of his younger cousin's shoulder. "You are a poet and statesman without equal, but I think we can handle this part."

The young Knight took Mia's hands and led her a few steps closer to Duncoin, who had grabbed Gregor by the shoulders and shook him with a hearty chuckle.

"Mia," Thomas began, and then immediately stopped and gave a breathy laugh as Mia's emerald eyes widened with anticipation. "Maybe I spoke too soon. Anargen and Seren made this look so much easier."

The laugh was picked up by the Ord audience and a few Ecthel courtiers that Anargen hadn't spotted before and lasted a good minute before Thomas held his hand up to signal he could go on. "Words always seem to fail me when it comes to you. When we were younger, I don't think love was ever something I worried about being lost between us."

Bouncing her brows once with a little smirk, Mia replied, "No, it wasn't."

"But then I met you. The you that is strong and compassionate and fiercely determined. The you who is quiet and thoughtful and careful. Gregor is right; we've each lost so much, but Anargen and Seren are even more right in saying that there is so much gain amid the loss. Because through the pain of my losses, I found the you who steals my words away. The you whom I will ever cling to, whatever we face ahead, and diligently rediscover for all the days of our lives, whether short or long."

For a moment, Mia's eyes were almost comically wide with surprise. "Oh, this is hard," she giggled and then covered her mouth. For just a moment, her face fell, and she tugged with one hand at the opal dress she wore. It was much finer than Seren's but still nothing like the quality she had doubtless dreamed of as a little girl.

Anargen felt a collective breath being held in for what she might say. Because it looked more likely with each passing moment that she would decline to speak further at all. As understandable as it would be, he hoped desperately that wouldn't be how his brother and sister in arms left things going into the hardest days of their lives.

Thomas seemed to sense the same. "It's all right, Mia. It's all right."

She shook her head, her ruddy ringlets shaking like a tree in a storm. A tear streaked down one of her freckled cheeks. "No, it isn't. None of this is all right." Gesturing to Anargen and Seren, she said, "Love like theirs deserves something better, something more." To Duncoin and the others in attendance, she addressed, "And those with such kind hearts ought to have many days to enjoy the fruits of loyalty and bravery."

Mia swallowed hard, her brows knitted with earnest, "And a boy who used to drive me mad as a child shouldn't be the one I'm standing across from on my wedding day, still driving me mad. Because for all his talk of losing his words, he has wrecked me with his."

Arching a brow, Thomas, like everyone else in the room, seemed unsure where Mia was going with this.

"I'm wrecked because, as beautiful as I wanted this day to be, and as sorrow-tinged as it has become for what we face after it, you have still made it more than I could imagine. You're always making more of my life and of me than I planned. At every turn and every slip, you've been there. Even with everything stripped away, at my very lowest moments, you kept kindled hope and baffling joy. I'm truly the one without words, because what words could describe someone who so far surpasses my childhood dreams and carries me through the real-life trials I face now and every day to come? The High King has been far better to me than I deserved to have you. Loving you, being true to you and by your side," her voice started to waver as tears flowed freely, "for all our lives, short or long, won't be a challenge. It will be ..." Mia sniffled and looked at him, her eyes fixedly intent and saying everything she couldn't.

He brushed away her tears and kissed her. Any doubt anyone might have about what she felt or meant to say dissolved as she wound her arms around Thomas in a fierce embrace, like a sailor clinging to the last bit of driftwood in a choppy sea. That is what they were to each other: a buoy, a harbor, a refuge from all that had ravaged their lives.

For Anargen, it was incredible to see them. It was like looking at a painting, so different from his and Seren's in composition, but with the same theme and elements in each. Perhaps that was why he couldn't help clapping for them before anyone else did.

When the pair pulled back from their embrace to take it in, Duncoin strode forward a step. "And once more, I'm left with little more to say. By your profession of love and commitment and my honor as regent of the Ords and servant of the High King of All Realms, I declare you man and wife."

Thomas and Mia didn't need the reminder to share their first kiss as husband and wife. This one more reserved, more conscious of those around them than their previous. Which was fortunate, because Gregor pushed forward again.

"And as heir to Ecthelowall's throne, I also bestow on you each my blessing and as one my blessing. Hale, hale, hale morrows be yours as golden as the orchard of Ecthalon's leaves, fruitful as its boughs, and stalwart as its trunks. Always under the banner of the High King."

Nodding to his cousin, Thomas said quietly, "Thank you, Your Honor."

With a thunderous clap of his hands, Duncoin returned the attention to himself. "Now, let this evening be one of dancing, eating, and rejoicing for these young couples. Hale evening, indeed!"

With that, some of the Ords toward the front of the Knight Hall struck up tunes on their woodwind instruments and one on a stringed instrument. Those who had largely been in attendance crowded around the couples to give their blessings and celebrate in lively Ord dances Anargen had never seen before. But it soon faded from his thoughts, because it was eclipsed by the wonder of twirling hand in hand with Seren across the stone floors of the secret Knight Hall. His father close at hand, clapping and joining in the dances occasionally. Laughing and sharing stories with Thomas and Mia. All of it so improbably far from what he could have guessed. So, he stored it all, every sight, sound, and sensation deep within.

It wasn't what he had wanted for this day with Seren. But in their loss were greater gains that he would cling to in the coming days when he knew all would feel dangerously near to being ripped away from them.

FATE SPOKEN

They were trapped! An army to their back and before them an emissary of darkness.

As if acutely aware of his thoughts, Melania called out, "There's no point trying to turn back. Why don't you come on over here, closer, and we can talk."

Not a chance of that happening.

Melania had been the first girl to hold his affections. Years ago, before he had run away from the monstrous family he had been born into. Even from this distance, he could see her crooking her finger, beckoning him in the playful way she always had when they'd been together. He was only a child then and had grown up enough, even before becoming a Knight, to know she had been using him. During their last encounter, she had ratcheted things up still further by revealing her dabbling in witchcraft and her servitude to his brother, Dorian. She'd almost killed Defender Black after he'd been captured, and she would've killed Aria and him too if she could've done it. So, no. There was zero chance he'd play right into her hands.

"Really, Jason. Must you play hard to get?" she used her best pouting ploy. From this distance and given the circumstances, it rang hollow, which she must know.

Then why is she—

"Guess we'll just have to give you some encouragement." To the soldiers around her, she instructed, "Toss them over."

Faster than he would've believed possible, the three

kneeling Jhi'ish contacts were jerked upright and dragged to the edges of the stone bridge. Two were flung over the opposing sides.

Their screams punctured the night air and faded out of hearing. Jason looked over the edge of the bridge and realized that here, Jhi City was on the edge of a cliff. Below was a jagged field of broken remnants from underwater caves uncovered by land reclamation, a pointed plane created by redirecting the Jhire River's waters. The towering pillars of the metal suspension bridge of the modern Jhi City dropped down into the fog-shrouded recesses below, giving the sensation of crossing over the gaping maw of a massive beast.

An older stone bridge appeared to help form part of the supports for the new bridge base. If Jason had to guess, there were maybe another forty feet from the top of the stone bridge to the pointed stone bed below.

"One more left? Ready to come have a civil chat?" Melania taunted.

"Nanxi," Yúzé commented ruefully. His fists were clenched tight at his sides.

Cinaed looked toward the teetering young man in the distance and let out a sigh that seemed as deep as the drop beneath them. "Servants of the Dark Prince are like animals tormenting their captured prey for sport. If we oblige, it will only deepen the sport for them."

"What choice do we have?" Aria pointed out.

In that moment, Jason did not envy Cinaed the decision before him. They were caught either way, but before them lay the choice of fighting until the very end or surrendering themselves to all manner of torturous wiles on the hope of Nanxi being spared.

"Hmm, not the compassion I expected," Melania tsked. She

waved to the man holding him, and he shoved Nanxi off the side of the bridge.

Jason gaped, watching as the Jhi'ish Knight of Light disappeared below. Such capricious cruelty! Some part of him hadn't really believed Melania could truly be so cold-hearted. Cinaed was too generous, comparing this to animals enjoying the sport of their catch. This was the sort of malignance that made this war worth fighting.

Yúzé seemed to agree. He dropped into a fighting stance that Jason guessed the Jhi'ish had developed and drew a long, curved blade that had been concealed behind his back in his loose-fitting *shenyi*. Flames traced up its length, and it gleamed like the stars dotting the night sky on the horizon. Without a word, he was a blur, closing the distance to Melania and her minions.

There was nothing else to debate or ponder. Even if Aria and Defender Black hung back, Jason was already on Defender Guo's heels. His spiritsword drawn, he struck with a sizzling crackle as he brought it to bear, severing a Jhi'ish soldier's rifle in half. With a fiery flash, he pivoted and was behind the man and elbowed him in the back of the head before he could react. Melania might have been a practitioner of witchcraft, but her guards were ordinary soldiers.

Another Confederate cocked his weapon and was about to fire it at Jason, but a sudden crackle from his side halted the infantryman. Without verifying, he knew the burning rapier-like blade that ended the attack belonged to Aria. To his other side, Sir Cinaed was bearing down on still another of the murderous Jhi'ish soldiers.

If his estimate at that moment was right, there had been twenty of them arrayed to face the four Knights. Thanks in particular to Yúzé, that number had fallen to half that already.

Several feet back and slipping still farther away from the

melee, Melania watched with a decidedly impassive face. Almost sanguine as her trap fell apart. She had not even come in clothes practical for a fight. She was wearing a dark dress that hugged her bodice and ended in fringe that allowed it to dangle past her knees. High-heeled strappy shoes and decorative satin gloves reached past her elbows. A long pearl necklace hung over her bosom and a sheer shawl draped around her shoulders. Her only practical attire was the pins holding back her bouncy, ashen curls.

There wasn't a weapon on her, yet there seemed to be no hurry to her withdrawal, sashaying like a Rehalcy model rather than a retreating fighter. From Jason's vantage point, she seemed only to be casually interested in the fray. Though it was difficult to tell what her feelings on her impending defeat were, now that he was closer, he could tell the stoic expression she wore was a literal mask, faintly golden and cast to match the exact high cheeked and sharp-featured face under it. At least, as it would've looked before a previous battle with Jason marred half.

As the last of her squad dropped before Defender Guo, Melania began a slow clap. Every beat of her gloved hands coming together obnoxiously full of disdain. "Very impressive, I must say," she began. "I never would've expected you four to be coordinated enough to handle my Jhi'ish escort so handily."

They had dispatched them with greater ease than Jason expected, and now Melania was "appreciating" their efforts. Something wasn't right. Jason watched her expressionless faux face for several seconds, searching for a sign of what scheme she had planned.

Suddenly, she cocked her head to the side, as if watching for something. Jason followed her gaze and caught sight of the projectile just before it screamed into landing right beside them, blowing a chunk of the bridge into tiny bits of rubble.

Every tiny shard pelted Jason, forcing him to raise his shield in defense against their spray.

Smoke roiled off the impact site, and Jason waved it away from himself, his attention immediately turning back to Melania. Completely unfazed by the explosion, she stood there seemingly fixated on him as well, a hand on her hip.

He took a step toward her and another whistle screeched through the air just before the concussive blast shook the stones around him. This time, as he steadied himself, he heard a groan and looked back to see Defender Guo holding his leg. The shattered stones from the second blast pinned him. Aria and Sir Cinaed rushed to his side to tend to him.

"Poor Jason. You brought your marvelous little swords to what is decidedly a gun fight," Melania crowed. Hips rolling as she walked toward him, she gestured to a point in the distance. "My artillery needed to wait until you dispatched those imbecile Jhi'ish troops. My thanks for handling them."

Jason felt like he had just been the one blown aside by an artillery shell. "What? Why would you attack your own allies?"

"Why indeed?" The undeniable lilt of amusement gave her voice a sing-song quality. "You always were a step behind." She cocked her head as if looking past him and added, "But, mm, you made up for dullness in other ways ..."

He followed her line of sight to see that she was staring at Aria. His fiancée was still working to get Defender Guo seated up against the stone side of the bridge, but she went stiff for an instant, and he could tell the implication was aimed at her as much as him.

"Careful, Melania, you wouldn't want her to damage the other side of your face. Then all the petty jealousy hidden behind that mask will only double."

A hiss issued from Melania. "Your sharp tongue will cost you. And it will be your little phosphila wench who pays."

In contrast to her threat, Melania dashed away, all alluring show and poise discarded. Jason took off after her, only strides behind. She whirled around and blew on a whistle. Its shrill sound and volume brought Jason up short for just an instant. Just long enough for Melania to pull back and slam something squarely into his chest.

Landing and bouncing on the stone, Jason groaned. He struggled to sit up. As he did, he spotted in Melania's hands a long black glaive. She twirled it around, once more a hand on her hip. Confident. Condescending.

Though the blow had almost taken his breath, the stalwart armor of his *Thorax Dikaiosyne* wasn't even scratched. Back on his feet again, he closed half the distance between them before another whistle cut through the air. Then the second. And third.

"Run!" he bellowed as behind him the bridge exploded in flashes of smoke and fire. Bits of stone plinked off his armor, this time in chunks big enough that he tumbled back down onto the bridge. Without his armor, he would've been battered to a pulp. Smoke and dust from the pulverized stone billowed all around, and he couldn't see anything.

"Aria!" he cried out, horrified when he didn't immediately hear an answer. In fact, all he heard was a ringing in his ears and the gloating laughter of Melania, whose icy presence felt unnervingly near.

From beside his face, so near that he could almost feel her stinging cold breath blowing on his cheek as she spoke, he heard. "Well, now that we're alone ..."

Fury flooded Jason. "Ah!" he shouted, swinging his sword down to cleave her in two as he did.

She skirted the strike narrowly, a cruel smile playing on her lips. "You do have a temper. I see why the phosphila girl was so dear to you. She brings out your beastly side."

Scowling at her, Jason fought to regain his composure. He couldn't afford to let Melania goad and bait him. Not if he was to have any hope of defeating her and getting to Aria as quickly as possible.

"Ooh, don't pout so," Melania taunted. "I have a beastly side too ..."

With a sleek move, Melania removed her golden mask and muttered something. Jerking backward, she uttered a groan that became a growl. Her head snapped violently to and fro. She landed hands and knees on the ground, and Jason gaped in horror as she transformed from the cloying woman he had known into an enormous mass of wild fur. A werebeast.

Her icy blue eyes fixed on him, and she bared her fangs in a feral grin. Melania's bestial form wasn't quite like others he'd seen. Silvery and sleek, like the foxes of Knorland.

"You're full of tricks. Is this your true form?" he asked, kicking himself for sounding so haunted by what he saw. He knew the Melania he had thought he cared about never existed, and if she did, she was long gone. This transformation still carried with it a profound sadness. As though it confirmed she had fully left behind all humanity.

Melania bellowed a monstrous cry and bounded to his left. He whirled to guard, but she had already sprung to the right and then back again. Then her head crashed squarely into his shoulder, sending him tumbling.

Jason fumbled back to his feet. From where it was stowed on his back, he produced the little buckler shield he'd received at Vif the elf's directing in Brackenburgh. Vif—if only he had the aid of the elf warrior now.

He raised the shield in a barely ready defense as Melania lunged for his throat, jaws snapping. Her claws raked over his shield.

Bringing his sword around, he forced her back several steps.

She landed with a skid. Caught her traction and launched herself again.

Jason positioned himself to brace against her claws and biting. But as she sailed toward him, she twisted, transforming back into her human self and then into a sleek back spear that zipped behind him, flattened to the wall of the bridge, and disappeared in the shadowy recesses of the night.

His heart thundered in his chest. How was that possible? She'd gone from werebeast to shadows in a literal second. It was as if she had all the powers and perils of every dark creature in the Lowlands at her disposal.

Turning around, he watched the night. Stars still gleamed from beyond the lingering haze of ashen smoke. And ... wait, no, that couldn't be the strange ball of light he kept thinking he saw.

The ringing in his ears was fading. He thought he heard something, faint and insistent. Familiar voices. His heart leapt within him. Aria—he heard Aria! And Cinaed. What were they saying?

The words finally began to form for him: "Jason ... watch out!"

His head turned just in time to see the stream of obsidian mist blasting at him. It coiled from over the side of the bridge and struck him like a locomotive on the express line. He tumbled, skidding into the opposing wall with a jarring smack.

He scrambled to his knees and had his shield up as the thing coiled and struck again like a giant ethereal viper. It seemed to twist and turn around the bridge and snap and strike at angles he could scarcely guess even if given all the time in the Lowlands. He had less than a second each time.

Great King, please help!

At last, his ears heard the familiar whisper, and he inwardly railed that he had seemed to be ignoring it all along. Blinded by rage and bitterness that weren't befitting a Knight of Light.

Rolling out of the way, he swung and scored his first hit against the shadow serpent. There was a piercing screech, and Melania spun out from the midst of the dark, twisting mass. She landed on one knee, her glamorous appearance restored, minus the wound seared on one shoulder.

She growled and once more was the werebeast. Bands of lithe muscle flexed. She charged and slipped under his attack to snap at his leg from behind.

Jason pivoted and managed to avoid the bite, putting himself off balance. A hard kick from Melania's powerful hind leg landed on his midsection.

Bouncing off the stone wall again, he raised his block, expecting a bite and instead getting slapped by her voluminous vixen tail.

Melania tried to capitalize on it, spinning to chomp down on his shoulder. A whisper of warning moved Jason to tumble forward. It wasn't graceful, but it carried him out of reach of those jaws. They may have been less imposing than others he'd seen, but could certainly crush his bones if given the chance.

Hardly thrown, Melania slammed her large vulpine head squarely in Jason's chest, and he landed near the smoldering, ruined portion of the bridge. Aches flared reports from all over his body.

Why am I taking so many hits? The High King warns me of some, while others connect freely. Why?

Out of the corner of his eye, Jason spotted Aria and Cinaed dragging Defender Guo away. They had gotten him several feet farther along the bridge. He hadn't noticed them moving at all through this fight.

That's why. While she's fixated on me, they can get him to safety. There's a purpose to this pain.

Fortified by the realization, he jumped up and tanked another headbutt using his shield. Giving only inches, he pushed off and whirled around, going for a stroke at Melania's neck.

She dodged easily, but it forced her around to keep Aria, Cinaed, and Yúzé out of her view entirely. He fought the urge to smirk, knowing it would give too much away.

A snarl roiled up from deep in Melania's throat, and she lunged at him. This time, the High King's whispered instructions came, and Jason side-stepped the strike narrowly. With all his force, he brought down the pommel of his spiritsword on the back of her head.

As she recoiled, he sprang forward and scored a solid hit that landed near her hip. Smoke roiled off the glowing gash and elicited a squall.

The werebeast fumbled backward on the ground and morphed into Melania , teeth gritted as she waved away the smoke roiling off the site of the sword stroke. It would have wounded Jason, too, to see her in such pain, even with all she'd done, if the blankness on the left side of her face didn't remind him that Melania wasn't truly here. Only the witch that bore her form.

Walking over to her slowly, cautiously, he pointed his spiritsword toward her. She strained away from the crackling blade, the very sheen of its light on her seeming to intensify her wounds' stings.

His resolve about her slipped again. Insane as it might have been, he couldn't just see her as the monster. Not while she was solidly in the form of the maiden he had known.

"It doesn't have to be this way. You don't have to let the darkness poison you and destroy you. Yield to the—"

"Oh please, save your pity and ploys for someone else. You and that wench belong together ... rotting beneath the corpses of all your fool Order!" She screeched as the glowing gash on her leg stretched, burning deeper into her leg. Through her clenched teeth, she hissed, "Either finish me or do the courtesy of bending low so I can sink my fangs into your neck. Will you?"

The way her icy blue eyes narrowed at him was something Jason knew he would never escape in his nightmares.

A familiar hand grasped his arm, and he covered it with his free hand. Aria leaned against him. "We should go," she murmured to him. "Those troops on the other side of the bridge won't hang back forever. Who knows what other tricks she had in mind for us."

"What tricks indeed!" Melania squealed with wicked glee, and her lower half morphed from legs into a spiked serpent's tail. The barbed thing slung around whiplike.

"Watch out!" Aria yelled and shoved Jason out of the way, raising her own small *Thyreos Pistis* shield to deflect the blow.

Struggling to his feet, Jason could only groan in pain. An obsidian dagger zipped across the air and struck him in the chest near where the first hit. He staggered backward. As he fought to keep his balance and push away the pain, everything seemed to move faster than he conceived possible.

Melania's new tail coiled around Aria's legs, tripping her. Before Aria could act, she slammed her against the bridge and then produced the whistle from earlier, this time giving such a long note, he wondered if she would exhaust her lungs' air completely.

Booms and screeches of artillery fire filled the air. Jason turned to check on Cinaed and Defender Guo. They were more than a dozen yards away. He had to get to them before the artillery shells did!

Sprinting toward the Defenders, he knew he'd only have seconds before the first shell hit. Pushing himself, he reached

Cinaed and grabbed for Defender Guo. "We have to move him!"

"No!" Cinaed bellowed. His eyes weren't toward the danger. They were fixed behind Jason.

Jason's heart seized as he spun around and watched a shell impact the side of the bridge beside where Aria and Melania battled. The impact reverberated through the stones and knocked Aria off her feet. The Melania beast writhed, having taken most of the stony shards and shrapnel herself. More shells were incoming.

Jason managed to take three steps before he was jerked to a halt. He whirled around, ready to deck whatever servant of the dark was keeping him from Aria. But it was Cinaed. His eyes were fixed with horror, but he shook his head as the next shell hit the bridge and tore a chunk out of the stone and Melania's serpent tail. Aria didn't move.

Another shell and another hit. Melania's screams managed to pierce the booms that were already deafening Jason again. More shells rained and began moving toward them as whole sections of the bridge gave a stony moan and fell away.

Cinaed tugged Jason backward, forcing him over to the other Defender and placing one of the Jhi'ish Knight's arms over each of them. Jason numbly followed, unable to comprehend what he was seeing. What was happening. Only after his feet left the ancient bridge and they stood before a new tunnel did he stop.

What am I doing? I have to go back for her!

The same strong hands were quick to grab him again. "No!" Cinaed insisted. "No."

"I have to go back for her! She's hurt. I have to—"

"No, my child. No ... agh," Cinaed's voice hitched, and his grip faltered. The pitiful sound from the old storyteller, who was steadier than a mountain, transfixed Jason to the spot. He looked at his mentor's face and saw his eyes were glassy, his hands were shaking now. "I ... can't ... lose you both," he wailed and dropped to his knees.

Jason dropped to his knees as well. His eyes felt like they couldn't close. He couldn't blink, couldn't move, couldn't breathe. He had completely miscalculated Melania's vengefulness and cruelty. Cinaed and Guo weren't her targets, Aria was. All he could think over and over was, *"This isn't happening. This isn't happening. I can't have lost her. This isn't happening."*

Except he must have been saying it out loud, because Cinaed's arms wrapped around him in a fierce embrace, and he sobbed into them.

"I'm so sorry, lad."

The Day After

"One breath's space. That's what it seems we are granted. Still, it is perhaps the sweetest breath I have taken since departing Black River for my first journey to Ordumair."

Anargen's King's Day Journal
16 Fylleth 1610 Middle Era

Anargen blinked. Deep inside Ordumair's mountain, it was impossible to tell the sun had risen. Thus, a special bell was rung on all the rounds to signal to Ords the start of a new day. Whether he had heard the morning toll or simply been acclimated to rising with the dawn, Anargen was awake.

"Mmm," Seren murmured beside him, snuggling up closer to him, still deep in sleep.

For a moment, Anargen just lay there, feeling the warmth of Seren's body close to his. Her head was resting on his left arm, and he traced his fingertips through her long, dark locks. Was this truly real? This incredible sensation of comfort and contentment? They had been married for less than a day, yet felt interwoven. No longer two, but one. It had always seemed a bit of a cliché, but in this moment, he understood it.

There had been more passionate ways of expressing that unity. Things they had reserved until their first night of marriage. Though that was certainly enjoyable, there was something about the simplicity of this moment, the peace, the implicit trust, and ease that made him enjoy this facet of their new life together even more. For however long that might be.

Unconsciously, he winced. It had been easier to face that his life might be ended within days before he had experienced this. Before he had seen the fascinating beauty of Seren sleeping, her rosy lips parted as she breathed lightly. Her form fit perfectly to his, and it seemed now a double tragedy loomed, as though the loss of either of them was compounded by the fact that "they" would also be lost even if one of them managed to survive what was ahead.

Anargen refused to regret this. Refused to regret finally being tied to Seren for life, because life wasn't a fixed length. No guarantee existed in the best of times. Whether it was war or old age or any other woe of the Lowlands, until the King's Day and joining him in the Highlands, this was the curse all people bore.

"You look awfully thoughtful for such an early hour, husband," Seren noted drowsily.

Anargen grinned. "Getting a solid start on one of my life's most important tasks."

"What's that?" she asked on a yawn.

"Keeping my wife safe from every harm of which I'm able."

Her cocoa eyes held his gaze fast for an instant before she reached up and kissed him. He wasn't in any hurry to end it. When their lips parted, Seren sighed. "You've been doing that for a lot longer than this morning. You've always made me feel safe." Her voice took on a distant, reflective quality. "Not just from external harms. My love always felt safe in your care."

Brushing her forehead with another kiss, Anargen murmured, "It's my aim to always care for you so. And better, with time."

Seren gripped him tightly. "There may not be much time," she reminded him.

"Maybe, maybe not. Whatever time we're given, though," he brushed her cheek, wiping away a single stray tear, "I will treasure."

A slight smile spread on Seren's lips, the sort that never failed to transfix him. Anargen leaned forward to kiss her, a heat familiar from the night before rising in him.

KNOCK. KNOCK. KNOCK.

"It looks like someone else is up early," Seren commented, a note of disappointment unmistakable in her velvety voice.

"I'll answer it," he said on a sigh and pulled on his tunic and boots. He rubbed his face to help massage away the remaining vestiges of the idyllic morning's hold on him, so he could focus on whatever prompted the visit. The fifth knock piqued his interest.

Opening the door, he found his father standing there, preparing to knock again. The older man stepped back. "Sorry to disturb you, son," he said, appraising Anargen's still disheveled appearance. "There's grave news, I'm afraid."

"What is it?" Anargen asked, shooting a concerned look back at Seren. She had already slipped on her dress and was hastily braiding her hair.

Glewdyn waited for his son's attention to return to him before continuing. "Would that I could spare you this after such a short respite, but preparations for a defense of the fortress are underway. Tengrath's men were ambushed last night."

"Ilyron's forces made it here sooner than expected," Anargen mused.

"Not exactly," Glewdyn sighed. "It appears last night Elder Feingohl attacked and tried to murder Elder Tengrath."

"What?"

"Or at least a creature posing as him did. The attempt

wounded Tengrath, but his men were able to slay the Feingohl duplicate before he could finish Tengrath."

Anargen shook his head. "He was a doppelgänger and no one realized it."

"Perhaps. The scout couldn't confirm that the false Feingohl was faceless, only that he 'transformed' after death."

"I suppose it doesn't matter greatly what specifically posed as Feingohl. Just that it infiltrated Ordumair without notice." Icy dread traced the length of Anargen's back. "How many others here might be doppelgängers ..."

"A month ago, Feingohl had gone missing in battle and returned a few days later, claiming he had escaped enemy imprisonment. That's when they think it happened. So many in Ordumair have served abroad, any of them, even the Thane, could be compromised."

Gnawing on his lip as he thought, Anargen gave a vigorous shake of his head. "No. Thane Duncoin is himself. There's too much that felt the same about him, even if initially he seemed to act erratically." He refrained from adding that if anyone felt off, it was Iaegon. His mentee, who had been notably absent from the wedding and avoided Anargen broadly. But Anargen couldn't bear the thought that he was gone, replaced by one of those blank-faced, shapeshifting horrors.

"Is Tengrath pulling back?" he asked instead.

Glewdyn shrugged. "Not by appearances. I wanted you to be aware so you can be on guard. The Thane has decreed that no one except Urald and Cerelah bringing you things as needed may disturb you and Seren this evening." The latter he said with a fatherly chuckle that faded into a somberness. "It is the very least that can be accorded to you both. That, and this." His father produced a small grey pouch tied with a fine blue cord and palmed it into Anargen's hand.

Bouncing it up and down, Anargen tested its weight. "Light ... what's in here?"

"See for yourself," Glewdyn replied, his smile tight from barely restrained emotion.

Undoing the blue cord, Anargen opened the pouch. Immediately, the scent of what lay within reached him. A fragrance of cloves and oranges wafted to him from within. "Mm, good tea. Where—"

"A gift from all of us, as I said. It's Avon-caroon orange-blossom tea if you both fancy the taste and ... have the chance to venture off to get more another day." Glewdyn cracked another thinly spun smile. "You are brewed now."

"Brewed" was the word used in Black River for a closing wedding tradition in which a newly-married couple would go into their new home and brew their first pot of tea together. Or coffee or cocoa. The latter being a new twist on the custom, though hardly as elaborate a one as some couples who had an entire meal laid out and made an affair of it for the whole village.

He and Seren weren't keen tea drinkers or partiers and planned to choose a quiet cocoa to be "brewed" when they had dreamed together of their wedding, but neither coffee nor cocoa was in ready supply here, and he guessed this tea was quite precious coming from the besieged nation of Albaron's artisanal enclave at Avon-caroon.

Anargen hugged his father tightly. "Thank you."

Glewdyn returned the hug and patted him on the back. "Well then, I'll leave you to your bride."

As his father started to leave, a thought struck Anargen. "Oh, wait, what about Thomas and Mia? They'll need to be alerted to what's happened as well."

"Gregor is seeing to that." Glewdyn chuffed. "That boy is

rather something. What that something is, I haven't yet decided."

Anargen couldn't fight back a smirk. "You spent the evening together?"

"We each couldn't sleep and stayed out in the parlor. It certainly made my night ... less quiet."

Anargen stifled a laugh and only half caught it. "Thane's decree or not, if you need rescuing, come to us."

Glewdyn nodded, grinning. "Thank you." More earnestly, he added, "Hale morning, son."

"Hale morning, father."

The door shut with a heavy thud, even though he closed it gently. Anargen called out, "I don't know if you heard, but we've been brought tea for our being 'brewed.' I know it's not cocoa, but—" When Anargen turned back to Seren, he saw she was sitting on the bed, hands in her lap, staring at the floor.

Dashing to her side, Anargen looked her over, anxious. Seren's eyes were glossy with tears. "Beloved, what's wrong?"

She looked away, wincing. No other answer came.

"Did you overhear the conversation with father?"

She nodded but continued to lean away, eyes squinted tightly shut as tears freely trailed down her pale, soft cheeks.

"I know it's upsetting, but there's a good chance it was only Feingohl who was compromised."

She drew in a shuddering breath, a sob catching in her throat. "It's not that."

"What is it then?" he asked, genuinely perplexed. He took one of her hands and rubbed it gently.

She turned to rest her head against his chest and groaned. "I know I'm awful to be so selfish, given what everyone is facing and that Elder Feingohl is likely dead, but when you hugged your father, it reminded me that I haven't seen my mother or brother for more than a year. And now ..."

Anargen shushed her gently as sobs rocked his wife's frame. Arms wrapped around her, he soothed, "I'm sorry, my love. I've already been a poor husband to forget how much you're missing at a time when we should be surrounded by family and friends."

She shook her head. "You haven't failed. You've lost so much too. I just can't stop thinking about how I'll never see them ..." Sobbing overtook her words and turned them to a wail.

"We don't know what the future holds. Only that it's in the High King's hands."

She leaned into him, her arms gripping him fiercely. "Everything but you being by my side is so awful. You're handling it so much better than I am."

He kissed her on the top of her head. "Having you here makes it difficult to despair." He tilted up her chin and gave her a crooked smile. She rolled her eyes but managed to quirk up a cheek amid the shudders still besetting her.

"Hard as it may be now," he added, "one day soon all of this hurt and pain will only be a memory as indistinct as clearing fog. The High King will bind up all our wounds inside and out. We'll be with him in his Kingdom, and the joy there will make all the hardships till then seem like feathers on life's scales."

Seren nestled into him, her breathing becoming more regular. "Mia spoke it well. I needed you without ever realizing how much."

"I need you too." He leaned back so that they both lay there wrapped around each other. Sheltering each other from the hard things waiting beyond the walls of their room and holding dearly onto the hope that the High King would set all right for them, and for everyone in the end.

"WAKE UP. ANARGEN! WAKE UP."

Anargen jerked awake. Seren's arm was draped over him. They had fallen asleep some time ago. He recalled them being brought dinner and all the intimate and tender hours after. What time must it be now? Their candles were all burned out, and hazy smoke trails still drifted off some of them.

One in the morning? Two?

What had woken him?

His thoughts finally focused enough to realize Seren had shaken him awake. Her eyes were wide with concern. "Did you hear that?"

A clear keening note echoed faintly to him. He waited to hear the sound a second time to be sure.

"It's an Ord rallying horn."

"Is this it then? The fortress is under siege?"

He shook his head. "No. That sounds different. This is blown to alert the dwarfs within the city that defenders are dispatched abroad. To be mindful of their courage and yearn for their victory. Tengrath and the others at Valesgard are locked in battle now."

"How long do you think they can hold back Ilyron's forces?"

Scooting to sit upright in the bed, he rubbed his face. "Um, that is in the High King's hands. But holding them for more than a few hours would be a great success."

"Shouldn't we go wake the others and prepare ourselves?"

"We should wake them, but not for a fight. We should plead for Tengrath and the others' well-being before the High King. Ilyron is a monster, and he'll wait till there are hours of night ahead to advance on Ordumair."

Seren sighed. "I had tricked myself into forgetting that our time together was just a brief reprieve."

"This was more than a reprieve. It's the beginning of our

life together. Whether the end is tomorrow night or a hundred years from now, I treasure what we have."

She brushed his cheek with a kiss. "You never let me lie in despair."

"That is something we do for each other. I'm just repaying you for keeping me from giving up in the woods outside Kirke."

She nodded. "We keep each other from falling."

"Always," he agreed.

"Always," she seconded.

Interlacing their fingers, he kissed the back of her hand. "Let's wake the others."

BY THE TIME Urald arrived to summon them all, Anargen, Seren, and the others had been awake for hours. Sometimes talking among themselves, often beseeching the High King to intervene.

From the quiet way Urald carried himself, the summons to see Thane Duncoin was not to join a victory celebration.

Entering his audience chamber, several Ord elders were already present. Duncoin's chin rested on his fist. He roused from an introspective stupor at the sight of them. "Hale morning, friends of Ordumair."

From his tone, it wasn't truly hale. "Hale morning, Your Honor," Glewdyn replied on their behalf. "You summoned us?"

Duncoin sighed. "Valesgard Pass fell earlier. Our scouts report a sedan approaches, borne up by a quartet of Monarchist honor guards."

"That's a bold move for Ilyron," Gregor scoffed. "Trusting Your Honor not to draw and quarter him in his arrogance."

A near growl rumbled from deep in Duncoin's chest. "Aye,

I find it a test of my mettle not to order such. It's futile either way. What will come upon us is set. His army will carry out his will whether he is dead or alive."

"You would have us meet him with you?" Thomas surmised.

"Aye," Duncoin admitted and rose from his elevated seat. "If I must face that monster, best to do it with those who bear fire for slaying beasts."

Looking across the five of them, Glewdyn drew his spiritsword. Flames raced up its length with an audible *whoosh*. "Then our blades will be your defense, dear Thane."

FLANGE CLIMB

"Jason? Lad, did you hear me?" Cinaed pressed, his voice earnest, concerned.

"Mhm," Jason murmured in response, disinterested in actually addressing what the old man wanted to speak about. Outside, the train blew its whistle, and Jason jolted in his seat. It was so loud and just shrill enough to evoke the sounds of the shells sailing through the air to hit ...

He closed his eyes. There was no fight left in him.

It should have been me. I should've been the one.

That was the first thought he had once his mind had unseized enough to think past his disbelief. That first awful moment when his mind betrayed him and accepted the reality that Aria, his beloved, his betrothed, his soulmate, was gone. Every sinew, inch of skin, even every follicle of hair felt raw and jagged as if a piece of him had been violently torn away. And it had. That moment before they left the gardens, standing before the Aperture of Fate, they had made their vows to each other.

It may not have been a "real" ceremony like fairy tales had with poofy dresses and dashing suits, sentimental melodic strains, and ripples of excitement permeating the air. But it was real in every sense of the sincerity, passion, commitment, and love between them. He had unequivocally vowed to bind himself to Aria until death parted them. That time ended up being shorter than the length of time he, Cinaed, and Defender Guo had stood in wait at the platform before boarding this train. He had wanted a thousand lifetimes with her and had only minutes.

"Just hand it to me, okay," he said for the third time since they'd taken their seats. Their overstuffed, scratchy, bland seats —the kind she would have hated—on the first train out of Monzu Regu, bound for Centros. They would be sitting on these miserable seats for days, and he did not want to start the trip with another squabble with the heartbroken old man in the other seat. "She wanted me to finish it."

Huffing, Cinaed protested. "She wanted you to understand how she felt. To comprehend the significance of the story. Before you both ..."

He didn't have the guts to say it. Maybe it wasn't fair of Jason to hold that against him, but Jason sure wasn't interested in giving Cinaed any extra slack when he had none to spare for himself. "Before we started our lifetime of happiness together? That didn't work out. So, I need to know what was worth the waiting, the trepidation she felt. Why we couldn't have even one full day together as husband and wife before I lost her."

"We lost her, but I don't want to lose you too. You have to face the grief before—"

Closing his eyes for an instant, Jason felt the snap of his last nerve. He leveled a gaze burning with barely restrained fury on the older man. "Face my grief? Do you even hear yourself, Cinaed? You sound like a hollowed-out husk, a caricature of Aria's grandfather. Don't tell me about 'facing my grief,' you sure as—" He had to catch himself lest he launch into curses and expletives and further criticisms that he would never be able to unspeak.

Cinaed's grave old face grew fierce as a storm. "Don't you dare try to tell me how to grieve my granddaughter. You loved her for, what, a couple of years? I've loved her her whole life. I held her as an infant and cared for her after her parents' deaths. The weight of their passing only adds to the sorrow of Aria's."

He softened some, the storm fading from thunder and lightning to a steady rain. "I see your devastation. I know all too well what it is to lose the woman you love. You only sampled a morsel of it. You grieve your imagination of a life together. I know what its weight and texture and contours are truly like. To have grown so close to your wife that there is only one life, not two, and the absence of her leaves a cavernous wound that can't be filled because nothing is precisely her shape, her fit in your life.

"You may heal, but the scars never fade completely, and the thing you have is memory. That and the promise that we make as those who survive to not just exist but honor their memory by living and resembling still the person they loved. To serve the High King all our lives so that when we reach the end of our own days, we will be able come before him unashamed and find the hurts of our lifetime absolved, cured as they can't be now."

Cinaed's jaw tensed and untensed in quick succession and he seemed to realize he was letting his thoughts sweep far past his initial point. It was all true, but unfocused, difficult to harvest and consume. Huffing, he reined himself in. "Weep. Moan. Cry. Grieve as you must. But recall that as by comes to by, we shall see the Light."

Jason scowled. In Cinaed's words were the steady beat of a broken heart, but he couldn't see how Cinaed could actually understand what he was facing. He talked about how much worse it was to lose his wife after a lifetime together. A lifetime. Besides, he didn't need Cinaed's changing moods to tell him neither of them was handling Aria's loss well. He could say that, tear the man apart. End whatever was left of their bond to each other.

Rather than go down that path, Jason stood up and threw open the door to their private seating area. He stalked through the train, passing overly helpful porters offering in Hilanese to do something or other for him. He didn't speak enough of the language to care to do more than wave them off. Aria loved Hilanese and the country of Vov Hilan that birthed it. It was the soaring jade and emerald canopies of the Uhil Forest that most captivated her. Thousand-year-old trees, wide as a train car, soaring over a hundred feet into the sky. The brightly colored birds, frogs, flowers—all of it. The rainforest's breadth and depth of life resonated with the woman whose very essence seemed to be in harmonic resonance with it. Both were so full of life ...

Finding himself alone at last in a luggage car, Jason sat on a beaten old trunk, his head in his hands. He couldn't keep doing this. Lashing out at Sir Cinaed. None of this was the old man's doing. In fact, if Jason hadn't been so bent on fighting on the frontlines of the war, then they might have been with Cinaed when he first met with Defender Guo, and none of them would've been caught on that bridge.

My fault. It always circles back to my fault.

Scratching his face as he pulled his fingers down from it, he knew that if he didn't right himself and settle back onto the tracks, then he would wreck, and that would be the end of it. Feeling like everything he did, or thought, or said somehow doomed his love for Aria made it hard to cope. His mind kept writing them into their fate-spoken end. But what was he supposed to do? There was no escaping this. No mending it. Pain from an injury like this could fade, and he would go on, even if crippled, for the rest of life. Unless the phantom sensation of the loss lingered and never let go.

Jason was almost certain this was going to be the latter.

Through gritted teeth, he pleaded. "Please, my Great King,

I'm trying to hold on, but it's hard. So. Very. Hard. I don't understand this. And I can't accept it. But I have to, because people are counting on me. The Lowlands needs all of us united against the dark. All I can think about day and night is how it hurts and how it won't get better."

He waited for a response, even the faintest whisper of one. Silence loomed over him, filling every inch of the room until it threatened to choke him.

Standing, Jason clapped his hands together. "Right. Well ..."

Marching back into the compartment with Cinaed, he grabbed the journal from out of the older Knight's pack and gave him a look that dared him to intervene.

There was no fight left in the Defender's eyes, no deep, scouring look that could see through all of Jason's walls. Just quiet acceptance.

Jason made sure to make the sound of him opening the journal dramatically loud. Flipping through pages and crinkling them on purpose. Jason knew it would rankle the old man. Whether he consciously acknowledged it or not, to some degree, he did blame Sir Cinaed and was indeed punishing him. All the more, because Jason's efforts to spite him largely seemed to have no success.

15

THE GATHERING DARK

"It has begun again. The danger. The death. All the terrors from which I plead the High King delivers Ordumair. And, in the midst of it, that I do not falter in upholding my oaths to Him. Even if the worst, which is by appearances unavoidable, befalls me."

Anargen's King's Day Journal
17 Fylleth 1610 Middle Era

The sun's rays were undeniably fading into twilight when the bier borne by Monarch Ilyron's personal guard stopped in front of Ordumair's assembled ambassage. Thane Duncoin pulled all of the Ords who lived in the modest farming village outside Ordumair's gates within the fortress walls. Even so, he insisted on forming a defensive perimeter well past the village for meeting Ilyron.

A chilly wind rushed down off the mountains to the west and stole away any lingering hints of warmth in the valley, bearing with it a strong chance of ice and snow. It bit fiercely enough that Anargen shut the faceplate on his helmet. The glowing fire that traced the inscriptions on his armor, divine words of the High King himself, gave off more than enough warmth and light to help him bear up under the frigid bluster. At his sides, his wife and father each were handling the deteriorating weather well. Such was true also of Thomas, Mia, and Gregor, though the latter quaked a bit, seemingly from nerves more than anything else. Those Ords and Restoration Ecthels present to complete the guard were less stalwart, but impressive in that they did not have the same protections as the Knights.

Six honor guards accompanied Ilyron's litter. Four carrying it and two marching before it, banners bearing the sigil of the Monarch. A procession with all the airs of royalty but lacking scale and ceremony.

Anargen shot a glance down the line of those nearest him, but like himself, the other Knights all had their faceplate shut against the cold.

Coming to an abrupt halt, the guards stood there without acknowledging anyone. Up close, they were massive, towering brutes. They were each a good foot taller than Anargen, which meant they were well over seven feet. Not giants per se, but still cruelly ironic choices given the tallest Ord present was Duncoin, and he wasn't much more than five feet tall. Heavily armored with black tinted plate mail, they had not shifted a hair's breadth since stopping, rigid and emotive as stone.

The longer Anargen had to look at them, the more unease he had about these soldiers. Every one of them reeked of dark sorceries. Minutes passed without the faintest hint of motion from the Monarch's entourage nor discernible through the dark tent curtain draped over his bier, which bore the emblems of his monarchical title.

"I have stood here waiting out this fiend long enough," Duncoin grumbled. Projecting his voice and not bothering to school his tone, he shouted, "If the dread Monarch Ilyron has anything to say, then let it be said quickly. Otherwise, be prepared to die here—you and all your men with you."

Another full minute passed before the guards lowered the bier to the ground. Two of them moved to flank the litter's exit flap and pulled aside the coverings. From it emerged a figure darkened with shadows that did not seem to respond to the failing day's light. Troubling as that was, it was less than half the story. Ilyron wasn't the one who stepped out.

"What nonsense is this?" Duncoin protested. "Tengrath? Is that you?"

The almost startlingly diminutive dwarf with such furious sentiments less than two days prior stepped out and stood deathly still. His armor had dents and was scored from serious hits. He wore no helmet, not even attempting to mask who he was any more than he offered a clarification on why he was the one striding out from Ilyron's personal litter.

Why would Ilyron spare Tengrath and send him now? Is this his attempt to feign peace once more?

As unsettling as Tengrath's armor's state and the untended wounds were, they were nothing compared to the vacancy in his eyes. Tengrath was a brute, a boor, and a bully; but inasmuch as he was all those things, he was by that same nature fiercely charismatic. None of what typified Tengrath remained in his gaze now.

"What have you done to him?" Duncoin demanded.

The guards did not respond. Did not move. Anargen strained, hoping to hear them at least breathe. The horrible notion that these were some sort of animated armors, empty of real life, was almost as unnerving as the numbed Tengrath before them.

Slowly, with a bit of jerkiness, Tengrath raised a parchment clenched tight in his hand and unrolled it. Like a herald at a tournament, he began reading. Though his voice hardly sounded like the boisterous Ord's. It was like an echo of his voice across an arid desert. "His Eminence, Maldes Ilyron, Monarch of Ecthelowall, Baron of Halifax, Baron of Emeral, and Prince of the Middlebane Islands, bids you greetings."

"Tengrath? What folly is this that you're acting as Ilyron's mouthpiece?" Duncoin looked like he wanted to cross the divide and shake the man, but had better sense than to do so.

"His Eminence spared my life to deliver this message. Ordumair will fall, and all who dare to defend it will die."

Tengrath was so void of any emotion as he said it that Anargen wondered if he had been replaced by a doppelgänger. As he focused, he realized it was worse. Much worse. There were striations on his greying skin. Difficult to spot due to his bushy beard and armor. Blackened veins that stood out like a spiderweb of chains. Tengrath was a carrion now. A mindless slave to the Monarch's will.

Duncoin seethed. "You traded even a few hours longer life to betray your people and dishonor yourself and your family's banner in this way?

"You may tell your new master that whatever substance he found you to be made of, if he imagines the rest of the Ords to be crafted of the same, he will be the one to die and all his maniacal plans come to nothing!"

Tengrath cocked his head and bleated like a goat. It was a hideous sound, raspy as his voice had become.

Duncoin looked at those around him, his brows knitted in question. There were no answers to explain the bizarre behavior.

Again, Tengrath bleated. And again. Duncoin tried to speak, but each time, Tengrath just bleated louder.

"What in the Lowlands are you doing?" Duncoin shouted.

"Meeehhh," Tengrath screamed back so loud that the veins in his neck bulged.

"Arraggh!" Duncoin charged forward and slugged Tengrath in the face.

The other Ord's head lolled back. Slowly, ever so slowly, he righted his head and turned it to face Duncoin. Blood dribbled from his lip. He smiled hideously. "Mountain goats, all of you mountain goats for the slaughter."

As sudden as a viper strike, Tengrath's deadened eyes grew wide.

A feral screech erupted from his mouth, and he rushed past the Thane to launch himself at Gregor. Fueled by his unbridled fury, his full weight crushed Gregor to the ground.

Yelping, Gregor tried to push the hefty Ord off, and though the fiery inscriptions on Gregor's armor scorched Tengrath's fingers, the wild Ord tore at Gregor like a fox would a turtle.

Two Ords and an Ecthel bodyguard grabbed at Tengrath to jerk him off the boy. But he just threw down the Ords and snagged the dagger from the Ecthel's belt, slashing him and then slamming the sleek blade into Gregor's chest plate over and over.

"Stop!" Duncoin bellowed and reached for Tengrath.

In a series of swift moves, Thomas stepped forward and brought his spiritsword around, battering aside the stolen dagger and then embedding the burning blade in Tengrath's back.

The Ord Elder wailed and recoiled, his hands frantically straining for his wound, which sizzled and crackled. Thomas let him take a few wobbling steps away and then jerked free the sword.

With a strangled cry, Tengrath collapsed to the ground. As Tengrath fell, Duncoin dropped down, one hand hovering over him as though he feared to burn himself by touching the fiery wound.

Anargen's eyes darted from the felled elder to the Monarch's guards. If the six thought or felt anything about what just happened, they didn't express it at all. Though Anargen was willing to bet the dark figures would be all too ready to engage them in battle if directly prompted.

Duncoin snapped out of the shock of what had just taken place and drew himself up. In his authoritative voice as Thane, he commanded, "Go back to your 'Eminence' and tell him petty tricks like this will certainly not be enough to overthrow Ordumair, now or ever. If he withdraws before morning, then there will be peace. If not, then he, like his ancestors, will discover the full fury of the Ords."

The guards silently turned to leave and then paused. From the ground came a hissing sound. Tengrath raised up, his breath a raspy wheeze. "Nothing will save you, Duncoin, last Thane of Ords, from the slaughter."

Tengrath fell still. A chill greater than the icy wind wound its way around Anargen, and from the way Seren shuddered, he knew she felt it too. Whatever Duncoin's bluster, it would take far more than their courage and stories of the Ords' past to survive what lay ahead.

When the silent sentinels were out of earshot, lost to the deepening twilight near the valley's mouth, Thomas spoke up. "I'm sorry, Your Honor, for striking down Elder Tengrath." He and Mia stood beside a visibly shaken Gregor. "I could not let him harm the Heir Apparent."

Duncoin waved dismissively. "Aye. You are pardoned. As much a thorn as Tengrath could be, I hate the manner in which Ilyron"—Duncoin spat the Monarch's name—"used him. He deserved a warrior's end."

Shaking his head, Duncoin looked at those still assembled. "All of you, take up the defensive positions we prepared. The Monarch will not delay his attack. I shall come with further orders once you're readied."

When Anargen and the other Knights started to follow, Duncoin held up a gauntleted hand. "No. You all must join the Ecthel forces Thomas brought. Wait till Ilyron's army is in position and come around and flank them. Our best chance is to surprise them under cover of dark and hope they turn on each other in the fray."

Anargen's brows raised. "What about your people's distrust?"

"It is because of what has transpired since allying ourselves with the Ecthels that my people do not wish to trust," Duncoin chided.

"It's not our fault—" Gregor began heatedly and then just as quickly fizzled out under Duncoin's withering gaze.

"I know you meant no ill. We have suffered beyond precedence. Having you aid us in the battle may yet cost me my seat as Thane, but I will give it ten times over if it delivers my people."

Looking them over once more, he added, "Go. Prepare. May the High King be with us all."

As Anargen watched Thane Duncoin trudge off to the fortress gates, he heard Seren at his side whisper to Mia, "Does this mean we have a chance? Now that your army will join the battle?"

"I don't know," Mia answered gravely.

16
A Sundering Blow

Darkness hung heavy upon the landscape, and it had only grown colder in the hours since the Monarch mocked them with his puppeteering of Tengrath. Looking out from his concealment, Anargen noted the tenebrous mass of Monarchist soldiers tainting the lower reaches of the valley. There were more of them than he'd feared. So many. As the number of their foes arrayed before the fortress swelled, holding onto his hopes they could defeat them felt more and more like trying to grasp a cloud.

Sensing someone's approach, he glanced up to find his father to his left. As the older man surveyed their enemy much as he had, Anargen asked, as loudly as he dared, "How did you and Mother do this?"

His father's brows knitted in question.

"Follow the quests given you, knowing you might lose each other?" Anargen clarified.

Glewdyn sighed. "In honesty, son, your mother and I never faced anything quite like this. We were part of a handful of quests for the High King together, before you were born. What we've been called to face here is something no Knights for maybe fifty generations have seen. We may well be on the edge of seeing the King's Day. If so, then nothing has ever been or ever will be like this."

Anargen did his best not to let his disappointment show. It was silly. He understood how momentous the times were, how dire the stakes. Fortunately, the dark masked much of the anxious fidgeting of his hands.

"It's not as though Seren and I haven't faced danger before. In Stormridge, outside Kirke. Death was very near. But I …"

His father placed a hand on the pauldron over his right shoulder. "It's different now because you've had a glimpse of what you could lose. I knew from the first time I saw you and Seren together that you had found your wife. But having made those vows, having dared to dream, even for a moment, it changes you to the bones. I don't believe the High King would rebuke you for your heart being pressed for your wife. Mine is certainly heavy for you. For you both.

"You can't let those thoughts distract you, though, no matter how natural they are. A vessel emptied holds more, so cast all your anxiety down before the High King, and he will fill what's lacking. Understood?"

"Yes, sir," Anargen replied.

Glewdyn arched a brow. "You're staring at me like there's something more you want to say."

Anargen flashed a winsome grin no one else would see. "I'm just thankful to have you here with me. To face this."

"Ten thousand armies of ten thousand could be arranged against us and still the High King will have ensured we have everything we need to face what we must in his service. Such as the Ecthel soldiers having used the time they were forced to wait outside Ordumair's walls to learn every pathway through and around the mountains of this area," Glewdyn pointed out. "The vantage from the Highland is far greater than what he can see."

That was true. Had the Ecthels not been seemingly sent away, Anargen was certain the Thane's plan would be utterly impossible to follow. These Ecthels had shown them ways to circle around through the steep slopes surrounding the Valley of Ords that Anargen didn't know. Perhaps even the Ords didn't. Even so, his small battle group, far closer to the front than Seren and Mia's, was not poised to escape this unscathed. He had been encouraged at the proper moment to say his goodbyes to Seren and the others.

There was a faint sound of gravel sliding down the rock face to their back. Thomas crept up beside them. "All groups are in position," he informed them. "As soon as the cannons open fire, we are to charge from behind and take them. We'll be favored to reach them, but if we do and can disable them, Ordumair's chances of surviving this are incalculably better."

"You do your people proud, Baron Fenwrest," Glewdyn said.

"Ah, it's Baron Halifax, actually," he corrected. "Thank you, Sir. Would that I could have done more ... and had more by my side to face this."

That sentiment Anargen understood. Thomas hadn't spoken much about the circumstances surrounding his adoption by Ecthelion and the Viceroy's sudden death in battle. Its sting was still too fresh. Even if it wasn't, Thomas already knew the pain of losing both his natural father and his mentor before. The last was something he and Thomas shared.

What would Sir Cinaed say in this moment?

"There is nothing more that the High King would have us do than be faithful to our oaths in whatever time and place we are called to do so," Anargen mused, hearing Cinaed's deep, melodious voice in his head.

"Cinaed couldn't have said it better himself," Glewdyn patted his son on the back.

"I wish I could have—" Thomas began.

BOOM.

Sounds of cannon fire echoed off the stern stone mountain faces. If it was not Anargen who trembled from their force, then the mountains themselves were.

"That's our summons," Thomas announced. "Stay with me."

"To the end," Anargen agreed."

"May the High King be with us," Glewdyn pronounced.

Thomas stood and produced a brass horn and sounded a long, hearty call. As the sharp notes sliced through the darkening evening air, Anargen spotted those with them rising to charge. In the distance, the horn sound was repeated as each of the other regiments echoed the call to strike hard and fast.

Anargen rushed down the slope, heart hammering. This was it. The Ords. The war. The Quest. All of it hung on this battle.

The back ranks of the Monarchists took notice and spun to face the sound and fury descending on them. They were mainly plain longbowmen by the look of them.

Most of the horses had been reserved for the regiment in which Seren, Mia, and Gregor were placed, with all three mounted to make a quick return to the fortress if it came to that. Anargen's group had a few horses, which were racing down the slopes as well, but Anargen, Thomas, and Glewdyn were all on foot. They were no worse for it; their boots, the *Evaggelion Eirene*, were endowed with the fiery inscriptions of the High King, which lent them speed surpassing what they could usually achieve. If the wind whipping past him as he closed the final feet between himself and the first archer wasn't clue enough to the degree of their alacrity, the startled faces of the Ecthels just before him certainly sufficed.

The first archer he encountered hadn't even notched an arrow. He blinked in disbelief as Anargen was on him.

Swinging his shield around, Anargen smashed the archer and spun off the impact to knock over the bowman beside him with a well-placed pommel blow to the back of that Monarchist's head. The next row of archers hastily began loading their bows and stumbling backward, but it was too late. He cleaved one bow, then another into singed ruin, and battered down the next archer as the sounds of the rest of the troupe crashed into the Monarchist lines. Sounds of steel battering steel and shouts and grunts as the Ecthels of each side vied against their brothers filled the night air.

THWACK.

Anargen jerked to a halt at the familiar whispered instruction from the High King. Another archer dropped next to him. One of his own had felled him in an attempt to take Anargen down. Shooting a look in the direction the arrow came from, he saw a small group of archers aiming at him. Shield up, he pressed toward them and then immediately dropped to a crouch and rolled to the side as instructed. A hail of arrows landed where he'd been.

The Monarchist nearest him tried to take advantage of his situation and deliver a kick to his side. Anargen let it connect, rolled up behind another Monarchist and battered the archer down, knocking over another of servant of Ilyron with him. Pivoting, he caught the latest arrow aimed at him on his *Thyreos Pistis.* The divinely engraved shield burned away the arrow, which could never overcome the protection it afforded.

Springing forward, Anargen dispatched three more Monarchists before breaking out into an opening in the field between the line of archers and his goal of the artillery line. Had there been such a gap when he'd watched their movements earlier? It certainly hadn't seemed so.

Once more, the cannons and mortars arrayed before him

launched their sulfurous projectiles at the stony face of Ordumair, forcing his attention back to his objective. Though he could not hear it, he knew that whatever walls of the fortress were repaired wouldn't take much of that sort of bombardment, let alone the weakened areas.

He spared a glance back to find Thomas coming up on his side. Gesturing toward the artillery with his spiritsword, Anargen called out to him. "To our goal?"

"Till we fall," Thomas affirmed.

The two young men dashed across the rolling grassy plain and reached the first cannon seconds later. The crew was relatively unprotected. A single guard and two soldiers for loading and firing the destructive field equipment. None put up much of a fight, and Anargen felt his spiritsword's burning blade cut through the wooden frame holding up the cannon's barrel with satisfying ease. No weapon could compare to the *Machaira tou Pneuma*. The spiritsword's fiery inscriptions burned bright in the dark, defying any to oppose the High King's favored.

Four more artillery pieces likewise fell to their efforts, and for just a moment, Anargen dared hope that they would destroy enough to allow the Ords waiting in the gatehouse's mustering area to stream out and join the battle. Might they not have a chance pressing their foe from two fronts?

No. This is too easy. Ilyron himself is here, somewhere. He is arrogant, but surely not this reckless and poor a tactician.

The keening notes of a horn reached his ears. It was the tune chosen for sounding a retreat. Not from the Monarchists, but the Restoration. Someone in their ranks was calling for a retreat to their failsafe point. The hidden postern gate to Ordumair that led to the secret tunnels of Ordumair. Last time Anargen fought on this field, they'd needed it as well. But this was too soon—how could they be turning back already when they were so close to breaking the Ecthel ranks and overturning their siege line?

Anargen's jaw lolled open as he peered at the source of the repeating, almost frantic call. A huge swarming mass of figures clamored over each other in a mad sprint toward where Seren, Mia, and Gregor were initially positioned.

No! No!

They had selected that side specifically because it was weaker, less densely grouped. Now a living tidal wave was rushing to crash down on them. Carrion literally climbing over one another in a scramble to reach their targets.

AROOOWOOOO!

Anargen knew that howl and loathed it. Somewhere in the dark lurked werebeasts, no doubt ready to pounce on and rend to shreds any and everyone in their way.

"They tricked us! I don't know how they knew, but they're sacrificing their artillery to destroy ..." Anargen couldn't bear to finish saying "our loved ones." Some rational part of him also understood it would be aimed at Gregor above all others, just as the Tengrath carrion had been.

"No!" Thomas wailed. "If we don't finish off the lines of artillery, we won't be able to prevent them from breaching the fortress. They'll tear it open and destroy everything."

Anargen tried to work moisture to his mouth. Thomas was right, but how could he say that? "If we don't get to Seren, Mia, and Gregor, they'll be overwhelmed. We have to aid in the retreat!" Anargen insisted, his heart thudding in his chest.

"I know! I know." Thomas looked down. "I may be a noble, but you're the more experienced Knight. What should we do?"

That was the last thing Anargen needed to hear that moment. An appeal to his wisdom and relationship with the High King. In that moment, he felt neither wise nor the exemplar of Knightly virtue. He was torn between what seemed equally valid choices, though for vastly different reasons.

On one end of the valley appeared to be the fate of Ordumair and the Ords. Without silencing the cannons, there was no way their soldiers could exit the fortress safely and enter the battle, meaning it was lost already. But at the other end was the woman whom he loved more fiercely than his own life. And not just her, but Baroness Mia and Heir-Apparent Gregor, each of whom was crucial to the survival of the Restoration and the war. Choosing between the two was tearing him apart inside. Was it selfish to choose to aid the side with his wife? Was it callous and forsaking of his vows to her before the High King to fight first for the Ords?

"I ... I don't know," Anargen admitted. His heart was an anxious mess, more chaotic than the battlefield. What did the High King desire of him? What was the right choice?

"Leave the cannons," he blurted out, surprising even himself with the finality of it. "We can't let them overtake your army." With it was the implicit addition of their wives and Gregor.

Thomas wasn't so divided as Anargen. "Then let's go!" Producing his horn again, he blew it, charging to the western end of the battlefield and continuing every so many strides to blow, drawing his troops and those battling the archers and artillery toward the route happening across the field.

At their backs fell a steady sprinkle of arrows, following them in their sprint to aid the others. Leaving off the work of the cannons meant also allowing the archers to regroup and take aim at them. Anargen felt so foolish to have overlooked that fact. As he peered over his shoulder and leaped to the right to avoid an arrow without breaking his stride, he was certain some of their troops would fall simply due to the shift in objectives. The weight of their loss was heavy on him, slowing his pace. Thomas began to get ahead of him.

Should I turn back? Act as a rearguard?

It would make him a target almost certain to be hit numerous times over. How could he live with himself, though, if he let others fall for his rash decision? Unless it was the right one?

Coming to a stop, Anargen turned. He had to do it. He couldn't let anyone else perish for his choices.

Just as he took his first steps in that direction, one of the fleeing soldiers stumbled, veered off course, and crashed squarely into him. Both men tumbled onto the evening-dampened grasses of the valley. Anargen shook his head and got to his feet before the Ecthel.

The man was cursing Anargen's idiocy right at the moment Anargen battered him aside and caught two arrows with his shield. Arrows that would have pierced the man's back. For a few precious seconds, the Ecthel regarded the arrows with wide eyes, then gave a wordless nod and ran on, leaving Anargen to heave in a shuddering breath.

AROOWOOOOO.

No. Please, not werebeasts. Not right now.

It was. He spotted their ochre eyes glowering in the near distance. They were closing in on him. Even as arrows continued to land sporadically around him with muddy *thuks*, the beasts bore down on him. A few arrows glanced off their high arched backs. One of the monstrous creatures didn't even slow as it leaped high over and past Anargen to skid along the ground behind him. The brown and black speckled creature loosed a rumbling growl from deep within its chest. Its eyes, like all of its kind, were hungry for his murder.

Another, this one tawny and sleeker, battered aside an

Ecthel it had overtaken. As it stalked into position, the pair had Anargen pinned between them.

Glancing from one fanged foe to the other, Anargen drew in a steadying breath. Silently, he pleaded, "My King, you have my life, and I have your sword. May neither fail till Ordumair is delivered from these fiends."

A rush of warmth wound up Anargen's arm, emanating from the blade as it glowed hotter. Anargen could see the insidious creature's eyes squinting against the light. Its lupine lips curled back, revealing its fangs. A bitter snarl issued from its maw.

It took a step toward Anargen's left, sinking its claws into the dirt. Quick as a viper's strike, it launched a clump of soil at Anargen, showering him in a spray of dirt.

As Anargen batted it aside, he heard a whisper telling him to duck. He dropped and felt the rush of air over his head as the speckled werebeast to his back took a swipe at him.

Wheeling around, he dodged the tawny beast's attempt to capitalize on his distraction. The creature smashed into its compatriot, leading to a short row between them punctuated with snapping teeth.

It wasn't realistic for Anargen to hope they would forget him or that they would defeat one another. All the same, he had to push down his disappointment as they turned to face him, a team once more.

Another howl echoed across the plains, and he knew at least one more monster was closing in to join them. He had no idea how many were coming. Doubtless more than these three.

The pair that first approached him began working back into opposing positions around him, keeping just enough distance to allow the third monster to join them.

This was a bittersweet development. Their focus on him meant other Restoration soldiers were making it safely to aid

Thomas in rescuing Seren, Mia, and Gregor. It also meant his odds of victory were diminishing.

Each of the three creatures sensed that too, tensing to leap at him.

The High King has delivered me from worse ... but if this is the end, then, my King, may I do what is needed to safeguard the others and honor you to my last breath.

Heat pulsing through him, Anargen didn't wait for the werebeasts to strike. He charged forward at the one nearest him, sword arm pulled back to deliver a stabbing blow. A step away from reaching the monster, it leaped back with ease. But his aim hadn't been for it.

As the creature got out of reach, Anargen spun and struck without hesitation.

A barked whimper was his reward as his blow landed against the beast that had been at his back. The shaggy grey-haired thing reeled and whined as it edged away, pulling its abdomen off Anargen's spiritsword. A steaming trail traced from the burning sword's tip to the smoldering wound delivered. With a groan, it collapsed.

One down.

Victory was short-lived. He fixated too long on the bested beast and didn't react quickly enough to the one at his left. Its brawny arm connected with his abdomen, sweeping him off his feet and sending him bouncing along the ground.

Struggling to stand, Anargen raised his shield and gritted his teeth as the monster's claws screeched down its steely length. He pivoted and blocked a hammering blow from the speckled creature. Stumbling backward, Anargen was suddenly very much on the defense as the tawny creature followed up with claw slashes and snapping jaws. Anargen managed to deflect each, but his chest burned. He still had not managed to draw a full breath since being struck.

From the corner of his eye, he caught the speckled werebeast crouching to lunge. He feinted a swipe of his sword at the tawny one directly in front of him and whirled around, bringing his shield up.

The impact reverberated through his shield and sent him crashing to the soggy soil. His only consolation as he fought his aches to get back to his feet was that Speckled was shaking its head and whimpering from where its face was singed on impact.

The contentment was short-lived. Tawny bore down on him, using its snout to flip him into the air. Anargen came down hard.

"Ugh," he groaned. Tawny's jaws were open over him, a line of drool dangled from bared fangs.

Anargen raised his shield and had it bashed aside and his arm pinned. His sword arm was also gripped with vise-like pressure from Tawny's other wickedly clawed hand.

He struggled against their hold, but it was no use. It may as well have been a mountain on top of either arm.

Anargen stared into the monster's cruel eyes and knew they both fully understood this was the end for him. There was no saving himself from what would come next.

Tawny reared back, a snarl of victory in its throat. Jaws wide, it chomped down on its prey.

The first bite was tentative. Testing if it could bite through his armor. By the High King's favor and endowment on the armor Anargen wore, it could not.

"Arrr!" the beast yelped in fury. It bit over and over from different angles. Anargen bore each one with the growing certainty that even though it failed to find his soft flesh, the sheer violence of each bite would eventually snap his neck. Already his head throbbed, and his vision blurred. A haze of toxic smoke spread as bestial saliva dripping from the werebeast's jaws was burned by his helmet's fiery inscriptions. The miasma blinded Anargen completely.

My King, please, no more!

The beast bit down once more, but this time it held tight, and he could just tell this time it would give a violent twist, one Anargen wouldn't survive. He closed his eyes, knowing that when he opened them, he would see the Highland.

ALIGNMENT

J ason really, really hated copping to it, but Sir Cinaed was right. He never should have read Anargen's journal, because all it did was make things worse. A tragic love story, fate-spoken like his own, except Anargen and Seren had had so much more than he and Aria. They may have only had a couple of nights before the battle began, but those were nights they filled with meaning and moments worth treasuring until their last breaths, which they had time to prepare for mentally.

Reading only made Jason all the angrier. Why in the Lowlands did Aria think reading this would've mattered? Did she worry he'd run if things were tough? Or not understand the value of holding dear the time you have with someone? Worst, his anger was increasingly focused on Aria herself, because her inane insistence on his reading the drivel had kept them from even having what Anargen and Seren had. If she hadn't been so enamored of the romance of two dumb youths from centuries ago, they could have been making their own story richer and fuller.

"Hmph," Jason huffed, running his fingers through his hair and fussing with his father's cap he'd taken to wearing again. It was his fifth time doing so. What else was there to do? They were stuck here in Quilona, their first stop in Keraxlaco. What good did it do, railing against his dead fiancée? What good would any of this do? Because ultimately, Aria was right about one thing. There wasn't really a solid definition of "happy ending" that he understood, apart from being with her. The

Lowlands Total War could burn everything down, and what would any of his deeds matter? Or did the Lowlands being reduced to ash ultimately matter? It had all been cursed already anyway.

"I spoke with the conductor," Sir Cinaed broke into Jason's broodings from behind him.

"Yeah?" Jason replied, arms crossed over his chest.

"Mhm," Cinaed replied, a bit of sardonic edge to his tone. "It appears that there's fighting going on along the border of Mbisai and Jhi. They're delaying all traffic to try to rush troops to the front to help keep the Jhi'ish from advancing any farther."

"So, we're trapped here watching while the Alliance stumbles toward a fall. Great."

The older Knight took in a breath and seemed to brace himself. But he didn't say anything. Which, of course, only irked Jason even more. "Well, go on. You clearly have something else to say."

"I do, if you're finished being a petulant child," Cinaed replied, his face stern.

"Sure, salty, lay it on me."

Cinaed narrowed his eyes at Jason and thrust a newspaper into his chest with enough force to stagger him. "With us stuck here, news from Jhi has had a chance to catch up. The attacks on the bridge and Posek weren't just meant to do us personal harm or even our allies. Those were calculated strikes designed to make the Palatini Lucis Aeternae Order seem treacherous and destructive."

Jason stared down at the newspaper, brows raised. This was the first thing that genuinely broke through his thickening walls of sarcasm and indifference.

The Storyteller barreled on, "Both the Poseki and Jhi'ish are blaming us for what happened in each incident. And it has given the Order one more hurdle to try to leap over in uniting, because we will be seen as dangerous and a liability. As though we were causing these events through either mischief, malevolence, or moronic stupor."

That wasn't good. Not in the slightest. Melania had said something to him before she attacked. Something about how all of those Jhi'ish soldiers being defeated was what she really wanted. "Now the Knights in those realms will be hunted and forced to work even harder to keep safe while also trying to battle Dorian's forces."

"Precisely," Sir Cinaed replied, though hardly sounding pleased that Jason well understood their predicament.

"That's insidious and so much more subtle than Monarch Ilyron's plans."

Cinaed pulled his duster tighter over his chest, eyeing a passerby and making sure his armor wasn't showing through his button-up shirt. "Indeed, it is far craftier. We are in an era where subtle evil is sufficient to direct us down wrong paths. Where the menace of the Dark Prince is implied to be imaginary and therefore of no danger. A man without his guard up is far easier to steal from ... and kill."

Jason scuffed his foot along the platform's tiles. "If we don't get to Centros fast, the Council of Defenders is going to fall apart. Isn't it?"

Cinaed looked down the rail lines and at the other disappointed passengers who were already abandoning the futile wait at the station. "It is a likely possibility. It took much to bring us all together again. A blow like any one of those we've received of late could be enough to undo it all. But—"

"We can't wait around here for them to sort out this business with Mbisai. We both know Jhi doesn't care particularly for that province of Mbisai. Their real aim is to divide Keraxlaco and Vov Hilan, keep the Alliance armies in each from supporting each other.

"Unless the Alliance pulls off some stunning victories right away, this station is likely to be tied up servicing troops and supplies for months."

"I believe you are right about that," Cinaed agreed, looking thoughtfully at Jason. Once more piercing, probing in his gaze. He had recovered much in the past days.

Fists clenched at his sides, Jason grumbled. "Why haven't you gotten us alternate transport? I'd rather ride horseback town to town, taking the full time for the stations to open, warning everyone along the way of what is needed and what is coming!"

"I'm working on it," was all Cinaed offered in response.

Yanking off his cap, he shook it at Cinaed, wanting to yell at the top of his lungs that it wasn't good enough. Instead of passionate indignation, all he felt was empty and aching at his core. The Council of Defenders wasn't going to happen. Aria had died for nothing. And if Jhi took that corridor between Keraxlaco and Vov Hilan, Jason would be set to win a bet that the war would take a very bad turn for the Alliance.

"It's all falling apart," was the most Jason could bring himself to say before he stalked off the platform. He had no idea where he was going, and the worst part was, he couldn't find a single argument at the moment to convince himself that it mattered. Especially after reading in the article that Professor Goulder was slated for execution for "his part" in what happened in Jhi City. Justice, honor, hope, peace—all of them seemed to be as dead and gone as the woman he loved.

17
SHADOWS AT NIGHTFALL

There was a horrific squeal, then a thump. The creature released its hold on Anargen's helmet and let him fall slack. Pressure let off his arms, and he felt the stinging sensation of blood once more flowing into his limbs as it should. Through the smoky morass, he couldn't see what was happening, but he heard his tawny tormentor bellow out a feral roar, then the sound of a blade swinging through the air and a sudden hiss and crackle. There was an animalistic gurgle, and a tremendous weight crashed down on Anargen's legs.

He coughed as he struggled futilely. Seconds passed in agony before he finally pulled in a few desperately needed breaths. Pain radiated all over his body. He kept his eyes closed because fresh smoke billowed off of whatever weighed down his legs.

Something hooked under each of his arms and jerked him out from under the dead weight. It sat him down several feet away with the delicacy of a friend. He dared open his eyes and saw the Ecthel soldier from before looming over him.

"Are you all right?" the man asked, but Anargen was too stunned to speak. He had never seen common weapons deliver an effective blow to a werebeast.

Another figure joined the Ecthel, his armor aglow with righteous flames. "The beast is vanquished," Glewdyn stated with solemnity.

Anargen's father looked down at him and offered his hand. "Lad, comfortable as you may be down there, you must come.

We cannot linger, or we'll all join you prone on the field and without rescue."

"You always know what to say, Father," he replied. But his voice was so hoarse and choked he was pretty sure all that could be heard was, "... Father."

His fingers closed around Glewdyn's offered hand. An instant later, he was hoisted to his feet, wobbling as he tried to steady his fuzzied head and pain-filled limbs.

Suddenly, he felt very self-conscious and managed to mumble, "The cannons ..."

"Aye. You had to leave them. I was able to disable a few more, but there's nothing to be done about that now. We must complete the retreat if we're to save any lives this night for tomorrow's battles."

There was no rebuke, only resolution. It was gift enough to buoy Anargen's steps. Gradually regaining his balance and senses, he followed his father and the Ecthel as they picked up speed from a canter to a sprint toward one of the most horrific sights he'd yet seen.

Ahead of them, the Restoration's forces were pinned partway up a slope and battering back wave after wave of persons who flung themselves forward without a hint of caution.

Carrion, there were hundreds of carrion swinging, punching, kicking, clubbing, biting—anything they could do to try to drag another defender off the rock face and into their midst, where Anargen knew waited a painful, protracted death by blunted instruments and fists. Thomas and what remained of his soldiers were fighting along the back of the group, but they weren't able to break through to reinforce the others or stop the horde's mindless fury.

"Any suggestions?" Glewdyn asked, sounding wearied enough for a dozen lifetimes. As Anargen caught up, he saw the

Ecthel who returned his rescue drifting nearer the valley opening, away from the mass of carrion. He looked terrified, but hadn't yet committed to desertion.

"Hey," Anargen called to him, his voice becoming steadier. "If we're going to survive this, someone will need to prepare the secret postern gate to receive us all. Due north of here, where the mountain's feet wrap around the fortress's base, is a large stone that will look somewhat out of place. Behind it is the release for the secret entrance.

"Go, get the door open and wait inside for us."

The Ecthel glanced from Anargen to the various points of turmoil on the battlefield—the carrion mob cornering the other Restorationists, the line of archers, arquebusiers, and artillery battering the entry and façade of the fortress, and to the seemingly inviting dark path leading out of the valley through Valesgard.

For an instant, Anargen feared the man would run off. Resolve seemed to form in him, setting his shoulders back and punctuating with a quick nod. The Ecthel took off running for the secret entrance as instructed.

Glewdyn sighed and chuckled mirthlessly. "Good suggestion, but not the solution for which I was hoping."

"You taught me to tend to smithing the smaller, easier items first, that way the harder ones will have a still hotter forge for when you attempt them," he reminded his father. How long had it been since either of them had talked about his father's now destroyed smithy? It felt so distant and silly that he had spent years worrying he would eventually end up taking up the trade his father hadn't desired either.

"Ah, well, since I'm so wise, did I happen to also provide something for hammering out this particular bit of stubborn work?"

Anargen shook his head. "I—I don't know. The carrion

won't ever stop. At best, if we come up from behind and attack them, some might turn and try to throttle us as well."

A tremor ran through the ground under them as, from across the field, a steady stream of stone from the fortress reconstruction and mountain slope tumbled down to the valley in front of the entrance to the fortress. For a moment, the cannons fell silent as a thick cloud of dust and smoke roiled off it. Much as the Great Bulwark's collapse had done at the First Siege of Ordumair, the only obvious entry to the fortress from the valley had been blocked off, as had its only exit.

As if unsure what else to do, the cannons began firing again sporadically. It was a puzzling turn of events, but one Anargen didn't have leave to explore.

"I think, lad, we're just going to have to fight with all we can muster and leave the rest in the High King's hands," Glewdyn concluded, pulling Anargen definitively back to the bedlam before them.

"I think that's what we're meant always to do," Anargen suggested.

"Aye," Glewdyn smiled and clapped him on the back. "Now," raising his spiritsword, Glewdyn nodded towards the carrion, "For the Great King!"

Father and son charged across the remaining space to join Thomas and his troops in jerking carrion backward, struggling with them. Even with their attention clearly fixed to those on the hillside, the pitiable lot still landed enough hits, kicks, and bites to make it dangerous work battling through from the back. There were just too many of them, and they were too fixated on their goal.

ARREEOOOO.

A strange horn sounded over the grunts and growls and thumps of the carrion army. As sharp and attentive as trained hounds, the carrion completely stopped fighting and turned as one. They faced the darkened path to Valesgard and took off in that direction without a hint of concern about those battling them.

The mysterious horn sounded twice more and then fell silent. In the stillness and without the mass of raging mindless marauders, Anargen spotted Seren and Mia. They were off their horses and tending to someone lying on the ground. Without even being conscious of it, he ran for Seren.

A few steps from the base of the slope, he caught a glimpse of Thomas on his flank. The briefest glance and nod passed between them before they were at their wives' sides and looking down on the victim to whom they were tending— Gregor.

The boy was groaning and looked like one of his arms had sustained a nasty cut. His helmet was off, too, and his young face had been bruised heavily.

As soon as Seren's eyes caught on Anargen's, she reached for him, gripping him in a tight embrace. It lasted long enough to calm the angst swirling like a maelstrom in Anargen since the battle started. The moment ended equally too soon for him, as Seren pulled back and informed him, "Gregor tried to defend everyone and lure them off. It worked for a moment, but they overtook him. Mia and I were only just able to pull him free of those brutes."

"We have to get him inside and treat his injuries," Mia added as she released Thomas from a similarly impassioned hold.

Thomas nodded, motioning to the commanders now clustering around him. "To the fortress. Unwanted or not, we're no good to anyone dying out here."

One of the commanders pointed out, "Our way into Ordumair is buried now. We should sound the horns and make for—"

"The secondary entrance, north, along where the mountain meets the western reach of the fortress. We have one of your men there waiting to usher everyone in now," Anargen informed him.

For just a second, Thomas blinked, surprise numbing him. He shook it off and said, "You heard him. Rally the men, bear up Gregor, and we'll follow Anargen. We'll make a stand with our allies, the Ords, within the walls of Ordumair!"

Familiar Ecthel brass horns sounded all around, and with impressive speed and efficiency, they were all en route to the secret postern entrance. About half of the group had made it when once more that odd horn rang out, this time with a different note.

Anargen looked about to see if he could spot where the horn issued from, and his eyes widened with shock. From Valesgard marched not only the carrion but another thousand Monarchist soldiers. They were headed straight for the secret entrance.

"We seem to be hard pressed again," Glewdyn commented. "We need to inform Duncoin what is going on and then get these soldiers routed through the tunnels. Thoughts on doing it?"

Anargen nodded. "You warn Duncoin we're all coming. There should be a tunnel path that takes you to where he will be overlooking his muster area. Take the first right, a left to as far as it goes and then a right," Anargen instructed.

Glewdyn glanced back at the Monarchists marching toward them from the distance and grimaced. "Take care, son," he instructed, and then was off on his task.

"Seren and I can get Gregor to an infirmary with a little help," Mia spoke up.

"Uh, two rights. A left ... another left ... and then a right!" Anargen recalled.

The two women helped Gregor, who was still dazed, to the passageway. Just before they disappeared inside, Seren shot him a concerned look. The pleading in her eyes was a silent shout: "Be careful. Come back to me."

He shot her a crooked grin, which faded quickly after she was out of sight. From his left, he heard Thomas ordering the outspoken commander from before, a Captain Strathmore, to lead the men into the fortress at his command.

As the captain bustled about his new orders, Anargen commented, "This is all so familiar, almost a re-enactment of sorts of the last siege. Ilyron isn't so petty and self-absorbed as to insist on rehashing it and winning this time, is he?"

"I don't really know," Thomas admitted. I was pretty young when I got pulled out of the noble circles, but I recall Ilyron wasn't around much. He mostly spent time in Rehalcy with his mother's relatives."

"It's a wonder Rehalcy isn't on his side as well," Anargen commented.

"They aren't known for fighting battles they aren't certain they can win," Thomas pointed out with a shrug. "I guess they haven't seen enough to feel confident he'll come out on top."

Anargen whistled. "That's unexpectedly encouraging."

"I guess we'll take all we can get," Thomas said with a chuckle.

"Can't say there's anything we're getting worth grinning over. It looks like they're surrounding us," Captain Strathmore commented dryly.

Anargen joined Thomas in whirling to find the Ecthel soldiers coming to stand by their sides. Anargen only spared a moment for surprise. Around them, their numbers continually ticked down as more and more troops continued to retreat, even as their enemy stood there watching their flight.

"You were supposed to be leading the men into the

passages, stationing them at the proper junctures," Anargen heard Thomas chide as he scanned the blank expressions worn by scores of the Monarchists in front of them.

What are the carrion waiting for?

"Yes, Your Honor," Strathmore replied. "As much as I obey your orders, I also obey the Baroness's, and she told me to make sure you returned to her—alive. You have no business risking your life and your title falling into Ilyron's hands."

A murmur passed among the carrion, and they seemed to twitch at the mention of the Monarch's name. Which quite possibly was one of the most horrifically tragic things Anargen ever witnessed. Could they hear and understand the world around them as usual, but their bodies acted largely independent of their will? If so, the carrion curse was the cruelest slavery Anargen could imagine.

A huffed sigh from Thomas meant he saw no point in arguing his wife's prerogative nor Strathmore's logic. "You aren't meant to throw your life away for mine just because I was given a title," Thomas insisted all the same.

"You were chosen to bear that title, not just 'given' it," Strathmore countered hotly. "And begging your pardon, Your Honor, but risking my life for the sake of Ecthelowall is precisely what I've been training for since I was a boy half your age!"

An icy breeze gusted down off the mountainside. Anargen's hair stood on end. It was a natural sort of cold the winds carried. Had he just seen something passing among the carrion?

"With all due respect to you both ... be still!" Anargen demanded through his teeth. Things felt more and more off about this situation.

Anargen held his shield up in a wary guard. Unnatural as the carrion were, there was something more. Something fouler still stirring among them. Suddenly, it all fit. The incautious field arrangement, the feigned withdrawal, the sudden redeployment.

At his back, the stragglers of the retreat were almost all inside the fortress. Except those like Strathmore, determined to make sure Thomas made it into the fortress as well. Though it would leave him without the aid of another Knight of Light, he looked at Thomas. "You need to get inside the fortress, Your Honor."

"Oh, not you too. I'm not leaving you to face them alone," he gestured to the mass of carrion.

"They played us. They're going to try to infiltrate the secret tunnels! We have to get ahead to block them. Besides, we're never—"

A whispered warning reached Anargen and he ducked, but a half second slower than he should've. A heavy, dark mass impacted his right shoulder pauldron, clipping it and sending him spiraling to the ground. Pain exploded in his shoulder, and he looked up to see nothing but the carrion garbed in the shadows of the night.

No, not garbed in any normal shadows. The dark shifted around them, concentrating into the form of a man bearing a chain with a spiked ball hanging from one end. The ebony figure began swinging the spiked ball again, building up to sling it again.

Sombra.

As if the werebeasts and carrion weren't enough, the arcane assassins able to merge in and out of shadows and form them into deadly weapons were here as well. All the horrors of this black hour were being brought to bear against them.

This one wore the mystical hood that granted him his powers, and his entire face was wrapped in a grey cloth. Otherwise, his clothes were black and nondescript. The sombra's milky eyes swept over the remaining Restorationists, seeming to size them all up.

Thomas stood in front of him, his burning shield borne aloft. Strathmore crouched down beside Anargen. "Are you all right, lad?"

"Yeah," Anargen grunted and began struggling to his feet as the dark figure crowed, "Good. Good. I was afraid the Ecthel sorcerer's news that you were here was a ploy for my services. But no, here you stand, little phosphila, and soon you will fall forever."

The voice sounded familiar to Anargen, though placing it was not a simple matter. "I didn't know the Sombra were at Ilyron's beck and call," he retorted.

Once more, the carrion seemed to strain at the mention of their master. Whatever the repeated invocation of his name would cause wasn't likely to be good. "Careful. Your secret order is becoming common thugs for him, and he isn't known for rewarding even his loyalist retainers with anything but suffering on his behalf."

Striding into the gap between the carrion and Restoration soldiers, the Sombra seethed. "The Sombra do not serve such rabble. Our employer's aims align for now with the Ecthels'. What draws me here is to visit vengeance upon you for the crimes you've committed against our order. Falconcleft, Cattingsford, Kirke—for your transgressions, I, Wev, have the honor of cutting you down."

Wev. The name was familiar. His grudge seemed entirely personal, so it was possible whoever Wev was, he had been at one of the first two sites of Anargen's "transgressions" against the Sombra. The latter he knew wasn't the case. The only Sombra at Kirke had most definitely been destroyed.

A shrill whistle now accompanied the swinging of the flail, its pointed black curvatures blurred into an ebony ring. This wasn't the opportune moment to be fighting a Sombra, if such a time ever existed. But it could possibly work to his advantage.

"It seems like a warrior such as yourself would want to confront me in single combat. That cannot happen till the rest of these with me are inside the fortress."

At his side, he knew Thomas was glowering at him. It didn't matter, though. The raspy hiss the Sombra made wiped away any notions of safely delivering the others.

"There will be no bargains. You will face me now or fall where you stand. Let the others with you try to lend you aid, the outcome will be the same—all of you, dead."

Anargen tightened his grip on his spiritsword. For some reason, the blade felt heavier than normal, as if it didn't want to rise to the challenge before him.

What is it, my Great King? What are you trying to show me?

"Depart from here, shadow," Thomas demanded, trying to move to flank the sombra. "If your true master does not bid you serve Ilyron, you would do well—"

The piercing sphere of the flail shot forward straight at Thomas's chest. Raising his shield, there was a telling clanging sound. The impact sent him sprawling on the ground.

Strathmore was by Thomas's side in an instant. To his back, the sombra seethed, "No Ecthel commands me. If that fool Ilyron can't, then you certainly don't."

Anargen noticed the carrion seemed to briefly turn their collective gaze to the sombra. It was so overt, so coincidental with his denigration of Ilyron, that it had to mean something. Silent agreement or rejecting it was the question. Anargen spared a glance at Strathmore, who gave a nod that Thomas was mostly unhurt. He had managed to block enough of the sudden strike.

Once more, the dreadful whistle of the whirling mace resumed. Around him, Anargen became aware that several soldiers were staring at the sombra in horror. They hadn't experienced such a thing. They were only supposed to be scary stories, not real dangers to face amidst the carnage of battle.

"If you want to face me, then do so in the open field. Away from your fellow servants of Ilyron."

The desired effect of agitating the sombra caused him to slam his spiked ball into the ground inches from Anargen. "I do not care what Ilyron desires. He and his pathetic army may turn to ash!"

The response from the carrion this time was undeniable. They growled and began inching forward, swaying and bumping into the sombra from behind.

Wev spun to face them and bellowed, "Back, you mindless grubs!" He slung his mace around, battering aside half a dozen carrion with each swing, left and then right.

The carrions' growling intensified, but they held their positions. Stoic and unaffected by so many of their number being dashed to bits.

Why did they react so violently ...

Anargen ducked and rolled to the side. The air off the spiked ball was frigid as it shot past him to land where he just stood.

His natural impulse was to close the distance between himself and the sombra, but he felt again a resistance. It wasn't just his sword; all his limbs felt heavy and planted to this spot. He was being held back. From the corner of his eyes, he watched as the flail's end was dragged back to the sombra, grinding through and gouging the ground as it was recalled.

The shadowy assassin glared at him with narrowed eyes. Anargen's behavior threw him as well. Like a viper, he struck again, not bothering to build devastating momentum.

Anargen's arm responded freely, and he deflected the less potent blow without issue. Both he and the sombra stared for a second at the flail on the ground between them, equally shocked, even if the sombra didn't know it.

Suddenly, the tumblers all clicked into place for Anargen. Putting on his most condescending airs, he called out, "No wonder the Monarch sent an army of carrion with you. He must have realized after the Sombra failed at Falconcleft, Cattingsford, and Kirke that you are all just as substantial as the shadows in which you hide."

The sound loosed from Wev's ashen form was a war cry and wail in one. Forming obsidian daggers in his palm, he spun around and flung them into a pair of carrion, screeching, "Sombra do not serve that weak nothing Ilyron. He is just a puppet, as much as these witless dregs. I do not need them. In fact, they deserve to die just as much as you!"

Dagger after dagger formed and flew from his hand as he turned, downing carrion in a wide arc. Just as quick, he whipped back around and launched a series of dark dirks at Anargen and Thomas, to no avail. Each burned up on contact with their ardent shields.

Wev wailed in frustration and began to draw himself up into a tornadic cloud of shadow, slinging his flail around wildly as he screamed a flurry of curses in a blur of ancient Tislatnean and Ecthelish. The carrion came alive again, closing around the sombra, which only further infuriated him. He began shouting over and over, "Curse Ilyron! Die! DIE!"

Anargen tapped Thomas on the shoulder and gestured toward the secret tunnel. Now was their chance to slip away.

A wild, guttural cry rang out, and suddenly the carrion were passive no more. They swarmed onto the dark form of the sombra, grasping, biting, punching, flailing.

Wev battered aside wave after wave of them, but they just came all the more furiously for him. They began pulling him down from his swirling height. With a yelp, he crashed onto the valley floor and was buried under a pile of carrion.

There was no time to revel in the victory. Some carrion began stumbling toward Anargen and the others. They were only two dozen feet from the secret entrance, but with all the chaos around them, they were the twenty-four most dangerous feet in the Lowlands.

"Time to go," Thomas declared and motioned for the last of the soldiers to run.

Anargen bashed backward the first two carrion with his shield and caught a third trying to sneak around to his back with the pommel of his spiritsword. Nothing felt heavy anymore. He had found the path out of their predicament that the High King led him to. Along with a host of questions to mull later, like who was directing the Sombra, if not Ilyron? And who could be malevolent enough to pull his strings as Wev the Sombra had suggested?

Anargen dashed toward the secret door, knocking back another carrion. From the center of the churning mass of them came a shout, and Wev's dark mace shot out, crashing through the carrion and catching Anargen off guard. He blocked the surprise blow and wobbled back, keeping on his feet.

Wev reached into his cloak as he strained out from under the tangled mass of bodies still assaulting him. Slashing back two carrion, and another, and another, Wev staggered toward the Knights. Five black daggers arced out in an array.

Anargen intercepted three, slicing through them with his spiritsword. Thomas caught another with his shield, but the last found a mark, embedding in Strathmore's chest just below the shoulder as he ran back to protect Thomas. He cried out in pain and dropped to his knees.

Two more carrion closed on Anargen and he dispatched them. He ran over to Strathmore and Thomas and helped bear up the captain. He awkwardly struck down another carrion and then a fourth as they reached the door and passed under its archway.

There was a strangled yelp of terror at their back, blended from raspy to normal human register.

Anargen didn't spare a glance to see for sure, but he guessed Wev's enchanted hood had been pulled off by the carrion, rendering him as human as anyone and tragically another victim of Ilyron's carrion.

"Ugh," Strathmore groaned as they dragged him several paces away from the door. His pain helped undercut the swell of sympathy in Anargen. His pity would be better shown for all those in Ordumair. Now, as before, they were trapped inside the fortress waiting for their enemy to bear down on them and tear at them with the same relentless fury that had just overcome a sombra.

THE SHARPEST SWORD

A faint squeak of the door's hinges protesting being used was the only thing that interrupted the silence the warehouse had been ensconced in. Jason groaned. "Looking for me?"

"Of course," Sir Cinaed replied. "You've been missing since our train arrived here. Two days ago," he made a pointed pause. "I thought to give you time to face the realities you flee from and grieve as needed, but—"

"Hmph. Thanks, but no thanks. You can keep your—"

"My child, no. No more of this," Sir Cinaed insisted.

Jason was ready to continue the petty game of interruptions until he heard, "My child." That was the first time Cinaed had called him such, the first time he had implied Jason was part of his family.

Seeming to sense he had a firm hold on Jason's attention or at least had stilled his tongue, Sir Cinaed continued. "This spiral you've entered is poison for you and ultimately ensures only harm comes to the Lowlands. I do not expect you to simply move past what happened, but as the Defender of the Northern Realm, and your friend and family, I cannot let you abandon your oaths to the High King. Not without a fight."

Shaking his head, Jason pushed back. "What's the point? It's all over. Me. The Quest. What does any of it matter?"

Clenching his fists before Jason, but in a pleading manner, the old storyteller groaned. "The King's Day matters. It's not over."

"Isn't it? How can it even come? Even if it did, what is it that it could overturn this?"

Sir Cinaed closed his eyes and seemed to steady himself, as if he had just taken a hard blow. The tight line of his lips stayed sealed shut until he tossed a bundle across the room to Jason and backed away. "You must take this, and after you've tried to practice with it for at least an hour, I'll return to let you out of here. Till you've done as instructed, whether it is today or ten thousand years, you will not be permitted to leave this room."

Jason gaped after the quickly retreating Defender Black's back. The whole thing was so bizarre. What could he possibly be thinking? He wanted Jason to leave the warehouse, so he was locking him in here?

Looking down at the bundle he'd caught, he undid the binding on the fabric and retrieved from it his spiritsword. He hadn't touched it since that night on the bridge. Its leather grip felt both foreign and familiar to his fingers. As he held onto it, the flames did not immediately spring from its inscriptions as they should have, and the coldness of the metal, its seeming deadness, startled him.

He debated putting it down. Part of him wanted to very much. To lay it down and never take it up again, certain only pain would come of trying to wield it once more. Greater within him, however, was an urgent need not to let it slip from his fingers. Within a minute, Jason held it aloft and dropped into a defensive stance to begin practicing with it as he had in the past.

With it came the sound of swipes and slashes as the blade sliced through the air in a sort of dance that was almost muscle memory to him at this point. There was no crackle from the fire, no rush of its heat and warmth. No whisper from beyond himself guiding his steps, instructing and infusing him. Lacking it all left the whole exercise feeling cold, dark, and futile. Words that were coming to define his life as a whole.

Why won't you speak to me?

There was a stirring, a tingling sensation within the blade that traveled up his arm. An inscription gleamed like the glowing coals of a nearly spent fire. *"Everyone who asks, receives; everyone seeks, finds; and to everyone who knocks, the door will be opened."*

Jason sucked in a sharp breath. Those words carried with them all the ache he had expected, and that portion of him that did not want the hurt railed at him for inviting in the pain. But he didn't let go, he pressed on, hungry for answers and the faintest hints of warmth he sensed within them.

"Haven't I sought you?" he challenged aloud.

New lettering lit the blade with a searing sting that nearly made him drop the sword. *"You will find the High King when you seek him with your whole heart."*

Fair enough. Perhaps he hadn't been seeking the High King's wisdom and will in recent days. "What would it change? It's not just that Aria's gone. Everything is gone. The whole Quest is in ruins!"

"And the High King is able to make all grace abound to you, so that having all sufficiency in all things at all times, you may abound in every good work."

These fresh words sizzled, and his hand felt now as if it had been burned to the hilt. Still, he countered, "How? How can the Quest be salvaged? We were outmaneuvered. Time is slipping away. If only we had known what would happen, we could've avoided—"

Before he had even finished his protest, the letters crackled to life on the latest inscription. *"He is the one, '... declaring the end from the beginning and from ancient times things not yet done, saying, 'my counsel shall stand, and I will accomplish all my purpose,'"* Immediately after those words, another section of the blade lit with, *"Is anything too hard for the High King?"*

Now the hurt of holding onto the sword was almost too deep to stand. "How? How will you make any of this worth what we—what I—lost? How can this be rescued from ruin?"

New words blazed to life, and Jason felt the air around the sword heating up, filled with energy as if ready to ignite the inscription, the sword, and Jason any moment. *"Behold, I am doing a new thing; now it springs forth, do you not perceive it? The High King will make a way in the wilderness and rivers in the desert."*

Before he could speak, the intensity of it increased as another inscription revealed itself with fiery flourish. *"Stand firm, hold your position, and see the salvation of the High King on your behalf."*

And though he could scarce stand it any longer, there followed, *"Have I not commanded you? Be strong and courageous. Do not be frightened, and do not be dismayed, for the High King is with you wherever you go."*

"But ... what am I fighting for? Why am I going on with all of the hurt and the sorrow? Every day I try and I try, and I try to keep moving forward. But I can't! I can't get past it. All I can see is the emptiness around me and feel it within me."

Tremors ran through Jason's body as he fought the urge to burst into sobbing when he had no tears left to shed. He wanted this whole thing to be over, but couldn't bear it to end. Why though? Why couldn't he let it go? All of him hurt. Inside, outside, it was like he was being torn apart. He shouted from deep within, "I feel like it would be better to be dead than go on like this. I need ... I need ... you. I need you here with me, and all I see is emptiness and devastation around me!"

A whoosh of fiery air rushed off the spiritsword so intensely that it blew back Jason's hair, sending his cap flying. He squinted against the sudden luminance emitted from the blade. Every inch of him, from each sinew to the deepest core of his bones, felt like it could be rent asunder by the force of the blast, but he couldn't let go, not now.

The spiritsword glowed brighter and hotter and brighter and hotter and brighter and hotter until the whole room was consumed in it. Swelling beyond the bounds of the sword's metal planes, everything was ablaze! Everything melted, consumed in a brightness that itself burned his arid eyes like the tears that wouldn't come. He wanted to gasp, but could draw no air. There was a sensation of tumbling, but he couldn't move to catch himself.

All at once, the overwhelming press of the heat and the light and searing, winding its way through his flesh to his deepest core, intensified ten times. A hundred. A thousand times, and he wasn't standing; he was kneeling. More than that, he wasn't crying, gasping, falling—none of them were possible. He could not speak, and dared not look up from the lesser light that filled his eyes, because he knew where he was: he was before the High King of All Realms. None of his wit or weakness or woes could stand before that magnificence of the One enthroned in light and with a righteous presence that was a consuming fire.

Burning, he was burning within; everything that had bound him was being reduced to ash, just as it had the very first time he had seen the High King. The day he had pledged himself wholly to the One True Ruler.

"I ... I'm ..." he couldn't find words. But the one before whom he was now summoned had not brought him here for him to stammer on.

A voice more striking than a roll of thunder and more commanding than a rushing waterfall bade him come closer. At first, he struggled to obey, the first step being the most halting and heavy. Each step he took eased in reluctance but became graver. He was approaching the One who, while undeniably good and benevolent, was more severe than any storm.

Jason found the closer he drew, the more he was overcome, not with unsteadiness, but a determination to give way, to defer. All around, the air grew hotter and hotter, becoming charged with such anticipation that there were actual peals of thunder and the ground seemed to quake. The most mesmerizing and terrifying part was that Jason could very nearly perceive things around him. A city rose up all around, with towers that shamed Falkirke and made the most exquisite architecture of Lyrscony, Zilnen, Jhi—everywhere in the Lowlands—seem the imitations a child would craft of their parents' work. There weren't simply buildings, though. The city was alive with a river flowing down its center from the raised dais of the one enthroned.

And there were plants. So many trees, bushes, vines, flowers, and some things for which he had no words to describe. Still more incredible was the splendor of the light shining from the one seated on the throne. It was brighter than if he were standing directly before the sun. Yet every rock, branch, and blade of grass was discernible, intricately detailed, and most notably straining toward the figure in a deep, palpable yearning that transcended speech and pulled at Jason's own heart till he could hardly bear it. It had to stop, but the light brightened, the heat, the pyrocastic intensity in the air, heightened and heightened until every bit of the land around him hummed with an ancient tune only known to the elements and the one who forged them—they still knew their maker's name.

Jason was on his knees and was convinced that if he didn't speak, if he didn't cry out with them, he would be consumed. He had to—he longed to as he had wanted nothing else in life. The instant he did, all of the light that blinded him, the heat that incinerated him, and the power emanating through the air crushing him intensified by an order of magnitude. Yet, in a wildly joyful realization, he knew that he wasn't devoured by flames, but rather he had been submerged before this moment, and now he surfaced. Before starving and now well fed, thirsty but now drinking from the most delightful waters. The pain had been the cure for all those needs visited upon him with such force and volume that he was torn out of need's clutches to look on all his heart had ever wanted without knowing it.

He knew his Lord was before him without opening his eyes. From where he lay, still as a dead man, but so filled with life he had no imagining of death or decay, he could just feel the radiance of the High King's presence.

"This is what awaits," he repeated to himself, knowing the Mighty One had spoken it. "I won't lose heart again."

Jason slowly sat up on the warehouse floor. He hadn't been violently jerked from the vision, but he felt the deepest longing to return to it. To be back before the High King once more. He had imagined the Great King's majesty had been breathtaking in the first vision he'd been granted that night as he hung dying in his brother's dungeon. This was something else, something more, as much as the cosmos was more than the Lowlands. Further, it was breath-giving. A foretaste of real glory. Real majesty. Jason had believed he was ready to die for the High King after he broke the chains that bound Jason, but now Jason was determined to live for the High King with the memory of what awaited seared indelibly into the fabric of his heart.

He gripped his spiritsword, which flashed with burning brilliance along the blade. The warmth wove in and around and through him, familiar and forceful as ever and then some. He had to get back to Defender Black. They couldn't stop, not now. Now that he understood what the King's Day was and why the old man pined for it so deeply.

18

CONFINED

"They beat and batter against the barriers we lay. One by one, they're falling--defenses and attackers. Our defenses will exhaust long before their numbers."

-- Anargen's The King's Day Journal
28 Fyelleth 1610 Middle Era

"Move, move, move," Glewdyn instructed. "Hrrmph." With a grunt, he placed the last weighty stone in place, sealing off the passage. "That ought to hold them for a bit."

"Just long enough for us to find and seal the next breach," Seren commented darkly. After the chaos of the retreat, Anargen would rather she have been kept safe in the infirmary with Mia and Gregor or the vault with Thomas and Thane Duncoin. Unfortunately, there was no convincing her otherwise.

"It won't hold that long," Anargen disagreed. "Werebeasts can tear through stone as easily as flesh. But as long as we keep the fighting to these corridors, we can reduce the harm they cause the city. Maybe even eliminate them."

"What comes after the werebeasts?" Seren asked as she slid down the wall and brushed bits of stone out of her hair.

"If their tactics are the same as last time, then normal infantry and arquebusiers. But last time they had no sombra to aid them, and who knows what other horrors Ilyron will bring to bear against us."

"Don't fixate on what the enemy will do," Glewdyn said, wiping sweat that was quickly cooling from his forehead. "Hold on to the knowledge that we serve the High King. He will see us through this to the end he ordains."

"Forgive me, sir, it is so hard to believe that right now," Seren admitted. "It is so hard not to think that having all of us here, clearly convicted we are serving the Quest to protect the Tower of Light, we will certainly overcome anything. Yet, have we gotten it all wrong? Could we have gone awry and deceived ourselves that we're doing as the High King bade us, and instead, we're on the precipice of disaster and ruin?"

Anargen rubbed his face. Hadn't he wondered that a dozen times himself?

Glewdyn glanced about the passage they were in. No other Ecthels or Ords were nearby. There were too many more vital passages to defend and smaller ones like this to block to spare any more than a handful at each spot. Apparently, whatever Glewdyn had to say, he felt would benefit from the privacy it afforded.

"I haven't questioned whether this is the Quest the High King would have us on. You both know, of course, that what victory looks like to us may not be what the High King knows to be best."

That was perhaps the thing Anargen struggled with the most. To yield to the idea that his death, his father's death, his wife's death ... that those could all be for the High King's greatest honor. Even to be humiliated or injured as he had been would be hard to reconcile, but especially reconciling his kind, compassionate wife's harm as ultimately good ... it nearly broke him to even think about it. No wonder Seren struggled, after all she had seen befall Gregor during the retreat.

"Steady, dear ones. I can tell that it is a difficult thing to confront, but our oaths are to one greater than the Lowlands. And they will last far longer than Ordumair or Kirke or Ecthalon. Even the ancient Centros where the High King walked among us will pass away before our bonds to our lord do.

"Bear that in mind when the troubles of these lower realms beset you. Over them looms the higher realm, and it is the one to which we truly belong."

Tracing the glowing lettering on the armor she wore, Seren's expression was pained. She sat that way for several moments before asking, her voice halting, "What then do you question, sir?"

Glewdyn stroked the tangled mess of a beard he hadn't shaved since leaving Port Jarreth. "Whether we understand our Quest fully. Whether the Tower of Light is truly just that, or is it something more?"

"More?" Anargen asked as he settled beside Seren and let her rest her head on his shoulder. She took his hand, lacing her fingers with his as much as they could through their gauntlets.

The elder Knight sighed. "You and Anargen have better words than I do. I suppose I mean something beyond a single physical tower. Something more profound. Even, perhaps, abstract. I've brought the matter before the High King a number of times and haven't yet been given clarity."

Clarity was something Anargen was in short supply of as well at the moment. Yet there was something, something gnawing at the edges of his thoughts, struggling to get in, to be given light. Some detail, a memory even, of something significant. At least something that could be significant.

"I know that what you tell us is wise and true. Anargen has shared those very insights with me before." Seren began and gave a tight chuckle. "I remember repeating for him the sentiments that 'we must make a stand, even if it won't end in victory as we imagine.' Right now, in the midst of all this pain and fear and sorrow ..." She began to tear up. "However true, it's just so hard."

Anargen remembered that moment when he needed to be reminded of that truth. How difficult it had been, how desperate and defeated he felt. Seren had helped pull him up out of despair's depths that day. He wanted fiercely to be able to take that pain away for her, to rescue her from the horrors that awaited them. He recalled clearly what she'd said that day, how it had reforged his resilience and perseverance when he thought the Quest was at an end.

How can I recast those words to help her face the pain, the dark, marring our world? Others see us ...

His eyes widened. The mental fog from earlier was gone, burned away like morning mist struck by the brilliant rays of the rising sun. Anargen had it. He could see clearly what the visions meant, what they were meant to be protecting.

Hurried footsteps echoed down the hallway, undercutting Anargen's thoughts. It was an Ord, a bawrnig under Elder Valen's banner. Dread seized Anargen, gripping him like a walnut's shell being cracked open. Elder Valen was an ardent supporter of Duncoin. Whatever brought his highest-ranking soldier careening to them, sweat-soaked and streaked with dust and blood, must be nothing short of tragedy.

"Knights," the bawrnig—Nikol, Anargen recalled—began, doubled over, hands on his knees. His nasally voice was higher-pitched from breathlessness. "The Thane has commanded all soldiers to withdraw from the tunnels. There's been a breach!"

"A breach? There have been a half dozen tunnels breached, and we've not abandoned all of them," Anargen replied. "Why would this one require a full withdrawal?"

The nostrils of Nikol's prominent nose flared in agitation.

"There is precious little time to speak of it—it was the central gateway."

"The main passageway that links the city and the fortress?" Seren pressed.

"Aye," Nikol confirmed. "We suffered a betrayal at the hands of the one tasked with guarding it. All of the secret tunnels those carrion have packed were unblocked."

Anargen shook his head emphatically. "No. No, that's not possible. Sir Iaegon was securing it. There's no way he would betray his people."

Nikol sighed. "I see we canno' do this quickly as needed. No fault to you. We're all taken aback. Elder Iaegon wasn't securing the passageway. Only something made to look like him. More wicked magics from the Monarch."

As the weight of what those words implied hit Anargen, he let his helmeted head clank against the stone wall. He had no reply, just pain, guilt, defeat. Iaegon was only a few years younger than him when they met, so Iaegon would be seventeen now. The same age Anargen had been when he set out on the journey to Ordumair. For the months they had been at Ordumair years ago, Anargen had been Iaegon's mentor after he, too, became a Knight of Light. After leaving, he had failed to keep up correspondence with the boy. The cool reception he'd received on arriving from him had almost made sense, felt justified. Now the awful truth was laid bare. Iaegon, the real Iaegon, was already gone. Slain and replaced by one of the fiendish doppelgänger servants of Monarch Ilyron. And as unreasonable as it might be to do so, he blamed himself for not being there for Iaegon when he needed him.

A gentle pressure on his hand brought him out of his thoughts. Seren was looking at him with empathy in her rich, cocoa eyes. Without saying anything, she clinked her helmet against his, her head and his supporting each other, their hands linked with greater ardor than steel chain. His pain was hers now.

Another sensation entered into the binary world Anargen shared with Seren, and he realized it was his father patting him on the back. "Son, we have to go. Grieve, and grieve deeply, but for now, you must not let this loss keep us from being an aid to others."

Drawing in a shuddering breath, Anargen looked to apologize to Nikol and found the Ord already having departed. His father must have traced his gaze, because he added, "Our messenger ran on ahead of us. Apparently, the Ecthels cleared much stone away, and when the imposter threw open the gates on our side, hundreds—thousands—of troops poured in. Everyone who wasn't already holding the line for the city has been summoned there. Except us."

"Why not us?" Seren asked. For which Anargen was grateful, he wasn't sure if his voice would ever return to him. It, too, may have been murdered by the vile creature that ended Iaegon's young life.

"We're being instructed to go straight to the vault. The Thane believes Ilyron will come for the wyvern straightaway."

Glewdyn's voice wavered in a way Anargen hadn't ever heard from his father. Steadfast as stone, steady as steel. That was his father to him. In that moment, his father's face was tight with worry, with a sorrow Anargen was sure he wouldn't know until he had a child of his own. Something his father's expression decreed would never be.

"This is the hour we've been preparing for," Glewdyn managed to say. "May the High King be with us and give us the strength to see it to its end."

"Whatever end it may be," Anargen offered, his voice guided back to him by the pull of his father's distress.

"Whatever end it may be," the older Knight affirmed.

The three of them—Anargen, Seren, and Glewdyn—raced through the winding passages of Ordumair toward the vault. None of them wasted air on talking as they ran. Every breath needed to go toward keeping them moving faster, and faster, around every twist and turn. Up and up into the heights of the fortress. Nothing could or should be worth stopping for, nothing except what was immediately ahead of them.

Anargen, who was leading them, skidded to a halt in front of the enormous stack of stones barring their progress. His chest heaved up and down as he fought to catch his breath in the dank, narrow confines of the secret tunnels. At his back, Seren and Glewdyn soon came to a stop on either side of him.

"What's the matter?" Glewdyn asked breathily.

Picking up a fist-sized rock, Anargen tossed it against the larger mass of stones. "It looks like the Thane ordered this passage blocked. We can't go straight to the vault now."

"Then how ... do we get ... there?" Seren asked, hands on her hips as her chest rose and fell with deep breaths.

Removing a gauntlet and undoing his faceplate, Anargen rubbed his face. He had to think of another route. There had to be another way there. Anything would be faster than removing all of the stones here. Seconds stretched into more than a minute of frantic thinking.

"There's one way," he blurted out as he reapplied his gauntlet and closed the faceplate of his helm. "We'll have to cut through the city to reach it."

"Through the battle?" Glewdyn asked, his breathing steady now.

Gnawing on his lip, Anargen wasn't sure whether he hoped it would or would not do just that. Encountering the battle would be dangerous and likely force them to join in the fray to save the city, but at the cost of protecting the vault. Thus, the impossible predicament of choosing between trying to rescue the Ords in Ordumair or the Restoration's peoples. And their presence could guarantee neither.

Glewdyn grabbed his son's arms on either side. "Keep together, lad. We have to hurry."

"We shouldn't have to," Anargen answered, hoping he didn't sound as conflicted as he felt about it.

Apparently, it was stable enough, because his father released his hold and gestured for him to once more lead the way. Anargen obliged by taking off, not sparing a glance behind to see Seren or his father follow after. This route would take longer, and whether it terminated in assisting those defending the city or those in the vault, he was sure neither could last long without aid.

Rounding turn after turn, he led them back down and then unexpectedly burst out through a hidden panel into a street of the city. Outside the tunnel, he was immediately beset by the echoing sounds of attackers' and defenders' steel clanging against each other and the report of arquebusiers firing rounds. Those were the sounds of battle Anargen dared to hear. There were other noises, tragic ones—screams and stone edifices collapsing under the occasional boom of a cannon.

He had brought them out on the eighth round. Here, there were no Ords out in the streets, and he guessed that everyone had been evacuated to the higher rounds. He cautiously approached the wall ringing the central open space that ran from base to top of the city. Peering over the side, he quickly averted his eyes. All he could bear to relay to Seren and Glewdyn as they too emerged into the streets was, "They've been pushed back to the fifth round."

He marched toward the next leg of their trek to the vault. Somehow, the finality of that choice having been made for him still weighed heavily. As if he regretted it being so that they would defend the vault, even if he knew the reverse would have been true if they had been forced to fight on the Ords' behalf. Back into the tunnels they hurried until they came upon it: the massive stone archway demarcating the entry to Ordumair's vault. The mosaic tile representation of the High King's symbol on the floor gleamed in the torchlight. It was a good sign the symbol was not marred, a petty act almost certain to take place once Ilyron's forces reached this point.

Foolish and perhaps even childish as it was, Anargen's heart raced as they entered the expansive chamber that housed the once lost library and treasures of Ordumair. Soaring marble columns dominated its enormous space, with the trees of the golden forest still lush and vibrant alongside the famed dual springs with their hot and cold-water sources. Beyond them stood the impressive shelves containing all of the library's tomes and a raised platform on which the sarcophagus for Thane Ornand the Orderer was placed. All was as Anargen remembered it from the last time he had passed through the ancient chamber imbued with such rich history and significance that it was like entering the beating heart of the Ord and Ecthelish peoples.

What was new, however, was more than fifty of Duncoin and Thomas's best soldiers arrayed in wait, weapons drawn and quick to intercept Anargen and the others. The guards, thankfully, recognized Anargen and allowed the trio to cross the space to join the Thane and Thomas under the boughs of the remnants of the golden forest.

Anargen walked up just as Thomas commented, "I never thought I would ever see the golden forest." He reached out his hand and rubbed a golden leaf between his fingers. "Just like the one on our seal. Like three small oak leaves forming a larger maple leaf shape. They're so silky to the touch. Not to mention the sweet smell ... Incredible. I finally understand why my people wrote so many poems and songs about its beauty.

"Mia would have loved them."

"Is Mia ill?" Seren asked, coming up alongside Anargen.

Thomas and Duncoin's attention shifted to the new arrivals. "No," Thomas replied. "She is well, but with things as they are ..." he began and left off. His face was contorted in an agonized mask as he struggled with what he wished to say. "We've held each other together and through so much. It's still my duty to protect her, and it's so hard to accept that everything is at an end. I failed to give her the life of peace and safety she deserves."

"You cannot give up hope," Anargen insisted. "None of us know what the High King may yet will for us. Only what He has asked of us in this moment."

Duncoin huffed. "And what might that be, lad? To die?"

"To keep to the Quest," Anargen countered, trying not to return the harsh tone Duncoin's cynicism had sparked. There were enough foes outside this room without making them of each other as well. "Honoring our oaths to him to the very end. Seeking justice, loving mercy, and walking humbly before him. Trusting we are in his care and all that transpires will work out for good according to his wisdom."

A deep rumble was all that Duncoin responded with. Thomas, in turn, leaned back against the nearby tree and closed his eyes. "I fear we won't have to hold on to our trust much longer."

As if to confirm that a crash echoed from the chamber

leading directly to the Vault. Sounds of tiles being cracked followed, then heavy footfalls.

Everyone around Anargen tensed. He felt Seren slip her hand into his and hold on tightly. Utter silence reigned as the first Monarchist poked its head into the pristine space.

To say it was ugly was an understatement. It looked like a bull and man's face had been smashed together, and it had a wiry series of bearded tassels attached to the chin. Or what passed for one. The creature pushed forward into the room, looming tall, at least ten feet or more. A clublike tail lazily dragged in after it and punctuated each of its massive-footed steps with a *thump*. Stony protrusions stuck out from all over the moss-garbed body. Under a shock of messy hair, like a cluster of tall grasses, were large, glowering eyes that scanned the room with a casual disdain. It snuffed like a pig and worked its protuberous lower jaw as its tusk-like incisors glinted in the room's lighting.

Anargen had never seen anything like it, though he had heard a story once from Sir Cinaed. One that the Defender loathed to tell, about how his father had died at the hands of a creature just like this.

As the stench of the monster filled the room, Seren coughed and whispered, "What is that thing?"

"A boggart," Anargen answered. "The Ecthels call them trolls."

A second such creature, even fatter and wilder-haired, stalked in.

Each carried huge stony clubs and bumped carelessly into one another with resounding impacts.

The soldiers nearest them backed as far away as they could, giving the pair room to spread aside and allow a cadre of those dark armored guards from the other night to ghost in silently. Anargen had not expected to ever think they looked small, yet next to the boggarts, they seemed like children dressed up.

At their back was a final figure. He wore a black coif and armor similar to the guards, but in his hand was a staff with pointed barbs at the end. With him came a chill like a gust off the snowy mountain slopes, but there was no wind in here. Smallest and slightest of all, this last figure carried with him a dark pall so deep there was no mistaking him for another. This was the fiend behind all the dark and torment they had all suffered for these long, fraught years. The blood of thousands was on his hands, and on his brow was the threat of ruin for all the Lowlands in the golden, radiate crown he wore. Monarch Maldes Ilyron stood within the walls of the Ordumair Vault.

The two parties, defenders and attackers, looked at one another across the space. Anargen felt as if the whole of Ordumair had to be holding a collective breath.

Without uttering a word, Ilyron banged his pointed staff on the floor twice. The instant he did, the trolls bellowed and shambled forward. On their heels, the dark guards advanced, seeming to almost hover across the floor.

Looking over at Duncoin, Anargen watched the Ord leader's stricken expression harden into resolve. Raising an axe overhead, he bellowed, "For Ordumair!"

He charged forward and was quickly overtaken by the Ords of his guard, halberds ready. The Ecthels joined an instant later as Thomas surged after the Thane.

Anargen looked at Seren and to his father, who nodded. The elder Knight drew his spiritsword. Flames rushed up the blade's length, and he said in a reverent tone, "For the High King."

Drawing his sword, Anargen felt more than heard the rush of heat as the fire caught on his spiritsword. He tensed, taking one steadying breath, and dashed into the battle.

Directly ahead of him, two Ecthels were trying to hold back one of the dark guard's strokes from the long-handled axes they wielded. It looked as if both men strained with all their might to hold back its attack. From behind Anargen, the snaps of arquebusiers firing reached his ears, and he watched as the lead balls plinked off the dark guard's armor. If they dented it at all, Anargen couldn't tell.

With a surge of force, the guard tossed off his attackers and drew back to cleave one of them in two.

Anargen forced his legs to move faster and leaped forward, holding his shield up to receive the blow. The impact sent tremors throughout Anargen's body, and he immediately struck the stone floor with jarring force.

Groaning as he rolled over, he saw that the Ecthel soldier had managed to scoot away. Both he and his compatriot stood watching, as if unsure what to do. Anargen couldn't tell them even to move aside before another sweep of the axe came round, and Anargen had to scramble to his knees and intercept it with his shield once more.

The blow sent him sprawling backward. He felt like the teeth in his head were shaken from the attack.

His foe didn't accord him recovery time. It marched forward with mechanical determination but ethereal fluidity.

What are these things?

The hulking armored attacker held the axe over its head and brought it down. Stone chipped and cracked where it struck, inches from where Anargen had rolled to get away.

Wriggling around, he tried to sweep kick the guard's feet out from under them. It was like striking a statue. He recoiled in pain, fighting his leg's protests as he rolled away from another axe swipe.

He had just struggled to his feet when the axe smashed his barely readied shield and Anargen went down again. This time, he didn't immediately try to get up. Where he lay, he felt tremors rolling through the thick stone floor. He looked up to see the nearest boggart casually ignoring the best attempts of two Ords and an Ecthel to pierce its hide and was focused on slamming its stone cudgel into the floor, over and over again.

What is the boggart—

A whispered warning alerted Anargen to move. Black metal slammed so hard into the floor that it cracked. His guard foe had tried to stomp him.

Bringing his sword around, it clanged off the side of the thing's legs. A shimmer, green as poison, rippled over the spot he struck.

That settled the question of whether these were simply powerful men or dark conjurations from the Monarch.

I can't believe I couldn't cut through it with my sword ...

An almost immediate rebuke fell upon him. His sword? No, this was a spiritsword, entrusted to him, but both he and the sword belonged to the High King.

Perhaps it shouldn't have surprised him, but the moment he relinquished his fixation on his failure and recalled the real power behind the blade, it flared hotter, brighter.

Bringing up his shield, he caught the next attack and closed his eyes, pleading for strength from the High King beyond his own. The axe fell heavily, but his shield held in place. In fact, he could tell the guard was straining against it, but it wasn't overpowering as before.

Deflecting the blow to the side, he took another swipe with the spiritsword and this time scored a glowing arc across the enemy's torso.

Black mist spewed from the gap in the armor and the thing stumbled backward. Its posture told him he'd come as close to surprising it as possible. On his feet in an instant, he blocked its counterattack with his shield. He slashed, grazing the chest plate. Dodging as it jabbed its axe pole at him, Anargen hammered aside the weapon with his shield and plunged the spiritsword deep into the chest plate and pulled it free in an upward arc. The split in the armor looked like the thing was cleaved in two.

It stood there shuddering, smoldering as more black mist poured off it. As it did, the glowing hot metal from the cuts caught on the mist, and suddenly there was a bright burst like a firework.

Anargen threw up his shield and braced himself as the concussive force of the mist's combustion scooted him back several paces.

That's one.

Would that defeating one was enough. Even as the dark mist was devoured by fire and cleared away, Anargen could see his next opponent stalking toward him.

IRON SHARPENS IRON

The door to the warehouse swung open with far less hesitation than Jason expected. He worked to coax his parched throat to speak, feeling utterly consumed.

No utterances were able to coalesce into a single word before Sir Cinaed burst in. In three long strides, almost a charge, he was on Jason and gripped him in a tight embrace. Tight enough that Jason began to cough and then chuckle in spite of himself.

"You ... ehem ... you already know what happened in here, don't you?"

Cinaed chuckled and released Jason. He gave the young Knight's arm a smack. "Of course. Do you think I wouldn't be aware when our Lord reaches out from the Highland to one so near?"

Jason bounced his brows. "I suppose that's something that would come with time."

The Defender shrugged; his aged cheeks lifted for the first time since they had lost Aria. Jason felt different, directed, full of zeal to push forward, and there was joy, but he wasn't quite ready to smile.

Cinaed seemed to sense that and sighed. The exuberance on his face faded to a more cautious terrain for the ridges and valleys lining his old face. "You are returned, but you still grieve?"

"Yes," he admitted, not bothering to mask the depth of the hurt in his voice.

Cinaed nodded. "It is a hard thing, the sorrow we bear. I suspect we shall both carry it with us all our days left in these Lowlands."

He held up a finger, again a step ahead in guessing Jason's coming protest. "Of course I'm buoyed from my grief. I have received back my son and brother-in-arms. No doubt finally appreciating exactly what the King's Day means."

For a second, Jason just stared at the elderly Knight. He had called him his "son." It was the first time he had been so direct in claiming him, either through Aria or through the part he played in Jason pledging himself to the High King. "I think I do understand ... better."

"Mhm. No eye has seen nor heart imagined the fullness of what awaits us on that day. A celebration to forever bind our wounds."

"Yes, sir," he agreed. Working some moisture to his mouth, he gushed, "The Great King showed me so much. But he didn't show why. Why we have to bear such grievous wounds here in the Lowlands ..."

How was he supposed to explain? Being fully committed to the High King once more and full of hope. Hope that all of the labors and sorrow would pass, but still finding himself struggling, pushing, fighting through the thick muck of the present.

The wizened gaze of the old Storyteller was fixed on him for a moment. He gripped both sides of Jason by the arms and said, "I do not presume to complete anything the High King spoke. I will, however, tell you what I have been shown in my years. Every pain has a purpose."

Jason sucked in a sharp breath. "That is what I struggle with. How can Aria's death serve a purpose for me? I—"

Cinaed waved his hand in dismissal. "Aria's life and death are a matter entirely apart from both of us. She belonged to the

High King as much as either of us. Her worth, personhood, what transpired regarding her life in the Lowlands, and its end is independent of us. The High King's ways and wisdom are above ours and he is a capable lord to decide what he permits for each of his servants. For you and me, the pain we feel as we are touched by those events of Aria's life ..." His voice faltered for just a moment. Drawing in a deep breath, he pushed forward.

"We are being refined by it. That process of heating to remove what isn't proper for the Highland within us. How can we not expect aches, deep ones to come?"

Jason shook his head, not sure what to say. Not sure if there was something to say.

Cinaed's mouth quirked like an artist dissatisfied with his canvas, bristling his beard. "Perhaps I do not rightly depict it. I have often thought of it as anchors, mooring us to these Lowlands. Every anchor a desire, however deep, to remain here. The High King is always at work slipping each one, so that when the King's Day comes, our allegiance, our desire for his Kingdom, will be undivided. The Highland, to be in his court before him, is our deepest longing and desire, even if we do not always consciously face it as such. And so, the painful snapping of tethers to this lower realm is needful."

"It doesn't lessen the hurt." Jason closed his eyes to hold in the tears that already stung his eyes as they encountered his deeply dried eyes. "Maybe dulls it."

"And one day cures it. You're right. though, woes won't fully leave us till we are made fully hale on his Day. It is enough to make the journey till then bearable."

The last wasn't posed as a question, but Jason felt sure it was in some way one. A check to see if he could and would press on. "Bearable," he agreed.

Giving his arms a final pat, Cinaed drew back and wiped

some wayward drops from his eyes. "Very good, lad. Then perhaps now I may give you some welcome news I received while you were in counsel with the High King."

"I would relish something positive right now."

Jason certainly sounded it, and Cinaed's eyes briefly clouded with a sharp pain of his own. Pulling free from it, he clasped his hands. "Word has reached me that there is a service line running southwesterly in Keraxlaco that we may use to get around the war mobilization. It will be a harder ride on older, less reliable engines, but it will get us back on track."

A little chuckle told Jason the old man delighted in the pun. Humor still escaped Jason.

"We also have some allies coming to help secure the Council of Defenders. A contingent of Knights has fled Jhi and seeks to ensure the pains they endure in their homelands do not spread to all the realms."

Jason wanted to speak, to say how wonderful the developments were, but he couldn't. Words weren't forthcoming. All he could do was smile, but even that felt like it took more of him than he had to spare that moment.

Brow furrowed, Sir Cinaed pulled Jason along toward the warehouse door. "Come, lad. You could use a rest, and the train to take us south will be ready shortly."

Following in silence, Jason's gaze fell to his spiritsword, still gripped tight in his hand. A surge of warmth, soothing over searing, traveled up his arm on currents swirling around the burning blade and he watched as fire traced a particular inscription, standing it out from the rest:

"And behold, I am with you always, to the end of the age."

A nother of the ethereal, armored sentinels rushed toward Anargen. Steeling himself to deflect the attack, he watched as his foe made it half the distance between them and then slid in half at the waist. A glowing streak lined where the armor was separated.

Anargen's eyes flicked to the side to see his father standing there, his chest heaving. Just to his left was Seren, also watching. Had they been fighting together while he tried to go it alone? Of all people, he should be by his wife's side. Not two, one. Even if they had fought side by side before, it was different now. A new dimensionality and importance to it.

He took a step toward her. "Thanks for the—"

Under his feet, the floor shuddered. Not enough to throw him down, but undeniable. He remembered the boggart smashing its club onto the floor almost as mindlessly as a carrion would. Except Sir Cinaed had made it clear from his tale that boggarts, while perhaps not the brightest creatures, were very strong-willed and far from mindless.

What is that fiend doing?

Whatever it was, it couldn't be good. Scanning the unfolding battle, Anargen found the other boggart doing the same. Except it seemed all too happy to take a brief break to bash aside the Ecthel soldier trying to spear it with his halberd tip. The poor man went flying into the bookshelves several feet back. A dozen old parchments dropped to the floor with him.

"We have to stop them," Anargen and Seren said to one another almost in the same instant.

Silly as it may have been, Anargen's cheeks flushed over the familiar twist of conspiratorial pleasure at how in tune he and Seren could be. Even behind her faceplate, he could see from the way her eyes fluttered that Seren felt the same. It was something to hold onto, because the next thing Anargen must do wouldn't be pleasant at all. They had to bring down both of the boggarts before the creatures achieved their mysterious aims. By all appearances, they were nearly impervious to damage and could crush a man like a grape in their enormous, crude hands.

Definitely not pleasant.

"How do we go about it?" Glewdyn asked, cocking his head downward as though peering over his nose pointedly at the young Knights.

Anargen nodded, eyeing the chaos around them, knowing he had to think faster. "Well ... in Sir Cinaed's account, he turned himself over to the High King and was able to get on the boggart's back and attacked. The spiritsword will cut through its stone hide, but he finished it by striking a soft point."

"Cinaed faced one of those things alone?" Glewdyn sighed. "Would that he were here with us now."

Sucking in a sharp breath against the swell of pain the wound of Cinaed's absence still induced, Anargen pointed with his spiritsword toward the creature. "You distract it, and Seren and I will climb on its back to bring it down."

With a smirk and shrug, he added, "Between the three of us, we should be able to manage to do what Sir Cinaed did on his own."

"Not on his own," his father amended. "The High King was with him and is with us as well. We do this for his honor."

"For the High King," Anargen agreed.

"For the High King," Seren seconded.

Crossing the raging battle, Anargen caught a glimpse of Thomas felling another of the Monarch's sentinels. That left only three. Even with his forces depleted, Ilyron had not moved to engage anyone nor summoned the additional troops he surely had readily at hand. One sentinel in particular stood beside him, also not moving, not engaging. For reasons Anargen couldn't quite grasp, he felt loath to even look at that one.

CRACK.

The boggart had busted up the marble flooring and was tearing away chunks of the slab, tossing them like a child throwing aside a rock they didn't fancy.

Glewdyn took off faster and dodged the latest hunk being discarded and, without breaking stride, raked his spiritsword across the monster's knuckles.

Instead of reeling in pain from the blow, the boggart yelped and grabbed for the older Knight. Its thick fingers scraped across Glewdyn's back, sending him stumbling across the stones.

The boggart huffed in annoyance at missing its prey. Ambling after him, it slapped its club into walls and pillars, wildly swiping at him. Those efforts failed, and it slammed its fists onto the floor in a tantrum-like rage.

Shockwaves like a minor quake rolled through the floor and Glewdyn lost his footing at last. There were only about a dozen feet between him and the boggart.

"My love?" Seren inquired, pulling Anargen to a stop as they pursued the monster to leap on its back.

Jerking to a halt, Anargen almost tripped. His wife's voice was steady, but the hand that had tugged at him was shaking.

"You trust me, and you trust the High King?"

"Always," he answered, though trusting in that moment came with a heavy dose of anxiety.

"Then you keep to the plan, but I'm going to try something."

"What?"

But she was off, dashing at an angle to the creature. Glewdyn's flight had led in a wide arc back to where it had started. Seren stormed past the creature, but at the last second cut back and, with her momentum and sword raised, cleaved through the monster's club. The maneuver sent her spiraling to the side, rolling along the floor.

Anargen's heart was like a blacksmith's hammer crashing over and over onto the anvil. Seren was bold. Too bold.

No, he knew her. She was clever and insightful and careful. He had to trust her and the High King that this risk was exactly what they needed.

The boggart dimly assessed the smoldering nub of its club and slammed both fists onto the ground, resuming its petulant fit. It uttered some strange words in a language Anargen didn't know, but he guessed it was profanity and curses. The hulking monster turned its great bulk toward Seren and, with a bellow like a bull, charged.

That's my opening.

Sprinting towards the creature, Anargen dodged a twitch of its spiked tail and leaped up onto its back, hanging off the rocky protrusions. Scaling the stony plates, he reached the point where he could slash most effectively with his spiritsword.

"Aaaiiieee!"

Seren's scream reached Anargen as he precariously balanced on his perch. The fiend had caught her by the leg and was dangling her upside down in the air. It made snorting sounds like a hog about to have the best meal of its life. Instead of biting at her, however, it whipped her around as if it was about to smash her down like a rag doll.

He had to act. Now.

Fighting to keep his balance, Anargen gripped the hilt of his spiritsword in both hands and slammed it down in between the plates. Hoping it struck true.

As soon as the fiery blade cut into the boggart, it screeched and threw Seren aside.

Anargen lost sight of her. The beast fumbled wildly, thrashing as it tried to reach the spiritsword to jerk it free.

On its back, Anargen was slung left and right, bashing into the hard plates over and over and over. Aches flared all over his body, but he held on tight, refusing to let go of the spiritsword and risk losing it.

Boggart curses were all Anargen could hear, and everything was a whipping, snapping blur. Something suddenly gripped him, and he was pulled off the boggart's back, spiritsword still in hand. An instant later, he sucked in a sharp breath as the other hand of the boggart slammed into him and began to press against its other palm.

"Little Knight, you'll squish like berries," chuckled the boggart in a bizarrely accented voice.

Struggling with all his might, Anargen couldn't free his arms, and the pressure was only tightening. It was already getting hard to breathe.

He tried to flick his wrist to nick the monster with his spiritsword.

No good. The fiend flinched away from it and gave Anargen a violent shake that almost blacked him out instantly.

Woozily, he watched as the beastly thug's glower turned to a wicked, inhuman grin. "Time to die," he crowed and started squeezing again.

This shouldn't be happening. How is this the end?

Had he honored the King with this life? Would his death be what the others needed to rally against their foes? Or was he just the first of his family to fall?

A flicker of motion caught the corner of Anargen's eye. An edge of flame bounced from the floor to the thing's propped-up leg as it kneeled. The young Knight's eyes darkened before he could see what was happening.

"Aarrgghh!"

Suddenly he was falling and crashed to the ground with a resounding clang. Breaths came in ragged wheezes that hurt as much as they were hungered for.

A heavy thump sounded next to Anargen. He looked up. Once more, his father stood over him, working to catch his breath as well. He grabbed Anargen's forearm and hauled him up without asking if he was ready.

There was a tightness around Glewdyn's eyes and a slight hunch to his back. Whatever he had done to rescue his son had really taxed him. "Thank you, that's twice," Anargen croaked.

"Seren," was all Glewdyn replied, his voice hoarse.

Anargen whirled, his heart suddenly jolted back to quadruple its normal speed. He found her lying beneath a pillar a dozen feet away. There was no measuring the time it took him to reach her. It must have been almost nothing, because Glewdyn hobbled over several seconds later. Anargen was already cradling Seren's limp form in his arms. He'd opened her faceplate and found her eyes shut and her lips parted, but heard no breath passing over them.

"Seren. Seren! SEREN!"

She wasn't moving. Why wasn't she responding at all?

Glewdyn gripped his son's shoulder.

Anargen flung his hand off. "No. NO!" he insisted, tears already beginning to form.

The older man opened his face plate, wincing. He sucked in a deep breath as if to steady himself for what he had to say. "Stay with her. Thomas looks like he's injured too. I'm going to go check on him."

Looking past his father, Anargen spotted Thomas halfway across the room and about a dozen feet farther back. He too was braced against a pillar, his head slumped.

Great King, please, no. I know I spoke boldly about giving my all, about each of us giving our all for you. But please, please ... don't let them be gone.

He couldn't bear to look up, couldn't bear to look away from Seren's face. Inwardly, he roiled. Rage, sadness, fear—all crashed down on the foundations of his resolve. The walls of courage, loyalty, and devotion to his oaths were swamped by the surges.

CRRRAAACCCKKK.

There was no ignoring the loudest sound Anargen had perhaps ever heard. Louder than the Great Bulwark's collapse, than Stormridge's dam breaking. He watched in horror as the marble floor at the room's back trembled and then fell away. Everyone near it, Ord, Ecthel, and Monarchist minion, dropped into the dark recesses opening beneath them.

More and more chunks of ivory and ebony swirled stone broke off and plummeted as if only just becoming aware of gravity's pull. Even from this angle, he could see it was a perilous drop with jagged cave stalagmite points glinting at the bottom and plenty of distance to injure or kill all on its own.

Anargen struggled to his feet and dragged Seren back, back, back as far as his taxed muscles and battered body allowed, before he collapsed. The hungry maw of the opening crept toward them, ready to swallow them both.

COUNCIL IN CONFLICT

J ason fussed with the bow tie he wore. He couldn't remember the last time he wore a full suit. Particularly one like this. The crisp white shirt was tucked into his starch-stiffened black pants. His hair had been trimmed and was slicked back. The rough scraggle of a beard he'd been sporting was shaved clean.

Looking in a mirror, he barely recognized the put-together, urbane young man with the red pocket square in his black blazer. An ironically Western style of dress, not exactly in line with how those in Centros were usually garbed. Though in fairness, Centros had a convergence of cultures. Hence why they were able to find the outfit he wore.

The man in the mirror watching him in kind blinked. He didn't look overconfident, cockiness verging on brashness, like the old scoundrel version of himself. Nor did he resemble the grizzled, seasoned warrior who had fought across the Lowlands against the Confederacy of Nations. About the best he could say was that he wasn't a lost man who was ready to lie down and die, either. He had been all of them; he was in some form still them, but also not.

"You do not need to be so nervous, Sir Landsby," Defender Guo commented to him. The Jhi'ish Knight glanced in the mirror, adjusting his own suit. His also included a sash around the waist to designate his rank as Defender of the Northeastern Realm. It was the only such extravagance taken to differentiate the dozens, perhaps hundreds of Knights of

Light gathering in Centros for the long-awaited Council of Defenders.

Part of Jason wanted to ask if there was word on the Jhi'ish Knights who were meant to come and lend them aid in securing the event. He managed to hold his tongue on the matter. Better not to broach the subject so close to the opening of the meeting.

"We've been longing for this for so long," he settled on. "It feels not quite surreal but super-real if that makes sense?"

Guo looked at him quizzically and Jason wondered if he had stretched the other's understanding of Ecthelish. At length, the Defender seemed to decide on an interpretation and replied, "You believe the King's Day is upon us?"

"Well, I ..." Did he believe that's what waited on the other side of this council?

He never got to distill his feelings and thoughts into an answer. The door opened to their dressing area and a Knight from Keraxlaco poked a tanned head in. "Hale day, friends," he said in the spritely manner typical of those from that country. "They are ready for you, Defender Guo."

"Very good," Guo replied and motioned for Jason to follow. He had been chosen as one of a handful of other Knights permitted to watch the proceedings in person.

Following the other two Knights, Jason glanced at their surroundings. The corridor they were walking along was nondescript. A sandstone passage that ran beneath a small hovel, miles outside of the actual eponymous city of Centros. If he had to guess, it was at least two hundred years old. Built well before Centros was granted nation-state status again and guaranteed neutrality in the conflict between long rivals Ecthelowall and Rehalcyon.

That was a period of time in Centros when being a Knight could mean being disowned and exiled by a community at best and being publicly executed at worst. This complex was the sprawling secret hub of activity for Knights of Light in the region since that time and still remained a largely unknown locality. At least Jason hoped so. It had been risky bringing everyone here, and even more so to hold such an important meeting during a phase in the war when a solid victory could turn the tide either way. Though he was beginning to see their role in the conflict was more than just fighting on the frontline and would continue irrespective of the political outcome, who was winning still mattered to him. He hoped dearly that the Alliance could recover from the faltering of Arnuk and Posek.

They had walked roughly a hundred feet down the corridor, with doors that branched off to dormitory-style sleeping quarters that were little more than bare rooms with multiple holes carved in the walls for sleeping. There was also a modest library and sparring arena for training. All of it very utilitarian. Though he didn't necessarily think drab was the right word for it, he had a bittersweet smirk knowing that Aria would've called it just that and suggested where well-placed color would do much for it.

Try though he might not to dwell on her, she was always going to be with him. In the opening of every book, the taste of a fresh-baked roll, the smell of cinnamon, and the abundance of plants matching the green of her eyes. Ironically, this now admittedly drab, dusty hallway even evoked her for him, by virtue of its contrast to her. Stiff, old, sparse—her dynamic, young, vibrant, and buoyant.

Up ahead, they finally came to the plain cedar doors that would usher them into the expansive chamber for meeting and resolving matters vital to the twenty or so Knights of the Hall that met here year-round. As the doors pushed open, Jason swallowed back his shock. The room was packed. In the center was a square cedar table. Around it were twelve chairs for the twelve Defenders, ringed by dozens upon dozens of others here to witness this historic moment and discover what path the Order would be charting through these uncertain times.

Getting everyone here was, by Sir Cinaed's own admission, actually the easy part. Getting them all to agree on what to do next would take something truly incredible.

"It is remarkable to see so many of the Order from all across the Lowlands here," Defender Guo commented to Jason. "It is a shame my fellow Jhi'ish were not able to reach us in time to see this."

Jason nodded somewhat absently, distracted by the noise of dozens of conversations taking place simultaneously. It did not help that the room's acoustics only amplified the commotion. "It is a shame. What held them up?"

Guo looked down at the floor and glanced up at Jason. The latter only caught the briefest flicker of conflict in the Jhi'ish Defender's expression. "There is a wounded Knight they are bringing with them. It forces them to travel more slowly. It will be days before they arrive."

Before Jason could inquire further, a loud, coarse voice broke through the chatter: "Much silence, now!" It was the Defender of the North-Central Realm, the Knorish Knight, Boris Tooadama. It was particularly amusing to see the boisterous old Knor up in front. Paunchy but still quite imposing, he eyed everyone in the room, daring them to speak.

Satisfied as the last strands of conversation withered under his cool, blue-eyed gaze, he added, "Defender Black now speaks."

Jason watched Sir Cinaed stand. He was commanding, and even though he wore a suit, he still felt as humble and approachable as he did in his duster and plain slacks. He was also the oldest Defender by a wide margin. The youngest being Kaveed Amine as Defender of the Southwestern Realm. A bittersweet twinge struck Jason as he recalled that Kaveed's bride, Tirzah, was very much pregnant and not able to be here. It bought Jason some time telling her about Aria. Which was going to be miserable, given they were like sisters. It might be craven, but he thought a letter might be all he could handle.

No. Don't be a coward. You owe it to Aria to tell Tirzah in person. Aria would've wanted it that way, and you're going to honor her in this, even if it kills you.

"Welcome, my dear ones," Cinaed projected. Once again, he was the Storyteller in tone and bearing. "We meet precipitously to discuss a matter of eminent importance."

Cinaed paused, attention turned to Jason. The gaze lingered long enough for Jason to become anxious about himself. Was he doing something silly? Breached protocol or committed some afront? Had he accidentally had his pants drop?

Not the latter for certain. Cinaed's time-worn face was grave. "In addition, I have something I must announce ... something personal."

He's going to tell everyone about Aria.

"But first," Cinaed continued, "The matter at hand for us all. As you all know, the Lowlands Total War has consumed all the realms in a brutal conflict."

"That is an understatement," challenged a speaker Jason didn't recognize by sight or sound of voice. He spoke Ecthelish with only the faintest accent, but it was enough of a hint to guess he was Rehalcy.

Jason did a double-take. He had spotted the speaker and realized the man strode to stand beside the assembled Defenders rather than maintain any semblance of deference and respect, hanging back like everyone else not on the Council. With him were two others. One a rotund Zilnian man with a sour expression on his curly, black-bearded face. He wore a robe of fabric that resembled his beard. Another was a bony woman with close-shorn hair, who was likely Yusbilsani with her billowy yellow dress.

"Friends," Defender Guo spoke up. "You are permitted to be in these proceedings to observe, but only Defenders of the Twelve Realms may speak."

"Indeed," the Rehalcyon man replied. Pointing to the Zilnen man, he announced, "This is Esau Mosem, Defender of the Southwestern Realm."

To the woman he assigned, "Defender of the West Central Realm, Ishte Egaba." His gaze flicked cooly to Sir Cinaed, and he gestured to himself. "I am Gerard LeVanseaux, Defender of the Northern Realm."

The tensed silence in the room was thicker than setting concrete. Defender Rindo del Miguelso of Vov Hilan endeavored to speak up. "You have an odd sense of humor. The Realms you named all have Defenders present. Why jest like this?"

"It is no jest," the woman, Ishte, snidely chided. Her thick Yusbilsani affectation made it difficult to understand her. "We were appointed by the Emperor of Rehalcyon to serve the Realms the Empire rules."

Immediately, the room exploded into a chaotic fit of challenges and questions. The three "Defenders" stood looking on the bedlam they induced with expressions ranging from smug superiority to disinterest to sly pleasure. The lattermost on the Rehalcyon man's face told Jason everything he needed to know.

Dorian. He found out about the Council, and this is how he plans to ruin it.

"All silent!" Defender Tooadama demanded over and over until everyone complied. Once the room quieted, he pointed to the Rehalcyon man, "You, I have seen you. Long time ago. In court of Knors. You secretary to Emperor."

"Department of the Foreign Ministry, yes," the Rehalcyon man freely admitted.

Boris slammed a heavy fist down on the table. "You are not the Defender. Sir Cinaed has been for longer than we both lived!"

Sir Cinaed patted Sir Tooadama on the arm as though soothing a guard dog.

Shooting a glance Jason's way that told him he had put it all together as well, Cinaed said, "The Emperor of the Rehalcyon Empire may only appoint a new Defender if the prior Defender is unable to perform his duties and no other successor was named by the elders at the Hall from which they served."

"Precisely," Gerard said slick as a serpent. "None of the three Defenders replaced can discharge their duties unbiased, because of the war. Regrettably, the Halls to which they belonged also seem to have no ability to choose replacements either. Thus, we are here to serve the peoples of our Realms at this auspicious gathering." Tapping his finger on his cheek, he added, "And, in fact, I'm not sure these proceedings can formally continue. Doesn't the Defender of Central and Lower Highlands Realm preside over the meeting as the Prime Defender?"

Once more, bickering broke out.

The notion of the Defender stationed in Centros being preeminent among all the Realms was not something interpreted or accepted uniformly across the Lowlands. One look at that Defender in question, Yohanan ben Davidiah, told Jason the Centrite didn't want to take the role being thrust on him. More than that, there was an edge to the manner in which Minister LeVanseaux regarded him. Had Dorian directly threatened Sir Davidiah? Perhaps warning that the Rehalcyon

Empire would invade Centros if he didn't comply with this sabotage?

The Empire had invaded and conquered almost all of Yusbilsi, despite its neutrality. Honestly, the notion that Centros was safe in its own was naïveté at best.

Jason noticed that Defender Kazim Cuzibaum looked as if he was going to break off the piece of the table he gripped. From Yusbilsi himself, the only reason the entire nation wasn't in Rehalcyon's hands was because he had carved out around his headquarters at Siğmacaq Yeri a breakaway nation representing true Yusbilsani interests. The Sykonos Republic was barely holding out, making his presence here all the dearer. The way Ishte leered at him made Jason wonder if something awful wasn't also afoot there.

Back and forth across the room, Jason could almost see the conflict deepening with every added dispute. Nearly all immaterial to their purpose being there. They threatened to send it ever farther over the side of the proverbial cliff. Worst, the three Knights most capable of steering the discussion and with the most potent positions—Defender Black, Defender Amine, and Defender Cuzibaum—were the three implied to be invalidated. Those closest to Sir Cinaed—Defender Tooadama, Defender Guo, and Defender Miguelso—could hardly stand for him without looking like they were meddling in the succession of other Realms. A thing viewed as tasteless at best and morally repugnant enough for dismissal by vote at worst.

Glaring at Minister LeVanseaux, Jason caught the man glance his direction, and the wicked curl of his mouth into a grin sent a shiver down Jason's spine. If his suspicions about Dorian's meddling were in need of confirmation, that was certainly it. Years of work, thousands of miles traveled, risking the lives of hundreds of Knights and soldiers of the Alliance across the Lowlands ... losing Aria ... all of it to bring about this

Council. This moment to stand united and carry the High King's banner as one Order dedicated to erasing the darkness with the unending light ... And all of it was being torn to shreds by dragging a stealthy dagger across old wounds.

Jason closed his eyes, trying not to imagine his brother's dark eyes gleeful over his torment. A slight smile on his young mouth that was as evil as any werebeast's slavering maw. Gloating, mocking, relishing the pain this would bring Jason, and the darkness that could swell across the Lowlands unchecked, because of it.

This was it. The end of the Quest. The end of the Order ...

"No!" Jason bellowed, bursting from his place in the wings. In one swift move, he drew his spiritsword, brandishing the fiery blade and slamming it point-first into the stone floor. Its burning tip flash-melted the stone and sank several inches into it.

The gesture was enough to silence the room for a moment as all eyes turned to him. Many of them stunned. But only for the moment. Any second, someone would call for him to be seized.

Uh, oh. Gotta think of something ...

A whisper rushed to him, the whisper that guided him in battle. And why not now? This was certainly a battle, if of a different sort. "Fellow *Palatini Lucis Aeternae*, Knights of the Unending Light, how are we so easily thrown into disarray, drawn into petty quarrels? We are gathered here today in service to the High King, for his cause and his purposes. How do you think he looks upon us all squabbling like children? Especially those who are his most noble servants!"

Jason swallowed, his heart hammering in his chest. So far, the words had guided him and seemed to find their mark, but every second of silence was an opening.

A rush of warmth from his spiritsword drew his eyes there.

A series of inscriptions glowed and huffed a light laugh. "By the High King's own words to us, borne on every one of our spiritswords:

"... walk in a manner worthy of the calling to which you have been called, with all humility and gentleness, with patience, bearing with one another in love, eager to maintain the unity of the High King's Spirit in the bond of peace."

"Over and over, we are exhorted to be '*one.*' To be '*of one accord.*' To be '*likeminded.*' What have we done so far at this, the first attempt in centuries to be one Order? Do any of us desire to be one as the High King bade us?"

A murmur of assent rose among some. Others quietly mulled the words. Minister LeVanseaux looked as if he wanted to run Jason through. Stamping his foot, the Rehalcyon envoy demanded, "Who are you that you lecture us? Hmm?"

Cocking his head to the side, Jason just smirked.

This guy. He really thinks using the "he's a nobody" argument is going to distract from the clear truth.

LeVanseaux seemed to be savoring the words as he said, "This man is Jason Wernstrum. Yes, of THE Wernstrum Crime Syndicate, which plagues Rehalcyon's citizens."

Jason's mouth almost dropped open.

A nargen cradled Seren in his arms and closed his eyes. "We're ready to come to you, my King," he whispered.

The cacophony of stone collapsing grew fainter until it faded away entirely. Even so, Anargen took several seconds to open his eyes. Though he tried not to, he looked down into the gaping pit that had been created. It stopped short of Seren and his feet. Importantly, Monarch Ilyron, the despicable villain who had tormented them, was nowhere to be seen.

He leaned back and let out the tension wracking his body in a deep sigh. "Thank you, my King."

Almost instantly, he remembered his father and Thomas. Head whipping around, he spotted them. They, too, were perilously close to the pit, but safe. Both Knights were up, leaning against a pillar, the next one back from the one Thomas had been initially braced against. The first pillar was now broken in half, with the portion still remaining pointing jaggedly down like a snake's fang.

There was a stirring in Anargen's chest. Relief, thankfulness. Precious after the harrowing minutes he'd just endured. He steeled himself because he knew the fresh air of hope might not be enough to bring him back from the depths he was about to plunge to as he examined Seren.

She still hadn't stirred, and his hands hovered over her still form with futile energy. He wasn't a physician or apothecary. What he knew of human anatomy was minimal, acquired from reading the scant texts on it he had encountered over the years. Nothing to tell him what to do. Should he remove her armor? Leave it? Move her? Let her lie here?

He cupped her cheek. She still felt warm, but there wasn't the same rosiness in her soft, pallid cheeks that came from the flush of emotion or effort. The overwhelming ache of certainty that he was losing her struck him over and over like a club.

A tremor began in his hand, and he knew that he was close to going into shock or madness or both. He kissed her impulsively, his tears beginning to fall and drip onto her face. This couldn't be it, couldn't be how it ended for them. He had to say something to her to tell her one more time that he loved her. That she had redefined beauty not simply because of her looks, but her heart. The tenderness and compassion she had shown ... oh ... it ached to even think about how gentle and thoughtful she had been.

By compulsion, he took off his gauntlet and hers and laced his fingers with his wife's. They felt as soft and well-fitted as ever, but cool. Chilled as he'd never felt them.

Putting his head between his knees, he started rocking, trying his best not to shatter like the floor had. When he began humming and then singing, he didn't know. Time, where he sat, his voice—all felt meaningless until he realized what song he'd slipped into singing.

"Summer's here, there's wheat to tend,
Over our eyes, we sun rays defend,
Missing word from any—Did you send?
Will you be home again?"

As he sang, he shuddered, as if each note was pulling him farther and farther from Seren. How many times had he sung this song? Sad as it was, had it ever stung this pointedly before?

"When all our journeys' ways mend,
Will you be home again?
Will you be home again?"

He was only through the first verse and chorus, but he couldn't bear to sing another word. If he made it to the end with its brutal finality, he knew he would crumble, and no one but the High King himself would be able to reassemble his fragments. It was enough to leave him numb. Pain had exhausted his capacity to feel for the moment, and in its void, he could be resilient enough to let her go.

Beginning to unfold himself and rise, he felt a tug and realized his hand was still linked to hers. A wave of bitter revulsion opened new grounds of agony he hadn't realized he could sink into at the thought of her body already having stiffened. He tried to extricate his fingers from hers and, frustratingly, couldn't.

"You stopped singing ..."

Had he said that? Anargen looked over and saw Glewdyn and Thomas sitting there, heads in their hands. Grieving for him. For Seren.

"... before you got to our verse."

A jolt of hope and panic coursed through him. He looked down. There, blinking with faint awareness, were the cocoa eyes he could stare into for hours. The slight pull of lips into a smile that could reshape a mountain of sorrow into happiness for him.

"It's ... yours ... to sing," he choked out, unsure he could even remember how to breathe, let alone speak.

She gave a ragged chuckle. "Maybe later."

In an instant, he was back down on the floor at her side. He helped get her upright, wincing with each twinge that twisted her face. Color was already beginning to return to her, and gradually her hand warmed. "I thought I'd lost you," he croaked, aware he was once more a mess of tears and torrid emotions, but chief among them was thankfulness that pervaded every fiber of his being.

"You almost had," she replied with a cough. Her voice was becoming steadier. It took all his willpower not to place his ear over her chest to listen to the blessed music of her heartbeat. "The High King told me we aren't done with the Quest yet, though."

There was definitely a renewed edge of determination to her words. "You have to help me up. Monarch Ilyron, he's—"

"*RRRRRRAAAAARRRRRRGGGGGHHHHH!*"

A chill with blizzard force rushed out of the hole at their backs and encircled Anargen. Every hair on his body felt as though it might stand on end and flee if it could. That sound was both familiar and yet slightly different from what he recalled.

On his feet again, Anargen hauled Seren up and draped her arm around his neck. This was bad. Very bad.

Thomas and Glewdyn jogged over to them. "I know that sound," Thomas said, his voice frigid with wariness. "But it's slightly off."

"That's because we've all heard a wyvern's cry," Glewdyn said solemnly. "That, lads, however, is something no one in the Lowlands has heard for centuries. That was a dragon."

VEILED THREATS

*O**h. Oh, no. This LeVanseaux is shrewder than he seems.*

Shrewd as a serpent. The Rehalcyon Minister gestured dismissively to Jason. "Now he's here among you, preying upon you during the most tumultuous hour of all our lives."

"This meeting isn't about the war," Jason protested. As soon as the words came out of his mouth, Jason almost gasped. Had he just said that, after arguing for so long that the Knight Order absolutely needed to meet here for that very purpose?

Yes, that was true. That was what he had thought. But deep within him, he knew that wasn't what this was about anymore. Not after what had happened with Aria. Not after his vision of the High King.

"Isn't it, though?" LeVanseaux challenged, breaking into Jason's thoughts like a proverbial Surcalido bull into a Jhi'ish porcelain shop. "Isn't it just one more ploy by Ecthelowall to try to save its power and profits by manipulating all of you?"

"This meeting isn't about the war," Jason insisted, seeing many eyes now looking very carefully at him. Scrutinizing him as though he were a dangerous sort of vermin that had to be dealt with, but only with the greatest caution.

"It's not about the war," he repeated. "It's about something bigger, more important."

"More important than the biggest conflict the Lowlands has ever seen?" scoffed LeVanseaux. "This is why you shouldn't let non-Defenders speak at such a meeting."

There was an edgy murmur of laughter from some. Mostly, the room was taut with attention to see if there was a rebuttal.

Jason shook his head. "The Lowlands Total War isn't the biggest conflict the Lowlands has ever seen. There is one far older and far greater that has been fought by every man, woman, and child in the Lowlands. Rebellion against the High King has been man's oldest story and battle. Each of us has taken our stand on the side of the High King—even I, who once was a Wernstrum, once a despicable servant of the dark.

"No longer are any of us of the dark. We are Knights of the Unending Light, and we are here to make sure that light never fades, never fails to push back the darkness that incites men to rebel against the rightful rule of the High King of All Realms.

"So, dismiss me, disregard Defender Black, cast off all of us that this clever puppet of Rehalcyon has besmirched. The Quest remains the same. The High King's honor will not be diminished, but it is our sacred duty to keep our vows and fight with all in us to continue shining the High King's light for all the Lowlands to see. In war. In peace. Whatever the Lowlands may bring us."

CLAP. CLAP CLAP.

LeVanseaux made a show of his applause. "Such fine oration. It is a wonder you did not join the Ecthel parliament!"

Murmured commentary passed throughout the room. A strong reminder that not everyone present held fond sentiments toward Ecthelowall and the Alliance.

"High praise from a high government official in Rehalcyon," he shot back.

"Touché. It seems perhaps the war does matter, even here."

Jason ground his teeth together. He had walked right into that rhetorical trap. Shooting a look of pleading to Sir Cinaed, he found the old man stroking his bushy beard. To Jason's surprise, instead of stepping into the argument, he waved his hand for Jason to continue.

He wants me to fight this battle. The Defender has to know I can't win it.

Around him, the room was shifting. In a moment, nothing he said would matter; the direction of the meeting would be altered, and whatever came of it would be the result of his failure.

Please, my High King, help me.

Once more, the tingling sensation of heat coursing up into him from the spiritsword drew his attention to it. This time, however, no one inscription stood out. The entire blade seemed to glow with the same steady luminance.

"Thinking about resorting to violence and swinging that sword around, eh, Wernstrum?" LeVanseaux taunted. "It only makes sense given you don't think wars matter."

For a brief moment, Jason had to force down the urge to oblige the Rehalcy with the violence he mockingly suggested. But no. That was not befitting a Knight of Light, no matter how loathsome his foe may be.

Wait. Knight of Light. Foe ...

"Perhaps it would be best for you to avoid goading. Given none of you three appointees are Knights," Jason pronounced.

Whispers surged, washing over all in attendance. How had they failed to note these interlopers weren't emissaries of the High King?

Fussing with his high collar and bowler cap, LeVanseaux splayed his hands. "As if you know a man's heart and allegiance."

Jason smiled broadly. "You're right. I don't, but the High King knows his own."

He pulled loose the sword and, taking it by the blade, he offered the hilt to LeVanseaux. "Here, take hold of it and show me the liar. If you can take it and fire catches, you are a Knight of Light. If you aren't, then beware. The High King is a consuming fire. Claiming you are his while you oppose him carries a grave consequence."

"Grave?" The Zilnian man finally spoke up. "As in, we go to the grave?"

"That has been the case," Kaveed confirmed, fighting a knowing grin.

LeVanseaux backed up, as did his two cronies. "This proves nothing! I'm not bound by any rules to take hold of this blade like a barbarian."

Now the whispers and rumblings of the room had changed. They were turning against the false Defenders.

"You take great sword!" Sir Tooadama demanded.

"I will not," the Rehalcy refused, unconsciously wiping away sweat beading on his brow from the proximity to the burning blade alone.

A whisper enveloped Jason, and he called to his flustered foe, "We could always resolve this with a dispensation from Defender Davidiah. You did say you acknowledge his primacy in these proceedings."

The other man seemed conflicted for a moment. As if unsure whether to lay hold of this offered gift or not. He seemed to settle that it was a misstep on Jason's part. "Yes, Defender Davidiah. Give us a ruling. Who is Defender of the Northern Realm? Who between me and this vagabond is the genuine article? And who between us must leave these proceedings immediately?"

All eyes naturally turned to the reluctant Prime Defender. He wrung his hands. There was no getting around having to choose to which side he belonged. His dark eyes shot back and forth between Jason and LeVanseaux. Just to his back, barely noticeable, Jason spotted that strange shimmer from before.

"Uh, I declare, in accordance with the rules of the Order ... that we ... must ... vote."

This didn't sit well with LeVanseaux, his superior demeanor faltering. "A vote? By whom?"

"The Defenders not in question," Davidiah replied with a shrug. Having rendered a decision at all seemed to grow his confidence, bolstering his words. To the Defenders assembled, he addressed, "Whom here agrees that Sir Kazim Cuzibaum is the rightful Defender of the West Central Realm?"

Of the three, he was the most interesting to contrast with his opponent. No one would struggle to apply the word severe to both candidates. But where they differed was in the quality of their austerity. This Ms. Egaba exuded a bitterness that had not softened once in all the proceedings. Even now, her lips were set in a tight line as she glared balefully on all, laying upon each who saw her the guilt of an offense that they could not ever ascertain nor recompense.

Kazim, on the other hand, had been through enough humbling and heartbreaking circumstances to have no use for games and politicking. His home was between the jaws of a great beast, and he would defy it to his dying breath. Unwavering, fierce, noble. Those were the words he conjured as he stood slowly and bowed his head respectfully to the other Defenders. He took up his place at the Rehalcyon puppet's side.

"Cuzibaum!" Tooadama enthusiastically called out.

"Cuzibaum," Miguelso agreed.

"Cuzibaum," Guo confirmed.

Egaba narrowed her eyes and shot a look at LeVanseaux. The latter splayed his hands to the group. "Have any of you been benefitted by former Defender Cuzibaum's brash tactics? Why has diplomacy with the legitimate government of Yusbilsi not been pursued? Does he leave you feeling any safer,

Defender Vesslo? Your Far Southern Realm has suffered a blockade of goods from the war. Goods that could have flowed freely if not for the so-called Sykonos Republic disrupting trade routes through the Imperial port of Suselah."

Burgha Vesslo, a thick-jawed man graying thoroughly throughout his bushy shock of hair that was pulled back into many braided tails, drummed his thick fingers on the table at which he sat and then called, "Egaba."

After him joined Defender Kiva Ishtai, whose Eastern Realm home in Zhoulong was also striving to maintain neutrality to protect itself. "Egaba."

"Egaba," Peshno Dublon called next. As the Knight who held the dubious title as Defender of the Lost Realm, which contained Tislatna, but was based out of Puertolica, far to the south of the ruins of the famed Tislatna, he too was in a tight spot. Puertolica desperately clung to its neutrality to keep its twin islands out of the crossfire between Ecthelowall and Rehalcyon's navies.

Marcus Shinneson of the Far Western Realm did not hide the conflict on his face. His home in Garcenilles had been protected and colonized by Ecthelowall for more than a century. But trade with Rehalcyon had been a key source of income before the war. Scratching anxiously at his curly tufts of slate hair, he mumbled, "I abstain." His head stayed down thereafter, eyes fixed on the table.

That left Mattai Johannon, who lived in Mbisai. The same Mbisai that was currently under siege and, though part of the Alliance of Realms, in serious danger of broader occupation. His wife and children were no doubt still in the capital Apisidisi, which was perilously close to the front lines. Furrows of worry lined his dark face. Though a large man, he didn't wield his size or imposing presence like a brute. He seemed to epitomize a gentle giant. In the Lowlands Total War, the gentle were all too often becoming victims of those who could be brutal. "I abstain too," he said in his thick accent.

Intimidation and the threat of loss and reprisals. Those were the bargaining chips that would erode the edifice of the Council's unity. Worries of the Lowlands clawing away devotion to the Highland. With those two abstentions, the vote was deadlocked. Everything hinged on the one remaining voice to be heard.

"Davidiah," prompted LeVanseaux. "It appears you will decide the matter."

There was such menace in it that Jason didn't begrudge Sir Davidiah when he swallowed with noticeable anxiety. Nor when he failed to speak one way or another. Torn would be a gentle way of describing how he looked as his brown eyes shifted from LeVanseaux and Egaba to Sir Cuzibaum and at last locked on Jason. As if startled by a sound, he stared down at the hilt strapped to his side. Drawing his spiritsword, he walked around the table to stand beside both Yusbilsani contenders.

Its light cast awful shadows on Egaba's sharp features, and she seemed to lean away from the blade, either unaccustomed to Knightly practices and therefore squeamish around the sword itself or repulsed by all it represented. Jason presumed the latter. Beside the sour little woman, the stalwart Sir Cuzibaum reacted as well, bowing his head lower, one fist pressed tight against his chest in a Yusbilsani display of respect.

Flames crackled from the blade, and Sir Davidiah lifted it high. "By the will of the High King and his alone ..."

The man's voice wavered, and Jason sucked in a tensed breath of his own. The High King had led him on this path to whatever end. If the worst happened now, he would not back down. Not until the end of his days.

"I choose Sir Kazim Cuzibaum," he said at last, touching the flat of the spiritsword to either of his shoulders.

Without missing a beat, he added, "I move we vote now on the Defender of the Southwestern Realm."

With Kazim added to their number, the whirlwind of votes called out now swung to approving the true Defender, Kaveed, without even needing Davidiah to tiebreak.

"And now, for the Northern Realm."

"I must protest," LeVanseaux spoke up, a growl in his voice.

"Don't tell me you're rethinking your position on the primacy of the Defender of the Central and Lower Highlands," Jason jeered, borne on a rush of elation. They were going to stop them! Foil their nascent plot to derail the Council. The light would not be so easily snuffed out.

Pointing a furious finger at Defender Davidiah, LeVanseaux snarled. "If you do this, you can be sure that your biased choices will cost Centros its neutrality. All the privileges and protections you've enjoyed here will be gone in an instant." He gave a snap of his fingers for emphasis. "Think very carefully before you condemn yourself and all you know and love to the horrific ends you know will come upon you."

That was as chilling and direct a threat as one schooled in double entendre and surfeit of subtlety like LeVanseaux would give. It certainly leveled the Knight at whom it was aimed. Davidiah took a faltering step back, quavering like water under a strong wind. As he did, he was steadied by the worn, resilient hands of Sir Cinaed.

He exchanged a look with Defender Black, those piercing eyes boring into him. Deep waters, however troubled on the surface, are unmoved beneath. The old storyteller had a way of deepening one, becoming a steadying stone wall on which to lean.

Turning, the Centrite Defender projected his voice in a manner he had failed to before, one worthy of the Prime Defender. "By threat of violence against the Order, you,

Gerard LeVanseaux, are disqualified from service as a Defender. By such, the title falls back to Sir Cinead Black."

As the flat of the sword touched each of his shoulders, Jason could tell Sir Cinead was quietly savoring the confirmation of his role. Perhaps even finding amusement, given he had been Defender of the Northern Realm since before Sir Davidiah's father was old enough to sire him.

Pointing his spiritsword at the trio of charlatans, he demanded, "Leave now or suffer the consequences of challenging the High King's will."

The Zilnian, Esau Mosem, looked stricken, and he edged without hesitation away from the fiery sword. Tiny slits of annoyance peered back from Ishte Egaba's scrunched face, but she, too, did not long linger. That left LeVanseaux standing there, arms crossed over his chest, behaving for all the Lowlands like a disappointed parent.

"You could have had a good life. Tasted rewards you only dreamed of," LeVanseaux addressed the Prime Defender. "Now ..." he snapped his fingers as he had before. "Gone. All gone."

Almost as if that had erased the sword-bearing Knight, he stepped past him to glare up at Jason. "And you ..." A cruel grin spread on his lips as he strained up to whisper in Jason's ear. "A pity what you lost in Jhi. A greater pity that your friend is on a train bound for Brackenburgh, destined to become the sacrifice by Monarch Ilyron's arts that will awaken the grand dragon of Rehalycon."

Giving Jason's cheek a pair of pats that verged on slaps, he added, "Your brother instructed that I relay that message to you. *Salut*."

Quick as they entered the proceedings, the three emissaries of Rehalcyon all ducked out. Their presence, however, had tainted the proceedings, jumbled them. No one was going to forget who had voted with the fiends. Certainly not Jason, whose heart hammered in his chest. He had been unguarded against this latest strike. All his thoughts had been on mourning Aria, clinging to the High King to keep from faltering. Then this Council and all the legendary glory surrounding it.

Surely that snake had been trying to goad him. A parting shot meant to unsteady him. And yet, what part of it rang false? Monarch Ilyron? A friend from Jhi becoming a sacrifice? A grand dragon, whatever that even meant? It didn't really matter which, if any, of those things were false. If any were true, then he could not wait for the Council to rebuild itself and act. He had to get to Brackenburgh.

Immediately.

22

FALSE IDOL

"It can't be," Thomas insisted. Though he sounded more hopeful than confident in his assertion. "How did he find a goblin and complete the ritual so quickly?"

"Does it matter?" Glewdyn replied and shuffled toward the edge of the gaping hole to peer down.

Seren gave a faint nod in that direction, so Anargen helped her over as well.

There was an eerie glow emanating from below. A deep orange pall was on the ruined stones of the floor all the way down into the cavernous chasm opened by the boggart.

As Anargen's eyes swept the debris, a shiver traveled the length of his body. A strong urge, almost a plea to get away from this place, struck. It was eerily similar to the one he'd had when looking on Ilyron's right-hand sentinel.

Revulsion swept over Anargen. "I think he brought a goblin with him. One of the sentinels that didn't combat us."

"As if suits of armor filled with evil mist wasn't creepy enough," Thomas grumbled.

A low rumble issued from the pit. Then a shrill squeal pierced the air, echoing in the otherwise silent chamber around the Knights.

"What do we do now?" Anargen asked of Glewdyn as the sound faded.

"We have to go down there," Seren spoke up. "We have to stop it, that's what the High King showed me. If we do not want the Tower of Light to fall, then the dragon must be destroyed."

Anargen almost shared his earlier revelation about the Tower of Light and its nature, but held back. This wasn't the time. It didn't change the reality before them nor lessen the danger.

"Can you make it down?" Thomas asked, eyeing her obvious reliance on Anargen for support.

"I will manage," she shot back more heatedly than was usual for her.

"Hmm, perhaps, but none of us is in our best condition," Thomas observed. "It may make sense for one of us to slip down there and assess the situation, while the rest of us find a way to get Seren down there."

Seren shot a scowl his way, and he quickly amended, "And for myself as well."

"We have to move swiftly. We have an advantage while that beast is contained in Ordumair. Once it is free ..." Glewdyn shook his head, dour as a night rain.

"I'll go," Anargen announced.

"Anargen," Seren keened. She didn't plead for him to stay. Someone had to go, and there was no point arguing whether it would be him or Thomas. Ultimately, they all would end up facing whatever was down there.

He helped her over to Thomas, who bore her up so gingerly she might have been made of glass.

Before he turned to walk away, Anargen brushed her lips with a quick kiss and then closed his face plate. Though he had aches of his own, he pushed the pain to the back of his mind and sorted out the best path downward with the debris, making it to a tenuous stack some feet down. With a deep breath, he leapt the five or so feet into the hole and landed on it.

The shattered remnants of flooring shuddered under the impact, and his knees mirrored the complaint. Especially as the stones began to shift.

Oh no. No, no—

The rubble began to collapse. Anargen tried to keep his balance, but it was too late. The whole thing shifted under. Down the shards he careened, sliding, hopping, and scrambling —anything to keep from plummeting straight to the cave floor or being buried under the debris.

Ten feet from the ground, he leaped away from it and shoulder rolled across the uneven natural stone of the cavern floor.

New pains rejoined with the old ones in decrying his choice. A wave of dust from the collapsed stack rushed over him, forcing him down. Precious seconds slipped away as he lay there pulling himself together.

Close by, he heard whispers, too faint to make out with the more boisterous crashing of stone still echoing through the cavernous space.

There was another sound too. A grating sound like a pickaxe's tip scraping over rock. With the last reverberations of the collapse passed, Anargen was able to identify a wetter, meatier slapping interspersed with the scraping. Chills ran down his arm as he guessed the source of the sound, but couldn't bear to say it even to himself.

He struggled to a sitting position. This cavern was sweltering, and with some focus he heard the steady crash of water from above, though he couldn't see it. A haze of dust still lingered, and the dark chamber's preternatural orange lighting was even more nightmarish now that he was deep amidst it. The aura of light from his armor's flaming inscriptions offered his only respite from the gloom.

The dark won't be such a concern once I'm face-to-face with the dragon.

The thought sobered him. It was silly to have forgotten in

the chaos of his sliding and collapse, but somewhere in this stony enclosure was a horror unlike any he had yet faced.

Keeping low and taking care to move stealthily, he scuttled across the field of broken cave rock and cut marble, moving instinctually toward the bizarre sounds he heard. Halfway across the space, his hand sank into something soft and wet.

"Ungh!"

Anargen jerked back and fumbled onto his bottom. His hand was slick and, in the orange light, looked darkly stained.

Blood.

He had found one of the combatants. Since it was neither a hulking boggart nor ethereal mist within a steel suit, it must have been one of their own.

How did he survive the fall?

That's when he caught the shimmer around the prone form. It was faint, so terribly faint, but he could make out the delineations of the glowing inscriptions. There was only one other Knight of Light in that room.

"Thane Duncoin!" Anargen said as loud as he dared and crawled over to the fallen Ord's side.

Duncoin's head tilted toward Anargen and he saw the tightness around the aged Ord's eyes. He was in terrible pain. "Lad ... my legs ..."

Leaning back to where the Thane's legs should be, Anargen grimaced. That was what he had touched that was blood-slicked. Enormous shards of stone lay across each leg.

"You wore only some parts of your Knight armor, not the full suit," Anargen noted, annoyed with himself for not having noticed it earlier.

"Aye ... I wore leggings of my ... ancestor ... Ordumair the II. It ... was sentimental ... and ... prideful."

Duncoin gasped out a tight-held breath. "Now, I ... pay the price."

Unsure what to say, Anargen focused on finding a way to help free him. It would be quite a lift, but he thought with his father's help, he could hold the stone up long enough for Thomas to tug the Thane free and then get him to a physician. It was risky, but this was beyond even what a tourniquet could aid.

"I'm going to get Thomas. We'll have you free in just a moment." Anargen started to stand and take off for the edge of the hole, but felt a surprisingly strong grip from the Ord on his arm. "No," Duncoin insisted. "Do no' leave. I ... I need ...you to take ... thas."

Releasing his hold on Anargen, the thane's hands shook as he held them aloft and slid, with some difficulty, a thick ring off his hand.

"Your ... hand ..." he grunted.

Dazed, Anargen held out a hand. Duncoin palmed the ring heavily into the offered hand and closed Anargen's fingers around it.

The Ord collapsed with a grunt of expended effort. Anargen looked into his clenched fist and recognized it immediately. "This is the Signet of Thanes!"

"Aye," Duncoin affirmed weakly. His eyes were closed now, and he was wincing but looked more exhausted than pained.

"I can't hold this for you, Your Honor. You'll need this for keeping the nobles in line. Especially while you recover."

"The ... only ... place I'll be—" he sucked in a sharp breath. "Recovering ... is in ... the Highland with the Great King."

Anargen shook his head vigorously. "No, Your Honor, we can get you out of here. Get you help. Your people need you."

"No," his voice came out as a raspy whisper. "They ... need ... dragon ...stopped. Give it ... to ... Defender ... Cinaed."

Had Duncoin really told him to give the signet to Cinaed? That thought stole all the resilience from Anargen's body, and he slumped backward. Duncoin knew Cinaed was dead. Anargen's back found a slab of marble and he sat there, staring at the dying Thane a few feet away, feeling like everything was tilting off kilter.

Get up. There's no time for this. Grieve later.

There was no time to lose, but he couldn't bring himself to move. It was like he was losing Cinaed all over again. As though, with Duncoin, the last piece of his mentor was gone as well.

The dark seemed to deepen and creep up around him, his armor no longer emanating as strong a comforting aura. He, Seren, and Glewdyn had survived the collapse, but Duncoin, whom they had every intention of safeguarding at the price of their own lives, was perishing. Just as Thomas had said, Viceroy Ecthelion had died despite his best efforts.

Ordumair was overrun, the city slowly devoured by the insatiable army of the Monarch. If his father was right, they had failed. Ilyron had done it. He had summoned the first dragon in the Lowlands in hundreds of years, and with his other sorceries, every land from Garcenilles to Vov Hilon would burn.

"Are you there, phosphila?"

The voice was chilling for being so common, so plain in contrast with the menace of its undertone. This wasn't a voice with which Anargen was familiar. It had the accent of an Ecthel mixed with something else. Rehalcy, no doubt. Monarch Ilyron was calling out to him.

"Won't you answer? Surely a brave peasant like yourself would not try to hide from your deserved end."

Anargen closed his eyes. The voice sounded closer, the speaker moving towards him.

"Coming all the way from the backward woods of the Lowlands to die on the stones of Ordumair. Some would call that bravery ...

"I call it immeasurably foolish. You can sense it, can't you—the steady thrum of the dragon's heartbeat. Power emitted from it is pressing against you even now, curling you in fear as you face the awful truth. Your king cannot save you any more than he could those disgusting little dwarfs."

A shuddered breath escaped Anargen's lips. Cold descended on him, and he perceived with every sense available to him that darkness indeed was enveloping him. Suffocating, freezing, biting, stabbing, tearing at him from every angle. He felt ravaged, picked apart without even having attempted to make a stand.

Another voice, more sinister than Ilyron's, echoed around him. Buffeting him, over and over, like an incantation. "Failure. Failure. Weak, pathetic failure. You let them die. Why did you even try? You were never called to fight. Never chosen to be a knight. False. Weak, pathetic failure. Failure. Failure."

Clenching tighter into a ball, Anargen's teeth ground into each other, and his eyes were closed as tight as he could make them. This was the worst pain of his life, this attack that somehow scored him within and without with venomous bites that seethed and swelled until he thought he'd burst. Never mind standing against it. He couldn't think a clear thought. Couldn't even breathe.

Footsteps drew near him, but he couldn't really hear them. Everything was muffled and masked except that infernal scathing squall of "They're all gone now, because you thought you were something important. Little Iaegon and that blowhard Duncoin—dead. Your supposed friends Caeserus, Terrillian, and Bertinand forsook you. And Cinaed, oh, his death was your worst failure ... till now. False knight. Failure. Failure. Weak, pathetic failure."

"False. Weak. Failure," he found himself mumbling. Tears stung his eyes and ran down his dust covered face.

"It is too bad," the voice crooned from a few steps away.

Though his eyes didn't open, he felt sure he could sense a blade had been drawn and was raised high to finish him with one sadistic stroke. It hovered over the nape of his neck.

"You didn't turn back while you could. Now you will die and miss witnessing the real fire consume your homeland. And your loved ones."

"Real fire," he repeated to himself. "Real fire ..."

He had seen that once. Seemingly a millennium ago. When he was practically another person. Fresh, untested. Unbowed with the weight of guilt and shame and failure he had accumulated like flakes piling high into massive, crushing snow drifts. A benighted worm.

"Real fire ..."

"Yes, the real fire you will miss, because your story is at an end," Ilyron and wicked intonations of that other dark voice mocked together.

There had been One who called to him out of that real fire, so hot he could hardly stand it. Even as he longed for it to burn hotter still. A light so intense, he was blinded, but never had he seen with such clarity. The voice speaking out of the real fire was unbearable, but every reverberation of his voice was the most essential sound Anargen had ever heard. Though unworthy, that voice had beckoned from amidst the fire and the light to him. Called him out by name.

"Real fire. Real fire ... It's not about me ... Not my story ... It's his."

Another voice reached Anargen over the dragon's jeers. It called to him. *He* called to Anargen, reminding him, bidding him to rise.

"My King!"

Anargen's eyes snapped open, and his grip tightened around the hilt of his spiritsword. In a rush of heat, it seared up his arm, burning higher, hotter, than Anargen had ever felt it. The cold pressing against him wasn't dispelled; it was utterly destroyed. Flames traced around every letter inscribed on every plate of his armor, his shield, and the sword he swung out and used to deftly batter aside the one poised over him.

Engulfed in the fire of the High King, Anargen could see, hear, and think clearly again. Of course he had failed on his own. He had stumbled and fallen, but it was the High King who lifted him up every time. Not by Anargen's strength or wit or power or will, but by the High King's. Time after time, he had been reminded he was called not to be the answer to the problem of evil, but to be still and hear the High King. Not sired to bear the Lowlands up, but knighted to lift the banner of the One who would bear up him and the Lowlands. A servant of the indomitable One.

Through the flames, he saw the Monarch. Ashen-skinned, with hair that looked greyed prematurely. Wiry under bulkier armor than he should bear. Though his staff glowed with its evil essence, Ilyron looked far from the unassailable conqueror Anargen had puffed him up to be in his mind.

Wretched and furious within his cocoon of dark and shadow, Ilyron glowered. The villain had backed several paces away and narrowed his black eyes at Anargen. "You should have yielded, phosphila. It would have been a quicker end for you."

"I did yield," Anargen asserted. "To the High King of All Realms. The only, true, rightful Monarch."

Ilyron's eyes widened, and he uttered a guttural snarl and rushed forward. An obsidian blade came around in a furious hack.

Blocked.

Again, Ilyron slashed.

Deflected by his shield.

Screaming like an embittered banshee, Ilyron charged again, slinging his sword around wildly. Striking over and over. Every blow, meeting its match, until Anargen parried and slammed his shield into the Monarch's face.

Stumbling backward, Ilyron tripped over the stones on the floor and landed hard on his back. Though he wasn't down long, Anargen could see the shock of it reverberating through him.

Anargen glanced to the side at Duncoin. The Ord's eyes were open, and though he wheezed, pitiful and pale, a smirk played on his lips.

Ilyron saw it too. He screeched and dove for Duncoin, but Anargen was there. With a keen swipe, he battered him back. His shield caught two more hits. With an eagle's swiftness, he struck another hammering blow directly into the tyrant's face.

The Monarch spat dark blood from his split lip. Growling like a child more than a monster, he retreated a few feet. To the back of the cavern, he bellowed in a strained voice, "What are you waiting for? Get him, you daft buzzard-lizard!"

It was then that Anargen finally perceived an irregular mass abutting the far wall of the cavern. Deep in its shadows was something massive.

It strode forward, a jet of hot steam shooting from its nostrils to fill the space with a sulfurous odor. Between its claws were the limp remnants of a boggart. The dragon tossed its meal aside. It sauntered out on powerful forelegs, keeping huge, maroon-feathered wings tucked up. This space that had seemed enormous moments ago was quite plainly too tiny to contain such a beast. The dragon reared up onto its reptilian hind legs, which, like the rest of its body, seemed to have hard, silver osteoderms like thousands of small sets of plate armor barely concealed under its wings. Twitching its barbed and plumed tail back and forth like a cat considering a mouse, its crocodilian head cocked to the side and bared teeth, each long and sharp as a short sword.

There was a certain beauty to the creature. Some would be tempted to call it majestic and admire the powerful bands of muscles and regal feathering it sported. The fluid way it moved and its imperious bearing. They would be buying the lie. The truth was in the eyes. Black without adulteration of whites and containing such malevolence, such cogent malignancy, there was no denying what he saw. This was a brutal, devious creature. Any animal grace and marvel of design and form it had held as a wyvern was supplanted by the darkness controlling it, seeking to deceive through its appearance anyone unwary or insensitive enough to the darkness it exuded to draw near in admiration or, more despicably, reverence.

If anything, the legends had undersold how vile this creature was to its very core. This was a true monster in every sense.

Anargen set his feet, ready to face it.

For all its might and menace, the dragon's dark eyes were clearly on Anargen's burning blade. It did not move as it peered across the chamber at Anargen and regarded the spiritsword he bore.

"Do not forget I summoned you," Ilyron shouted. "I command you to destroy this foolish cur!"

Anargen saw the sneer on the dragon's reptilian lips. Something about it felt even more unsettling than when it had bared its fangs.

"I command you to attack!" the Monarch bellowed, his voice cracking.

The dragon's eyes rolled, and its long, serpentine neck arched up as it fixed a withering gaze on the Monarch. "Silence, human. You mistake your place."

"Mistake my place?" he shouted back and slammed his staff on the floor, its poison green glow flaring. "Do you forget who forged you? I am your—"

The dragon huffed, a cruel, coarse sound. "You think that because you served your purpose, you have authority over me? You do not. You are my slave, little human."

"Slave?" Ilyron seemed to shudder with rage. "I'm the most powerful sorcerer the Lowlands has ever seen! I have power over—"

The dragon snorted and bashed Ilyron aside with a deft swipe of its enormous foreclaws. The Monarch was launched into the air like a leaf on the wind.

He landed several feet away and only managed to keep to his feet. Even with the distance, Anargen could see that his armor was dented near the site of impact. That casual smack could easily have broken bones if Ilyron hadn't been wearing such sturdy armor.

Anargen started. Was he really concerned about what happened to that brute Ilyron? After all the harm he had done, including murdering an entire civilization to summon this beast?

A twinge of shame reverberated in his heart. It wasn't the way of a Knight to bear grudges, especially in the face of undiluted evil. And there was no mistaking that that was what the dragon represented. The air felt thick with its lashes to bind its prey in dark chains. Given the chance, it would rend apart all that was noble and good in the Lowlands.

For an instant, the dragon's attention moved toward Anargen. No doubt it could see, even beyond the stone barriers between them, that he was there. An emissary of the light, which it could not bear to exist any more than he could suffer this abomination to remain in the Lowlands.

"You will obey!" Ilyron shouted. "I know the Dark Prince's arts and I am master over them, over him!"

The dragon's attention diverted sharply to Ilyron, its voice molten with disdain. "Slave, you will be silent! You are nothing but a tool. Expendable, if you continue to rant so before your master. Whatever powers you think you possess were granted solely to serve this end. To grant my arrival into this world ahead of the Dark Prince's. Now, kneel and beg forgiveness!"

With a roar, it slammed its clawed fist onto the cave floor, sending a tremor through it that fissured several feet of rock.

To Anargen's horror, Ilyron, clearly struggling, cried out and slammed onto the ground. The wretched man wailed. His resistance lasted just long enough to prove he was powerless before a stream of pleas rushed from his mouth.

A chuckle deep and mocking echoed off the chamber walls, and the dragon lifted him up. "There is no mercy for one like you, even if you are still of use. Finish the phosphila in this chamber and your death will be quick and painless. Otherwise, you have never known the torment that awaits you."

Tossing him aside again, the dragon leaped toward the hole above. It was trying to climb out!

"Watch out!" Anargen shouted, abandoning his hiding place. "It's trying to escape!"

The dragon's head whipped around. Its jaw snapped open, spewing a stream of green-tinged flames.

Anargen leaped out of the way. Behind him, the rocks boiled, instantly melted.

There was no time or point to seeking stony cover. He brought up his *Thyreos Pistis*, trusting the High King's power to keep the shield stalwart against any attack. An instant later, he felt the gale-force pressure of the stream of flames strike his shield and knew there was a torrid heat surrounding him, reducing rock to magma all around.

He pushed back, his shield holding firm. Still, it was like trying to lift a boulder.

The stream ended in a roar from the dragon. "Slave, end him or end yourself in the attempt!" It turned back to climbing out.

Please, my Great King, help Seren, Thomas, and Father to face it! Be their unassailable tower of defense!

A flicker of motion caught Anargen's attention. Ilyron sprang at him, barbed staff slinging around to bludgeon his skull.

Anargen caught it with his shield and staggered back, putting space between himself and the Monarch as the other landed. Ilyron seemed empty now. A husk of what he'd been. Surrendered fully to the goblin within the dragon and thus to the dark forces he had foolishly believed he could command.

Once more, pity welled in Anargen. If only he could get through to him ...

He had to dodge as the Monarch shot out a dark line of shadows which formed into a barbed whip, just as a sombra might. It jerked back to him, and he howled, swelling and distorting into a midnight-black, horned werebeast. Massive, the black bulk of it crashed down onto Anargen, battering him back farther into the cavern's recesses.

I guess he has the powers of all the foul things he's conjured.

Once more, Ilyron conjured his shadow whip and cracked it at Anargen. This time, the young Knight dodged and then lunged forward, scoring a grazing hit on one of the beast's powerful forelimbs.

The Monarch screeched and lashed out with his staff, which reformed into a long spear with a shortsword blade affixed to the end. As Anargen ducked it, he felt the chilly air off it tugging at his tunic. Those heavily muscled arms weren't totally illusory. Ilyron's bestial state was genuinely as dangerous as it appeared.

He shoulder-rolled away as a clawed foot stamped where he'd just been and shattered the rock underneath. Ilyron snarled and cracked his whip.

Bouncing it off his shield, Anargen spun, chopped the whip in half, and parried a spear stroke, sneaking in a quick slice on Ilyron's spear arm.

As Ilyron recoiled, he glowered at Anargen and bellowed something in what Anargen barely recognized as Tislatnean filtered as it was through his monstrous form's guttural intonations.

Watching with disgust, Anargen edged away just as bat-like

wings exploded outward from Ilyron's back. Holding his shield up in guard against the sudden gust of air as the creature took flight, he watched warily for whatever came next.

Rraaarrrggghh!

The sound of the dragon's roar above wrested Anargen's attention. What was happening up there?

A whisper told Anargen to focus, and he forced his attention back just in time to throw up a messy block. The impact of the spear on his shield sent shudders through Anargen's whole frame and sent him tumbling backward.

Wincing, he was thankful that at least he hadn't been skewered by the opportunistic spear dive. Flying about the chamber, the menace of Ilyron's attacks doubled.

Anargen had few options for offense. For now, he was forced to keep close attention to where the dark blur had swooped and be ready to defend.

The monster dove at him and knocked him flat on his back. He could taste the dank dust of the cavern floor kicked up by his fall. Before he could get up or return a strike, the thing was already in the air circling, for its next attack.

No beast that bulky should be so fast.

He was a mouse hunted by a hawk. He had to get the Monarch back onto the ground.

Diving out of the way of another attack, Anargen got to his feet and kept turning to keep himself facing his foe. At this rate, Ilyron would soar around taking cheap shots until Anargen was too exhausted to keep up his defense. He couldn't let that happen, never mind what happened to him. The real fight was taking place above. Ilyron, like Count Eidolon before him, had been a misguided piece in a game bigger than either of them.

"You know, it's a pity you weren't there to see your teacher, Eidolon, fall to the wyvern," Anargen chided. "Maybe then you wouldn't have blundered into the same mistake he made. Even if goblins weren't masters of deception, you both were so eager to throw your lives away!"

The Ilyron beast snarled and launched itself at him. Anargen was ready, throwing himself behind a subterranean pillar that helped hold the remaining floor above in place. Rolling, he heard Ilyron crash into the pillar behind him.

Anargen scrambled to his feet and charged. One of Ilyron's wings was broken, and he was shaking his head as if to clear it when Anargen slammed his shield into the monster's side.

The black beast tumbled over, but instead of crashing face-first into the ground, the whole creature dissolved into a shadowy pool and then reconstituted, facing Anargen once more.

To Anargen's annoyance, the broken wing appeared to be repaired by the act. Despair threatened to creep back in to strangle him, except he noticed the Monarch's labored breathing. This fight was wearing on him more heavily than on Anargen. The favor of the High King was no doubt buoying Anargen's fortitude. Perhaps like Eidolon, the attempt to summon the dragon had been a costly drain on Ilyron's strength.

Not giving his foe a chance to rally, Anargen sprang forward. Following guiding whispers, he raised his shield and caught a spear jab, glancing it off to the side. The blow was already forespoken to do so, and Anargen took the opportunity. "Hrrahh!"

He swung with all his might and severed the spear shaft from its head just above Ilyron's clawed hand. Immediately, he braced for the counterattack and had his shield ready. It landed harder than expected and drove him back a step, but he pivoted, came back around, and pressed the attack, swinging his sword around in bold stroke at Ilyron's midsection.

The monster didn't have time to conjure a new weapon, or

perhaps couldn't with his arcane staff now a smoldering ruin on the cave floor. Desperate, he grabbed the spiritsword's flaming surface with his bare hand and slung Anargen aside.

Tossed like a rag doll, Anargen hit the ground and bounced, hard. He crashed into a stalagmite.

"Ungh," he groaned. There was no time to assess his injury or lament fresh pains. Fighting back to his feet, he hobbled back at the Monarch, refusing to give him the chance to launch into another aerial campaign.

The creature was busy with his own worries, thankfully. Screeches and curses rolled off its black tongue as he shook his clawed hand. From a glowing incision along it roiled a trail of smoke.

Anargen didn't give the fiend time to recover.

Once, twice, three times Anargen slashed, connecting with the monster's raised forearm, then its shoulder, and last across its chest. Pulling back, Anargen slammed his spiritsword's burning blade forward, driving it deep into Ilyron's abdomen.

Like all his minions to take similar form before him, Ilyron screamed in agony and fury at the wounds. All of them charred, smoking, burning away his dark form. Unlike the lesser creatures, however, he had enough strength to bash Anargen away, sending the young Knight crashing into a pile of rubble some eight feet away.

From where he lay, Anargen could see the Monarch writhing and wailing. His bestial form faltered, and he reverted to his human shape, wounds still glowing. Ilyron stumbled into the pillar he'd crashed into earlier and used it to bear himself up, one arm wrapped around his smoldering midsection. His breathing was undeniably ragged now. His eyes landed upon Anargen, dark with hate, and if he could but will Anargen to be instantly eviscerated, there was no doubt it would have happened a hundred times over.

Mercifully, such power was not Ilyron's to wield, but in his free palm, he conjured a black throwing knife and launched it. The projectile half dissolved in flight and plinked largely harmless off Anargen's shoulder pauldron. This earned a hiss of frustration and then a groan of renewed pain as the wounds the Monarch endured glowed brighter, hotter.

Once more, Ilyron tried to launch knives. Each one failed to maintain substance. The last one, Anargen was able to block with his shield. With every failed strike, the Monarch slunk closer to Anargen and appeared more and more ashen-faced and wobbly.

A pair of arm's lengths from Anargen, who had just forced himself up, Ilyron launched a spiked mace which struck Anargen's shield, threatening to topple him once more.

Unlike Ilyron, Anargen's strength wasn't his own, and he felt himself being held steady, his body mastered through surrender to its Maker. Digging his feet in, Anargen bore another heavy clang of the morning star weapon on his shield, and this time tensed for a counter. With a satisfying clink, his blade swung around and severed the shaft.

The black spiked ball hit the ground and dissipated. A growl was all Ilyron seemed able to conjure in response.

Poised in a guard stance, Anargen cleared his throat, weary and addled as he was, "You don't have to perish this way. The dark can't claim you if you yield to the High King. Even after all you've done."

Confusion contorted Ilyron's grey face as sweat rolled down from his brow. Tremulous, he seemed to totter there, unable to move forward and embrace an offer he had perhaps never before considered.

All at once, his face tensed in pain that coalesced into fury, and he gave a shout. Lunging at Anargen, the young Knight sidestepped and delivered another blow deep into the enemy's back. Monarch Ilyron gurgled and dropped.

Anargen staggered back several steps from the felled sorcerer. Bitter as ever was the taste of a victory that saw another man refusing to find light's deliverance out of the dark. Ilyron's looks weren't so different from Anargen's. They were close in age, height, and build, now that he could look on him without the augmentation of the other's sorceries and battle focus.

But for your unmerited favor, that could have been me, my Great King. Deliver us from the dark. Your light and Kingdom are all I long for.

Tears might have come if fatigue, pain, and the demands of the greater battle still had not pressed upon him. From the twitching of Ilyron's frame, the other had not yet perished, but he seemed determined to cling to the dark until it destroyed him. Then, all at once, there was a searing swell of flame and light. Maldes Ilyron was gone.

Breathing out his tension, Anargen looked over at the rubble. It would be a feat to climb out of here under good conditions. These were not good conditions.

Overhead, he heard the beating of the dragon's wings and shouts. Shouts from those he loved as they struggled against their true foe. An emissary of the darkness who gulled men into forsaking the fellowship of the High King for which they were made. A darkness that would not stop until all of the Lowlands and its peoples were destroyed.

Sheathing his spiritsword, Anargen stretched his weary limbs and got into a tensed crouch.

My King, give me your speed and your strength to reach the battle ahead.

Feeling a flood of heat rush into his limbs, Anargen sped toward the rubble pile. The cavern blurred around him, including the rush of water cascading from above, which had kept this tepid place cool enough that the wyvern had not woken for centuries.

His feet shod with the *Evaggelion Eirene* hit the edge of the rubble pile. Leaping from one stone, kicking off another, bouncing over a collapsing stack, Anargen crouched and jumped, launching himself at the section of vault floor hanging overhead. Eager fingers gripped fast, and he pulled himself up, flinging himself over the edge and back into Ordumair's vault. He barely gave himself space to draw a steadying breath before he stood and turned to face the dragon.

HASTY EXIT

A gust of warm wind encircled Jason as he stood on the train platform. He would miss that when he arrived back in the far more frigid Brackenburgh. Never mind all of the more significant reasons for this being a regret-filled departure. Missing out on the Council of Defenders as it truly took place, not the infiltrated and stymied affair that, thank the High King, was resolved.

Tapping his foot on the wooden platform, he glanced at a nearby clock. The train was running late. He had told Sir Cinaed goodbye, but it rang hollow. Saying goodbye to the man who had completely changed the course of his life was one thing, but to reveal that his brother was attempting to aid the evil Monarch Ilyron in summoning a monster that would destroy the Lowlands ... what words are there for that exactly? The very best Jason could hope for was that it had been a bluff. A skilled gambit by his brother to lure Jason to a trap that could no doubt lead to an incredibly painful and violent death.

Jason gripped his father's cap in his hands, twisting it as if he could wring out all of the evil from it. Hoping to excise with it all of the darkness that had tainted the sweet boy who had been his younger brother. Dorian, who had been too meek and compassionate to kill the ants that would invade the kitchen of the Wernstrum compound from time to time. Dorian, who had sheepishly suggested a yellow daffodil he'd found as Jason's first overture of affection to Melania years ago. And Dorian, whom he'd known was crying into his pillow as Jason slipped out on that fateful night when he had abandoned their family and its sordid business, foolishly thinking his brother would be safe without him.

Closing his eyes, Jason tried to force down a storm of emotions. None of them would serve him in the days ahead. Because neither sadness, regret, guilt, nor foolish nostalgia for his very lost little brother would deliver anyone from what could come.

Indeed, he really doubted he would prevent anything, but perhaps might delay and damage the schemes Dorian had contrived long enough for the Council of Defenders to act. Mobilizing thousands of Knights across the Lowlands in a final campaign against the dark and ushering in the King's Day.

"Mmm," he could still recall the majesty of the Highland. Fleeting and veiled as his glimpse had been, because he could not yet handle the reality of such a place.

"Having yourself a snack before our trip?" a familiar voice called to him.

Snapping out of his pleasant reverie, he found Sir Kaveed standing there, arms crossed over his chest. "Did you really believe you could sneak away like this?"

He shook his head. "It's not sneaking away ... I just ..." There wasn't a positive spin to him hating having to say one goodbye so much that he just skipped the others.

"Need to wait a moment," Kaveed finished for him.

Arching an eyebrow in question, the Zilnian Knight gestured for him to look into the train station. Inside were Defenders Guo, Cuzibaum, and—as dreaded—Black. He must have looked as stricken as he felt, because Kaveed added, "It wasn't hard for us to guess after that snake LeVanseaux whispered to you what you are doing. Rushing to face your brother alone is rather foolhardy."

"Wha? How did you figure that out?"

Extending his arms and giving a slight bow, Defender Amine said, "The High King gifts us Defenders with great insight and discernment. You will have it too one day."

I'm not a Defender, and if I succeed, then I won't live long enough to develop it.

Telling Kaveed that, of course, was not what he should do. At least he hadn't mentioned—

"Besides, what would Aria think of what you're doing? Where is she, by the way?"

Thankfully, the other Defenders walked out onto the platform at that moment. If Yúzé or Cinaed had overheard the conversation, neither seemed inclined to divulge to Kaveed that which Jason failed to. They were also each sporting a bag of their effects. "You cannot except us to ..." Cuzibaum struggled for the Ecthelish words he wanted.

"I think what our dear brother-in-arms means to say is that you cannot expect us to watch you take such a risk alone," Sir Cinaed spoke up. As he walked up and placed a hand on Jason's shoulder, he felt so much more the weight of it. The set of his old jaw, the glint in those eyes. If none of the others knew his precise reasons for going, it was entirely believable that Sir Cinaed did. One of a number of reasons Jason still wondered at times whether the old man was the original Cinaed of Tislatna from the Ancient Era.

Shaking his head, Jason said, "I suppose I should take comfort in the depth of insight you each possess, and that you think I'm worth being rescued. You're right, this is reckless and a terrible idea on its face, but you four are the very last people in the Lowlands who can help me."

Cuzibaum cocked his head to the side, his face scrunched in incomprehension. It wasn't clear whether he really didn't understand Jason or if he had understood it properly, but found it so absurd that he doubted himself.

Jason addressed Defender Amine first. "Kaveed, it would be an honor to have you fighting by my side again, but you're about to become a father. Aria would never forgive me if I were the reason Tirzah's child never knew you. Never mind what Tirzah herself would do to me."

A little twitch at the corner of Kaveed's mouth told him that he had hit the mark squarely as intended. Before he could speak up, Jason added, "It's not a matter of devotion to the High King over all others. Don't break apart your family to help me face mine."

Gesturing to Cuzibaum, he quickly pivoted, "You're even less fit to go with me." Once more, Cuzibaum's expression of confusion was so comical that Jason had to fight to keep his thoughts in order. "You cannot, because not only would your family mourn your loss, but you have an entire newly formed nation to defend. If you aren't there to continue guiding the Sykonos Republic, it will fall, and Centros soon after."

From the way Kazim stiffened, Jason could tell he'd been correct. The Yusbilsani had understood him from the start.

"And what of me, young Landsby?" Sir Guo asked, stroking the dark hairs on his chin. "I have neither a family nor a nation to safeguard. Surely you don't think my skills so insufficient as to—"

"You cannot come for the same reason our young friend believes none of us may," Sir Cinaed interrupted. "We're each Defender of a Realm, and with the Council convened, to halt such a momentous meeting would do more harm than his life is worth in the grand tapestry of matters."

Oof. Well maybe a bit blunter and more direct than I would have been, but man if he isn't on point.

"He's right," Jason confirmed, his voice cracking a bit. Not because his own life was so dear to him, but because of the way the old storyteller was looking at him at that moment. His unspoken accusation that Jason was taking himself from the old man so soon after losing Aria. Wise as he was, he had to know it was worth the risk and loss to make sure Dorian didn't win.

"Which is why," Cinaed began again, breaking the heavy silence that had fallen over the small group. "All of you shall stay. I will accompany Sir Landsby on his quest, which I believe to be integral to the Quest."

Holding up his age-spotted hand to preempt Jason's protests—which were very much ready to be unleashed—Cinaed concluded, "There are enough votes to secure the path forward we must take without me. I have confidence in Defender Davidiah to lead the Council in wisdom and honor."

"Your own wisdom is in doubt, old friend," Defender Guo said. "Your charge is zealous, but we all know well the dark things of the Lowlands are gathering their might. We convened the first Council of Defenders in centuries precisely because none of us can handle this threat by ourselves or even with the might of a single Realm."

Sir Cinaed eyed Jason expectantly, which threw Jason off. It wasn't like him to be so roundabout. If he meant to stop Jason, he would've just ordered him down directly. That meant he really did intend for them both to leave, and it was up to Jason to justify it.

"My brother Dorian has Professor Goulder," Jason blurted out. "That's what LeVanseaux whispered to me. If I don't go help him now, he won't just be killed but die horribly. The only reason Dorian has him is because he sacrificed himself so Aria and I could escape."

Guo's brows knitted with displeasure, but Jhi'ish culture had a long tradition of repaying kindnesses with equal grace. Jason owed it to Goulder to come to his aid. Guo had to respect that. Somehow, though, the Defender seemed to suspect that the capture of the professor was only part of the story.

"My brother-in-arms," Kaveed spoke up. "This is a grievous injury for us all, but I cannot see how you and Defender Black risking your own deaths will serve the Lowlands or the High King. I think we should wait and let Aria weigh in. I'm certain she wouldn't want either of you to come to harm."

"She's my fiancée, and I think I know her heart well enough," Jason snapped. Immediate regret colored his cheeks with rosiness befitting his thorny sting. "Forgive me, Kaveed, I ... I cannot bear the thought of my brother being the death of a friend such as the Professor. Only with Aria being with me can I move forward, of that I can assure you."

Astute as ever, Defender Guo huffed. "Reason has failed. You have already decided upon this fixedly as the stars above. There is no point now in quarreling over it. Tell us, at the very least, where you intend to go to find the Wernstrum darkling. Perhaps I will be able to send my people to aid you when they arrive."

Jason didn't have the heart to tell him that the reason Professor Goulder was captured was that the contingent of Knights bringing him was intercepted. Minister LeVanseaux doubtless would've boasted many captives would be sacrificed if there were any to do so.

"Better still for them to remain by your side and join with those present for the Council in seeking the High King's guidance for the days to come," Cinaed spoke up. "While I've made it clear I believe our course is not to fight directly in the war that embroils the Lowlands, it is not my intention that we pretend it is not happening all around us, either. Great care must be taken. Through the darkest days, always trust that the High King guides us to the true good, irrespective of what circumstances cry."

"That sounds like a farewell address," Kaveed noted solemnly.

"If the High King wills it be so, then it is," Sir Cinaed replied, not quite shrugging as though it were of no consequence, but neither treating it as gravely as those around him.

Cinaed turned as though to leave, and Defender Guo lunged forward and grabbed hold of one of Jason's suspenders, jerking him over to him. Not unlike the unsavory LeVanseaux, he whispered heatedly into his ear, "We both know what became of Aria. Since you are not forthright about that which I know of, I can only assume other things are in doubt as well.

"At the very least, you must divulge where you are going. I owe my life to Defender Black, and you are indebted to me for keeping secret your deceit."

A chill ran through Jason. It wasn't precisely deceit that he was intending to engage in, but it was difficult to dismiss the validity of Guo's request. Perhaps it would be best to have someone know whence they went.

Under his breath, he muttered, "Brackenburgh."

The other man leaned back, looking at him like he was about to denounce him as a charlatan then and there. But he drew up short of it. Rubbing his chin as he was in the habit of doing, he nodded. "Very well. Look—"

A long whistle from the train as it finally pulled into station cut off his words. Jason thought he asked him to, "Look after him." Meaning Defender Black. As though he could do anything else at this point.

"I will," he called out as he took the opportunity to extricate himself and stepped back.

Once the train came to a halt, hissing steam and making its metallic groans, Jason hurried over and presented his ticket to the conductor as soon as the portly man stepped off the train. Pulling on his spectacles and rubbing his bald head, the conductor evaluated the ticket. With a shrug, he punched it and returned it to Jason. "Not many are heading westward if they can help it."

Since the man's Ecthelish was particularly good, Jason guessed he was a seasoned conductor. "I suppose it's because I cannot help it."

Behind him, Cinaed walked up and presented a ticket he must have bought before even stepping out on the platform to confront him. "Hale afternoon, friend."

The conductor gave a nod. "Hale indeed, and hotter than a sand scourge's breath." He punched the ticket and returned it to Cinaed.

"No, it really isn't," Jason mumbled to himself rather dryly. He had faced a sand scourge deep in Zilnen's deserts, and the fire-breathing sand lizards, cousins to the wyvern and dragons of greater renown, were nothing Jason ever wanted to trifle with again.

But it wasn't worth fussing with the man who was already soaking with sweat after only a minute in Centros's arid air. Jason also didn't wait for Sir Cinaed to join him. He made it to his private seating area and dropped onto the chair. A moment later, Cinaed was seated across from him, giving Jason one of those stare-downs that Jason was sure would cut through steel and stone to see through to the truth.

"So," he began.

"You're going to Brackenburgh to confront your brother," Sir Cinaed surmised. He didn't state it like a question. "You left in a hurry, ergo it is an urgent matter. My child, I cannot shepherd you if you keep running like this."

"I had to, sir," Jason replied, not bothering to hint at anything like an apology. "LeVanseaux said he has Professor Goulder and that Dorian is going to sacrifice him to summon a dragon."

It felt good getting it all out into the open, though he could scarcely explain why he'd so freely divulge what he'd kept so carefully hidden.

Once again, Sir Cinaed acted unfazed. "The professor would be an understandable target. A lesser man in his position would be a danger to us, revealing all manner of secret locations for meeting. Since he was captured, I feared they would try to use him in that way.

"A dragon, however ... It is well that we are on our way. Though some may trust in the tools of war being employed across the Lowlands, a dragon is of an entirely other sort of danger. You were right to withhold this from the others, for the moment, because if it proves true, the danger will be immense. Disrupting the Council at this critical juncture could do still more harm."

Jason blinked. "Are you commending me for trying to sneak off?"

"No," the old man was unequivocal. "Your shrewdness aligns with what prudence would bear out in the end. Ends do not justify means, because the High King looks at the intents of our hearts."

"Oh, well then, I apologize, sir."

Cinaed huffed through his broad nostrils. "You are brave, Jason Landsby. Brash too, but learning to seek first the High King's will is something that can be learned. Willingly laying down your life for another, that is only accomplished genuinely by the High King's mark on our hearts."

He reached out and patted Jason's hands with his leathery old one. "Do not keep anything from me going forward. Understood?"

Brows knitted, Jason dithered over granting that request, but ultimately replied, "Yes, sir."

"Good." Settling back into the seat, Cinaed laced his fingers and lay his head back onto the seat, looking ready to take a doze. "You might as well break out Anargen's journal and read some more. We may yet face that which it chronicles."

Producing the journal, Jason brushed his hand over the leathery cover and gnawed at his lower lip. "There are very few pages left, sir. Perhaps I could save them, and we can discuss how exactly we're going to sneak so deep into Rehalcyon's lands. Given we're both on Dorian's hit list and ..."

Jason trailed off as Cinaed began waving off his concerns. "You read. I will seek the High King's guidance on the matter of our travels. I have lived as an enemy of the dark for a long time, lad. He has carried me through far more problematic challenges than smuggling myself into the serpent's den."

As much as he wanted to protest, Jason kept his mouth shut and began leafing through the pages of Anargen's story. Where he'd left off had been particularly painful for him. He couldn't just ask Sir Cinaed to confirm the account ended happily. All of it was tied up in Aria. Their conversation about happy endings certainly at the forefront. Because Jason wasn't sure which would scour him more thoroughly—for Anargen and Seren to have lived through their ordeal, triumphing over their foe, or only one to have lived to carry the tale on. Clearly, they had not outright defeated Monarch Ilyron as Anargen believed, otherwise Jason would not now be preparing himself to face the ruler. Perhaps that is what the final pages contained. No matter their contents, it still weighed heavily on Jason that soon all of his questions would be answered, even those he could scarcely bear to ask.

24

THE DREAM REALIZED

A moment of pause was needed. Ready as Anargen was to face whatever end, seeing the dragon dominating such a huge space was sobering.

All the more as he saw one of his fellow Knights having to pick another up off the floor and drag them to shelter behind a pillar. The last of the four of them was standing, chest heaving and shield raised before the dragon.

He could not let himself fixate on which of them was hurt worst. Nor the state of whomever was dragged off. They might all be dead in minutes. Their fate was in the High King's hands, where it had always belonged.

Like the Monarch's beast form, the dragon's flight presented a challenge, but unlike Ilyron, it was so massive that it was really only able to keep three or so feet off the ground within the vault. Anargen sprinted around the edges of the gaping hole in the floor and leaped to land a quick surprise nick across the beast's jaw as it snapped at the lone Knight able to face it.

Both Knights dove behind the remains of a pillar to avoid the monster's fiery retribution. It was Thomas.

The teen barely reacted outwardly to Anargen's arrival, but whispered. "Are you hale?"

"Our Great King has seen to it."

Thomas drew in a breath as though readying himself. "And the Monarch?

"Felled. Who is injured?" Anargen asked, unable to look away from the prone Knight lying several feet back.

"Your father."

With a chomp, the dragon nosed behind the pillar, just missing taking a chunk out of Thomas. It bashed Anargen's shield and sent him reeling.

"It appears that fool Ilyron failed me again," the dragon snarled, a curl of smoke wrapping around its reptilian sneer. "You humans are all alike. Each thinking you are worth so much! For a hundred generations, I have watched your kind wither and fade like grass. You four, however, will have far more dramatic ends!"

The dragon's jagged tail whipped around, thick as a tree trunk and as fast as a gazelle. Anargen scrambled to his feet and dove over it, his armor grating along a spike as it passed. As much as his heart ached for his father and he longed to find out how badly he was hurt, keeping his attention anywhere but on the next step the High King had for him would be a good way to get himself murdered by their foe.

As Anargen struggled back to his feet, he found himself beside the gaping pit from which he'd climbed. He looked up to see the dragon watching him. It seemed to snicker, and its long, barbed tail swooped back toward him. Throwing himself forward, Anargen felt the tail pass overhead with a whoosh. Several of its barbs scratched along the back of his cuirass, testing his confidence in its resilience far more than causing any damage.

He got into a crouch, unsure whether the tail would sweep back lower or come at the same height.

It crashed after him, grinding a groove into the stone floor. He started to jump up to avoid it, but his legs were unresponsive. Just before the tail connected with him, it snapped upward, the spikes along it ready to gore him. They would have if he had tried to leap over it.

He breathed out a sigh, his heart thudding in his chest. Relief was short-lived because the tail disappeared, and he spun around just in time to stumble backward and throw up his shield as the beast's long-fanged snout bore down on him. Sharp venomous fangs scraped his shield's surface, and the sulfurous scent of its breath choked him.

He had thought the Monarch's beast form unreasonably fast for his size. This was something completely other. How had it moved so fast?

He rolled out of the way as it snapped at him again and again. It was trying to drive him back into the hole. One good hit from it and he'd be plummeting backward to his death.

Another bite hammered him back a step, and he felt for his next step to back up. His leg sank into empty space, and he struggled to keep on the floor.

The only option was to dive forward. Once more, he felt restrained from doing so.

Snap! Hard dragon scales ground against his armor as it chomped directly in front of Anargen. It had again anticipated his logical choice and was ready to punish him for it. Slinging his spiritsword around, he got a grazing blow along its snout.

It recoiled, looking indignant more than injured.

Anargen took the opening all the same, charging at the reeling beast. The next instant, he tumbled forward. At his back, the dragon fiercely slammed a clawed fist on the floor, sending fresh shards of it crashing down into the dark below.

Anargen made it to where he had stood moments ago near Thomas. The other Knight was a dozen feet away, dodging the whip-like strikes of the dragon's tail.

It can fight us both with such precision and speed at the same time?

A whisper warned Anargen to move, fast.

Rolling forward and slipping behind the nearest pillar, the dragon's crocodilian jaws ground its razor teeth across the floor. The near miss earned a sulfur-laced huff from the beast.

Perhaps it was simply shifting focus between them quickly? If that was the case, then a coordinated attack might work. Motioning to Thomas as discreetly as he could manage, he signaled for Thomas to go for an attack at the same instant he did.

Not bothering to watch and see what his fellow Knight did, Anargen dashed around the pillar and was already blocking as the dragon battered its head into his shield.

Anargen skidded back a few feet, then rallied and surged forward—slashing, shielding, and searching for an opening to do real damage. None opened.

A fiery blast forced Anargen back several steps. As he stood at the ready, fighting to steady his breathing, he heard it. Not the dragon's boisterous voice, but something silkier and more sinister. The intonations of the goblin, apart from the vocal covering of the wyvern's body which it currently inhabited.

"Be honest, you have no chance, little phosphila. Even your beloved Cinaed could not best a wyvern—a dumb beast—how could you hope to overcome me? You will never live up to the calling you imagine you've received. It is all a convenient fantasy, a tale you told yourself. This is reality, brutal and, for you, fatal."

Was it in his head? Reading his thoughts? Dread seized him and threatened to paralyze him. This was something wholly different they faced. Creatures of dark and impressive prowess had one by one fallen to them, but not this. Not raw power, speed, and incalculable malevolence with such intelligence that could probe into his deepest fears and lay them bare.

He began to lower his spiritsword against his wishes.

Overtaken by the sensation that an enormous pressure pushed it down, compelling him to surrender. From all sides it pressed, so much more potent than what he'd felt down in the cavern. Had the dragon only exerted a fraction of its prowess to compel, to control? Is this what it did to destroy Ilyron's will and truly enslave him in the end?

Anargen stared downward at the floor, not wanting to look directly at the dragon's face. He knew full well its eyes would be crinkled with pleasure. A pleasure that would give way to some devastating attack at any moment. But he couldn't do it, couldn't face it down. The fiend was right. There had to be a mistake. What was he doing here after all? Chasing the dream of a friend who had abandoned him? How many times had he resolved that he was truly a Knight of Light only to find himself questioning it again? Did the questions themselves prove his fears right—that he was a fraud and only adding to the weight of failures stacking up against the Order to which he longed to belong?

As he stood there, stricken, shadows began to gather. A darkening pool of tendrils lashed his limbs, and with them came the bitter cold. It was familiar but so much icier than any he had ever experienced. It worked with the shadows to harden the spectral bands into an obsidian prison of despair around him.

Fight it as he wanted to, quivering began in his arm, and he felt his grip on his spiritsword's hilt loosening. Something told him the instant it clattered to the floor, his life would end as well. Probably the goblin, gloating to him. It was just as well. Everyone was better off without him. Better off without the fraud, the one who never should have left Black River, never should've been a Knight.

No. That last thought—that wasn't wholly his own. Or at

least it was too saturated in the subtle suggestions from the darkness ensnarling him.

A glint of light from the spiritsword peeked through the gloom. If he were a fraud, then how could it be said he "never should've been a Knight"? What did it matter to the goblin if he was here or not, if he wasn't truly a servant of the High King? As a dragon, it had dispatched the second boggart without issue for the sake of slaking its physical host's hunger. What was he to such a creature?

The spiritsword's glint grew, tracing fiery letters along the hilt through the haze that would deign to obscure them. "... whoever comes to me I will never cast out."

Anargen gripped the spiritsword's hilt tighter. Heat rushed into him. These were the same lies, repeated a thousand different ways. The same torture self-inflicted and offered to his enemies to use against him. There was no accident that he was here, in Ordumair, standing against this darkness, however deep.

No more. Never again.

The High King's honor secured his spot in the Order. It was the High King who had favored him with these fiery implements and burned brightest in his weakness and insufficiency. All those emissaries of the Dark Prince had failed, not because Anargen was a great warrior and Knight of Light, but because Anargen served the Great King of Light, and his majesty would never suffer these monsters to overcome his servant. Not in the way it now attempted. There was no power, not even in the Dark Prince himself, to sever the bond between him and the High King. None that could overturn his oaths.

As the fire swelled along his spiritsword, the shadowy chains dissolved, and the sly deceptions of the goblin faded out of audible range entirely. Tilting his head up, he met the dragon's gaze and raised his spiritsword back up into the guard stance he'd held a moment earlier.

His enemy's nostrils twitched, its lips pulling back to reveal its fangs. A rumble, deep as thunder, began in its chest. There, in its reptilian expression, was something he hadn't noticed before: a haughtiness and defiance divorced from Anargen.

A new sensation rippled through Anargen: rage. A fresh surge of heat traced along his blade, up his arm, onto his armor, and seared his flesh to burn away the last vestiges of fear's chill down to his bones. This dragon represented all the evil and most heinous rebellion against the High King. All the malice of Ilyron's dark campaign found its focal point in the dragon. Every needless death. Families shattered. Treasures of time and memory lost. Cities and lands ruined. Sorrows of every sort perpetuated by its wickedness. Anargen shifted his posture from defensive to offensive.

A compulsion gripped him, and he called out to as much himself as much as the other Knights, "I have spoken often of making a stand, despite how that stand may end. For future ages and future lands to be encouraged by. That they may be emboldened to stay true to the High King knowing we never can estimate the impact of our faithfulness to our oaths.

"But here, today ... this is distilled evil. Embodied darkness, and it alone deserves to be resisted and combatted by our dying breaths. I have lamented dearly what I will miss if I fall here today. No more. Seeing such evil, I regret that I only have my life to give the High King and no more. Because I would give it a dozen times over if it meant expunging this dark."

From the periphery of his vision, he saw Thomas straightening on the opposite side of the dragon. His armor was aglow. And from the far left, his father and Seren emerged, their spiritswords drawn and burning with righteous indignation. They separated, almost as if by instinct, and soon

Seren stood across from Anargen, forming a box around the dragon. A shining beacon for the cardinal directions, not unlike the Tower they'd been tasked with safeguarding and the defense of which they were meant to shore up. Anargen almost gasped aloud.

"And here it is, goblin. The thing you've been dreading and scheming to prevent all this time. There are four of us. Four Knights of Light, gathered to protect the Tower of Light, and in spite of all your attempts to shatter it, the Tower of Light hasn't fallen. I know its secret, the truth. The Tower isn't a place. Isn't an object. It is the Order. Knights of Unending Light, standing as one to bear the High King's light to all the Lowlands.

"You would have that light expunged, doused for all time. But you have no authority to do it. No power to contend with the Great King's. Before this day is through, you will be banished from the Lowlands to await in dark chains for the judgment due you on the King's Day."

"Aye," Glewdyn called out.

"Aye," Thomas seconded.

"Aye," Seren finished.

The dragon's head snapped around in quick succession, its dark eyes squinting against the luminance of the Knights, which intensified further and further. A panic was brewing beneath its scaled brows, and Anargen could tell it sensed its end was truly near.

"Now!"

Anargen hadn't said it, and none of the others had spoken either, but the command was there, and they all four rushed the dragon at once.

Startled, its head reared back in a final act of defiance and unleashed a fiery torrent that covered all the room in a green blaze. It just kept pouring all its cruelty and hatred into the swirling inferno that struck with the force of a tempest more terrible than any Anargen had weathered in all his life.

Stones began to melt, precious tomes instantly incinerated. Nothing in the room would survive the firestorm.

Except that the dragon's fire was a fraud. Paltry imitation. Through it burst all four Knights, fighting as one, falling upon the dragon and delivering sundering blow after blow. Lines of fiery fissures opened in the otherwise impenetrable hide of the dragon. They knew they were doing real damage when the torrent of flames ceased, replaced by reptilian gurgles of pain. Over and over, it tasted the searing heat from the Originator of real fire through his chosen emissaries. An irrepressible crescendo of condemnation of all its dark schemes consumed its massive limbs. Shrieks of woe echoed in the chamber and were drowned by the sound of true flames catching and burning down the darkness.

25
STRUCK DOWN

The screeches and yowls of pain felt so out of place coming from such a massive monster. Gone were its mocking and thundering strikes. All around the room was ablaze with its infernal green flames, but the only fire that mattered was the High King's. It practically leaped off the spiritswords to score deep into the thick hide of the dragon.

The beast stumbled as it tried to move away from the quartet of Knights hacking it to ruins. It made it to the center of the vault before Glewdyn climbed up onto its leg and plunged his spiritsword deep into its hip. The older Knight was thrown off and landed roughly, but the dragon dropped to a knee, unable to support itself.

Thomas dashed in to slash its exposed belly. An enormous clawed hand swatted at him. Shards of the floor exploded from the impact inches from the young Knight. Rolling the blade over in his hand, he jabbed his spiritsword through the reptilian hand.

Their foe recoiled and whipped its neck around to chomp him. It was too slow. Thomas dodged and reached its abdomen, throwing all of his might behind the cleaving blow he delivered.

Giving a cry of agony, the dragon retreated still farther, swinging its barbed tail defensively. From the distance it imposed, Anargen could see that every strike had left a fiery gash in the smoldering dragon's hide. Its feathers had also caught fire, and their charred ruin made for a far less impressive specimen than when the cruel beast had fanned its opalescent plumage earlier.

All of this spelled its doom, but the dragon refused to yield. Its serpent-like eyes darted around the room. A wicked glint suddenly entered them. Faster than seemed possible for its size, it hobbled and scraped to the edge of the cavern and flared its wings. Launching across the pit toward the room's exit, Anargen had an awful realization. While its fate was sealed, the dragon would murder as many Ords and Ecthels as it could before it fell.

Charging after it, he leaped out over the pit and snagged hold of one of its tail barbs about midway along the swishing timber-like appendage. A faint grunt to his back alerted him that he wasn't alone. He whirled to see Seren gripping tenuously to a spike farther back.

There was no time to dispute what she'd done. To argue who should risk themselves to stop the creature. It was act now or live with the unconscionable consequences.

The dragon slammed into the vault's wall, shattering through the cut stones. It ambled through the corridor, half gliding, half shuffling. Every narrow opening it battered through. Shredding stone with the desperation of the dying.

Through the storm of sundered stone, Anargen and Seren moved up along its back. Bits of rock pelted off Anargen's armor. None of the passages were remotely big enough for the monster, but still it bored through all the barriers as though it was all paper instead of solid rock. Any moment it would be in the center of Ordumair, and Anargen was only onto its middle back.

A large chunk of stone crashed down onto the beast's dorsum and tumbled toward Anargen. He sucked in a sharp breath and threw himself against the thing's steely scales as the boulder-sized chunk of stone bounced up and off the creature's hip. He had no time to yell a warning to Seren.

He looked back, and his thudding heart threatened to stop. One moment she was there, the next gone. His mind couldn't grapple with what his eyes had just witnessed. She was just ... gone.

A flicker of motion caught his eye, and with a crackle of flames, Seren swung back around. She was straddling the dragon's tail, barely hanging on.

Anargen was by her in seconds, gripping a spike with one hand and reaching with the other to grab her nearest arm. With a choked groan of effort, he hoisted her back on properly. She looked up at him, and he could almost feel the relief, the hope radiating off of her.

The dragon bellowed a furious roar and slammed through a final wall. Amidst the shower of stone and dust, Anargen saw they were now in the city of Ordumair, looking down from maybe the twentieth round.

As the sounds of the dragon's roar echoing off the walls faded, Anargen realized the battle below was slowing to a halt. Every soldier must have trained their eyes on the hollowed core of the city's gradual upward spiral to see the mythic beast. Some with terror, others with vile glee.

At least until seconds later, when the dragon thrust its head downward and erupted a stream of its foul green fire that consumed allies and enemies without discretion. Dragons never truly keep allies among the men and women of the Lowlands. All are merely chaff for them to burn away. That was this monster's intention. Its time was short, and it would destroy as many people, whatever their allegiance, as it could.

Without a word passed between them, Anargen and Seren began the tenuous journey along the dragon's back, gripping its jagged spikes along its spine and coarse, steely scales as the air rushed against them. The creature dove, its fierce flames intensifying as it neared the greatest concentration of combatants and citizens of Ordumair.

Holding on was precarious, and Anargen's stomach felt like it was in his throat, choking him, but he had to reach the fiend's neck and finish it. He was almost there.

The beast's dark eye flicked back and caught sight of him. Anargen grabbed for the nearest spike and braced himself.

Pitching itself on its side, the dragon's tilt yanked against Anargen's hold, but he didn't give. Seren wasn't as solidly anchored and tumbled with a wind-muted gasp toward the dragon's shoulder and off it.

Anargen snagged one of her hands as she slid past. His hold was so tenuous, and she had her spiritsword in her right hand, so that only their left fingertips connected. Anargen's hand quivered as the dragon continued to twist in such a way that her full weight was held by those tips.

With a squeal, both their fingers gave. He watched with wordless horror as she fell.

Swinging around her spiritsword, she carved her blade in a deep path to its shoulder, where the smoldering scraps of its wing joined. The blade stuck fast there, and Seren managed to hang on as she came to a sudden halt.

The dragon writhed and contorted in midair, its damaged foreclaws fumbling to knock her away but having neither the angle nor the strength to do so.

White hot fire glowed and smoke streamed from the wound, forming a tornadic cloud as they spiraled downward.

With a sudden jerk, the dragon crashed into the wall of one of the rounds, and Seren's body was launched off like a doll being tossed by a petulant child.

Anargen couldn't speak, couldn't move, could only watch in horror. A fervent plea for his wife consumed every heartbeat.

She crashed somewhere on what he thought to be round twelve. There was no knowing how she took the impact. She rolled off into the shadows, and the dragon pitched and yawed, either from agony of its wound or trying to shake Anargen as its last tormentor. When it failed, it gripped the round wall nearest and launched them up, up, almost to the peak of Ordumair's interior.

Anargen knew this was it. The dragon's one wing would not support it, and it could not long outlast the High King's consuming righteous fire. The only recourse left to it was a final meteoric crash into the onlookers below to kill as many as possible—Anargen in particular.

The gut-jarring instant they began to drop, Anargen thought of Sir Cinaed. His noble sacrifice leaping off the shattering dam in Stormridge to plunge his spiritsword into the wyvern unleashed there. The sight of him disappearing into the valley depths below as a gush of frigid water surged down atop him, and the vanquished menace was emblazoned on Anargen's memory and so easy to recall now.

He knew what he had to do.

Seizing the spines nearest him, he pulled himself along them as the air whipped past with the rounds. The force of it threatened to rip him off the dragon's back. There was no yielding to the forces trying to thwart him. Every muscle, every ounce of resolve he poured into this last act, one last service to the people of Ordumair, the Lowlands, and the High King he loved dearly.

Fighting his way forward, his whole body shuddering against the effort of it, he reached the creature's shoulders, intending to plunge his spiritsword down into its neck. He just knew somehow it would instantly become fatal and cause the creature to disintegrate before it could impact below. Anargen would hit, but his much smaller body would hardly cause the damage and deaths the massive dragon's could.

He raised his blade to deliver the piercing blow that would end them both.

The dragon corkscrewed and snagged him in its good clawed hand. It drifted nearer the round walls as if to smear him along them all the way down.

Anargen struggled and couldn't get free. The wall rushed to smash him into a pulp.

Taking a breath, he entrusted himself to the High King of All Realms. He slashed his sword along the creature's knuckles with a one-handed stroke, and the moment it released its hold, he grabbed its arm with his free hand. Yanking against the dragon's arm with a might beyond himself that threatened to rip every sinew in his body to tattered threads, he flung himself into the air.

For the briefest moment, he was in parallel flight with the dragon, spiritsword scything through the air. He sliced its neck with all his might and yelled, "By the High King's authority, I banish you from all the Lowlands' realms forever!"

The sword severed the beast's neck, and with a strangled cry that was as hideously unnatural and awful as the goblin behind it, there was a tremendous flash of light and rush of heat and fire out from the spiritsword that engulfed the dragon entirely.

BOOM!

A dramatic concussive blast swelled throughout Ordumair, and the creature was gone. Not even a cloud of smoke remained to bear bits of its burned form.

Anargen had precious few seconds to take it in as the force of the spiritsword's explosive fury slammed him backward, and he found himself crashing into one of the walls on a round. This round had an enormous lattice with a hanging garden of sorts, and Anargen desperately tried to gain a hold on it, but he was moving too fast, tearing through the thin planks and ill-prepared vines.

It slowed his descent enough, however, that when his plummeting body came to the next round, he slung both arms over the round wall and, with a devastating crunch that he knew broke at least half his ribs, held onto the stone wall. One arm was dislocated at the shoulder, but what was that pain amidst so many others? He couldn't hold on, and he knew it. He could scarcely breathe at all after the impact.

There was nothing left now but to cherish the few extra seconds he'd been gifted to mentally bid farewell to those he loved. To glance down and see the crowds below returning to look up now that the danger for them was passed.

There was a furor of activity. Was he imagining that the defenders were surging back against the Monarchist attackers?

No, that had to be it! A surge of dots that were people—Ords and Ecthels alike—were dashing forward, pursuing those that had besieged them, expelling them like a man spitting out a grape seed. The Monarchists would suffer great losses; there were no clear paths of retreat, only the tight, secret tunnels they had co-opted to gain entry. The irony of the reversal in fortune that gambit had induced was a sweetness Anargen needed amid all the pain.

His grip was giving. This was it. In moments, he would be in the Kingdom of Light, forever in the Highland with his Lord.

"When all our journeys' ways mend ..." he murmured as his hands lost all grip and his body slid back.

Two hands grabbed hold of his right arm, locking tight around it. "You will be home again!" Seren half-sang, half-shouted in completion of the verse he'd taken up. His weight and total inability to help worked against them both, and she began sliding up onto the round wall, in danger of going over as well.

If he could've fought to extricate himself from her grip, to rescue her by dooming himself, he would have. But he couldn't. Anargen was truly dead weight, his right arm no longer responding to his commands at all.

Seren screamed with the effort and futility of it. In a moment, they would both be at the end of their lives. Fate-spoken, some would call them. Assigned to a tragic end. Romantic in its own sorrow-filled way ...

A jolt coursed through Anargen, and if he had been applying any effort, it would've wrenched his grasp free. Seren's hold on him was ferocious, though, and someone or something was pulling her back over the round wall.

They were hoisted in by inch, and another pair of arms grabbed for Anargen's left arm. These arms were stronger, so much so that Anargen was over the wall and smashing onto the stone floor of the round with an agonizing jolt.

"Ahh!" he cried out, surer than ever his ribs were broken.

An instant later, hands were on his helmet, undoing his face plate. He was looking into the rich cocoa eyes of Seren, rimmed red as tears flowed freely. Her face bore dark bruises, and he could tell from the way she held herself that her attempt to save him had been at cost of great pain to injuries she had earlier sustained.

With a wordless cry, her lips, split and bleeding though they were, were against his. Stealing his air, but filling his beleaguered heart with warmth and pleasure that for a delicious moment parted the waves of aches and pain crashing on him to savor the sort of bliss only she could bring him.

But air was dear, and she knew that well enough to pull back. As she did, Anargen could see his father and Thomas standing over him. Thomas dropped to the ground with an exhausted sigh and chuckled. "Almost got away from us."

"Couldn't let that happen," Glewdyn said, his voice choked with emotion as he crouched beside his son and held his hand tight.

"No ... sir," Anargen managed to mumble.

By now, a small crowd of others began streaming from other rounds above and below where citizens had been sheltering. Anargen saw two dear sights, Mia and Gregor, among them, hobbling over to join them.

After they reached Thomas and their embraces and cheers began, Anargen lost track of everything. It all blurred under the weight of his injuries' pressure, and he must have blacked out, because the next thing he knew, he was lying bandaged in a bed.

There was definitely soreness, but so long as he did not move, it was bearable. Seren was lying by his side, not quite clinging to him, but holding to him with the clear intention of never letting him go. Glewdyn, Thomas, Mia, and Gregor sat or stood, arrayed around his and Seren's guest room in the Thane's quarters. A new sort of pain presented itself stridently. Duncoin, Thane of Ords, Knight of Light ... he was gone. Perished in defense of his people.

"You're awake," Seren chirped, drowsiness and relief thick in her voice.

"Mhm, and you may ... rest now, my love," he said with a winsome smile.

She lay her head against his arm, but did so with such gentleness that he could squelch his arm's bitter protests and aches. Tender care as hers deserved so much more reward than to just bite back a complaint.

To his surprise, a few moments later, she was making the breathy sounds of her deepest sleep. He glanced over at his father, who smirked. "She's worth keeping, that one. More precious than rubies. Seren hasn't left your side for a half second longer than necessary to eat and allow a physician to tend to you."

Glewdyn walked over and placed his hand on his son's head and mussed his hair a bit. Again, with marked gentleness.

"Ordumair?" he croaked, daring to hope much.

Glewdyn's brow furrowed, his expression mixed. Cloudy, not stormy. "The Monarchists were routed. We managed to capture most of them. Captain Strathmore rode out two days ago to deliver word to Caldoness that the Monarch has fallen and his personal army was defeated."

"The war should be over now," Gregor piped up with no small wonder in his cracking teen voice.

"Just like that?" Anargen asked, fearing now to hope so much.

His father shrugged. "It will take months for word to spread sufficiently to stop all fighting. Then there will be peace negotiations and all manner of politicking I don't care to imagine, but, yes. There's no reason for the Monarchists to keep fighting. They did not have a cause as we did, only a leader with a vision. One that may have been imposed on them with dark sorcery, in fact."

"A good many of the Monarchist soldiers seemed to come out of a trance state after the dragon's end," Thomas clarified. "Those that weren't carrion, that is."

Anargen was silent. Good news in such abundance was almost as hard and heavy to process as bad. "Our quest. It's at an end?"

"Is it?" Glewdyn asked, an amused lilt to his voice. "You're the one who deduced that the Tower of Light is our Knight Order. I imagine the Quest will go on till the King's Day comes. Which, sadly, wasn't this day."

"Or any of the week since," Gregor clarified needlessly.

Once more, Anargen found himself introspective, examining all this in the addled recesses of his mind. His heart was sufficiently content to embrace it all with an almost choking joy.

"Then what comes next?"

"The road goes ever on till we arrive at the Highland. One day," Glewdyn replied and patted him on the head as he stood again. "For now, rest, take comfort from your wife's love, and mend. We have much to be grateful to the High King for, and by appearances, the time in which to fully explore and express that thanks."

"No," Anargen disagreed, causing his father to arch an eyebrow. "There will never be enough days with all their hours devoted to thanking the High King for the favor we've been granted. Not in my lifetime or a dozen."

Glewdyn nodded, shooing the others out as he must have noted fatigue was dragging Anargen's words down, along with his fluttering eyelids. "Then perhaps you can write all that has passed, and through it ensure the thanksgiving echoes for many ages beyond us."

Anargen's lip flicked into a brief smile. "I like that. I think ... I will. For the honor of the High King."

"Aye," Glewdyn agreed. "For his honor."

WHAT HAS COME BEFORE

That was it. The last pages. All the tale was told. Yet, how could it be? There were things left unsaid, unresolved. Answers that mattered more to Jason in the present than they may well have as they were being born out in the past.

Okay, don't get overdramatic. Just ask him.

"Sir?" Jason began, sounding all too much like a much younger version of himself, when he used to foolishly approach his grandfather with questions only to come away with a smarting mouth and better sense of his value in the old man's eyes. He hoped Sir Cinaed would have a very different manner of resolving unpleasant inquiries.

"Yes, lad?" the old storyteller replied, setting aside a notebook he was using to jot something down.

"It's finished?" Jason asked, feeling oddly expectant for more, though the story had concluded.

"Is any story ever finished?"

Jason shrugged and sighed. A direct response from the poster for esotericism was probably a bit much to expect. "You would know better than me."

Lips pursed, Cinaed gestured to his young compatriot. "You have questions then?"

"Ha," Jason gave a punctuated laugh, unsure of any greater understatement. What did he honestly need to know? "I suppose ... what happened next for everyone. Though, more than anything, I want to know why you told me this story. Or stories ... Or ... I don't know."

Reaching over and giving Jason's knee a squeeze and a shake, Cinaed pointed to his effects. "I thought you might have that question one day. Retrieve the red-backed book from my bags, if you would."

By now, Jason had learned to just go with the old man for a distance. Even if he did feel so very heavy, having just reached the end of the story. It had started him on the Quest and put him on the path to serve the High King. The weight of its significance made his movement mechanical. What did it all mean?

His hand gripped the red-backed book, and before he even knew what he was doing, he read aloud: "A Brief History of the Western Lowlands – Ancient to Modern Era, by Francis DuBois, PhD."

Cinaed retrieved the book from him and flipped through the pages quickly to a particular point. With a satisfied nod, the old storyteller turned the book around and handed it back. "Read from the middle of page three twenty-two."

Jason eyed him for a moment. The other just raised his bushy brows as if to say, "Go on." Drawing in a preparatory breath, Jason launched into it.

"Thus ended the Ecthel Civil War. Though combat continued sporadically for months after, word of the Monarch's mysterious disappearance—no reasonable accounting of his death exists—circulated broadly. In terms of meeting the lofty objectives Viceroy Ecthelion Halifax held for the Commonwealth, perhaps one success can be tallied. Considering a young Gregor Fenwrest was granted the Monarch's throne nearly a year after, the notion of the Commonwealth only lived on through the power plays of Gregor's older cousin Thomas, who happened to be adopted by Ecthelion shortly before the Viceroy's death. Such circumstances are naturally suspicious, but the zeal with which

Thomas Halifax seized power and redirected the course of history is one of the marvels of the transition from Middle to Modern Era in the Lowlands.

"Wedding Baroness Mia Sornfold consolidated his holdings across Ecthelowall into the most formidable portfolio of assets and influence of any Ecthel noble. And with his 'reluctant' acceptance of the role of prime minister for his simpering cousin, Thomas undercut the new Monarch by enshrining the role of the council of nobles in the administration of the Commonwealth's affairs. It is through ambitious projects begun by him and continued by his line—he had five children with the Baroness, and their grandson ascended to the Monarch's throne during Thomas's lifetime—Ecthelowall became the nation we observe today.

"True enough, Monarch Gregor Fenwrest's marriage to the daughter of Albaron's Laird cemented Albaron's effective annexation by Ecthelowall, but that would only have succeeded in maintaining Ecthelowall's status as a regional power. Thomas Halifax's reforms transformed it into *the* power of the Lowlands, even as its rival Rehalcy made significant strides toward its present imperial regality. Indeed, many scholars, myself included, argue as to whether the Modern Era truly began with Thomas Halifax's tenure as prime minister or the fall of Kirke to Rehalcy's coalition. Given how coincidental they are from a broader perspective, the question is a pedantic one. However, it only underscores the fluidity of society in the closing years of the Middle Era as a disgraced squire boy could become the most potent political player in the Lowlands of his day."

Finishing the passage, Jason looked up at Cinaed. "It sounds rather skeptical of Thomas's motives. More so than one would expect. Or at least more than I ever would be."

Grumbling, the old man took the book back. "Now let me

tell you what really mattered. Thomas did indeed become prime minister, but at Gregor's request and need. This 'historian' misses both men's humility and compassionate care. He utterly neglects to mention the reestablishing of Ecthelowall's Knight Halls' forgotten duty to care for local communities, especially the poor and the ill across the Commonwealth. They neglect Thomas's own writings, which brazenly credit all good he experienced to the High King. And Mia has no voice nor role at all, even as she was the perfect complement to Thomas, and their combined efforts were far greater as one than apart."

Snapping the book shut, Cinaed's tone and demeanor grew severe as a storm. "So, my child, you've wondered why I tell the stories I do. This is part of that greater mosaic. Because men actively rebel against the High King, resolving to misunderstand and reduce through bitter skepticism all that is good to the basest view of events and people. In so doing, they lose truth, heart, and the impulse to admire and emulate virtue."

He paused suddenly, as if remembering himself to be an elderly man of dignified composure. Cinaed cleared his throat and finished, "They do a disservice to themselves and their readers."

"No doubt," Jason replied, striving not to sound patronizing. Cinaed was right. Though it hardly sufficed to distract Jason from the ache gnawing him to nothing. Preserving real history, truth, was noble enough. It just didn't begin to sort out for him how he had been pulled into all of this. How these stories directly mattered to him. But he guessed that if Cinaed really wanted to tell him the full reason for telling this story over the years, he would have done so. For the moment, Jason would have to settle for more targeted answers. Further lessons. There was perhaps a comfort in thinking that more might lie ahead, and he hadn't learned all the old man had for him yet. "Does this Dr. DuBois mention Anargen, Seren, and Glewdyn?"

With a wry smile, Cinaed replied, "Of course not. They were commoners, and their involvement and their roles are only remarkable when considering how the High King of All Realms used them marvelously. It's incomprehensible in a framework to which so many in the Lowlands want to be and are in fact beholden."

Frameworks. Systems of self-deception and willful naïveté. It was all still heavier to digest than the possibility that there were no further stories to hear, which he might as well admit, stung mightily in that he had initially become their willing student only because he'd been smitten at first sight with Aria. Aria, whom he would've married and loved for a lifetime. Aria, who was the perfect complement to him. Aria, whom he had lost and scarcely been allowed even a breath's space to mourn.

"Well," Jason prompted when a minute had passed without Cinaed saying anything further.

"Well," Cinaed pushed back, arms crossed over his chest. That piercing look he had when first they met was there. That almost ethereal penetration to gaze into the deepest recesses of Jason and examine every ounce of his mettle. Years now he'd been with the old man, and still that gaze shredded through Jason's nerves.

"Well, what happened to them? To Anargen, Seren, Glewdyn?"

"Anargen, Seren, and Glewdyn stayed on in Ordumair for a few more weeks. While Thomas, Mia, and Gregor left for Caldoness. There, Gregor was named the new Monarch of Ecthelowall with Thomas his prime minister. They began sorting out the task of reforming Ecthelowall into the Commonwealth it is today."

Jason started to interrupt that he already knew about Thomas, Mia, and Gregor. It felt like the Defender was being dodgy. Leaning forward as a sudden realization that perhaps whatever happened next to Anargen was in fact its own full story or in some way answered so many of the questions he had lingering, questions about Cinaed himself, pulled Jason in like a magnet metal. "All right, so, Anargen survived and wrote the accounts we've been reading?"

"He did," Cinaed replied, settling into his chair and closing his eyes. "Though the accounts I carry are copies. The originals were too fragile to tote around and expect to last almost four centuries. Not that these are exactly freshly printed. They're about a hundred years old each."

For some reason, that detail surprised Jason, though it really shouldn't have. He knew parchment wasn't the most durable material. Fleetingly, he considered asking if Cinaed thought they were faithful copies, but that seemed unnecessary. Cinaed Black wasn't the sort to peddle stories he felt weren't well preserved or were in some way untrue. Besides, he had a feeling the answers he really sought were tantalizingly close at hand. "What happened to Anargen after recovering in Ordumair? And to Ordumair and the Ords, for that matter?"

Cinaed began again after a lull with no indication on his face of whether he approved of Jason's inquiries. "By the time spring came round again, it was clear that Ordumair wasn't a viable home for the Ords any longer. Of the hundreds who survived the Second Siege of Ordumair, only about two hundred made it through the winter. A brief civil war ensued once it was discovered Anargen had been given the Signet of Thanes. Even if he and the other Knights were heralded as dragon slayers, it disgusted some that he held the signet. He offered to turn it over, but they reached no consensus as to who should take up the ring. With Duncoin's death in the siege and the confirmation that Iaegon had been lost some months before, the line of thanes stretching back to Ordumair I was broken. It was without parallel in their entire history.

"Fighting was intense. Injuries, illness, and poor conditions from the harsh winter added to the losses and ravaged them. Anargen and his loved ones eventually were able to bring the remaining Ord nobles to reason before the feud destroyed the Ords entirely. No Ord would be bestowed the dear signet. Even so, putting their wearied and battered people back together with some new agreement, a democracy, or anything to maintain harmony and hegemony, remained elusive. Sensing their presence and the signet's may only further complicate the matter, Anargen and his family concluded they would leave Ordumair. They offered for as many as wished to have a fresh start to join them. Some Ords insisted on staying in their ancestral Ordumair, while others traveled with Anargen and his family to the spot they had decided to settle: Bracken."

Jason's eyes were wide. "What? Why would they possibly have gone to that dreary place? With all the horrible memories from when the Grey Scourge slaughtered the villagers there to ambush Anargen and the other Knights ..." Jason gave a shiver and grimace for emphasis.

Cinaed's thoughtful eyes lifted from him, and he once more closed them and leaned into his seat as if to sleep. "Now isn't the time for that. We need some rest after what we've been through. Time. In time, I'll reveal what you're really wanting to know."

Gnawing on his lower lip and tapping his fingers in rapid succession on the tight brown upholstery of the chair on which he sat, Jason felt like a fish on a line. He wanted to bolt, but he was hooked. Hooked, and Cinaed was just going to leave him there without reeling in for who knew how long. Maybe another tack was what he needed. A new avenue to get to the door he needed opened. "So, what about Caeserus, Terrillian, and Bertinand? They just seemed to drop out of the account. What happened to them?"

By now, the heat of Cinaed's ire was cooled fully and cast to something more akin to pensiveness. "Those are stories I can tell you and should. They are not the stories you need today."

"Which do I need?"

"All those that I've given you. And all that have come before."

Jason scooted down on his chair, edgy despite his own weariness. His body felt like worn leather that had been wetted and beaten over a rock. "I need to know more."

"You shall. But a story first heard isn't all that it will be. Once heard, it begins to work on us, and what it will mean, what you will know from it, isn't fully told even after you have reached the final page and turned it to find the back cover."

Classic Cinaed. There was no point continuing if that was all the old man was willing to give. It might even be detrimental to Cinaed's health for Jason to keep pushing the way he had been. If Cinaed Black was a mere man like Jason, then everything they'd been through—the escape, losing Aria, the Council, rushing away to face a potential nightmare—any of them would be enough to finish off most men of his presumable age. Never mind having to tell Jason stories for hours and be grilled and pressed relentlessly for all his deepest-held secrets.

"Thank you," Jason found himself saying before he'd even realized he would.

There was a wavering around the old man's lips as though he wanted to smile, but just couldn't right now. "Aye."

WHAT IS NOW

Rain fell heavily on the darkened stones around Jason. It only felt right that a storm had beset Brackenburgh shortly after they reached the city limits. A feat, which, if Jason was honest, was made eminently more achievable with Sir Cinaed accompanying him. The Defender hadn't exaggerated the extent of his inroads and contacts spread across the Northwestern Lowlands. Even if he had spent a considerable amount of time running the Black River Inn before the war, he had been a true servant of his Realm. Going far and broad among its enormous expanse, much of it controlled by nations like Rehalcyon and Knorland, which were openly hostile to Knights of Light. It may have been silly, but he hoped they lived through this, if for no other reason than to hear from him the stories of how he and Aria had skirted being found and brought in by the authorities serving the darker forces in the Lowlands.

Dorian.

Jason dashed down the street and rounded a corner, keeping out of sight from the more active thoroughfares. Even at night in a storm like this, Brackenburgh wasn't totally without some activity, especially downtown. It was funny how much development had taken place since he had last been here. The proliferation of more and newer models of cars. Smokey jazz dens and gleaming movie theaters had popped up in greater numbers. Much as though no one had told

Brackenburgh's citizens that Rehalycon and all the Lowlands were at war.

Dorian.

He doubled back and motioned for Cinaed to follow him. As the old man slipped past him, moving at his usual surprising speed for his age, Jason made sure no one noticed them or followed.

None of the papers he'd seen in Rehalcyon made mention of the war. Other than to say the Emperor observed the efforts across all fronts and was "pleased with their progress." That phrase alone made Jason want to throw up, never mind the insipid images of the Emperor attending to affairs of state that dominated the remaining space on front pages. Were the people of the Empire oblivious to how much of a pawn Emperor Han Dikeriakesan was truly? Maybe when Monarch Ilyron revealed himself and the darkest forces of the Lowlands became inescapably present in their lives, Rehalcyon's people would finally perceive the peril that had seeped into the nation for centuries until at last the whole levy was ready to burst.

Dorian.

"This way," Jason called to Cinaed under his breath. Together they slunk through the pooling along the streets as the drains struggled to swallow all of the water crashing down on them. At this point, Jason moved fast enough that his splashing was loud and obvious enough if someone wanted to give care to hear him. At this point, were they to be caught, it wouldn't slow them any further. After all, they were coming up to the block on which the towering Ministry of Justice building stood. The ironic tower that, along with a collection of other government and commerce buildings, loomed more than a hundred feet high over the sprawling Elkland Square.

Even from here, he could see that since his last visit, they had finished adding the electric streetlights around its perimeter. From their modest light, the buttresses, soaring columns, and arcades of the buildings looked like giant hulking beasts, many-limbed and brooding as they looked down on the Wernstrum Fountain at the plaza's center. In stone, the centerpiece fountain boasted Rehalcyon's triumphant dragon, which shook off its shackles and rose proud after being laid low by its foe, the bear. The mythic symbolism still wasn't clear, but the irony that soon they could be facing a flesh-and-blood dragon was inescapable.

He stepped out into the street, marching toward it, ready to face whatever lay inside the Justice building. No matter how mythic or menacing.

HONK!

Faint lights approached, bearing a pronounced growl, and he raised his hand to his eyes to help see their source. Jason was jerked out of the way just as the flivver—or perhaps more fairly the roadster—zipped past. The next instant, Cinaed pushed him against the wall of the nearest building with a clank as the heavier, more obvious plate armor and tower shield they bore for this task struck the bricks.

"Lad, are you all right? Even my old eyes and ears couldn't have missed that vehicle barreling down on us."

Shaking his head, Jason replied, "I'm fine. I'm fine." That wasn't true. A shiver ran through Jason.

Cinaed leaned forward and gave him a hug. The gesture was almost as surprising as the car encounter. As the Defender pulled back, he patted Jason's arm. "None of us can face what is ahead without trepidation, even without the complexity of your situation."

My situation? Right. Dorian.

Jason took a shuddering breath. Remembering to breathe, to focus, shouldn't be such a challenge. This was what they'd traveled thousands of miles to do. Rescue Professor Goulder. Slay a dragon. Stop Dorian.

Of course, it was the last that gave him a pause that felt so unbearably weighty. His younger brother, who had been behind so much evil, had essentially issued him an invitation to come and engage in a final showdown. A battle that would determine not only their familial conflict but the tenuous balance of the war.

"You know the worst part of all this is ..." Jason began and decided to just drop it.

"I have my guesses, but even if I'm right, it would do you good to speak it aloud," Cinaed said quietly as he watched for any signs that the car from earlier was doubling back to investigate the odd pair of people in the road. They had abandoned subtlety in their choice of armor and shields tonight, so it wasn't a bad idea to keep a wary eye out. Nor should they linger long in this spot. Not when they were so close.

Taking a few steps toward the building, intending to disregard Cinaed's advice, Jason suddenly stopped and closed his eyes. "The worst part is that I know he caused Aria's death, so part of me isn't sorry to have to face him. Part of me wants to utterly crush him for what he's done."

Rain continued to plink off their armor and keep its steady sigh of falling. Jason wondered if he shouldn't have been so open and unapologetic about his dark thought. At length, Sir Cinaed said, "What you are facing is not unique to you. I, too, struggle with seeing our foes as fallible creatures that the High King would redeem and be reconciled with if they would but choose it. Our own brokenness makes it hard to accept another's. Neither of us has much hope of approaching this wholly without biases. We will simply be forced to focus closely on that to which the High King leads us."

Again, the rain was the only source of sound between them for close to a minute before Jason asked, "Are you ready, sir? Once we go in, there is no coming back out without succeeding."

"I'm ready, lad. On we go."

Drawing in a breath, Jason verified no cars were coming and dashed out into the open, Sir Cinaed following him. They rushed past the turnoff into Elkland Square and then onto the next block, cutting back and making the long loop around to come at the Ministry of Justice from behind. As he had when he'd tried to trade his freedom for Dorian's, before discovering Dorian's dark nature, he crashed through the secret entrance that led into the Wernstrum mob's headquarters.

They made it into the first parlor, and there was no one. Fancy upholstered chairs and dark green carpeting with the counter bearing a coffee pot and assortment of liquor bottles in the far corner made it seem more like a gentleman's club or upscale bar than a staging room where thugs would wait for their "fresh meat" to arrive before pummeling whomever had crossed the family into a softer cut. Last time Jason had been here, he had experienced that warm welcome.

Passing beyond it into an interior salon, Jason found it to be utterly empty as well. Had he misread the challenge from LeVanseaux?

No, this has to be it.

There was no turning back. So, he just kept pushing on and up toward his grandfather's office. Every hallway, every room they passed through was empty, but he could all but feel the dark pulse beating within the building's concrete confines. Working farther and farther into the Wernstrum's hidden operation until at last, there was the long hall leading straight into his grandfather's office.

Faint light from wall sconce-mounted electric lights kept it from being dark, and also reinforced the impression that, for all appearances, the building was empty and abandoned. The fixtures had changed from the conventional Dag Vogtere solar reliefs to dragons that bore the bulbs between their wings. The visible tilework along the hall had also been changed from geometric patterns to what looked like the Tislatnean pictographs he'd seen in the Ruins of Gerisk necropolis.

Jason glanced at Sir Cinaed. Just ahead were the enormous mahogany double doors to his grandfather's office.

BANG.

The doors to his grandfather's office flung open of their own accord, crashing heavily into the walls to either side. Waiting in the entrance to the expansive room just beyond stood Dorian.

DEVASTATION

"Ah, brother, you have arrived early. I suppose you have truly changed," Dorian commented with a note of amusement. "And you brought the old storytelling phosphila, excellent."

Jason couldn't speak. The person standing before him sounded like his brother, but older, with the deeper intonation of manhood. He was taller as well. Not quite as tall as Jason, but close.

He was in a midnight suit with a shirt of matching color, his hair was slicked back, and his face was pale, gaunt. The dark around his eyes was so intense that they appeared bruised. Dorian looked as though he had been abused and passed on the treatment to others, barely standing on his feet and projecting power, control, and menace at the same time.

"What is happening to you?" Jason blurted out, unable to hide the hitch in his voice. Images of his innocent kid brother rushed past like those on a picture reel.

Narrowing his eyes while still smiling, Dorian replied plaintively, "Are you going to pretend to be concerned about my well-being now? You're seven years too late, big brother."

Jason clenched his jaw. The last time they had seen each other, Dorian had revealed he didn't care about Jason's absence. Even if Jason did immensely. Either Dorian lied and did deeply care—which meant he was reachable—or he was lying now—which meant he was just manipulating Jason's emotions for sport and thus lost.

"Where is Professor Goulder?" Jason demanded.

"I'm sure I don't know," Dorian replied with a shrug. He turned as if to walk off, seeming to be bored.

Taking several strides toward the darkened office ahead, Jason jerked to a halt. Cinaed had both hands on his shoulders, holding him back. He just shook his wizened grey head.

"This isn't a game, brother. If you have to murder a Knight to appease your master Ilyron, why not me? Hasn't that been your goal since you tricked me into coming back to Brackenburgh three years ago?"

Sitting on the huge mahogany desk lavished by the shadows, Dorian clapped. "Bravissimo. Such a compelling performance. You have fulfilled your knightly duty, offering yourself in place of another.

"Professor Goulder is fine where he is, "resting in peace," and I have no intention of allowing you to swap places with my chosen sacrifice. That would ruin all of the fun of watching you disintegrate as you futilely attempt to mount a rescue."

Jason tried to pull free of Sir Cinaed's hold, but the Storyteller was surprisingly strong as always and did his best to keep Jason where he was.

"Lad, open your eyes!" he grunted.

Blinking, Jason started to ask what his mentor was talking about, and then he saw them. Dozens of ochre eyes, fixed on him from the shadows. Bestial shaped, but with the attentiveness and expressions of men.

Werebeasts.

Now the faint lupine shapes and the delineation of their sooty tufts of fur and fangs could be discerned. His grandfather's office was packed with them. Dimly he wondered if this was where all of the Wernstrum bruisers had gone to, transformed into slavering monsters.

"Oh, you old prune, always spoiling the best sport. He had

almost stumbled right in. Wouldn't that have been something to see?"

Dorian slapped his knee, his tone utterly deadpan.

"You're sadistic," Jason accused, feeling the pain of those words and their truth through to his very core.

"From your vantage point, my, yes." He kicked off the table and snapped his fingers once. All of the werebeasts leaped out of their places toward the door with a barking, ravenous burst. Before they reached the door frame, another faint snap could be heard, and they all froze in place, some leaning toward Jason and Sir Cinaed, drool dripping from bared fangs, their posture tensed as if every muscle yearned to rend them to shreds but couldn't possibly comply with that driving desire.

"Remember, the prize you seek is in the awakening chamber beneath the building. I'd hurry, though. My pets are hungry."

Jason couldn't move. He felt as if he'd already been torn apart. Two things felt inescapably true of what Dorian had said. One, Professor Goulder was not here. Two, Jason was far too late. Whatever he had told himself and convinced himself of in the time since he last escaped Dorian's torture, he hadn't stopped believing he could reach his brother, draw him back to the light. But this ... this felt impossibly evil. Beyond redemption, as much as it was beyond him to reach out and grab the moon with his bare hands.

Cinaed jerked back on him, towing Jason down the hall. "Run, lad, now!"

Jason spun, stumbled, and took off after Sir Cinaed at a sprint. At his back, he heard the snap of Dorian's fingers echo in the corridor. An immediate burst of barks and howls and scrambling, scraping claws followed.

"Get to the elevator," he instructed Cinaed. Surging alongside him in the sprint. Whomever was down below, they had to reach them. If Dorian thought it would destroy him to witness their death, Jason fully believed Dorian was cruel enough for it to be true.

They were only a few floors above ground level right now. Grandpa and Grandma Wernstrum had been firm believers in being the power in the shadows. They didn't need the penthouse suite atop the Ministry of Justice to control it, and the less noticed they were, the easier it was for them to keep their grip tight.

Dashing down the hallways, Jason could hear the beasts closing behind them. Whirling around, spiritsword drawn, he almost fell over backward. One of them was only a few feet away and scrambling along the wall up onto the ceiling to allow its fellow monsters to surge forward down the middle of the hall.

The beast snarled at him and leaped down, arms extended, claws and fangs bared.

Jason backpedaled and brought his fiery sword up and around, nicking the creature's cheek. It whimpered and pawed at the singed fur around the glowing scar it had received.

Not waiting to see how it would feel once its ache eased, Jason sprinted after Sir Cinaed and found him waiting at the elevator bank, opening the doors to the car.

The elevator chimed as it slid open, revealing another werebeast. The silvery monster snapped at Sir Cinaed, who just managed to scramble out of the way of its wicked, sharp teeth. Drawing his spiritsword and sliding on his shield, he called to Jason without looking away from his furred foe. "How are things the way we came?"

"Not better," Jason replied, skidding to a halt and slipping on his shield just in time to bring it up. A shudder ran through his arm as the claws from another werebeast raked along its burning surface.

There was a yip, and Jason shot a look to see that Sir Cinaed had baited the creature before him into an attack that had left it overcommitted and plunged his spiritsword into its exposed back. He left it there a moment before pulling it free. His opponent hobbled backward, flailing to reach an injury it could not cure nor ease.

An urgent whisper forced Jason's attention back to his side of the attack. A clawed fist slammed into his face, sending him sprawling to the floor. The groan of the price paid for his distraction hadn't yet left his lips when the monster was over him, pinning his arms and leaning in to tear at his throat.

A fiery flash sailed over Jason's head, and there was a meaty sticking sound. Crackling smoke poured off the creature. It shrieked and recoiled.

The fumbling of the fiend bought Cinaed time to help Jason to his feet. "Can you fight?"

"Yeaaahh," Jason replied as he touched his helmet where his jaw had been struck. It would've been shattered if not for the armor of the High King he wore. Any more of that kind of fighting and he probably would be down for good.

"Be wary," Defender Black instructed and shifted back and to the side. Two more creatures edged toward them, hackles raised and heads down, growling at them.

Beyond that pair, another was engaged in the same trick of climbing the walls, looking on him as it hung upside down, furious and pleased in one. A dozen more lingered in ranks to come, and who knew how many more would come after.

"Um, how about that elevator?" he asked.

"Arrah!" Cinaed bellowed, and Jason heard the sharp slice as his blade connected. The monster at their back must have rallied. With a cry, the beast fell smoldering to the floor. It was obstructing the elevator entry. Not that it mattered, getting onboard it and safely headed down would be impossible with these added creatures bearing down on them.

I thought Dorian wanted to torture me before he fed me to his pets.

Jason's thoughts trailed off as he swung his sword in a wide arc, keeping their attackers back for a few precious seconds. How were they going to get out of this?

A werebeast lunged and chomped down on his rebrace, jerking him forward like a rag doll. Not bothering to try to free his forearm, he let the momentum carry him forward to slam his shield into its head. The moment its grip on his forearm slackened, he twisted the blade around and slashed across its open jaws.

Not waiting to see how he did, he spun to face the other werebeast and blocked its expected attack. Jason was tugged violently back. Barely keeping on his feet, he watched as the werebeast from the ceiling crashed down heavily in front of him. Little fissures in the marble flooring radiated out from under the long black-and-green runner on the floor.

"Thanks," Jason mumbled to his mentor, knowing he had been the source of the rescue.

"It is but my duty," someone else replied.

DESCENT

A familiar spherical glow hovered before him, this time with an arm extended from it. There was a flare of brilliance, and from it stepped an imposing figure, garbed in gleaming armor that looked like molten bronze. Though Jason had only ever seen it once, this was without doubt an elf.

"Vif?" he inquired hopefully.

"Well remembered," he replied. "Duck."

Jason complied, half dazed. Over his head, the elf brought his shimmering curved sword around and sliced a deep gash into the werebeast tentatively sortieing.

"Behind me," Vif compelled him as he strode forward.

The monsters seemed both repulsed and fascinated by his glowing presence. He met their interest with a complex twisting swoosh of his sword that terminated into the floor, leaving a blazing wall of fire between them and their prey.

Without wasting a breath's space, he was back to facing Jason and gestured to the elevator. "Take it down as far as it will go, then use the passages down to the dark grotto beneath. You must face what awaits there. Be bold, and know that our Great King is with you."

"Aren't you coming with us?" Jason asked, glancing to Sir Cinaed, who seemed to be sharing a very intense gaze with Vif. It was as if they were speaking without uttering a word. Statue-like, they remained that way as the fire raged behind Vif and the cacophonic chorus of howls and barks and growls continued from behind its protection.

"Um, hello?"

"I have done what I may directly. I cannot aid you in what comes next, not down there. My kind and I are fighting with and for you all throughout this shadow-stricken town.

"Now, go quickly. What you must do is of great import."

Nodding, Jason backed away from the gleaming being of legend. It wasn't as though he could argue with him on the matter. No matter how vexing it was that Vif had appeared and so handily disarmed Dorian's trap, only to vanish when they would be facing a far greater threat. An "important" one at that. At least Jason managed to keep his misgivings to himself until both he and Cinaed were on the elevator coming to their stop.

"I don't understand why Vif would appear suddenly and then just leave us to face this threat alone. With an army of elves, we could end Dorian's threats and the Lowlands Total War in weeks, maybe days. Why not just send them into battle with us?"

Cinaed's voice was lower than before, and implanted in his demeanor was a kernel of anxiety that Jason didn't dare ask after. "The elves fight battles we cannot see, on a plane we cannot access of our own. Every once in a great while, you will see the light of them glimmer, a reminder they aid us."

Jason stiffened, recalling the instances of the glow he had witnessed since the attack on Kezmarepos. Had there been aid from the High King he hadn't recognized in all of those places? Aid against things seen and unseen?

The elevator doors opened to a poorly lit tunnel, not for lack of electric lights. Something oppressive hung over this place. Jason felt it, like he'd shouldered a heavy pack that was weighing him down. An unpleasant chill clung to the air, clawing at him. All of this he'd experienced when the forces of the Dark Prince were arrayed to oppose them.

"Looks like this is the way," Jason commented offhandedly.

"Hmm," Cinaed huffed and stalked down the hall. There were several offshoots, but he seemed to be ignoring most as he forged a trail through the building's labyrinthine basement.

Not wanting to fall behind, Jason jogged and caught up. He wanted to ask why the Defender hadn't answered his question about the elves more directly. It was good to know they weren't abandoning them, but why not let them fight this battle? Though, for that matter, why didn't the High King simply banish all the darkest enemies from the Lowlands altogether? It was within his power to do so. Dark beings like these only obscured the light.

There's a purpose to this pain.

The phrase returned to him then, and he felt the weight of it in counterbalance to the heaviness of the shadows crowding the tunnel. Or perhaps it was of the same substance. In that moment, he longed to be away from not just this place but the Lowlands as a whole. There was a weariness to living in a land filled with such brokenness and suffering. The promise of truly being in the High King's presence was a yearning that cloyed deep within him so that every fiber of his being ached after it. He was willing to forsake all his ambitions for the privilege of kneeling before his Lord.

Pain pulls us off our paths and onto his.

Ahead, Sir Cinaed stopped abruptly and swung his arm out, slapping it across Jason's chest, barring him from proceeding farther. Yawning beneath them was an enormous underground cavern system.

"Oh, thanks," Jason said breathily, his heart racing out of introspection to that moment.

"A ladder," the elder Knight observed and gestured toward the extra-large handles anchoring it to the edge of the sheer drop-off. Its rungs descended straight down into the roughly oval limestone opening below. Stalactites could just be made out hanging from the ceiling interspersed with other pillar like stony protrusions within the opening.

Again, Jason sensed in Cinaed a trepidation he hadn't encountered before. "Sir ..." he hesitated.

"Yes?"

"I ... what ..." Why couldn't he bring himself to ask after what troubled his mentor? They faced awful things before, and they had not shaken him. What could be different now?

Grabbing both his arms, Defender Black pinned Jason down with a heady stare. "Later, lad. Questions, concerns. They are not for this hour. Your brother's arrogance may have led him to deliver us to this moment, or it may be his arrogance that leads him to think we cannot stop him, even knowing his intentions. Whatever the case, pride precedes a downfall."

Now Jason fell under a cloak of pensiveness.

"Come," the old man patted his arm. "You are loath to see that come. I do not begrudge you your hope, but guard your heart."

"Yes, sir."

With a curt nod, the storyteller made his way to the ladder and paused as he gripped the top handles. He looked up and around and breathed out. "Why don't you go first, lad. Speed is essential, and my years are harder on me today than most."

Jason scoffed. "You outrace most men my age on your worst day."

His wrinkled face quirked up in a smirk. "Perhaps," Cinaed replied. "Please, humor me."

With a shrug, Jason took hold of the handles and began his descent. The distance to the top of the opening from the ladder's handles was maybe ten or so feet, but there proved to be several times over that from the opening to where it finally ended, riveted into the damp limestone floor. If Jason had imagined the dark to be domineering above, it was absolutely tyrannical at this level. He couldn't imagine it being this frigid, even on the Northern Ice Shelf. The light afforded by the glowing inscriptions of his armor was all he had for seeing.

Drawing his spiritsword and holding it aloft, he felt as though the dark was viscous and his blade had to cut through it. Flames burned brightly on his blade, crackling as it pushed back against the ebony oblivion of the cavern.

"Umph," Cinaed grunted behind Jason as his feet landed at the ladder's end.

Jason didn't bother looking back to check on him. What he could make out looming in the darkness beyond was already more than he could process.

Soaring limestone columns, natural constructs of the cave's erosion, were joined by towering cranes. The heavy machinery appeared to have been used to stack some of the largest cut stones he'd ever seen to create the pillars. They were reminiscent of those he'd seen at Gerisk and arrayed around a stone dais or platform of some kind that had a square wall around it, but there were enormous gaps between the three corners he could make out.

"Guess we caught them before they could finish it," he commented somewhat numbly, not bothering to tame his shock at the effort it must have taken to bring the cranes and stones down to this cavern. Never mind that in all his years living in Brackenburgh, he had never once been told about cavern systems like this being in the area, let alone below the Wernstrum's effective headquarters.

"They did finish," Sir Cinaed said rather breathily. "They've created a giant replica of Tislatna's symbol. A circle with chevrons to the four cardinal directions."

"The top looks flat, though. Shouldn't there be a relief or statue of a dragon in the center?"

Cinaed glanced up at him meaningfully. "It isn't decorative, lad. This is the first recreation of the summoning portal since Tislatna's fall."

"Summoning portal?" Jason asked, following Cinaed's trudging pace toward the structure, which he realized was larger than his initial assessment and that a sort of incline had skewed his perspective on it.

Much larger.

Whispering now to him, Cinaed explained, "In some of the oldest legends, it was mentioned that platforms like this were used for the ritual of binding greater dark elves, hobgoblins, to wyverns to create the most devastating dragons. Details and dimensions of those designs have been lost for thousands of years."

Jason shook his head. "I don't understand. Monarch Ilyron didn't need it in Anargen's day. The journal clearly recounts a dragon being summoned there."

Shuddering slightly, the old Knight pointed to it. "This blasphemous monstrosity isn't just for summoning them. It's where people were brought in sacrifice to appease the dragons and from which they demanded adoration and obeisance of those under their rule."

"How do you know all this?"

"Only a handful of people in the Lowlands would, I imagine," he replied, but left it at that.

He's going to answer that one for me later ... High King willing there is a later for us.

If before he had felt an aversion to this place, it deepened to a complete revulsion. Every fiber of his being raged against all that this structure symbolized. All of the wicked perversions and cruelties he had witnessed at the hands of their enemies since being drawn to the Quest paled before this. Had Dorian really gone to such lengths to recreate an abomination that had sealed Tislatna's destruction millennia ago? One that required forbidden knowledge, lost to the ages as well.

A sickening realization overtook him.

Dorian didn't just build this; he's really going to use it.

Try as he might, Jason couldn't bring himself to take another step forward. His heart felt like it was being torn in two. Every step, every twisted scheme and darkling wile had pushed Dorian further and further from the innocent child he'd known. But this was inescapable. It was ...

"Jason?" Cinaed asked. He had walked another ten yards closer to the raised platform that stood more than twenty feet tall before them. Steps ringed upward to its summit.

"Dorian is really gone. I had considered several times that he was beyond redeeming, but this time I feel it in my heart. I have to let him go."

"The High King can redeem any willing to forsake their rebellion," Defender Black replied, but it was clear from the way he said it that the matter wasn't settled.

"But?"

"After walking this far in the darkness, few would be willing to renounce their error and yield."

Several seconds passed between them before sounds of scraping and groans broke the silence. They were coming from atop the platform.

His victim. Dorian is readying his sacrifice.

Suddenly, all the icy regret and reluctance that had frozen Jason in place flash-thawed under the torrent of righteous indignation coursing through the spiritsword in his hand and rising within his own heart. Jason rushed past Cinaed, bounding up the stairs. He didn't slow as he reached the top and raised his spiritsword, ready to rush to the rescue of Dorian's captive.

Jason made it to within a few strides before startling

Dorian, causing him to leap back a half dozen yards away, unnaturally spry and agile. The monster that looked like his brother called out, "You escaped those daft mongrels. You defied my expectations. I anticipated it would take you at least a few minutes longer. I haven't finished preparing my offering."

He edged closer to his victim, bound with steel chains and lying on the stone platform. They were wrapped in a blanket, but it immediately struck Jason that they looked a little small to be Professor Goulder and feminine in contours. Which meant he was intending to use Dr. Jing for the ritual. In turn, that meant Professor Goulder was likely somewhere nearby, his punishment set to be watching the woman he was enamored with die horribly in front of him. Tislatnean symbols created a rectangular area that seemed to indicate where to position the sacrifice, and she was currently half-straddling that space.

Pointing his spiritsword in warning, Jason instructed, "Stand down, Dorian."

The shared look between them was so intense, it felt as though the air would spontaneously ignite. Dorian's eyes darkened. "No. I don't think I will."

"I will end you if you take another step forward."

Cocking his head to the side, almost bird-like, Dorian asked, "Do you still have Father's cap?"

Blinking, Jason suddenly felt the weight of the thing tucked into his armor, its significance galling him. He pulled it out and threw it down in front of Dorian.

Raising his brows, Dorian whistled. He bent down, made a show of dusting off the cap. "Such verve. No wonder Grandpa Wernstrum wanted you so badly as his heir." Clucking his tongue, he applied the cap with a deft tug to his head. "Pity he didn't realize how little spine you really have."

Dorian took a step forward.

"Don't make me do this," Jason instructed, but the plea in his voice was already icing his resolve of moments earlier.

"I can't make you do anything. Isn't that the point of justice? We freely choose to do as we will and we are held accountable for those choices. That's how your king works, is it not?"

"What?" Jason asked, puzzled over Dorian's inquiry.

Dorian strode another step forward.

"Surely you must wonder why I would freely choose to do such awful things."

"Hmph, you're just like the others—Eidolon, Ilyron—you think you can control the darkness, that you can rule the Dark Prince and challenge the High King. You can't!"

A smile curled Dorian's lips, and he took two more bold strides toward his victim. "No fears, I'm not a fool like Eidolon or Ilyron. The Dark Prince's powers aren't something I can both summon and control. What utter silliness. Nor do I foolishly believe that either I or the Dark Prince will ever overpower the High King."

The tip of Jason's sword dropped several inches from level. "What? But why then? Why build all this and defy the High King? If you freely acknowledge he's the rightful sovereign, you could yield to him. The High King turns away no one who comes to him."

From the distance, it wasn't clear whether Dorian rolled his eyes or merely blinked. In either case, he didn't seem impressed with the declaration.

"While that's a lovely gesture, you do not understand. I am painfully aware the darkness has no power to destroy your king. I also have no desire to serve him or his notion of justice. My aims are to slight him, wound him, force him off his mighty throne in those unapproachable Highlands of his."

Jason shook his head. It made no sense, less than no sense.

"How could this," Jason gestured to everything around them, "possibly do that?"

Clasping his hands together, Dorian took three more quick paces toward Dr. Jing. "Ah, but that's just it. 'This' even existing defies his authority, and if I complete the ritual and a dragon takes command of the Rehalcyon Empire in the middle of this war we have lovingly nurtured and cultivated to its present state ..." He uttered a breathy sigh. "All of it will force the High King to intervene. To destroy the Lowlands himself. Which, as I'm sure you know, is not his plan at all."

As much as Jason understood, it was the High King's intent on his day to bring forth a new Lowlands, to establish his reign over lands that were as much renewed as his own servants in the Knights of Light had been.

Dorian seemed to take Jason's silence as a confirmation. "If he must do that which is against his own will, I will have made the divine bleed, and all of the realms must be overturned. All of it must be ended to hide his disgrace!"

With his faceplate down, Dorian no doubt was missing the effect of Jason's mouth hanging open. Many possible impetuses for the wickedness he now observed in his brother had occurred to him. Chief among them the sycophantic allegiance to Monarch Ilyron, though it now appeared plain that Ilyron truly was dead. Unmitigated pride and ambition to lay claim to powers beyond himself had seemed another likely possibility. Even straightforward devotion to the Tislatnean ethos and the Dark Prince. This, however, was something wholly other. A depth of debased thinking that defied explanation, and to refute and correct it seemed as feasible as Jason with his bare hands carrying all of the stones of the Summoning Portal and throwing them into the volcano on what remained of Tislatna.

"You're mad," Jason concluded.

Shrugging, Dorian took another four steps. He was back

before Dr. Jing now. "Am I? I suppose you will just have to watch and see, brother."

"I won't let you harm Dr. Jing!"

Whether he heard Jason or was lucid at all, Dorian did not respond. He simply bent down and began to fuss with the cloth covering his victim. "Just a moment, and this will be over for you," he crooned to her. From a sheath within his vest, he produced a short, black dirk.

"NO!" Jason surged forward, closing the space and with one swift slice sent the dirk flying backward to clatter along the stones several yards away. With another snap, he brought his shield around and slammed it into Dorian, bashing him away.

Dropping down to his knees, he jerked free the remaining cloth and gasped. His heart hammered in his chest and threatened to go still in fits. Lying there, her eyes fluttering open to gaze at him, was Aria.

BEST LAID PLANS

J ason felt tremors threatening to shake his sword and shield from his hands. This couldn't be real. What he was seeing had to be a trick. An illusion.

A little groan came from Aria. She was bruised and her lip bloodied. One eye was partially swollen shut. There was no denying it was her face, though, her lips which parted and with some effort called out, "Jason ..."

"Aria—I—is it ..." he stopped himself and took a step back. This had to be some kind of deception. A doppelgänger or some other sorcery designed to torment him and tear him apart from the inside out.

"Help me ... my leg," she pleaded.

At war with himself, he still snapped to respond, slicing away the fabric wrapped around her legs and the chains there to reveal her lower half, still garbed in the tattered remains of the Jhi'ish dress he had seen her in last. Oh, her leg! He turned away and brought his forearm to his face, the rebrace clinking against the faceplate. A choked cry caught in his throat. One leg was badly broken and poorly bandaged. The other had a burn that needed treatment.

This was impossibly awful, either a cruel trick or, equally bad, it was truly her, and she had been suffering for weeks. Both were enough to turn his bones to water and shatter his resolve.

A sharp clank registered in his ears at the same instant he was spun around by a dark dagger clattering off his pauldron.

Dorian was up again, an obsidian throwing knife forming in his hands from shadows like a sombra. "You always had a habit of spoiling the best surprises."

"What ... have you ... done?" Jason struggled to get out and to get up at the same time.

A deep chuckle echoed off the walls. Dorian sounded wickedly gleeful. "You should thank me for your reunion. And the role you each get to play in the end of all realms. Such esteemed positions!"

Jason spared a glance down at Aria. There was a quiver to her lips, but her eyes, swollen and injured as they were, showed a resolve that was one hundred percent her. A degree of stalwartness that a copy would be hard-pressed to fake.

"Jason, watch out!" she cried hoarsely and tried to lift herself up.

Two more throwing knives plunked off of Jason's armor and he tumbled backward. They'd connected on either side of his armor, seemingly aimed to find a space between his cuirass and his helmet to embed in his neck. Both had failed. More importantly, Aria had tried to save him by taking a knife and sacrificing herself. She was his Aria.

Somehow his wobbling, wavering will recast itself, harder than steel once more. Back on his feet, shield up, he deflected the latest round of knives. He pushed ahead, forcing Dorian back several feet. Jason crouched low to provide Aria as much protection as he could manage.

More black blades sailed across the space and found their end on Jason's shield. Forced into a constant dance of defense, Jason had to stretch to block knives thrown at all angles, each one clearly intended to injure Aria over him. He desperately needed to go on the offensive, before he slipped up and failed to stop one. The trick was doing that without risking harm to Aria. Despair rushed in on him like the incoming tide, submerging him and wearing away at him with each blade's impact.

A gentle pressure on his back almost broke his concentration. He couldn't spare the attention to see if it was Aria or someone else come to attack them. All he could do was maintain his wavering defense.

"Ahem!" Dorian demurred. "Bring her back, you old sloth!"

Defender Black. Of course! He's pulling Aria to safety.

Knowing she was being cared after, Jason surged forward. He was on Dorian in blink and slammed his shield into him again.

Backpedaling, Dorian's shadow knives lengthened into shortswords, and he slammed one strike after another into Jason's shield, battering him back. The instant there was enough space between them, one blade morphed into a knife and zipped across the space.

Jason narrowly managed to intercept it. There were no pulling punches in this fight. Either he definitively stopped Dorian, or he risked Aria and Defender Black being lost.

Blocking the latest knife throw, Jason pivoted around and lunged forward, clipping past Dorian's guard with the shortsword and landing a grazing blow on his shoulder. The reaction was instant and dramatic. Dorian recoiled with a squall and grabbed his smoldering arm.

"Rarrgh!" he growled, the first show of frustration cracking through his façade of indifference and self-assurance. Witty words and snide comments at an end, he charged forward, forming himself a two-handed *zweihänder* from his shadow supply and hammering Jason's sword. It nearly broke Jason's guard. With another stroke, the impact on Jason's shield sent the Knight reeling.

Okay, he's definitely stronger than when we were kids.

The *zweihänder* had to be at least five and half feet long, making it tricky for Jason to close the distance again to attack. With the power Dorian put behind his blow, Jason knew too many hits and he'd be downed for sure.

At least it's less wieldy.

A dark blur crossed Jason's vision and Dorian was on him, swinging the sword like a bat. His shield was just high enough to catch it, but the blow struck so hard Jason went sprawling.

He tried to get to his feet again but only managed to reach his knees before Dorian was there again, crashing his sword down on Jason's hasty block. His shield dropped, and Jason received the pole-like hilt to his faceplate before he could even react.

Rolling on the ground, he struggled to push aside the dizziness after that blow and to get his shield back up for another block. His roll ended short as he bumped into something solid. Glancing up, his eyes widened in shock.

"Argh!" he flung himself to the side as Dorian buried the point of his enormous sword into the stone where Jason had just been. The dark sword pierced through several inches of stone.

Wary, Jason scrambled to his feet while Dorian calmly withdrew his sword. Once more, he looked urbane, though with an added edginess, as if on the verge of a manic episode.

Maybe I could use that to—

Dorian was on him, slamming the blade from over his shoulder into Jason's shield, then cutting back up and around from low to high in the opposite diagonal. He wielded it as deftly as a rapier.

Careening back to the portal's stone top again, Jason eyed the stairs downward warily. If he wasn't careful, he would go down them, and he wasn't sure he'd recover from that fall.

A timely whisper of warning reached him. Half-rolling back to his knees got him out of the way of a slice that scored a long scar into the otherwise polished veneer of the portal. He was already blocking before the next attack fell upon him.

Pushing off against Dorian's stroke, he surged to his feet. He'd been through enough battles with monsters of the Lowlands to let neither the icy oppression they brought with them, nor their overwhelming prowess and dark powers, lead him to despair. The High King was with him, he knew that, and if the High King willed it, none would overcome the fiery implements he wielded.

A scowl graced Dorian's face. Backing up a step, he coolly sized up Jason for his next sortie.

"You don't have to do this, Dory. I won't profess to understand how or why you've forsaken all reason. But I know from experience the High King can shatter any bonds if you are willing to be loosed."

Sneering, Dorian started to answer and then closed his eyes, wincing. He shook his head, and his countenance seemed to darken. It was as if a sudden gust of wind had snuffed out a brief flicker of humanity's candle in him. That there was even a flicker ignited a new flame within Jason: hope for his brother.

Only a faint hope, as Dorian at once renewed his attack. The clang of sword and shield meeting one another echoed in the cavern. They whipped about, a flurry of blocks, parries, strikes, sorties, lunges, and near misses. Dorian was faster and stronger than any minion of the dark Jason had ever faced. He was always there with another attack, pushing, pressing the offensive, and not readily taken off guard. It was impossible to know whether he held back at all. It certainly did not appear that way to Jason, except that if Melania had at her disposal all the dark powers he'd witnessed over the years, then Dorian almost certainly did as well.

Why is he holding back?

He decided to press that point. "You have some ..." he

blocked an attack that staggered him. "Impressive moves. Strange that you aren't using all of the abilities you possess. Melania didn't hesitate to transform into a werebeast to fight me."

Dorian pushed off, breaking from the fight for just an instant. He shook his head as if clearing it. Huffing in a breath, he nodded to Jason. "That is because she was a beast. A beast you murdered."

Jason gaped for an instant. With Aria alive, he had supposed Melania was too somewhere. "No, I—"

"Couldn't have done it? Of course you couldn't. Your nonsensical compassion inhibits you. Not so for me. I have no need for my greater powers, because you are merely an amusement. A tool of catharsis, as your blundering old fool appears to have absconded with my sacrifice."

Impulsively, Jason looked for where Aria and Cinaed were. He caught sight of the pole-like pommel end of Dorian's *zweihänder* smashing into his face too late. The blow landed, glancing off dead center just enough to prevent Jason's neck from being broken from the force.

Instantly, the room went dark, and Jason stumbled backward, collapsing to the ground.

While he struggled to hold onto consciousness, he received a swift kick that sent him bouncing down the stairs of the portal. More than a third of the steps had rolled past before Jason managed to halt himself. Pain radiated from all over his body, and he peered up. Dorian stood a few steps above him, sword raised to deliver a sundering blow.

"Farewell, brother. Whatever final fleeting thoughts bring you peace, know they are meaningless."

The shock in Jason's eyes seemed to please Dorian and bought a precious reprieve as the huge sword in his hands held its place. "Oh, your expression! I can even see it through your ridiculous helmet. You do not know the words of the sword you wield: '... *vanity of vanities! All is vanity. What does man gain by all the toil at which he toils under the sun.*'

"It would appear you should have spent more time learning about the pointless nature of the order you follow and less wooing one of its strumpets."

It was silly, but Jason's cheeks burned. "You take words from their context and make of them your own meanings—ironic that you would call them 'meaningless.' If only you stopped running from the Great King, you would find real meaning, far greater than those you've made for yourself."

Dorian scoffed. "Enough prattling from you, sir knight. You have wasted your final words even as you have wasted your life in the Lowlands." He tensed to deliver the fell stroke thus held.

"Poor Dory," Jason grunted as he fought the aches to lift himself up, arms quivering from the effort. The deepest ache was centered within his chest, but he refused to let that come through in his tone. "You still don't understand."

Jason's words worked. Dorian hesitated fractionally.

Strength surged in Jason's limbs and heat traced up them as he said, "You can't understand that the night is soon ended because you look to the darkened west instead of the burning east."

Eyes narrowed, Dorian was once again obsidian, dark and rigid. With a wicked glower, he struck. The sword didn't connect; Jason's shield was ready and bore the blow, deflecting it.

A shadowy ripple flared across Dorian's form. With a snarl, he swung his sword round as though he would chop Jason like a tree.

Warned by a timely whisper, Jason was already dropping flush to the stairs and then exploding upward, smashing his shield into Dorian's face and sending the younger man reeling.

Before Dorian could react, Jason slashed, grazing across his right upper arm. Dark smoke rolled from the glowing gash.

Unlike foes Jason had faced before, Dorian merely looked down at the wound and scowled. It was a furious, baleful glare that looked nothing like the Dorian he knew from youth. It was twisted, malignant, other.

"You don't understand that I belong to the High King, and whatever happens here today, his day is coming, and with it the unending light we are all longing for. Even you, if you will just turn back from this path long enough to see it!"

Dorian said nothing, raising his sword with a grimace. His wound made it more difficult to wield the massive weapon. For an instant, his gaze flicked to the side.

"Goody, my sacrifice is returned. Walked back to me no less."

Wary of a trick, Jason only flicked a cursory glance in that direction, but sure enough, Aria and Cinaed both stood there, looking ready to tear down the massive altar, the building, and all of Rehalcyon with them.

That Aria was standing meant Defender Black had enacted a healing upon her that was far beyond normal arts. Power from the High King that was rarely granted, and almost certainly a marvelous favor for which Jason would never stop being grateful.

He couldn't allow himself to look at her now. Even thinking about it threatened to choke him with tears and words, so many words that would be lost in kisses and an embrace that he resolved he would never break from.

All of that, all of the joy of having her back and whole, must wait. Because even the moments he had dwelt on it already were too many and endangered that imagined and hungered for reunion ever taking place.

"Give it up, Dory. You can't take all three of us."

As coolly as a man might peruse produce at a market, Dorian looked at each of the three Knights. His eyes suddenly flicked to his arm. It was still smoldering. He made his selection and slung the *zweihänder* around.

Though well out of range, Jason caught the hushed warning and ducked as the sword split apart and the tip slung out tethered to a chain. Over his head, the chilly caress of the blade's nearness sent a shiver down his back.

The blade, now more of a pointed sickle, returned almost instantly to Dorian's waiting hand. Claw-like tips had sprouted from each finger. Attached to the other end of his new weapon's chain was a large hoop with serrated barbs along the edges. This he began to twirl so that it made a keening whistle, unnerving as a siren's call.

"A *kyoketsu shoge,*" Defender Black commented grimly. "They were weapons used in the Middle Era by Zhoulong and Okyn in their wars with Jhi. Be careful of the ring. It's heavy, and most dangerous when thrown."

Across the space, Dorian laughed. "A little ring and rope. Is that the thing you fear?"

Shadows amassed in a great heap, gathering to Dorian, wrapping in layers like papier-mâché. In seconds, he swelled up, becoming something less than human. His legs were goat or perhaps bull-like, but thicker and nimbler. His back arched and became a broad, tough hump like the werebeasts. Armor plated around his body and horns curved up from his head as leathery wings sprouted out the back.

Jason gaped. Whatever remnants of resemblance to the boy he'd known were swallowed up in this monstrous form. Even Dorian's face, though retaining a semblance of humanity, was too disfigured by newly sprouted tusks and more gorilla-like contours to see the faintest hint of his brother. It was the most utterly horrific-looking thing he'd ever seen.

"You did ask for this, didn't you, Jason?" his voice reverberated, deep and raspy as if life's vital current had been dried from it for a thousand years.

"Dory ..." words died on a choked gasp. In all the nightmares he had ever had, lived and dreamed, the sum of them together could not have equaled this.

THE RITUAL

"Courage, dear ones," Defender Black called out. "No foe has ever found themselves the equal of the one on whom the High King's favor rests."

A snort, animalistic and human in one, sounded from the horrific amalgamation beast before them. With a powerful flap of its extended wings, it rose up. Not in total flight, but just high enough that it could not be reached while standing on the ground. Bile rose in Jason's throat as he recalled the similar behavior of Monarch Ilyron when he battled Anargen. True enough, Anargen had overcome the Monarch, but destroying Dorian would be a hollow victory.

"Jason!" Aria called out.

His attention snapping back to the moment, Jason leaped out of the way as the spiked ring shot past where he had stood. It jerked whiplike back to Dorian and began again its whirling. Its distinctive wail resumed.

"Thanks," Jason called out as he scrambled back to his feet. "How do we—"

He had to cut off his sentence as he caught the flicker of motion. Throwing up his shield, the ring ground against it and bounced off. Jason skidded back a foot from the intensity of the strike. It was like being hit by the *zweihänder* but with all the speed and distance of a whip.

"Stop him."

"Spread out," Cinaed instructed. "Get to his sides. I'll take the middle."

Jason watched as Aria edged away from her grandfather, her eyes intent on Dorian.

They're going to destroy him or be destroyed by him.

"There's no winning this battle," the beast called out to him, as though it knew his thoughts. Perhaps it did. One more chilling and deadly power it possessed.

No. The High King may know my thoughts, but creatures of the dark can only read me and my actions.

Running was an option. Retreat from an unwinnable battle was an accepted tactic.

Whoa, where did that come from?

Jason looked at the monster and saw that it was shifting its position as it moved, though its eyes remained fixed on him.

It may not read my thoughts, but it can certainly offer ones that are destructive.

Which meant he had to be all the more careful to keep his attention on the High King's guidance and not the wicked thing before him. Guidance he desperately needed as he reached the positioning specified by Cinaed. At least this form seemed to move more slowly.

The whistling shifted, and Jason blocked. Bouncing off, the ring retracted and then shot out lower, aiming for his shin.

From this, he leaped back. But the ring was already shooting out again for his chest.

Jason fumbled to block and was spun around by the blow. His back was exposed, and he braced himself for the shattering sting of its next strike.

In its place came a shrill clang. He spun around to see Aria jumping higher than was within her normal bounds of ability and taking a swipe at the creature's lower leg. The shrill clang was the ring spun on the chain being used as a kind of moving shield. Not very effective against arrows and other projectiles, or even their swords if the beast landed.

From the height the beast hovered at, it sufficed to frustrate their efforts.

At least until the next moment when Defender Black joined Aria, leaping still higher and giving a sundering swipe. Their monster foe managed to deflect most of the attack with his sickle, but the attack had come unexpectedly for it as well, and its left wing had been clipped. Smoke streamed from where its taut, leathery expanse was now tattered.

In a blink, the monster was back to warding off Aria, this time hacking with the sickle and nicking her pauldron. A tit-for-tat strike. Almost a blur, it was back to strike at Defender Black with its ring.

Back and forth, the battle continued. Roughly balanced. It couldn't remain so, even as the combatants moved around each other, zipping and striking faster than was believable, almost too fast to watch. The High King's favor was on Aria and Cinaed, but they weren't overtaking the creature any more than it was them. Could it go on this way indefinitely? It looked as though the beast was gradually losing height from the minor injuries incurred on its wings, but Cinaed and Aria were battered as well.

As if waking from a dream, Jason realized he had just been standing there watching.

What am I doing!?

Nothing. Absolutely nothing, because if he joined in, they might destroy the beast and any hope of rescuing Dorian.

Jason stared at the thing as its ring caught Aria's forearm, and she spiraled to the ground with a moan. He couldn't stand by. He took a step forward. It felt like his legs were boulders he was having to tumble. Images of Dorian as a kid flared before his mind's eye. Another step. Now a memory of him standing between Dorian and a school bully. One more step, and Jason gasped. He recalled the night he had slipped out of their shared bedroom and into the night, intent on never returning. Except now he saw as if from a still frame image that Dorian wasn't passively watching; his hand was raised as if he wanted to cry out and beg Jason not to go.

Eyes shut, Jason shuddered. He had abandoned his brother once; how could he do that again? Didn't he need to help? All he had to do was let the fight play out. Then he could go to him, reason with him. They could be brothers again.

The shrill cry of the ring terminated in heavy clang and a muted grunt. Cinaed was on the ground. He'd gotten hit hard and was completely vulnerable. Jason could see it, knew before it even happened that in a moment the beast would swoop down and land on his back and jab its sickle into him. With a backward swing of its ring, it could keep Aria from coming to her grandfather's rescue. Cinaed would die!

Kind, fatherly, compassionate Cinaed, struck down by that horrid creature. The truest brother-in-arms he could ever have, indeed, the truest brother he had ever had. Forged into fraternity by a blood bond deeper than any with which Wernstrum ancestry bound him to Dorian.

Suddenly, all the polite musings of how he could reconcile with Dorian evaporated like midnight mists in the dawn's light. Dorian would not, could not be reached with reason. This beast wasn't keeping him captive; it was Dorian. As much as it hurt, as much as he would never get past it, Dorian, the Dorian he knew, was gone. But Cinaed Black, who was his brother by oath and more a father or grandfather to him than any Wernstrum kin had been, wasn't yet.

All of the stony resistance of his legs shattered, and Jason was a bolt, streaking across the space. The monster had just landed on Cinaed's back and raised its sickle. Jason leaped.

The creature turned its head toward him.

Too late. Jason hammered his spiritsword down directly

into its chest and kicked off, jerking it back out. Landing, he crouched in front of Cinaed, his shield raised in a guard.

For a moment, the beast just staggered backward, looking at the gleaming wound on its chest and the smoke rolling off it. Disbelief seemed discernible on its inhuman face.

Aria was by his side and then down tending to her grandfather. Every muscle in Jason's body was tensed, ready for the creature's inevitable counterattack.

It did not come.

What did happen was as baffling as it was blinding. A sudden flare of flames erupted from the wound as dark fumes spewed from it. The fumes, however, twisted and swirled in ways completely unnatural. It was as though they were alive.

More and more, the sentient smoke poured out and coalesced into a cloud several feet back from Dorian. When the smoke stopped, Dorian let out a choked gargle and collapsed to the ground. All of the shadowy layers streamed off him, and he was just a man again.

He raised a hand toward the smoke, his voice strained. "No. No. I can still do this," he insisted to the black miasma.

The sentient smoke roiled and arced up high, almost as if it were drifting away like chimney smoke. Except it didn't dissipate, and it stopped once it reached a certain height, forming a dark cloud over Dorian.

"Your methods are too brutish. I will find a way. I always find a way," Dorian protested, clearly speaking to it.

A flicker of something seemed to move within the mass of dark air, and Jason saw Dorian wince. For the first time in a long time, a flicker of something akin to the boy he knew passed over Dorian's face. It was the expression he had been most accustomed to in their childhood: fear.

"Very well," Dorian stated, his voice as dead calm as a windless sea. He stalked over to a patch of the summoning portal's stone top that had been damaged during the beast fight and retrieved a particularly sharp-looking shard of stone. He stalked to the center of the platform.

Along the way, he had begun muttering something. It was hard for Jason to hear and even harder to understand. It wasn't in Ecthelish, Rehalcy, or Zilnian—the languages he knew best.

Which means it might be Tislatnean. What is he up to?

Standing there, Dorian began chanting loud enough that Jason could tell distinctly that it was Tislatnean, even if he couldn't understand what was being said. He looked over at Aria, who had gotten Cinaed upright. "Do you know what he's doing?"

She shook her head. Even so, her eyes were wide and filled with worry.

A tremor ran through the ground. Punctuated and brief.

A foreshock? What is Dorian—

The tremor returned and become a steady shudder in the ground. Dorian grew louder, and the shaking with it. Behind Dorian, it looked like a part of the cave had collapsed, with jagged stalactites breaking away from a huge grey slab of stone that had fallen off the wall. At least until that slab rose behind Dorian. Ochre eyes tinged with red at the edges. A stream of sulfurous steam rushed from its nostrils as the wyvern stretched to its full height behind him.

It wasn't like the wyverns described to Jason and depicted in art he'd seen. Long, serpent-like, its wings were mere flaps between its strong forelimbs. It looked just as comfortable walking crocodile-like as a quadruped as it did reared up the way it was presently. With those small wings, it reminded him of the sand scourge he'd faced in Zilnen's Ziljafu Desert. The stalactites he'd identified before were actually bony barbs that ran down the length of its spine. It had whiskers like a catfish, and its color seemed to shift slightly as it worked out the kinks in its taut muscles. If he understood rightly, this was an eastern wyvern.

Even if different, Jason understood now what Dorian was trying to do. This was the ritual for summoning a dragon! He was going to fuse a goblin with the wyvern.

Except Aria is over here. Does he really still believe he can sacrifice her after we bested him in combat?

"Oh no," Aria said suddenly, holding her hand over her mouth. "Jason, you have to stop him!"

It was only then that he noticed the makeshift dagger was raised to Dorian's throat.

"Dorian! No!" Jason shouted. He tried to scramble over to his brother.

Behind Dorian, the wyvern uttered a bloodcurdling screech, loud and high enough to make Jason stop and grab to protect his ears. Did eastern wyvern screech like sirens instead of using fire?

"Dorian," he called again over the horrible sound. "Don't do it!" Jason's heart hammered in his chest. He had to fight through it, get to his little brother.

He took one step and then another. Every time he did, the wyvern intensified its cry. It felt as if he took another step, the sound of it alone would shred him to pieces, and Dorian was standing, unarmored, in the midst of it all. If it didn't stop the screech, it could kill his brother.

"Dory!"

For an instant, Dorian broke from his Tislatnean chanting and locked eyes with Jason. They were cold, dark eyes. Empty. "I told you, brother. It is all meaningless."

"Please, don't!"

With vicious energy, Dorian sliced across his own throat and dropped to his knees. He gurgled something in Tislatnean and fell flat on the central stone.

The wyvern ceased its screeching and reared back. Above, the cloud streamed down to the wyvern, filtering in through its nose and mouth. Renewed quakes shook the cavern, and dark tendrils of shadow reached out like hands from the depths of the grotto to enshroud the wyvern, which now twitched and spasmed, releasing little growls and grunts and squeals.

Jason backed away, his shield raised, but completely uncertain about what to do. He had failed. Dorian was dead, and this thing, this terrifying creature of myth and legend, would wreak its havoc on the Lowlands.

DESOLATION

"L ad, back away!" Cinaed instructed, yelling over the commotion.

Jason half-turned back to see his mentor on his feet again. Aria still hovered by him, her hands ready to reach out and steady him if needed. Tears streamed down his face, but he knew they could not see that. If he tried to speak, it would betray how broken he was in that moment. Broken over a brother who had died a monster in the service of a darkness that would destroy so much and cruelly end so many lives.

"The battle isn't finished," Cinaed urged. He hobbled a bit as he came to Jason and physically pulled him backward. "Not till we're kneeling before the High King in his land."

The image broke through Jason's melancholy enough that he was able to push against his moroseness. Straining, shoving it aside for the moment. He didn't know if he would be able to hold himself together when it finally forced its way back to the forefront. For now, however, he was able to snuffle and blink away the sorrow that had begun to strangle him.

"What do we do, sir?" he asked pitifully, sounding like he was still a doe-eyed child. He gritted his teeth. No, he couldn't think about childhood. Not with Dorian's loss so fresh.

There was silence.

Exchanging a glance with Aria, whose face, streaked with dirt and her own tears, was just as tight with concern. "Grandfather," she pressed, gently.

Silence reigned for a moment more, at least between them.

At their backs, the sounds of the wyvern's transformation had begun to echo with the deep, gravelly intonations. Sounds of a frightened animal fading into the grim triumph of a monster.

"Grandfather!" Aria tried again.

He placed a hand on her shoulder and sucked in a sharp breath. "Stand firm, children. Remember the stories. What have I taught you?"

Aria gaped. "I, uh, well, so much ..."

Jason looked over at the writhing wyvern as the shadows began to solidify into its new form. Much thickened with now prominent wings, but still the serpentine body of before, arrayed with dark green plumage, it looked eerily like the image embossed on the central platform they stood upon. A true Tislatnean dragon.

Frowning, Jason took up the question Cinaed posed. "You taught us how to stand firm. No matter how dark it gets, those who serve the High King can overcome by his strength."

"Even slaying dragons," Aria mused, reaching out and placing her hand on his arm for the first time since discovering she was alive. Both what she said and the cascade of emotion her touch drew sent an electric current throughout every cell of Jason's body.

He reached out and took her hand in his, holding on, intent on never letting go. "Even slaying dragons," he agreed.

Cinaed's face lit up. "Aye, my children. And so we shall."

Some of the brightness diminished in Aria's eyes, which had just been locked on Jason's. "How, Grandfather? I always took Anargen's account to be condensed. That the battle was harder, more complex than he related in his journal."

The old Knight bounced his brows thoughtfully. "That wouldn't be like Anargen. All the same, this will be a different struggle." He gestured to the dragon that seemed to be settling. The shadows having wrought their miserable creation in full.

"The goblin affixed to this wyvern was a hobgoblin, as much superior to the goblin of Anargen's dragon foe as a high elf like Vif is superior to lesser elves."

"So, it's bigger and tougher," Jason said as though it didn't matter. "Big deal," his voice hitched at the end.

"You have no conception, mortal," the dragon boomed from across the cavern. Its eyes slid open, changed from the dragon's ochre to black, edged with a wretched jade. It maintained its chromataphoric talent for changing the coloration of its scales. Rippling through shades of grey to a deep slate and then to black, before settling on something close to it with streaks of the same fetid green hue. Its very coloration spoke a warning of poison and danger that instinctually unnerved Jason.

"If you bow before me now, then I will make your deaths the swiftest of all those in the Lowlands," it offered. It landed at the other end of the summoning platform and dominated the space. In fact, the cavern seemed to scarcely contain it. Over fifty feet tall when reared on its hind legs, its wings encircled half the platform.

It was the still form of Dorian, however, at the platform's center that drained all of the wonder and trepidation out of Jason. Striding forward, he drew his spiritsword, feeling its heat racing the length of the blade in such a rush that the wind off it ruffled the tunic he wore over his armor.

This dragon, like all the lesser emissaries of darkness they had faced, emanated a sort of frigid power that was meant to bow their backs and ice their resolve. No doubt the dragon's was the most potent he had ever experienced. Jason refused to allow it to embrittle his confidence in the High King. Live or die now, he would do it fully given over to the High King following his oaths.

"What boldness from one with such brokenness belying him," the dragon hissed. Waving its hands around, a dark void appeared, and from it slid shadows that twisted and arced through its arms and between its clawed hands. Grabbing hold, it held forth the now solidified conjuration of its design. A massive black chain, big enough to bind a building.

They can use Sombra-like shadow arts. That's great.

The dragon's forked tongue shot out like a snake and groaned with pleasure. "Ah, your fear, I taste it beneath your cocksure veneer. Is it because you recognize these chains from when I instructed your brother to hang you by them in the dungeon above? How did it feel to dangle there helplessly, knowing that your brother was pleased to see you suffer and die such a horrible death?"

Jason's grip tightened on the spiritsword. He sensed Aria coming up to his side, and he strode forward, toward the dragon. He pointed at it accusatorially. "You made him do that!"

A chuckle rumbled from the dragon. "My kind do not make any mortal do anything. Your kind is merely malleable to our desires. Your brother was, oh, so much so."

Aria grabbed his wrist, holding fast. Under her breath, she pleaded, "Don't. He's trying to separate you to pick you off first."

Jason closed his eyes and gave a curt nod. "Together," he mouthed to her. Cinaed was also in line of sight to see his proposition, though the older Knight was watching the dragon astutely. There was no doubting that the crafty Cinaed knew exactly what Jason had said.

To the dragon, Jason bellowed out, "It's good that you recognize that chain means something to me. It does as it did in that dungeon. The High King is the breaker of my chains!"

"We shall see!" the dragon bellowed, so loud that bits of rock from the ceiling shook free and crashed down.

Arching its back, the dragon snapped forward and

unleashed a torrent of flames that looked wide enough to cover the whole summoning platform. Jason skidded to a halt and dropped behind his shield. Next to him, Cinaed did the same, and Aria crouched behind the overlap of each. All around the dragon's green flames blazed, scorching the stone of the platform.

Jason kept his eyes shut, focused on pushing against the enormous pressure of the flames and trusting the High King to hold back the dragon's deadly attack. It seemed to go on without end as marble around them fissured and cracked with super-heated gas blasting up from it. Around them, some of the lower layers of the platform began to melt. How long it truly lasted, Jason could only guess, but at its end, he, Aria, and Cinaed were on a sort of island while all around them was a blackened, ruined mess.

Not wasting a moment, they all broke off and ran in separate directions. Aria took the left, Cinaed the right, and Jason charged down the middle. Their dragon enemy snarled and jumped onto the platform, slinging the chain it had conjured around and slamming it onto the platform. Jason dodged one strike and almost lost his footing. The links were over two and a half feet high, and the impact of the chain on the already damaged surface fractured a line of stone everywhere it struck. He imagined this was how a rat might feel being chased by a human.

Closing the distance, Jason halted sharply. Stone exploded in a shower of tiny shards that pelted his shield as the chain crashed down in front of him. Bringing his burning blade down on it, he hacked through the nearest black links and jumped across the crater in the platform it had left. Cinaed was almost to the beast's feet, as was Aria. Her boldness twisted Jason's heart with concern. She had less armor than they did without her helmet, but at least Cinaed had brought a second spiritsword. It was akin to hers, if more a saber than a rapier.

Roaring with disdain, the dragon bunched its powerful legs and kicked the summoning platform, its enormous wings flapping with forceful strokes that sent strong gusts of air down on them. It put the dragon up higher than expected, but it was only a matter of time. There wasn't sufficient room in this cave for it to fly freely with its size.

No sooner had Jason deduced this than the dragon seemed to also. With one powerful flap, it corkscrewed and latched onto the ceiling, climbing along it like a lizard with comparable speed even for its size. Jason watched with growing horror as it raced toward the hole that had ushered them into the deeper cavern.

Defender Black didn't hesitate, bounding back toward where they'd come in, his *Evaggelion Eirene* boots carrying him like an eagle past them. "Grandfather!" Aria called after him, but he didn't slow or hesitate in the slightest.

UPON THE HEIGHTS

Aria came up alongside Jason, her expression unabashedly pleading. "We have to keep the dragon from getting out. While I was held prisoner, I heard your brother telling one of his werebeasts that once the dragon is free of the grotto, it's going to destroy Brackenburgh. Though I don't understand why. Brackenburgh is firmly in Rehalcyon's grip."

Jason thought for a moment. "'Everything is meaningless.'"

"Pardon?"

"My brother said that this is all meaningless. It's not about the war. Rehalcyon is just as worthless to the dragon and Dorian's forces as any Alliance nation. The goal is to just destroy as much as they can in hopes that it forces the High King to wipe away the Lowlands."

"That's insane," Aria said and gave a shudder. "Even in Anargen's day, the evil was not so ... total."

He shook his head. "I read the remainder of the account. I think that the Dark Prince's servants have always had these aims. In past eras, they found servants who were greedy and ambitious and used them to their own ends, but Dorian ... he actually was a true follower. They didn't need to deceive him. He was so twisted he actually wanted to end everything."

Aria placed a gentle hand on his arm. He placed his on hers and squeezed it. There were no words for how badly he needed her that moment.

Quiet as a whisper, she reminded him, "I know it hurts, but we have to keep moving."

Jason let out a heavy, shuddering sigh and nodded. This wasn't the time. All of the pain needed to be faced and sorted out later. Right now, they had to push forward and stop the dragon before it could unleash its terror across the Lowlands.

Rushing over the uneven stone floor, Jason surged past Aria just before the ladder and leaped onto it, climbing the rungs as fast as his arms could take them. At the top, he found Defender Black, hands on his knees, drawing in deep breaths.

Above them, he could see the dragon working at clawing its way through the stone. Jason started to call out to Cinaed, but the words didn't have a chance to make it from his lips before the older Knight sprinted forward and jumped out onto the dragon's long, twitching tail.

Horrified the beast would notice, Jason called out, "Hey, duck-zard, what's the rush to leave? I thought you were going to grind my bones to powder or some other monster-boasting nonsense!"

The dragon halted. Twisting its long neck so that its upside-down head faced Jason. Its jaws opened wide, and a stream of fire shot out at Jason.

Jason dropped to a crouch, throwing up a hasty block. The force of it pushed him backward. If the attack hadn't been such a short burst, he would've been knocked over.

A close call.

Back upright in an instant, he was ready to antagonize the fiend again when he saw that the sickly colored flames had damaged the ladder, which Aria was still climbing!

Scrambling over, he grabbed hold of the last viable rung just before it snapped free from the rock face. "Ungh!" Jason now held the full weight of the ladder plus Aria.

"Ah! What's happening up there?" Aria called. She was three-quarters of the way up.

"Oh, the usual, angry dragon damaging the ladders again."

He tried to project ease, but couldn't hide his grunts of effort. It felt like his arms wanted to snap off. "Thought I'd lend a hand, make sure you make it up safely."

"Mmm, I appreciate it," she called back, clamoring up the ladder at a pace that would get her to the end faster but made the whole thing wobble in his hands.

"Ah, take ... your ... time," he called.

His body started sliding forward, jarred from its stable place by the movement. Jason tried to lift the ladder more firmly to regain his placement, but it was no good.

"Actually, maybe ... definitely ... hurry."

Each finger trembled and began losing its grip even as he found himself moving toward the point where he'd have to let go or tumble over himself.

No, I just got her back. I can't lose her now.

As much as he longed for his body to comply, he felt his arms giving. With a groan, the rung slipped away from his left hand.

Aria's face peeked over the edge, panic highlighting it as the ladder swung. "Jump!" he begged her.

She did, the force of which tore the ladder from his other hand and sent it clattering down to the stone below. The instant it left his hands, he grabbed hold of her shoulders, anchoring her to the floor until she swung her legs over the edge and got away from the depths.

Jason rolled over, his arms rubbery and aching. An instant later, she wrapped her arms around him, and he found the will to fold his around her in a fierce embrace.

The moment was interrupted by the sound of rocks falling away, and Jason looked up to see that the dragon had clawed a hole through the stone and concrete and was tearing its way upward.

Aria sprang to her feet, towing him up an instant later. "Which way do we go to get out of here?"

"Take the tunnel, we have to make it above ground before that thing causes the whole place to collapse!"

"Grandfather?"

Jason looked up and spotted Defender Black, still hanging onto the tail, picking his way up along the ridge of the dragon's back. He hugged tightly to it as the dragon shimmied through the tunnel it was boring.

"He's on the dragon," he answered reluctantly, unsure how she would take it. Neither of them could get on it from this distance to help, even with an incredibly boosted leap.

She thought about it for a moment and then said, "The dragon will probably climb a building to get an easier takeoff for flying. Does this building go up very high?"

Wincing, he nodded. "Yeah, this is the Ministry of Justice building."

A brief flicker of something passed over her face that she pushed aside quickly. "Good, we'll take the elevator up to the top. When the creature climbs up, we can attack it."

"Right," he said, taking her hand and pulling her down the hallway he and Cinaed had traversed to reach here.

Taking the elevator proved interminable, but he didn't break the silence while it went up. He held Aria to him. Her head resting against his chest was the most delightful and bolstering thing he could have in that moment. Silently, he thanked the High King over and over that she was alive. That he'd rescued her, even if briefly. He treaded over every thought he could not afford to say aloud, because there was a strong chance that uttering them would break him.

When the elevator reached the top of the building, he took her hand and led her up a final flight of stairs and another ladder, then out onto the roof. Darkness greeted them; Jason had forgotten it was deep in the night. Rain fell steadily, running off the sides of the building. Peering down over the edge, Jason stumbled back, pushing Aria toward the roof exit. "Run!"

That moment, the dragon's head peered over the edge of the building. Its long snout twitched with an animal pleasure as it took in the sight of Jason sprawled on the roof.

"Your tenacity will earn your death," the dragon commented with glee. Its jaws opened wide and it snapped its neck around, chomping at Jason.

He ducked and rolled out of the way, fighting to keep on his feet and to get his spiritsword drawn.

The monster's snout crashed into his shield that he held in block, battering him backward into the stairway door housing. He slid down the concrete, knowing it was cracked and perhaps his shoulder with it.

"Ahh!"

From the side, Aria came rushing. Spiritsword held high, she swung it round and scored a long slice on the dragon's jaw, severing one whisker-like tendril from its face.

The dragon reared back, shaking its head like a dog that poked its snout into a nest of bees. Before it could right itself and go for her, Jason had his spiritsword drawn and in two strides was alongside the opposite side of its head, striking it with another blow that left a burning streak on that side of its jaw.

"Impudent insects," it growled. "You think you've taken the high ground, no doubt. Your kind are always raising yourselves up for a devastating fall."

The dragon reared back and blasted the Ministry of Justice building floors closest to it with a torrent of fire. Glass windows across the building's face exploded. A rush of steam rose off the rain droplets flash-evaporated.

Jason watched, eyes wide. If they didn't stop the dragon quickly, it would render the stone and steel of the building molten on the floors it attacked, and the whole building would collapse.

There was no escaping down the building's stairs or elevator now, and the next closest building in height was still more than forty feet lower at its rooftop than where they currently stood. They were trapped, waiting to plummet to their deaths with the ruined rubble of the Ministry of Justice.

"We have to jump," Aria said to him over the din of the foul flames erupting from the dragon's mouth.

He took her hands in his and stared down at them. "We can't survive that fall, not unless the High King grants us to drop like leaves. And we can't use our spiritswords to rake down the building the way Anargen did in Stormridge. The dragon would never let us get past it that way."

She shook their joined hands. "No, no. I mean, we have to jump on the dragon. It's the only way."

He didn't bother telling her that it would be insane to jump off the building onto the dragon's jagged back. Nor that once they were on it, if they tried to slay the dragon and succeeded, they would be going down with it. In the end, though, she may have been fully aware of those facts.

"On three?"

"On three."

"One," they said in unison.

"Two."

"Three!"

Hand in hand, they ran to the edge of the building, ready to leap off of it onto the dragon's back. Jason held them back just before they did, because he caught sight of Cinaed. The old storyteller had climbed unnoticed all the way onto the monster's shoulder blades. He shot a look at them both that was hard to discern through the rain and smoke of the burning building. It looked bittersweet.

Balancing precariously on his position, he drew his spiritsword and, with both hands gripping the hilt, raised it over his head and jammed it down hard into the back of their foe's neck. The sword slowly carved through the rock-hard scales of the dragon. It immediately reared its head back, yowling in pain. Its muscular forearms swatted back futilely, unable to reach the spot Defender Black had chosen.

Jason couldn't breathe as he watched the old man dangling from its back, using its osteoderms to hang on. How long could he manage that?

Looking down, Jason saw that the dragon's long belly was exposed now. This was it. They had to try Anargen's technique of planting the sword and allowing it to burn through material, gradually slowing on the way down. Even if it was pure insanity.

He looked over at Aria and saw in her eyes the same conclusion. Each drew their spiritswords and called to each other, "Now!"

They jumped off the rooftop.

For a sickening moment, they were just falling, with nothing under them but the pavement below. They dropped and dropped and ... WHAM.

Two heartbeats separated freefall and the sudden jarring impact against the rain-slicked underbelly of the abominable creature. The impact almost knocked the breath out of Jason. The monster's long abdomen was so much harder than he'd anticipated. And the rain, it was so slick, he began sliding toward the curvature in its torso that was angled perpendicular to the street below.

Fumbling for a hold, he found no purchase for his fingers and jerked back his sword arm as far as possible and slammed it down. It struck and initially felt as if it might deflect off, but it couldn't. It absolutely couldn't, or they were both finished.

Please, Great King, help us!

The monster twitched back forward, bringing its belly closer to the building, and Jason suddenly had the crumbling façade of it to kick off against, applying the pressure to drive the point of the burning blade deeper into the monster.

As soon as the blade began to burn through, the dragon once again contorted, this time recognizing their attack. Fortunately, it couldn't reach them with its arms to pick them off and toss them like dolls. They just needed a moment longer; he was sure the blade would sink in enough and begin to shear through the resistive scaly carapace any second.

Their dragon foe twisted its serpentine body changing the calculus of their distance from its grasp. A clawed hand raised over both him and Aria to rake them off.

There was a shout, and Jason's eyes flicked upward. Defender Black had twisted around and, with the dragon's new posture, found means to jam his spiritsword into the space between the serpentine neck and jaw.

Another squall from the dragon echoed into the night. Suddenly, Jason was smacked forward into the beast, sinking the fiery edges of the spiritsword in to the crossguard. He felt himself beginning to slide down. Fast, too fast for his liking, the spiritsword sliced the dragon's torso and abdomen, careening toward the long stretch of its tail, which quivered and coiled. Sparing a glance to the side, he saw that Aria, too, was slipping down the enormous fiend. The plan was working!

Once more, the dragon became aware of them, but its attention was short-lived, because Cinaed was jerking his blade around, threatening to go under its chin and pierce its throat.

The monster was a good eighty to one hundred feet in length from snout to tail. Maybe they could try to jump back onto the Justice building? If they handled the landings well, they could try for an awning maybe fifteen feet above the pavement at street level after, but it was an awful risk.

The dragon's grip on the building faltered, and it dropped, claws thick as a man's arm grinding through the flame-damaged stone. Not to mention the pain of what Jason and Aria were doing had to be inescapable for it.

"We have to jump off," Aria shouted to Jason.

He shook his head. "Not yet, we won't get another chance at this."

"We won't need it, look at the dragon!"

Looking upward, he saw it. Only one of its clawed hands fought to find a new handhold. The other gripped at the dual lines of fire billowing smoke from its interior. Pain wasn't the word for what it experienced. They had brought agony to the beast, an anguish beyond its capacity to resist.

More than that, they had made certain it couldn't bother with Defender Black, who jerked back his spiritsword, gripped a whisker, and swung under the beast's chin and struck, shearing a fiery gash across its throat that instantly blazed with such intensity that the crevices between its scales glowed pale yellow.

Jason choked back a whoop of vindication; the poetry of its throat being slit after what happened with Dorian was not lost on him.

"Jason!" Aria yelled, and he saw the ground rushing to meet them. With a nod, he flung himself off the dragon's tail, aiming for the awning. He reached out his hand toward Aria, snagging her wrist and jerked her to him. Enfolding her in his arms, he spun so that his back was to the awning and closed his eyes. That way, his last sight in the Lowlands would be her face.

EVIL UNMASKED

A gasp burst from his lips as his back struck the awning and tore through the fabric and frame. He slammed into the concrete, the weight of Aria's body on his, crushing the last air from his lungs and at least bruising a few ribs.

Jason lay there, gasping as he watched the dragon's body contorting and crumpling on itself as it crashed thunderously downward. Its head and neck smashed into another building, busting through the brickwork as it tore through the buttresses and ribbed vaults of the opposing building. Everything in him longed to call out on Cinaed's behalf, but he couldn't speak, couldn't breathe, only lay there choking as an entire armada of aches and pains assaulted his mind at once.

He shut his eyes, struggling to breathe, the burning desire for air outstripping all other things at that moment. A weight eased off his chest, and suddenly he felt himself being jerked forward. Cool rain pelted his face as his faceplate was slid out of the way.

Blinking, bleary-eyed and wondering if he would ever breathe again, he saw Aria staring at him, eyes shimmering with panic, her soft hand caressing his cheek. She was okay, shielded from the fall as he'd hoped.

"Stay with me," she insisted.

With a faint shudder, he sucked in his first breath. It was the sweetest taste in the Lowlands, even tainted with the acrid smokiness of the dragon and burning building.

"You got it ... cinnamon cake," he wheezed and instantly regretted a chuckle.

Aria sighed and brushed his lips with a kiss. "When this is past, we need to rethink our pet names."

More seriously, she asked, "Can you get up?"

"If I absolutely have to," he said through gritted teeth.

Her response was to hoist him forward, throwing all her weight into pulling him up.

He helped as much as his battered body would allow. That's when he felt it, the shuddering beneath them followed seconds later by the sounds of groans: iron surrendering its strength, stone rendered insubstantial and buckling. A quick glance up confirmed that the Justice building was going to collapse any minute.

"We have to ..." Between his battered chest and his breathing having not yet steadied, it hurt too much to finish.

"Get away from here," Aria finished for him. "I know. Be careful stepping over the dragon's tail. It has some barbs, but I think even the feathers have sharp cutting edges."

"Of course they do," he groaned.

Relying heavily on Aria, he staggered, hobbled, struggled down the street, away from the downed dragon's body and the damaged building's area of potential collapse. The instant they reached what seemed to be a safe distance, Aria leaned him up against a building he didn't recognize and turned to charge back toward the danger.

"Wait!" he called, coughing as he did. Which hurt. A lot.

Squeezing his hand, Aria said, "I can't. I have to get back to Grandfather. He needs me!"

Careful to control how his chest moved, Jason pleaded. "Don't go without me. I'll help."

She shot him a look that said, "Yeah? How?"

"You can heal me, like Defender Black ..." he winced. Too

fast, too much talking. He forced out the words anyway. "Did for you."

Aria looked miserable. "I can't. The High King granted that to Grandfather. He has never healed like that through me."

"You could try?"

"Even if I could, there isn't time," she insisted.

"Rraarrrgh!"

At her back, there was a sudden shifting. The dragon's limp form shuddered and began to rise. As its huge form pulled free of the building it was partially draped through, something fell from off it.

Not something, someone.

A little yelp of surprise and horror escaped Aria's lips, and she made it two steps toward her grandfather before a spray of bricks and glass crashed down in front of her. More came after it, forcing her back to Jason's side.

A tremulous arm of the dragon pulled free of where it had been pinned, and Jason watched raptly as the convulsing beast flopped down onto the stones, doubled over at its serpent-like middle. Rain ran down the grooves between its hard skin, and smoke continued to roll off it. It looked like entire portions of its body were now molten magma, and its lips, only feet away, twitched, revealing the abundance of its serrated fangs.

Slowly, its jaws opened wide, so wide as to swallow a man whole. All the while, its vicious black eyes were on them. A terrible gurgled growl rose in its throat, and Jason readied his shield to block the fiery blast he expected to come. Assuming he could block it being so close and unsteady.

Smoke, black and thick, exploded from its throat and twisted up in a tornadic swirl, crackling with a wicked energy. This was no simple cloud. Jason sensed it in his very core and gripped his spiritsword, the touch of which was so hot from indignation that it felt as if even the hilt would explode into flames.

In less than a minute, the dark spiral condensed into a figure and dropped to the ground. For the briefest moment, it was resplendent. Grey-skinned and human-like, but more handsome in countenance than any man of the Lowlands could hope to be. Every feature sharp and balanced, its hair finer than spider silk but thick as a bear's pelt. When its onyx eyes found Jason and Aria, its lips pulled back in a snarl, revealing itself as the most horrid and beastly monster Jason had ever seen. His brother Dorian's werebeast form, as hideous and malignant as it had appeared, was nothing like this. It defied words.

It defied more than words, though. The heat he had felt in the spiritsword a moment ago was only the faintest taste of the fury coursing from the righteous blade. This being, towering over them at more than eight feet, was the hobgoblin which pulled the puppet strings of the dragon, Dorian, of perhaps the entire Lowlands Total War. Blood of thousands had been spilled at its behest, and it would tear down every good thing in all realms if allowed. Pure rebellion against the High King. Not misguided, misled, or blinded. This was evil in its undiluted, unrestrained form.

Jason took a step forward, no longer caring how he hurt, how his body raged with its complaints. When he raised his spiritsword, it was all he felt, all he knew. The fire of the High King's fury was his own.

"You have caused much trouble," the hobgoblin commented, almost absently. "It will take time to trace out a suitable new vessel. Both human and wyvern," it added with a wicked smile.

Aria rejoined Jason, pointing her spiritsword at the embodiment of all they strove against. "You will have no further hosts. You will not leave this country, this town, this street. Your end is tonight."

It cocked its head and then burst into laughter. Mocking, coarse. A string of insults filled with vulgarity and blasphemies unrepeatable spewed from its mouth as shadows coalesced into an enormous glaive in its clawed hand. The weapon was longer than Aria was tall, but the dark elf wielded it with one hand. In the other, it formed a short sword nearly as pointed and straight as an ice pick.

"First, I will roast your would-be-husband to ashes, just as his brother has been, and smear them over you. And when you die, phosphila," it said, "I will bring your bloodied corpse to your grandfather so that in those final agonized moments as he bids farewell to his life, he may do so in utter, complete, perfect despair." The last it said with pop of its lips that reeked of blood and decay. The grave's pungent stench emanated from every inch of it.

Out of the corner of his eye, Jason saw Aria's hands trembling, but not with fear or infirmity. In her expression was rage, raw and unfettered, such as he had never seen in her. Exploding like a cannon shot, she careened at the hobgoblin, fire from her sword streaking after her.

She slammed her spiritsword down on the glaive, battering it aside, and lunged.

The hobgoblin was startled, but recovered in time to avoid the lunge and stabbed with its pick.

Aria shoulder rolled to avoid the attack and whipped her spiritsword around and smacked aside the pick. Wheeling aside from its next strike, she scored a grazing blow on the hobgoblin's arm.

It growled and threw a punch. Its massive fist just missed crashing into Aria's face and slammed into the building, obliterating the blocks there. The goblin spun and shadows shot out like black barbed whips, sweeping to trip her up.

Fast as a blink, she was over them. Striking, dodging, blocking, and sortieing like lightning. It was a dance of blows and battle that defied anything Jason had yet seen. He felt frozen in awe by it. No, not by awe—he wasn't permitted yet to move. His every sinew strained to join her, yet couldn't.

Blow after blow hammered from each of the combatants, scoring the stones of the street and buildings around them with near hits and deflected attacks. Back and forth without slowing until the hobgoblin got in a sneaky blow to Aria's abdomen that doubled her over.

She threw up her spiritsword to catch the hobgoblin's hammering glaive in a block, her tiny arms tensed as she strained to hold back its muscular ones.

Jason perceived the restraint on him lifted. Quite the opposite now, he felt the torrent of unyielding fire pushing forth into him like a flood he could not resist.

"My Great King, for you, now and always."

When he took a step forward, he knew as soon as his foot kicked off on the stone that it wasn't his own muscles driving him forward. He wasn't a streak, a blur, a flash, he was a meteor, and when his shield slammed squarely into the face of the hobgoblin it was with a crack that echoed off the windows and shattered their splintered glass. The fiery impression of the High King's lion and radiant lamb was seared into the creature's visage, and it tumbled several yards down the street from the force of it. Jason was sure he heard a lion's roar.

He kicked off the curb again and crossed the distance of ten feet in a single bound, his spiritsword battering aside the hobgoblin's glaive. Blocking the short pick with his shield, he pivoted—the glaive that was ready to slice him missed entirely, and he stabbed his spiritsword into the hobgoblin's exposed shoulder.

Spinning back, he caught its responding attack, parried, and scored a quick jab into its abdomen before he had to backpedal and block with his shield.

Duck, dodge, block, strike. Over and over, and then an opening, ignored. The whispers that had guided him in the past were the shout of many waters coursing for millennia. Their flow unquenchable and his will totally swept up in them.

There was another voice, silky and strident in turn. It haunted him with cruel ghosts of guilt and anger and bitterness for every wrong and every pain and every failure Jason had experienced. It trilled about the thousands of ways Aria could die here. Battering Jason's bastion defense with an icy maelstrom of every doubt and uncertainty and fear that had ever beset him.

The mental assault was more potent and focused than any Jason had ever faced. The chill on the air, the pressure bearing down on him, crushing. Yet, he did not slow, did not waver. Because these were only the sum of things already faced, the total of obstacles overcome. Pains born. Fears braved. Doubts answered. They were those with which all his trials and travails in his life, and those read from Anargen's, had already struck him.

His jaw clenched, and he pushed against them, knowing that what had been built in him was greater than the sum of evils crashing against him. The greater shield he carried was not only for external but internal defense. Its mettle was not challenged in either arena. Every pain born had carried a purpose, and here on the battlefield in which it mattered most, he proved it.

The hobgoblin surged forward, anticipating its ploy would deceive him. It missed and stumbled forward. Aria was there in a blink and jammed her spiritsword down into its back. A strangled gurgle escaped its lips.

Aria leaped away as it flailed backward. It swiped wildly, but Jason had already dodged its attacks, hacking its hand and shearing through its glaive at its guard. Ducking, he slammed the shield into the hobgoblin's waist.

Doubled again, Aria was there, this time sliding under a swipe with its remaining blade and jamming her spiritsword up into its abdomen. She twisted it free with a jerk and wheeled away.

Jason weathered the responding blow with a block from his shield. And blocked the next. On a turn, he came up and around to catch the hobgoblin across its other shoulder in a slice.

The hobgoblin recoiled and bellowed so piercingly that Jason had to back away. His ears felt like they might burst. Ancient and cruel without yield, the hobgoblin swiped with each arm in turn, and dark jagged surges of black zipped at both Knights.

Jason faltered for a step. Aria didn't have a shield to block it.

He wanted to dash to her, but the shout demanded he stand his ground and block his own. In that moment, he saw in the dark spiked attack the choice of a thousand generations: obey or defy. There were no other choices, no matter how many shades of gray mankind had longed to add to justify choosing the latter. And though it would cost him the woman he loved more than his own life, it was not the cost, the circumstances, the nature, or timing of the command that mattered. Only obey or defy. He had vowed when his chains were broken in his brother's dungeon to never again allow shackles to bind him to defiance.

"My Great King, I'm yours now and always."

Gripping his *Thyreos Pistis*, the unbreakable shield that could move a mountain if the Framer of All Realms willed him to use it so, Jason slammed forward into the obsidian breakers, feeling them shattering against the shield like glass.

The waves didn't end and increased in height such that they looked like they would subsume him, but he didn't shrink back. Pressing forward as instructed, he knew he was close now and caught his next command.

Drop.

He did, and a black spear shot forward to impale him. It missed, and from his crouch, Jason saw Aria land with cat-like ease behind the hobgoblin. With two deft flicks of her wrist, she had scored hits on the hobgoblin's legs that sent him to his knees.

Now.

Surging up, Jason buried his spiritsword into the chest of the hobgoblin and yelled at the top of his lungs, "By the authority of the High King of All Realms, and in his magnificent name, I command you to depart this and all the realms of the Lowlands forever!"

Light and fire engulfed all that Jason's eyes could see, and in a flare that blew him back, still gripping his spiritsword, he watched as the shrieking hobgoblin was dissipated in the light, completely consumed and banished by it from the Lowlands.

Watching until the dark servant was gone and the light finally faded, Jason closed his eyes, the chilly drops of rain plinking off his armor. He dropped to his knees.

"Thank you, my Great King. Thank you. This was your victory. Your might. Your triumph. Thank you!"

"Truly, even so," Aria agreed, coming alongside him.

For just a moment, he looked at her as he raised up and lifted his faceplate. His throat felt parched of words.

In the same instant, they crashed into each other. He

hoisted her up into his arms and spun with her, laughter, tears, and cries of joy erupting from both of them.

They kissed, wildly, desperately, with gratefulness felt within every fiber of their frames, individually and singularly together. It was sweeter, more precious a moment than any he'd yet shared with Aria.

Of course, it had to end, because in the dark, the relenting rain's murmur was the reminder that they were in the empty and ravaged streets of Brackenburgh, and there was one more who needed to share in this victory. One who had bested the dragon when all seemed lost.

Jason didn't even need to say it. He just followed as Aria sprinted back toward where her grandfather had fallen. It was best that he didn't try to keep up. Some of his aches had been permitted to return. He wondered after why the pain wouldn't be removed, carried away in their overcoming the tremendous evil threatening the Lowlands.

Reaching Aria's side, Jason's heart felt like it plummeted off a mountain's heights. Cinaed lay there. The only movement he made was in the faint rise and fall of his chest. One old hand clutched with ferocious intensity his spiritsword. The other was gripped just as fixedly by Aria.

A whisper familiar and necessary as breath broke through the scene for Jason, and he sucked in sharply. "Aria, we have to get him out of here. Right now."

"Can he be moved?" she asked, tears streaming down her cheeks.

"He has to, we have to move now!"

DENOUEMENT

Hooking his arms under Defender Black's shoulders, Jason nodded to the old Knight's feet. "Grab them and help me move him!"

Aria looked down at her grandfather and then to Jason and then back again. Anxiety twisted her face, but she only delayed another pair of seconds before hooking her arms around his ankles and hoisting him up.

Cinaed's face contorted in pain, and Jason winced with him. There was no time to even apologize. Charging out of the rubble, wobbling as he did, and just hoping he wouldn't stumble and fall, he moved as fast as his own worn body would allow. Passing where the remains of the dragon had already burned away completely, they had only just cleared the block when the rumbling began.

Eyes wide, Aria called out through heavy breathing, "What is that?"

"It's ... going to ... collapse!" Jason called back as he tried to both pick up his pace and answer. His lungs were not pleased with him in the least.

Following the path that he and Cinaed had taken to reach the Elkland Square, Jason slowed up once he could only just make out the Ministry of Justice over the rooftops of the buildings around them. Thus, he had a solid view as the building suddenly dropped out of view and heard even better as the cacophonous resounding cry of the building's collapse echoed through the alleyways and almost tore the ground out from under their feet.

That wasn't the end of it. The whisper returned to him, urged him on. And he called to Aria, "Still too close, we have to keep moving. Where can we take him?"

"A hospital?" she replied as they both picked up moving. The quaking beneath their feet hadn't subsided. In fact, it was growing more pronounced.

"No!" Cinaed's paradoxically feeble but firm voice interjected. "The ... home ... take me ..."

"What?" Jason asked as he tried to avoid bits of roof tiles, pots sitting on sills, and other assorted debris dropping from the trembling buildings around them. People were beginning to come outside to see what was going on. Had they heard any of the battle that preceded this? How long had the entire thing taken to elapse?

"He wants us to take him back to the Inn," Aria replied, redirecting Jason's attention from his musings. "He means ... THE Inn."

"Is that safe?" Jason asked, dodging around a couple talking anxiously and pointing toward the direction where a plume of dust had risen up over sixty feet and was beginning to spread into all the adjacent streets.

"Safe as anywhere in Brackenburgh for us," she answered with a measure of resignation.

They were about halfway to the Inn when the most potent shudder yet threw Jason to the ground. He tried to use his body to cushion Cinaed's fall and let out a yelp as his own hurts were further agitated.

On her knees, Aria was sucking in as many breaths as she could draw. "You've ... really ... got to stop ... being ..." She swallowed and laughed a bit hysterically. "The Black Family's ... fainting couch."

Jason just stared past her, eyes wide. He pointed to where they'd come from just as the sound reached them. "Elkland Square ... the whole block. It's gone ... collapsed into the ..." he coughed as the sudden cloud of dust hit them and his throat seized up. In seconds, it threatened to pollute all of the fresh air his over-exerted lungs and muscles craved. "Grotto."

Aria just closed her eyes and tried to steady her breathing and ended up coughing. As the rumbling and quaking subsided, she suggested, "Let's keep going."

"Right."

Dust from the collapse hung in the air all around. With as hurried a pace as they could manage between its choking and blinding cloud, they reached the street they sought, and Jason felt a rush of emotion as they came up to the boarded entrance to the building bearing a hanging sign that had been defaced, but still faintly bore the words: "BLACK RIVER INN."

Setting Cinaed down for just a moment, he got a few boards ripped free and then switched tactics and slashed the remainder free with his spiritsword. A minute later, he shouldered open the door as he and Aria carried her grandfather into the dark and empty expanse of the grand room where Jason had first met them years ago.

While Aria tore some bits off her dress to bandage her grandfather's head, Jason gathered some candles and lanterns still lying discarded in the inn and brought them over. Arraying them around Defender Black's prone form, he lit each of them. Their faint glow and the scent of the worn old wood of the building, still strong after so long sitting in dust and disuse, seemed to revive Cinaed.

Those heavy, old brows of his lifted as he smiled. "Could use ... some sprucing up."

Wiping at some errant tears with the back of her wrist, Aria chuckled. "When you're doing a little better, I'll get right on it."

Cinaed's face fell somewhat, morphing from humor into concern. "My child ..."

"Don't speak. Save your strength. At your age, you need to conserve it. Defying your years is usually your specialty, but ..." Aria ran out of air and had to catch her breath. She was talking in a rush.

"Aria," Cinaed said with a shake of his head. "Aria," he tried again, giving her hand a shake when she refused to meet his gaze.

"Please, don't," she begged.

Jason sat down next to Aria and put an arm around her. He placed his other hand on Cinaed's shoulder. Immediately, he joined the war against tears as he took in the distant, glazed look in Cinaed's eyes. Never had he seen him not seem vibrant, vital, stronger, and sharper than any decades could define or diminish. It was so awful to see him this way.

Irrespective, the gesture by Jason brought on a fresh smile and a cough from Cinaed. His face twisted in agony for an instant before relaxing again. Sweat had broken out on his brow some time ago, forming a dark crust with the dust they had passed through. Mask-like, it was presently cracking and chipping.

Brushing away the bits of debris, Jason commented, "Perhaps it would help you to tell us a new story?"

Cinaed smiled, but it wasn't so broad, more satisfied than amused. "I have no more to tell but one. And it is one you already know. But one you won't know so well till you experience it."

Aria swallowed with some difficulty and again dabbed at her tears; this time, her hand was linked with Jason's. "The King's Day," she said like a reluctant student.

"Aye, my child. You always were sharp. The Lowlands are better with you in them."

"Not as good as if they have you," she protested, her face twitching as she struggled not to break into sobs.

"Hmm," he rumbled from deep within. "The best of me was never"—his breath hitched as though he had to work for it or to it—"of my making. It was my Sovereign. So, you too ... shall come to see in time."

Closing his eyes for a moment, he bounced his bushy brows. "Fortunately, you have this former ... scoundrel ... by your side. Don't think ... I didn't see ... what you did ... in the Jade Gardens."

"Oh, sir," Jason blurted out, suddenly self-conscious. "We were going to ask your permission—"

Cinaed coughed, and a little laugh was embedded in it. "No, no apologies. You've had my blessing. Take ... care ... of each other."

To both of them, he seemed to address, "Make ... each other ... better."

His attention turned to Aria. "Bear him up ... the burden ... is better borne ... when two ... are one."

Tears freely flowed down Aria's face, and she nodded. "Yes, sir."

To Jason, he motioned with faint tilts of his head. "Top pouch, under ... *Thorax Dikaiosyne* ... my chest plate. Don't ... forget ... the ancient names. Ancient meanings."

Reaching past the old storyteller's bushy beard, Jason felt how shallow his breaths were now. He found a silky pouch with the stiff contours of a ring within and extracted it. For a moment, he thought by its size it might have been a ring set for Aria. Maybe Cinaed wanted to conduct the ceremony himself while he could.

As Jason produced it in the light, he saw the pouch was a vibrant blue, even if weathered some, so that he understood it to be old. Undoing its argent tether carefully, he produced the ring, and his eyes went wide. Glinting silver in the light was no diamond bridal set, but a large signet ring bearing a tree at the center with fountains to either side framing it.

"Is this ..." Jason started to ask and trailed off, unable to hide his amazement.

"Aye. The Signet of Thanes," Cinaed answered and coughed. With a sharp breath, he seemed to fill and his voice became steadier. Commanding. "It has been passed by every Defender of the Northern Realm to his successor since my ancestor Anargen received it from Thane Duncoin for safekeeping. A sign of our commitment to serving the good of all placed under our charge by the High King of All Realms."

Cinaed's eyes seemed to clear, and their piercing power was in full force, seeing deep into the recesses of Jason. "Sir Jason of Brackenburgh, once a Wernstrum, once Landsby, I hereby confer on you the Signet of Thanes and the title 'Defender of the Northern Realm' and all the duties and responsibilities carried with it. Do you accept this charge, to defend the innocent, care for the needy, and safeguard the Knights of this realm as long as you bear this Signet?"

"I ..." Jason looked at Aria, whose eyes were a mix of emotions. Pride, sorrow, a palette of combinations linked and between them. He glanced down at the gleaming signet in his hand. This was unexpected, undeserved, unbelievable. Jason closed his palm around the ring and took a shuddering breath. "How could I—"

"Do you accept?" Cinaed cut him off pointedly.

Looking into those eyes again, Jason saw the intensity seemed to lighten just a fraction. Not cutting through him, never had they been doing that. He understood now. They had been carving, sculpting, polishing, preparing him. For this. He saw it all now.

"Yes," he said, the same surety and potency suddenly swelling within him.

Cinaed smiled, his lips quivering a bit as he pronounced, "By the High King of All Realms' favor and authority, I declare you to be the Defender of the Northern Realm. Long may you serve our rightful Lord and the *Palatini Lucis Aeternae*, Knights of Unending Light."

He swallowed with difficulty, his breathing suddenly ragged again, and looked up at them both. "Hold firm ..." he cleared his throat again, his voice fading. "To the end. Never ... stop ... looking for ... for ... forward ... to ... the King's Day."

Breathing out, Cinaed seemed to deflate, his eyes again clouding. Then they closed, and he sighed, falling still.

"Grandfather?" Aria asked, giving his hand a little shake. "Grandfather?"

"He ... he's gone," she wailed and buried her face in Jason's chest. Sobs rocked her body, and he put his arms around her, the Signet of Thanes still gripped tight in one hand.

"Why?" Aria cried, "Why didn't he ..."

Words dissolved into keening and sobs as grief stole her voice.

Rubbing circles on her back, it didn't seem to make sense that they should make it while Cinaed died. Just as it didn't make sense that his aches and injuries hadn't just been erased after the battle with the hobgoblin. Except ...

The pain has a purpose.

Jason looked up. He couldn't tell Aria this now, but he thought he understood it. Understood it in a way he hadn't before, not even when he'd thought he'd lost her, because he had to see it through this lens as well. A life of service and sacrifice to the very end.

Every pain had a purpose, and so often it served as a

reminder. The Inn wasn't the home Sir Cinaed had been wanting to go to. These Lowlands weren't their home, nor the end goal or aim of anyone living in them. A better land awaited. The Highland was the home they craved, and every pain of these Lowlands would only serve to sharpen the resolve that the King's Day would heal them for good. Everything until then would be part of the story, and every step in service to completing the Quest to keep burning the fires symbolic of the true unending light. A Tower of Light in the night until the Day erased all dark.

"Whatever happens next—no fear," Jason vowed.

FAMILIAR BEGINNING

J ason settled down into his chair. Aches raced down his back and shot up his knees, through to his hips. Beside him, Aria patted him on his sore old shoulder. Her wrinkled, bony hands shook as she did.

"Don't hold them too long," she instructed. "It isn't as easy as it once was to keep their attention."

"Isn't that what you do with your cinnamon cakes?" he countered, peering around her to the tray she had covered with a plastic lid.

She bent down, wincing as she did, and kissed his cheek. "You keep out of them till the children have had their fill."

His bounced a thick, silvery eyebrow. "You're the only cinnamon cake I need," he reminded her.

Her green eyes narrowed to happy slits behind her round spectacles. "Mhm," she replied knowingly. Then her attention turned to the back of the room.

Jason's gaze followed hers, and he spotted their youngest son's twin teenage daughters, Isabella and Suzanne. They were caught in a conversation with a pair of strapping boys wearing faded jeans and T-shirts from some televised program or digital medium. Some years ago, Jason accepted he would never be able to keep up with what passed for entertainment in younger generations, try though he might. At one time, he thought it might help him keep his stories relevant to them.

That lasted until his beloved wife reminded him that the stories they told were relevant because they were true at heart and in fact. Things that would seem dubious to many in the Lowlands more than seventy years after the Lowlands Total War ended.

The girls were level-headed, so he wasn't worried about them being led away by the sorts of scoundrels prowling the streets of Brackenburgh these days. Even so, he had mixed feelings, knowing just what could begin when one turned aside to hear a story from an old man because one fancied a beautiful girl. Love stories like that seemed a rarity now. Or rather, love that belonged as a thread of fabric within the greater tapestry of The Story felt rare.

Which was why he was sitting up here, of course. Promoting a book he'd written, a recollection of events from the lives of a great many Knights of Light. Events that would seem fantasy to those hearing with their ears attuned to modern frequencies of life.

That being as it was, the girls settled down and the smitten boys with them. Along with about twenty others. A decent crowd, as it went.

Jason clapped, rubbing his hands together, and the girls, coached by Aria, got the whole group quieted. Raising a hand to gesture to each member of the group, he said, "Thank you all for undertaking the journey to be here to hear an old man speak."

Eyeing the boys interested in his granddaughters, he said, "Like you two lads. What are your names?"

One of the boys, taller and lankier with a shock of dark hair, reddened noticeably, his eyes for Isabella jerked to Jason. "Uh, well, I'm John ... Wolfsglen, sir. This is my brother, Clive."

Wolfsglen was definitely decided on the spot, which made Jason wonder just what had drawn two boys who couldn't give their full names into the Black River Bookstore and Café. He looked forward to sorting that out. "Hale evening then, John and Clive. Good to have you."

He paused and, with a more thoughtful tone, added, "I must warn you, this tale is not mine. It began days long past in a land far from here, but it is one which I'm certain is true." Leaning forward, he looked intently into the eyes of each member of his audience, especially John's—you never knew for whom it would be a thing that mattered greatly. Jason began demurely, as if imparting a closely held secret. "This journey, like so many, began with a lad no older than some of you, seventeen to be precise, stepping foot onto a new road. His journey began late one night in his home village, where he had an encounter with the High King . . ."

EPILOGUE

The sound shook Jason, as he had not been shaken in so many years. It was hard to place, seeming so familiar, but he couldn't recall where he knew it from. How long had he been asleep? Certainly, long enough to have forgotten where the light switch was; that was the danger of growing old. And he was that, so much more so than he had ever expected to be. Perhaps older than Defender Black had been.

Ah, he had to be careful with that, thinking about Cinaed the Storyteller as Defender Black. That was what people had called him for decades now. In the absence of a surname he really felt was his own, he had taken Aria and Cinaed's. It felt right, as though he claimed the heritage that had shaped them as much as it had him.

Sitting up, he was pleased that he didn't feel dizzy. That had been happening so often in the recent months. All the more since he'd lost his precious cinnamon cake. Aria loved to hate that nickname to the day he laid her to rest. But he didn't like to think about that, to dwell on it.

Their eight children and numerous grandchildren certainly made sure to argue against him doing so. At least those of them who still spoke with him. Darkness was in the Lowlands again, so much deeper than he remembered, even from those bleak hours of the Lowlands Total War. Its subtlety and infiltration into every facet of life made up for its lack of bold, blatant embattlement of the Order. What was left of the Order, that is to say.

Jason stood and found he was up as quickly as he liked, with no aching knees, a complaining hip, or a stubborn back mucking it up. He must have slept well; he had not felt this way in years. If only he could see now.

Ahead, there appeared to be light coming in around a nearby doorway. Shuffling toward it, he found it stony, resilient to his efforts.

"Give it a good shove," a voice he knew as well as his own encouraged.

He spun and blinked. He couldn't see, but he knew that voice was impossible to hear. Not just because its speaker was dead, but because Aria had not sounded so youthful and hale for a long, long time.

"Cinnamon cake?" he called out, startled by his own voice. It was smooth, lacking the coarse rattle born of long years and much weariness. Stronger now even than perhaps he ever remembered it being.

Aria laughed, light and contented. "You never could just call me your love or dear or by my name."

He chuckled. "It's not my nature. Really, it's your fault for falling in love with someone like me."

Jason knew she was close, but guessed she could no more see than he until he caught the faint outline of her arm being highlighted by the door. He almost gasped. It was as sleek and supple as in their first years of marriage.

"Maybe we should try together?" she proposed.

"Indeed," he agreed. Placing his hands on the resistant entryway, he called out. "Three. Two. One!"

They each shoved, and the stone gave at last, not turning aside, but collapsing forward to land with a crack on the ground. Light flooded in, and with it the notes of the horn that was blowing. Jason stepped outside and his eyes widened.

"We're in a graveyard?" he asked, turning to see if it disturbed Aria.

If his heart did not feel strong and sure as never before in his life, it would have given out. Aria had stridden forth from the mausoleum they had apparently been in, looking more radiant than the day he met her, yet more distinguished than the final years of her life. All the wisdom and weight of the years seemed to balance in the face that looked far too young to have borne them.

Then it came to him in a rush, on the horn's commanding notes. They were in the mausoleum because they had both completed their lives in the Lowlands and been placed there. This was something new, and as the notes of the horn grew louder, closer, every sinew, bone, and follicle of hair felt the horn's pull. All the cells comprising him yearned for what he instinctively knew lay ahead. "It's the King's Day," he said with all the heady emotion of a good cry, but all the jubilance of the most wonderful celebration.

"It is," she agreed, beaming.

They stood there together, looking out at the commanding dawn as an enormous ship came into view. The ship was of an older design, one that would have been considered ancient even when they were young. Not to say that it was any more rickety than they were. Ancientness and fitness did not seem to be in conflict on this day.

More impressively, the boat wasn't floating to them on the sea, but rather sailing through the air. From either side, winged creatures deployed and swept down to them. In a few seconds, they became clearly identifiable as winged horses, and their riders had the molten magnificence of elves.

The elf pair stopped before them. "Sir Jason and Lady Aria Black," they called.

"Yes!" they both answered at the same time and shared a quick grin.

"The High King of All Realms summons you this day to join him in the Highland," the pair announced, and each held forth a hand.

Taking them, Jason and Aria were each swept up onto a horse in a heartbeat and were galloping through the air to be placed upon the ship, teeming with others. Thousands, it seemed, maybe many times more. The longer Jason looked, the bigger the boat seemed.

It wasted no time once they were aboard in proceeding onward, and he and Aria were permitted to mingle.

A strange compulsion to make his way to a particular area of the boat drew them both to what felt midway across but may have been far off from it. As they approached, a young man with the gravity of a planet in his bearing turned toward them. He grinned broadly and clapped.

"At last, you're here," he said.

Jason wanted to gape, but in the same instant of surprise, he felt quite sure he'd expected this as well. "Cinaed," he said at roughly the same instant Aria did.

It was interesting to hear her say her grandfather's name, but it didn't feel inappropriate or less tender than "Grandpa" or "Grandfather" as she had always called him before. Any more than it felt odd or out of sorts that his face was unwrinkled or his age-roughened hair and skin restored. Cinaed's voice was the most intriguing thing, because it was recognizable, but if not for this day, Jason would never have matched it to the gravelly and sanguine tone he'd become accustomed to during those far past days.

"I have waited so long for you to join, and yet so little time has elapsed. Marvelous, isn't it?" he replied.

"Marvelous," Jason agreed.

"It is wonderful to see you again," Aria added.

"Mmm," he demurred and added, "You'll have to introduce me to the children, grandchildren, and great-grandchildren you raised. When we get them, of course."

Not all of them, Jason was sure, but he was very much grateful to know, like many others he'd encountered in life in the Lowlands, a number would be boarding as well. "How long till they come aboard?" he asked.

Cinaed shrugged. "An instant, an hour, two hundred years? Perhaps, if you want a sense of time, it would be better to ask those who boarded before me."

Jason nodded and said, "Very well. Where are they?"

But Cinaed did not need to introduce any of them. As if summoned, there were arrayed before them all of those who had been within the stories that were integral to shaping him as a fledgling Knight of Light. Striding up to him were Anargen, Seren, Thomas, Mia, Terrillian, Ecthelion, Duncoin, Orwald, Iaegon, Hurstwell, and more, and more. Glewydn and Anargen's mother, Ailis—Anargen's family that preceded him, and those descended from him and Seren were there. Tracing up, of course, to Cinaed. And, with some wonder, he finally saw him. Cinaed Black's namesake. Meredoch MacCowell, the "Cinaed" of Anargen's day, who had mentored Anargen and been the guide he had needed at the start of his leg of the Quest.

Still farther on the ship, Jason spotted both men's namesake, Cinaed of Tislatna, and Helena. There were so many Knights that Jason longed to speak to, and seemingly he was able to chat with every one of them without feeling that he had been too brief with each or had exhausted much time. Once his and Aria's offspring, along with their spouses, came aboard, many new rounds of conversation began.

All the while, they had been flying ever nearer the Charis River, and then upon reaching it, they joined with still other ships of like kind and throngs of passengers. There seemed to be one ship for each realm. From ship to ship, they could speak, such that they were able to converse with Professor Goulder and Dr. Jing. Defender Miguelso and Defender Guo. On another were Tirzah and Kaveed and Dr. Antoni. Another had Defender Cuzibaum. Still another Defender Davidiah. They soared upwards beyond the reaches of the most impressive modern technological marvels in the Lowlands that Jason and Aria had lived to witness. Beyond it all to the brilliant point swiftly approaching in the near distance.

"You all did such wonderful things to keep the Tower of Light ablaze in preparation for this day," Anargen commented as he came to stand near both Cinaed and Jason. "Your assembling the Council of Defenders united the Order during some of the hardest days the Lowlands saw in that dreadful war and what came after."

Jason laughed. "None of it could have been done without what you did before us. Certainly, it was on your shoulders we stood."

Anargen smiled and looked at him. "We deserve no more credit than you. We all had a part in the High King's story."

"The High King's story?" Jason asked, puzzled.

Cinead put a hand on his shoulder as he had in days long past. "Yes, his story. Didn't I tell you at the very beginning that the story I related was not my own? It was not Anargen's. It was not yours. Nor any or all of ours on these ships. It was and will always be the High King's, and ours is the joy of being a part of it."

As Jason looked at Cinaed, he could perceive beyond the clouds around them the tremendous light was close. Surrounded by all those valiant members of the Quest of Fire throughout all of time, anticipation washed over him. He clicked his tongue. "Hmm. That time Aria told me about happy endings. She told me you had taught her everything she knew of them. Do you recall it?"

"Of course."

Jason clapped Cinaed on the shoulder and said, "This is the end that is truly the beginning. The King's Day is our joining him in the unending light, his story without end."

"Aye, even so," the group around them all agreed in unison.

A hush fell over them all as they passed beyond the heady mists encircling the Highland. From below, the clouds seemed dense and dark, but at these heights, a brilliant light could be perceived beyond such that the mists had a prismatic quality, shimmering with every color conceivable. In the void of speech and wonder at the mists flooded the sound of the Charis River's falls. They were so loud the boat trembled, but no one feared. The sound wasn't raucous or painfully boisterous but musical in a way. Its harmony swelled and engulfed them, carrying them higher as it filled every pore and worked its way into them, resonating within every sinew, every cell, every atom. The mist gave way and all could see the soaring buildings of the Kingdom. They were not all perfectly smooth and uniform as Jason had always imagined. Some were but, on the whole, they were variegated in design and so intricate that one could examine them for a thousand lifetimes without cataloging every detail.

The boats were now sailing up the headwaters of the broad River Charis. None yet spoke but a song was in them, the anthem of ages already humming within the immense city. They encountered a light unlike any other. The radiance of the High King of All Realms engulfed them. Close as they had ever dreamed. Close as they had ever longed. Close as they had always needed.

And what came next was truly beyond any description the Lowlands could ever hope to form. From beginning to beyond all the reaches of the endless era to come.

ACKNOWLEDGMENTS

Where do I even begin? This book is the culmination of twenty years of dreaming, writing, editing, publishing, and everything that goes into making each of them possible. For certain, I have to thank Marsha Brock, my High school creative writing teacher who asked me to write a fairy tale short story and graciously accepted a short novella that was the origin point for *Quest of Fire.*

I also need to dearly thank Erin Howard, Kathy Cretsinger, and Linda Fulkerson; each of whom gave *Quest of Fire* a chance and supported it even when it might've looked unlikely to amount to all it should. Linda in particular has been the most gracious and patient publisher the world has ever seen as she waited on me to pull together the threads that make up this book. I could not have asked for better editors and caretakers of this series.

My bosses at my day job, Andrew Neely and Daniel Mead, accommodated my need for leave and were immensely understanding as I struggled to get this manuscript completed. Pulling together this much story, with all its rewrites and self-applied pressure—they helped me keep from burnout by giving me the time and space I needed to finish.

Of course, the same is true of my incredible wife, Shelly, and my son. Both of whom allowed me to step away for hours at a time when late-night writing wasn't working out and to save me from becoming an addle-brained zombie from lack of sleep.

My parents, always there, always supporting me no matter the goals. And always patiently reminding me to not forget to get my rest.

Eric Dotseth, who very unassumingly has labored for years inking the maps and providing artwork for the series. He asked for nothing and gave so much to *Quest of Fire* and me.

The numerous authors, famous and friends, who have inspired me with their stories. Especially those whose faith has encouraged and instructed me.

All of my author and reader friends who have been picking up each book in *Quest of Fire* and through their feedback giving me the insights on what to improve and encouraged me to not stop or turn back from this journey.

Above all others, the Lord has been my shepherd through this. I could tell very clearly the moments where I was trying to work around or apart from Him and it is by His grace that this book was composed. I'm a rather crude, lazy, and stubborn brush in His hand even after all these years, but He continues to use me to create art and that is an incredible gift which I deeply treasure. He deserves all the honor for this book and so much more.

ABOUT THE AUTHOR

Brett Armstrong has been exploring other worlds as a writer since age nine. Years later, he still writes, but now invites others along on his excursions. He's shown readers haunting, deep historical fiction (*Destitutio Quod Remissio*), scary-real dystopian sci-fi (*Tomorrow's Edge* series), and layered, sweeping epic fantasy (*Quest of Fire*). Every story is a journey of discovery and an attempt to be a brush in the Master Artist's hand. Through dark, despair, light, joy, and everything in between, the end is always meant to leave his fellow literary explorers with wonder and hope. Always busy with a new story, he also enjoys drawing, gardening, and spending time with his wife and son.

MORE FROM THE QUEST OF FIRE SERIES

The Gathering Dark

Quest of Fire Series – Book One

2020 Selah Awards Finalist

After a thousand years of light, a teen's world teeters on the edge of utter darkness.

On the run from his past, Jason hides in an inn where he hears a tale from centuries past about Anargen, a teen on a quest to bring peace between Ecthelowall's men and Ordumair's dwarfs. But an arcane evil seeks to ruin the peace talks and ensure a lost dwarf treasure isn't found by those for whom it's meant. As he listens, Jason realizes the story is more than a fable and he must choose whether to join Anargen's quest, which has shaped and can destroy his world.

Get your copy here: scrivenings.link/thegatheringdark

Succession: A Novella

Quest of Fire Series – Book Two

The heir must prove his worth - or die trying

Son of the Northern Realm's Defender, raised among the dwarves of
Ordumair, Meredoch was anticipated to succeed his father. Some
whispered he would bring the longed-for peace between Ordumair
and their ancient foe, Ecthelowall. All of that changes when
Ordumair's Thane is killed and Meredoch and his family are exiled.

From prestige to poverty, the young boy must chart a new course.
Battling creatures believed only myths and racing against evil toward
the prize, Meredoch must face the truth of his place in the world and
claim his right of succession.

Get your copy here: scrivenings.link/succession

Shadows at Nightfall

Quest of Fire - Book Three

The hour has arrived ... with all its terrors.

The shadows of Jason's past have caught him. Having stepped into the Quest of Fire, Jason is pursued by a league of assassins formed of pure darkness. To his horror he discovers these creatures were also contracted to eliminate Anargen and his friends as they sought to understand the Tower of Light's oracle. To unravel the mystery of who wants him dead and how he fits into the ages old quest, Jason must travel the lengths of the Lowlands. He'll have to move fast, the darkest creatures in the Lowlands have long waited for this hour. With few concerned for the light and everything falling apart around them, Jason and Anargen will face the shadows of night's falling as their world hangs in the balance.

Get your copy here:

https://scrivenings.link/shadowsatnightfall

Desperation: A Novella

Quest of Fire - Book Four

Guarding his nation's last hope, a teen must escape enemy lands.

While Anargen, Caeserus, and Bertinand are held captive in Stormridge, the war to restore Ecthelowall's Commonwealth has been waged for months. Enter Thomas Fenwrest, an orphan and page to the captain of Baron Fenwrest's guard and tasked with escorting the children of Restoration nobility to safety at Castle Yerst. Things quickly spiral out of control when the Monarchists deliver a devastating blow to the Restoration. Ancient sorcery and bitter grudges combine to ensnare them. As desperation sets in for the Restoration and Thomas, to where will they turn for hope?

Get your copy here: https://scrivenings.link/desperation

Resurgence of Dawn

Quest of Fire - Book Five

Hope returns with the dawn.

Haunted by tragedies and failures, Anargen and Jason each struggle to find their way. Night has fallen in the Lowlands and neither teen has an easy road ahead. In Anargen's Era, Monarch Ilyron's powers and influence grow, forcing Anargen and his dwindling list of allies to travel the length of the Lowlands in a desperate attempt to keep the Quest and all they hold dear from falling into ruin.

Jason meanwhile must find Aria and her grandfather to help unite the Knights of Light from across the Lowlands against his brother, Dorian. But agents of darkness and painful vestiges of his past mix with vindictive new enemies to make the hope of seeing the dawn of the longed-for King's Day ever so faint. If either teen gives in and surrenders, doom will come swiftly on their world.

Resurgence of Dawn won Third Place for Speculative Fiction in the 2024 Angel Awards

Get your copy here:

https://scrivenings.link/resurgenceofdawn

Devastation

Quest of Fire - Book Six

Hope grows faint as disease, war, and betrayal devastate a teen's people.

With the added support of Libertias, hope is renewed for young Thomas Fenwrest and those dedicated to restoring Viceroy Ecthelion and the Commonwealth to Ecthelowall. That hope is short-lived. A terrible plague called the Devastation soon ravages the Restoration's soldiers and allied lands. The Monarchists press the advantage and attack.

At the same time, a series of betrayals within the Restoration directly threaten the lives of Thomas's beloved, Baroness Mia Sornfold, and his cousin, Heir Apparent Gregor Fenwrest. Thomas must risk everything to keep them safe even as the Restoration crumbles around him. Hiding within the mountainous lands of Albaron, they learn of a dark secret held deep in Albaron's Wyvares region. If this terror is unleashed by the Monarchists, it will mean the end of the Restoration and death for thousands all across the Lowlands. To stop it, Thomas must face an awful he may not be able to save both those he loves and stop the great evil. But to fail at either will destroy him.

Get your copy here: https://scrivenings.link/devastation

ALSO BY BRETT ARMSTRONG

Day Moon

Tomorrow's Edge Trilogy Book One

AD 2039: Eluding authorities, one teen holds the past and future's key.

AD 2039: Project Alexandria is an initiative to give all humanity safe and equal access to all recorded knowledge. But the prodigious teen Elliott knows something is wrong. There are dark intentions behind Project Alexandria and the key may lie in the last print copy of Shakespeare's complete works that contains a sonnet titled, "Day Moon." Racing along a path made perilous by federal agents and betrayals from those closest to him, Elliott must uncover the sonnet's secrets. All of history past and to be depends on it.

Get your copy here: https://scrivenings.link/daymoon

Veiled Sun: *Tomorrow's Edge Trilogy Book Two*

2021 Selah Awards Finalist

AD 2040: Every day the world slips further into lies.

AD 2040: Every day the world slips further into lies. Seventeen-year-old Elliott knows that better than most. Project Alexandria is rewriting history, shaping the world according to sinister goals. To stop it, Elliott must assemble the "Veiled Sun", a secret program written by his grandfather.

The only people he can count on are siegers—outlaws who use their coding skills for purposes almost as nefarious as Project Alexandria. Overcoming the schemes and betrayals all around him, he's the world's best hope to save reality, if he doesn't lose hold of it himself.

Get your copy here: https://scrivenings.link/veiledsun

Silent Stars: *Tomorrow's Edge Trilogy Book Three*

AD 2040: Past and future hang in the balance as the stars fall silent.

AD 2040: Barely eighteen, things have become much harder for Elliott. Reeling from the losses during the confrontation that brought Project Alexandria to a halt. Elliott feverishly hunts for the original files needed to finish it off. Finding only dead ends, he instead stumbles upon something dire: messages about the Babel Initiative.

Conceived as a successor that would make Project Alexandria's manipulations seem tame, this new threat once again forces Elliott into alliances with morally grey programmers known as siegers. Beset by continual setbacks and defeats, many siegers abandon the cause and go underground to survive the dangers ahead.

The bleak reality that Elliott and those closest to him are almost certain to die in the fight against Dr. Almundson begins to set in. But Elliott isn't ready to give in. He knows the cost of such a silent surrender will be humanity itself.

Get your copy here: https://scrivenings.link/silentstars

The Near Distant—Novella Collection
by Brett Armstrong, Erin R. Howard, and
C. Kevin Thompson

Awards for "By Far and Away" by Brett Armstrong:

2023 Selah Awards Finalist

2023 Realm Awards Finalist

2023 Carol Awards Semi-Finalist

On a day trip into the wilderness around Lake Tahoe, college students Ned, Tyler, and Everly stumble upon a monolith. No one knows its origin or purpose, but structures like this one have popped up all over the world, making national headlines. While not the local legend the group hoped to find, they decide to investigate, only to be engulfed by a blinding, powerful pulse of light. Instantly, the three friends find themselves in separate and drastically different worlds. They must quickly adapt to their new surroundings or perish.

Get your copy here: https://scrivenings.link/theneardistant

The Wonders Within the Starlit Inn—Novella Collection by Brett Armstrong, Erin R. Howard, Dawn Ford, and J. L. Burrows

"Asunder" by Brett Armstrong

A couple ready to give up hope on their marriage stops at the Inn and finds themselves trapped in frozen nightmare-scape of Vonlaus. As they race to save the planet and themselves, the fire of hope they mutually stoke in one another may be the only thing that can help them return to their world.

Get your copy here:

https://scrivenings.link/thewonderswithinthestarlitinn

Stay up-to-date on your favorite books and authors with our free e-newsletters.

ExpanseBooks.pub (an imprint of Scrivenings Press LLC)